THREE THROUGH TIME

BOOKS ONE AND TWO

SARAH ETTRITCH

NORN PUBLISHING
TORONTO, CANADA

Library and Archives Canada Cataloguing in Publication

Ettritch, Sarah, 1963–
Threaded through time : books one and two / Sarah Ettritch.

ISBN 978-1-927369-02-9

I. Title.

PS8609.T77T47 2011   C813'.6   C2011-907582-2

Editing by Marg Gilks
Cover design by Boulevard Photografica/Patty G. Henderson

Printed in the USA
v1

Published by Norn Publishing
www.NornPublishing.com

Acknowledgements

My thanks to Jennifer Brinkman (my lovely partner and wonderful beta reader), Marg Gilks (my fabulous editor), and Patty Henderson (my talented cover designer). My special thanks to the late B.G., for keeping a journal in 1911.

THREADED THROUGH TIME

BOOK ONE

For all the cats who have enriched my life, especially Fluff, Mouse, Morag, Zazzie, Hickory, Lucy, Henrietta, Daisy, Dozey, Sandy, Bluebell, Tubby, Tabby, Maxwell, and Grover.

Chapter One

Pam muttered under her breath as she dug through her purse for her keys. The plastic bag dangling from her left hand—the hand holding her purse steady as she groped—slipped from her fingers and thudded onto the steps. *Shit!* She pounded on the front door. "Robin!" No answer. "Robin!" she shrieked, not caring what the neighbours thought. Damn woman probably had her headset on. "Robin!"

She pulled out her phone and quickly dialled their number. "Come down and open the front door," she barked, then hung up.

Fifteen seconds later, the door swung open. Robin glared at her. "I couldn't find my damn keys." Pam picked up the bag and brushed past her. "We need to get the stupid doorbell fixed."

Robin shut the door and locked it. "We're in the middle of a boss fight and I'm the freaking healer," she wailed, dashing for the stairs. She was halfway up them when she stopped and turned around. "Aren't you supposed to be on a date?"

A date that would have lasted all of five minutes, if she'd had the guts to walk out instead of sitting through a boring dinner with a cheapskate. He'd shattered her visions of romance soon after the server had seated them: *I know you modern women like to pay your own way. I can respect that, so it'll be separate bills. Unless you'd like to pay for me.* Smarmy bastard. On her way out of the restaurant, she'd given him the finger—surreptitiously. What was it about men today? Was there a man out there who knew how to respect women *and* treat them well? "We didn't hit it off, so we decided to skip the movie," she said.

"Oh."

"I stopped in at Jake's on the way back, picked up a couple of things." She lifted the plastic bag so Robin could read the *Mathers Mystic Marketplace* emblazoned on its side.

"So it's Jake's now?" Robin rolled her eyes. "If it weren't for you, he'd probably go out of business." She thumped up the stairs.

Pam went into the living room and set her purse and the bag on the arm of the sofa. Now where were those damn . . . She fished around in her suit jacket pocket. Her fingers closed around metal. With a sigh, she pulled out her keys and dropped them into her purse. Today just wasn't her day; it felt as if the universe were conspiring against her. Jake had understood, had known exactly what she needed. Too bad he was already taken. She grabbed the bag and headed upstairs.

As Pam approached Robin's bedroom, she could hear her pleading, "I'm sorry. My roommate couldn't find her freaking keys. You all looked fine when I left."

Pam stuck her head around the bedroom door. "Sorry," she mouthed.

Robin glanced at her. "Look, do you want to take a fifteen-minute break, then try again?" she said into the headset's microphone. "It looks like I'm in for more roommate aggro." The responses must have been affirmative; Robin whipped off the headset and set it on her desk. "Now they're all mad at me," she muttered.

"I said I was sorry." Pam walked into the bedroom. "When you start playing again, do you think you can keep the shouting and swearing down? Jake recommended I meditate while holding rose quartz and tanzanite."

"And let me guess . . . that's what you just bought."

Pam nodded.

"And I didn't even have to tap into my psychic abilities," Robin said sarcastically. "What else did he—" her fingers formed air-quotes, "—prescribe? That bag has more than crystals in it."

"This is pretty cool." Pam rested the bottom of the bag on the edge of Robin's desk and slid out the large black book it held. She offered it to Robin. "What do you think?"

Robin's face screwed up as she waved her hand in front of her nose. "I think the last owner smoked."

Pam sniffed the air. "Incense," she stated. "But never mind that. According to Jake, this book contains sacred verses that were lost to us until they were rediscovered in the nineteenth century! They bolster the body, the mind, and reveal what the universe wants from us, the reason we were given life."

Robin shook her head. "You don't really believe all that crap, do you?" She set the book on her lap and gingerly lifted the front cover. "Ugh! The last owner drank coffee, too."

"There are a few stains—which Jake pointed out to me. But I just couldn't pass it up." She couldn't wait to recite the verses, either. Why not improvise? After meditating, she'd hang onto the crystals. The verses would be more illuminating if she read them while still in tune with her inner spirit. "Oh, apparently one set of verses will reveal the natural form of your spirit guide."

Robin barked a laugh. "I don't know why you waste your time and money on this."

"You're one to talk, Miss Elf-Healer!" Pam held two fingers against each ear and stuck her teeth out.

"You look like a rabbit," Robin said, her mouth twitching. "And you can take this smelly book back."

"Pearls before swine!" Pam snatched the book away and slid it into the bag. "I want half an hour of quiet, all right? After I've recharged, I'll go downstairs and watch a movie. You can make as much noise as you want then."

"I'll try to hold it down," Robin mumbled.

"Why don't you watch the movie with me? You can play with your elf buddies another time."

"You know I don't like old movies."

"Well, I need one of those old movies tonight." Pam clasped her free hand to her heart. "I want to watch Cary, or John, or Jimmy, or Humphrey, be swept back to the time when men were men and women were women."

"Pardon me if I don't share your enthusiasm for the old days." Robin reached for her headset. "Lesbians weren't exactly welcome back then."

"I suppose that's true." She ruffled Robin's hair. "But I wuv you, Robin. I do," she cooed.

Robin groaned and leaned away from her. "Go do your meditation . . . thing, already."

Pam blew her a kiss from the doorway and chuckled to herself as she walked down the hall to her own bedroom. Robin should spend less time in her fantasy worlds and find a nice girl to settle down with. But then she'd move out, and the place wouldn't be the same without her. Pam and Robin were more than roommates; they'd been best friends since elementary school. When Pam had inherited her mother's creaky old house that was too large for one person, Robin had been the perfect solution. Pam had loved her for agreeing to move in, instead of being her usual pragmatic self and suggesting that Pam sell up and find somewhere else to live. Robin had taken some convincing, but she knew how precious this house was to Pam. And moving in had allowed Robin to finally pursue her dream. She'd denied herself too much for too long.

Pam dropped the bag on the bed, changed into a t-shirt and sweats, and lit a few candles to set the mood. After dimming the light, she sat cross-legged on the bed and cradled the rose quartz in her left hand and the tanzanite in her right. She closed her eyes and imagined herself walking along a beach on a warm summer morning, the sand squishing between her toes and the sun—

"I said pull, not bring the whole mob down on us!" Robin shouted in her bedroom.

Pam groaned. With that damn headset on, Robin couldn't hear herself. It didn't help that Pam's door was open, but she hated meditating in a closed room. Air flow was important. Openness was key. Fortunately the house had two floors.

A minute later, Pam was in the exercise room on the ground floor. Okay, they'd yet to exercise in it and their treadmill was currently serving as a place to stack boxes, but whatever. She shooed Mitzy off the old chair in the corner and plopped into it, ignoring the dirty look the cat gave her.

Forget the damn meditation! Too keyed up, Pam looked down at the book in her lap, tracing the embossed gold letters of the title: *MAGICAL MOON RHYMES FOR ALL TIMES*. She opened the cover and flipped to the copyright page. Published in Toronto in 1882. Cripes. The book was old, yes, but more than age had yellowed its pages. Robin was right; this book had encountered a smoker, an incense burner, and someone who couldn't hold a coffee cup steady.

She pulled the crystals from the pockets of her sweats, selected the rose quartz, and held it in her left hand. With her right, she flipped to the first rhyme and read its introduction: *For those with too much time.* She snorted. *I wish!* But she dutifully read it anyway and moved on to the next rhyme—though the first rhyme didn't rhyme at all and, from the looks of it, neither did the second.

Pam was beginning to think that maybe the $35 she'd spent on the book hadn't been a wise purchase after all, when she reached page 17 and read the next rhyme's introduction: *For those who were born before or after their time.*

Oh my god! That's me! She always said to Robin that she belonged to her grandparents' generation more than her own. Pleased to finally come across a rhyme that resonated with her, Pam tightened her fingers around the rose quartz, then tutted when she noticed the coffee stain obscuring the verse's last line. Fortunately someone had penned in the missing words.

She silently read the rhyme:

> *when in the wrong time*
> *universe will not be kind*
> *until you align*
> *with swapping souls*

What the hell did that mean? She read it again, this time aloud.

1910

MARGARET PACED THE length of her bedroom, dreading the knock at the door that could come at any minute. Why did she feel this way? Her married and engaged friends were thrilled for her, and her single friends were envious of her. Mother looked as if she were having heart palpitations every time she spoke his name. Father's eyes shone every time the subject was raised at the dinner table. The only one who wasn't excited was Margaret. And she should be! She was about to receive what every young lady desired: a marriage proposal, and from Jasper Bainbridge.

Oh, the hearts that had broken when he'd invited her to the annual merchants' ball. That evening had been followed by the theatre, walks in the park, and quiet lunches in upscale cafés. When the invitation to dine with his family had arrived, she'd known it was only a matter of time. Then, one afternoon last week, she'd returned home from a carriage ride with Helena in time to see Father shaking Jasper's hand on the doorstep.

Helena's mouth had formed an "O" and she'd quickly ordered the coachman to circle the block. "Congratulations, Margaret," she'd crowed, her eyes bright with excitement. "I wonder what the engagement ring will look like. A diamond, surely. Lord knows he can afford it!"

Margaret had hoped her answering smile didn't look sickly. She'd sat in silence as Helena prattled on about when Jasper might propose, whether they'd marry in the chapel near the Bainbridge Estate, and who would be on the guest list. "I wonder if you'll beat me and Teddy to the altar?" Helena had mused. Then she'd nudged Margaret's arm. "Aren't you excited? You're going to become Mrs. Jasper Bainbridge!"

Yes, her fate had been sealed by a handshake. Jasper would *ask* her to marry him, but the question would be rhetorical. It would be scandalous to say no, and if she dared to respond that way, her parents would never speak to her again.

It wasn't that she didn't like Jasper. She enjoyed his company, shared his views on many issues of the day, and trusted him. But she didn't love him, and was starting to wonder if there was something wrong with her. She'd lied her way through all the breathless conversations with her friends about the boys, and then men, they'd kissed. To hear them talk, the kiss—touch—of a man produced some kind of delirious and pleasant state that couldn't be achieved through any other activity. Everyone always squealed in recognition as they listened to a girlfriend describe her bliss when her date had passionately kissed her good night. Margaret squealed and nodded too, but felt nothing but bewilderment. When she kissed a man, or accepted a proffered arm, she didn't feel blissful, or dreamy, or the titillating heat in her nether regions that Susanne always experienced on evenings out with Stephen. Nor did Margaret feel repulsed. She felt nothing. Nothing at all.

When she and Jasper kissed, her lips—and the rest of her—felt dead, and when she slipped her arm through his, she felt no different than when she slipped her arm through Grandmother's. It wasn't him; no male evoked the blissful state her friends raved about.

But she couldn't refuse his proposal. She was already twenty-three and didn't want to delay marriage any longer. Jasper would be kind; he would take care of her, and perhaps allow her to study at university—after she'd provided the requisite heir to the Bainbridge fortune. She, in turn, would be a dutiful wife and take care of him. As for love . . . she had to believe it would grow between them. He was certainly more interesting than all the other men she'd dated, and they *were* friends. Surely that was a solid foundation for marriage?

When a footman had arrived yesterday with Jasper's card, announcing his intent to visit and asking for confirmation that she'd be home, Margaret had known what would take place. Mother hadn't been able to sit still all day, and as the Wiltons' two housemaids had dusted and polished in the drawing room, they'd chattered about the upcoming proposal and the celebrations that would follow. If only Margaret could feel as excited!

She turned to the full-length mirror and displayed a broad smile. "Why yes, Jasper, I would love to marry you!" Her smile wilted. But what else could she do?

Margaret tensed when she heard the expected knock. "Yes?" she called, then raised her brows when Mother swung the door open, rather than a housemaid.

"He's here," Mother hissed. She pressed her hands together as if praying and studied Margaret. "Oh, my baby. My sweet, sweet baby." In a rare display of affection, she grasped Margaret's shoulders and pressed her cheek against hers. "Go on, now. Don't make him wait." Her eyes were moist when she stepped back.

"Yes, Mother."

Margaret descended the stairs to the drawing room, her heart sinking with each step. She briefly entertained the notion that perhaps she'd misinterpreted the handshake and the footman's visit, that everyone's excitement was misguided. After all, Father had never told her that

Jasper had requested his permission to propose. But he'd told Mother, and her demeanour since then, especially her exuberant anticipation of Jasper's visit, had told everyone else.

One look at Jasper chased away the last shred of hope to which Margaret still clung. He normally exuded an air of confidence, but not today. He paced the drawing room, his hands clasped behind his back and his eyes on his feet. Not wanting to embarrass him, Margaret stepped away from the doorway and cleared her throat. When she entered the room, he smiled and stepped toward her. "Margaret."

She extended her hand. He gently held her fingers and brushed his lips against her skin. "So nice to see you," he murmured.

"And you, Jasper. Would you like me to ring for tea?"

"Not yet." His Adam's apple bobbed; his eyes closed as he gathered his courage. Margaret reminded herself that she couldn't refuse him. What would she do? She had no money of her own, and no desire to work outside the home. Father's property would go to her brothers. They'd likely see to her needs, but the stigma . . . the sense of failure . . . Mother and Father expected grandchildren.

Jasper opened eyes now bright. He shifted his weight. "Margaret . . . darling . . . ever since our first evening together at the merchant's ball, my life has been blessed. Lately I find myself looking forward to our times together with an unbearable yearning. I admire your keen wit. You are pleasing to me in every way." Margaret's face flushed when his eyes left hers and travelled down her body, lingering an extra second on her breasts. He lifted his gaze, then dropped to one knee and pulled a small box from his inner jacket pocket. "Margaret, I would like nothing more than to have you as my wife." He lifted the box's lid and held the ring out to her. "Will you marry me?"

Her hand went to her throat; she stared at the glittering diamond. "Jasper—" A wave of nausea doubled her over. She clutched her stomach, surprised at the intensity of her physical reaction to Jasper's proposal. She felt as if she were being pulled in ten different directions, and shot out one hand to steady herself. Then, as quickly as it had begun, her discomfort passed. Gasping for air, she silently chided herself for being weak and childish. Jasper would think her mad! And be hurt. She must apologize, blame it on nerves, and accept his proposal.

"Margaret!"

She could hear the fear in Jasper's voice and raised her head to reassure him that she was all right. But . . . nothing was as it should be. Jasper had straightened and was wildly glancing around, his expression mirroring her confusion. What—

"Holy shit!"

Margaret turned toward the foreign voice. A wide-eyed and oddly clad woman sat in a chair, an open book on her lap. "Robin, get your ass down here, now!" she shouted.

Margaret shrank into Jasper and screamed.

Chapter Two

PAM STARED AT THE STRANGERS WHO'D materialized right in front of her eyes. The woman's scream snapped her to her senses. "Robin!" she yelled again, then drew back her arm, preparing to throw the rose quartz she still held in her trembling hand. "Don't move, or I'll bean you with this!" Though if they felt even half as petrified as they appeared, she didn't have anything to fear from them. "Robin!" Could Robin hear her with that damn headset on? Pam wasn't turning her back on these two! She lowered the rose quartz when footsteps thudded down the stairs.

"What is it now?" Robin shouted from the hallway. "It sounds like someone's getting killed! I'm going to get thrown out of my guild if—oh, sorry. I didn't know people were over." She stopped in the doorway and eyed the two strangers up and down. "Uh, you guys know Halloween's still a month away, right?" she said with a smile. "On your way to a costume party?" She frowned when nobody spoke, and shifted her attention to Pam. "Do you want to introduce me to your friends?"

"They appeared out of nowhere." Pam rested the crystal on the open book.

"What?"

"They just appeared—out of nowhere."

"Yeah, you already said that." Robin shrugged. "Okay, I don't know what the joke is, but I've got to get back upstairs." She turned away.

"No!" Pam shrieked. Something in her voice must have alarmed Robin, who spun around.

"What's going on, Pam?" Robin's eyes were now wary.

"I was sitting here reading my moon rhymes when these two just . . . appeared. Poof!" She snapped her fingers. "Just like that." If not for the woman's scream, she would have wondered if they were alive. They hadn't said a word or moved a muscle since. They just stood and stared.

"You seriously expect me to believe that two people appeared out of thin air?" Robin drawled. "Are you telling me you don't know them?"

"I've never seen them before in my life."

Robin squared her shoulders and glared at the couple. "Okay, I don't know who the two of you are or what you want, but if you're not out of this house in five seconds, I'm calling the police. In fact, maybe I'll do that anyway."

"The police!" the man blurted. "There's no reason to involve the constabulary. We mean you no harm. We're as shocked as you are. We don't know where we are."

"We're in my house," the woman said quietly.

Pam pushed herself forward. "I beg your pardon! You are most assuredly not in your house. You're in *my* house." Movement in the doorway caught her eye.

"Halfway house," Robin mouthed, tipping her head to the left.

Oh god, yes! A halfway house for those with mental health problems was only a couple of streets away. But how had they gotten into this house? And why were they dressed in old-fashioned clothing? No, wait—they *had* appeared out of nowhere. Or had she somehow blacked out? Had they slipped into the room while she was in some sort of meditative state, and their movements had brought her out of it? But if they were creeping around the house, why would they enter an occupied room? Then again, if they'd wandered away from the halfway house . . .

The woman was murmuring to the man and pointing upward. Pam followed their gazes and squinted at the high, decorative ceiling. "And this," she heard the woman say as the two strangers peered at the fireplace mantel.

Pam stiffened when she realized that Robin no longer stood in the doorway. Was this a weird dream? Who would appear or disappear next? Not wanting to alert the "guests" that she was alone, Pam tried to keep the rising panic from her face and silently willed Robin to return. She released a relieved sigh when Robin stepped into the room and put her hands on her hips.

"Okay, both doors are locked and no windows are broken," Robin announced.

"Did you call the cops?"

She shook her head. "I'm starting to think they are from the halfway house. I'd rather turn them over to the people there, not the cops."

Pam understood why. Robin's schizophrenic brother had spent a confusing night in the local lockup because officers had thought he was high. "But how did they get in?"

"We do have ears." The woman's voice was quiet but strong. "And this *is* my house. Though the furnishings and decor have changed."

"But when?" the man asked. "We were just standing in the drawing room."

"I don't know. But this," she pointed to a chip in the wooden panel beside the mantel, "happened when Uncle was demonstrating his golf swing and the club flew out of his hand. Father never repaired it because he didn't want to replace the entire panel for such a minor blemish."

Pam no longer feared them; she pitied them, especially the woman, who seemed to be living in a fantasy world. "Listen, lady—"

The woman raised her hand. "No, no. I'm not a lady. You may address me as Margaret."

After rolling her eyes at Robin, Pam said, "All right, Margaret. My family has owned this house for over fifty years, and I don't recall ever seeing you, your father, your uncle, or your companion here."

"That's impossible! Your family couldn't have owned this house for that length of time. My father had it built and still lives in it."

"My parents moved into this house in 1985," Pam said patiently.

The man paled at the same time Margaret gasped and grabbed his arm. "Did you say 1985?" he asked hoarsely.

"Yep, 1985. So you must be in the wrong house. Now, I don't know how you got in, but since you've been polite, I won't involve the police. But do you know the name of anyone who's been taking care of you in the big house a couple of streets over?"

"What are your names?" Robin asked. "Margaret what? And who are you?" she said to the man.

Margaret swallowed and placed her hand on her chest. "Something horrible has happened. Jasper and I—we were just standing in this room, but in 1910. What year is it now?"

Robin looked at Pam. "Great, they don't even know what year it is. I'll phone the halfway house, see if they're missing a couple of people."

"Wait!" Pam's mind raced. "Robin, I know you'll think I'm crazy, but they really did just appear out of thin air, right at the moment I was reading one of my time rhymes!" Oh my god, had she summoned people from the past? She grabbed her head. "I might have brought them here! Listen to this." She lifted the book, allowing the rose quartz to slide onto her lap.

Jasper's eyes widened and he pointed. "You practice the dark arts!"

Pam chuckled and waved the silly notion away. "No, no, this isn't magic." Or maybe it was. After all, she'd somehow sucked these poor people into the present—the future—no, the present. "These are inspirational rhymes, meant to help attune you with the essence of the universe."

Robin and Margaret tutted, then looked at each other, startled. Robin cleared her throat. "So you expect me to believe that saying a rhyme brought these people here?"

"What other explanation is there?"

"I don't know," Robin said sarcastically, "maybe that one of the doors was unlocked and they waltzed in off the street?"

Pam shook her head. "I saw you lock the front door, remember? And we haven't been out the back door all day. Or at least I haven't."

"Neither have I," Robin mumbled. "And the windows have been closed all day, too."

"And you keep denying what I saw with my own eyes!"

"And talking as if we're not here," Margaret said. "You also haven't told us what year it is."

"Two thousand and ten," Pam said.

Jasper and Margaret gaped at her. Margaret recovered first. "I may be able to prove that I live here." She frowned. "That I used to live here."

Robin folded her arms. "Oh, this'll be good."

"Robin!" Pam wanted to throttle her. "Will you please give them a chance? How can you prove it?" she said to Margaret.

Margaret hesitated. "Well, I keep a diary . . . in the attic."

"That's a strange place for a diary," Jasper said.

"It's the only way to ensure privacy."

"The housemaids?"

"No, Mother."

"I've never been up in the attic." Pam turned to Robin. "Have you?"

"I didn't even know there was an attic. Where's the access point?"

Pam shrugged. "I don't know."

"I do." Margaret stepped toward the doorway.

"Whoa!" Robin thrust out both her hands.

"Oh, for god's sake, Robin, if they were going to hurt us or steal anything, they would have done it by now. I believe them."

"You would."

Pam glared at her.

"Tell me where the attic is," Robin said to Margaret.

Margaret pointed upward. "It's at the top of the house."

Robin snickered. "I meant the access to the attic."

"I know." Margaret's voice held a hint of contempt.

"I haven't introduced myself," Pam said, hoping to defuse the hostility rising between the other two women. "I'm Pam, and that's Robin."

"I am Jasper Bainbridge," the man announced, "son of Mr. and Mrs. Sherwood Bainbridge, of the Bainbridge Estate. And this is Miss Margaret Wilton. Do you not have surnames now?"

"Oh yes, of course we do. My full name is Pamela Elizabeth Holden, and she's—"

"Robin Tillman." Robin's smile looked forced. "Pleased to meet you."

"Tillman?" Margaret glanced at Jasper. "The Tillman family used to live up the street from us—until Victor Tillman gambled away all his money."

"They might not be any relation," Pam said quickly. "Tons of people are named Tillman." Including Robin Elenora Tillman. Pam couldn't wait to tease her about leaving out the middle name she'd inherited from her great-grandmother—and hated. "Now, about that attic . . ."

"I'm delighted to meet you." Jasper stepped forward and held out his hand.

Pam stared at it, then giggled and extended hers. "Oh, charmed, I'm sure," she said breathily as he pressed his lips against it.

He turned to Robin. Pam stifled a grin as Robin grudgingly extended her hand. The moment Jasper's head lifted, Robin pulled her hand away. "Now that we all know each other, where's the access to the attic?"

"It's in my room." Margaret muttered something and shook her head. "The second room on the right."

"That's my bedroom!" Robin blurted. "You can't get to the attic from there."

"Yes, you can. If you'll allow me to pass, I'll show you."

"Hold on." Pam rested the book on the arm of the chair and the rose quartz on the book, then pushed herself up. "Let's go."

Jasper swept his arm out. "After you, ladies."

"Oh, thank you." The jerk at dinner could learn something about manners from Jasper! Pam felt as if she were in one of the old movies she loved to watch. She sighed when Robin stepped into the hallway and motioned for everyone to go ahead of her. "For all we know, he could knock us out the moment we turn our backs on him," she whispered as Pam passed her. "And let her lead us to the bedroom, to see if she knows where she's going."

Pam bit her tongue. Convinced that their two guests were indeed from the past, she wished Robin wouldn't be so mistrustful. They were representing the twenty-first century, here!

"This is certainly . . . different," Margaret said as they walked down the hallway. They climbed the stairs. Margaret didn't hesitate on the landing; she walked to Robin's bedroom and peered into it. "May I?"

"Be my guest," Robin said.

"Be careful, Margaret." Jasper waved his finger into the room. "We don't know what those contraptions do."

Did he mean the computer and the printer? Robin's dirty laundry was more likely to harm them. "They won't hurt you." Pam walked into the bedroom and twirled once. "See?" Margaret took a couple of tentative steps, then walked over when Pam beckoned to her. "Now you, Jasper," Pam said.

He shook his head. "It wouldn't be proper for me to enter a lady's bedroom."

"Well, that's all right, then. Robin's not a lady," Pam said with a giggle.

"And there's no way you're staying out here while we're in there," she heard Robin say.

"Very well." He stepped into the room and clasped his hands behind his back.

Robin remained in the doorway. "Go on, then. Show us the access."

Margaret started to open the closet door.

"Hey, what are you doing?" Robin stepped into the bedroom, then stopped.

"The access to the attic is through here. Where did you think it was?" Margaret opened the door and surveyed the closet's contents.

Pam peered over her shoulder. "What a mess! We'll have to clear out all that stuff on the floor."

"I'll do it," Robin quickly said. "You stand here. Both of you."

Neither Pam nor Margaret needed to be told twice. They silently watched as Robin threw shoes into a corner, rumpled shirts and pants onto the bed, and slid out a couple of boxes. She poked her head into the closet and looked up. "I can't see anything. They should have added a light when they wired the rest of the house. We need a flashlight."

"There's one in the basement," Pam said. "I'll get it."

"No! What about—"

"I'll be quick. If I hear any screaming, I'll call 911." Shaking her head, Pam headed for the basement. If she had the slightest suspicion that Jasper and Margaret would hurt Robin, she wouldn't leave her alone with them or go down into the basement by herself. Why would anyone dress up in early twentieth century clothing, break into a house, and pretend to be from the past? Maybe they were from the halfway house, but Pam was inclined to believe her own eyes, and desperately hoped that Margaret's diary was still there and would make Robin believe, too. Otherwise two visitors from the past would be forced to wander the streets, confused, hungry, and homeless—and it would be Pam's fault for being so careless with the power she hadn't realized she possessed!

MARGARET LISTENED TO Pam's receding footsteps and hoped she wouldn't take long to retrieve the flashlight. The curious creature staring at them from the closet opening made her nervous. At first she'd thought Robin was a young man. Then Robin had stopped shouting and had spoken with a low but feminine voice, and Margaret had noticed her hips and smooth face. Not a man but a woman, and a rather suspicious and gruff one at that. Margaret and Jasper were the ones who had cause to worry, not these two women from the future. If Margaret's diary wasn't there because it had already been discovered and removed sometime during the past one hundred years . . . Her heart thumped. There was no telling what Robin would do to them.

Of course, Margaret reasoned, perhaps she was dreaming, or had experienced a bout of nerves and was in a trance. It was hard to believe that she really had been transported to the future when she'd doubled over in the drawing room. Had her mind created this world to escape marriage to Jasper? No, she never would have imagined a world like this. Did all the women dress like men? Margaret hadn't seen a single dress come out of Robin's closet.

Robin's bedroom didn't look like a lady's room. Where were the vanity and the full-length mirror? The blue walls were drab and masculine; a multicoloured rectangular cloth hanging on one wall stood out in contrast. Was it supposed to represent a rainbow? It was the wrong shape.

She glanced over her shoulder when she heard Pam climbing the stairs. Were Pam and Robin related? Where were their husbands and families?

"Here," Pam said breathlessly, handing the flashlight to Robin.

She turned it on and swept it across the closet ceiling. "I do see what could be a trapdoor."

Margaret felt Jasper's eyes on her and turned to him. His brows drew together. "You climb into the attic?"

Blood rushed to her cheeks. "There's a stepladder in my closet. It's been there since I was a child. I think everyone but me has forgotten about it."

"We need a stepladder here, too," Robin said.

Pam sighed. "How about a chair? And not yours. You could break your neck if it rolls away." She snapped her fingers. "No, the stepladder we use to water the plants. I think it's in the guest bedroom."

"But what about your clothes?" Jasper asked Margaret, clearly struggling with the idea of Margaret scrambling into the attic to scribble in her diary.

Pam answered for her. "The closet's practically a small room." She jutted her chin toward Robin. "Remember how amazed you were when you first saw it?"

"I still don't understand why you didn't want this bedroom." Robin stepped out of the closet. "This thing's wasted on me."

"Because this was never my bedroom. I wanted *my* bedroom."

Pam had said the house belonged to her family. Margaret didn't think Pam and Robin were sisters. Cousins? "Are the two of you related?"

Pam drew breath to respond. "We're friends," Robin said tersely. "That's all you need to know. Are you going to get the stepladder, or what?"

"Yes!" With a sigh, Pam whirled.

Margaret didn't expect her to be away for long, and she wasn't. Robin took the stepladder from Pam and opened it inside the closet.

"I wonder what's up there." Pam sounded both fearful and curious. "If this were a crime show, a body would tumble out when we push that trapdoor open."

"A body!" Margaret edged closer to Jasper.

Robin looked at Pam. "You're scaring the guests. Do you want to go up? If I go, I expect you to keep an eye on them and not let them come up after me."

"Oh, for god's sake!" Pam climbed up the stepladder.

"Perhaps I should do it," Jasper said.

Pam chuckled. "Jasper, you'll find twenty-first century women are quite capable of doing things for ourselves."

From her vantage point, Margaret could only see Pam from the waist down. When she heard a thud, she could tell that the trapdoor had opened slightly, then thudded shut again. It had done so many times for her, until she'd learned how much momentum to put behind her shove so that it would swing fully open.

"Harder," Robin said.

A muffled crash told Margaret that Pam's second attempt had succeeded. "Light!" Pam barked. Robin handed her the flashlight. "Mmmm. Nothing much interesting here." Pam stood on tiptoe. "I don't see a diary. I don't see—aaaaah!" She leaped off the stepladder and dropped the flashlight. "Get it off me! Get it off me!" she cried, slapping at her head and making spitting noises. "Oh my god," she wailed, blindly moving around the bedroom.

Margaret snagged the cobweb on Pam's head, then ducked to avoid one of Pam's flailing arms. "It's all right. It's just a cobweb."

Pam's arms stilled. She lifted her head and eyed the cobweb draped over Margaret's fingers. "Oh." She slumped into Robin's chair. "I thought it was a daddy longlegs. I hate the little buggers."

So much for twenty-first-century women. Margaret deposited the cobweb in what looked like a trash bin.

Jasper smiled indulgently. "Let me do it."

"No. I'll do it." Robin picked up the flashlight and cast a suspicious glance at him. "You might have a diary tucked in your jacket."

"What, you're not worried they'll murder me while you're up there?" Pam said.

"I'm taking my phone." Robin snatched a rectangular object from her desk and slipped it into a front pocket. "One suspicious noise and I'm calling the cops." Flashlight in hand, she climbed the stepladder. "Where's this diary supposed to be?" she called, her voice muffled. "Because Pam's right, there's nothing up here except cobwebs and dust."

"One of the floorboards is broken," Margaret said loudly. "Father didn't want to replace it."

"Father sounds like a cheapskate," Pam murmured, followed by, "Sorry."

"It's all right. I share the sentiment." Margaret raised her voice again. "Once you're in the attic, walk along the southern side. You should spot it near the far end. Lift up the broken bit."

Robin's feet left the stepladder. Her legs dangled. "Pam, come give me a boost."

Pam snorted. "I'll try."

"Allow me," Jasper said.

"Yes, allow him, Robin. Please."

Robin sighed. "All right. Just give me a push after I've hoisted myself up a little more."

Margaret craned her neck, but Jasper was blocking her view. When he stepped back, Robin was gone and footsteps creaked overhead, moving away from the bedroom. Margaret heard what she thought might be a muffled exclamation, then the footsteps grew louder.

"I'm coming down," Robin shouted. Suddenly Margaret could see dangling feet. Jasper stepped forward and blocked her view again. She almost didn't believe her eyes when Robin emerged from the closet, a brown book clutched to her chest. My Lord, they really were in the future!

Pam gasped. "Oh my god, you found it!"

"Don't get excited yet." Robin nodded toward Margaret. "Let's see if she knows what's in it."

Margaret inwardly sighed. Would Robin ever be satisfied? Robin started to open the diary, then stopped and glanced behind her. "Um, why don't you stand with her, so I'll know you're not reading over my shoulder and telling her what to say?"

Jasper shook his head and walked to Margaret's side.

"Okay." Robin held the diary in front of her and lifted the front cover. "I have to admit, it looks old."

Of course it's old, it's been there for a hundred years! Margaret wanted to shout.

Robin turned several yellow-edged pages with care, then shut the diary, flipped it over, and lifted its back cover. "Let me find the last entry," she murmured. "And why don't you tell me what the date will be? If you're telling the truth, you should remember because you practically just wrote it."

Margaret seethed at the invasion of privacy, but she needed to gain the woman's trust. And Robin was right. Margaret had written an entry just last night, musing about— Her hand went to her throat and her cheeks burned. Her last entry was all about how she felt about Jasper's impending proposal! It was supposed to be private! What if Robin read it out loud, or asked her to tell everyone what it said? What if she gave the diary to Jasper?

"Ah, found it. What's the date?"

"September 18th, 1910," Margaret said hoarsely.

Robin's brows rose. "And let's see what it says."

Please, read it to yourself! Fortunately Robin did, but Margaret still wanted to die from embarrassment and couldn't tear her eyes away from Robin's face. The woman was reading her innermost thoughts— concerns, fears, and opinions that she never would have shared with anyone else. Robin would probably laugh, read Margaret's words aloud, and berate her. Margaret tensed when Robin finally raised her head. She forced herself to hold Robin's gaze, when what she wanted to do was lower her head in shame. How stricken she must look!

"There's nothing interesting in this entry," Robin said. "Just stuff you probably wouldn't remember, even if you'd just written it. I'll look for a more interesting one."

Almost swaying with relief, Margaret let out her pent breath and silently thanked Robin, who had a heart after all. "Try June 23rd," she suggested, partly to help and partly to prevent Robin from reading every word in her diary.

"That was the night we went to the theatre," Jasper said.

"Yes." He probably remembered because of the long kiss they'd shared in the carriage on the way home, a progression from the usual peck on the lips. Fortunately she hadn't mentioned it in her entry. If she had, she would have expressed her ongoing bewilderment that Jasper didn't affect her in ways he should.

Robin paged backward. "June 23rd," she murmured. "Uh, yeah, you did go to the theatre, but what else can you tell me?"

"That a gentleman sitting near us fell asleep and snored loudly until Jasper shook him awake." Margaret's reason for recalling the evening. "And that I thought the actor who played the doctor wasn't very good."

Robin lowered the diary and looked at Pam. "That's what it says."

Pam leaped to her feet and punched a fist into the air. "Yeah! And enough with the tests, Robin. Unless they somehow managed to sneak in here, get into the attic through *your* closet, and plant the diary—"

"And age it," Robin said.

"They're who they say they are—or rather, from where they say they're from." Pam's mouth dropped open and she clutched her hands in front of her chest. "I summoned these people from the past. Incredible!"

Frankly, Margaret didn't view her circumstances as a cause for celebration or wonder. She held out her hand. "Can I have my diary, please?" As Robin handed it over, she met Margaret's eyes again. Heat travelled from Margaret's neck to the top of her head. "Thank you," she mumbled.

Robin nodded. "So now what?"

"I want to go home," Margaret said firmly. "We don't belong here." Nor did she want to stay here, in her home that was not her home; in a strange world with strange machines; in a future in which women . . . Well, she didn't know what to make of them. She'd only seen the two, but they were most unladylike—especially Robin.

"I agree with Margaret," Jasper said. "Send us back."

Everyone looked at Pam. "Uh—I—you see, the thing is, I don't know how I brought you here. It wasn't intentional. It just happened."

"You said you were reading from that book," Robin said.

"Yes! Maybe reading the rhyme again will send them back."

"I doubt it. I think we're stuck with them."

Pam frowned. "Don't be so pessimistic. It's worth a try. Oh, but Margaret, first we should put the diary back where we found it. I don't know what would happen if two copies of your diary ended up in 1910. I suppose it's possible the entire universe would collapse."

Robin threw her hands into the air. "Great. Maybe I should make a few phone calls, to say good-bye. Then again, I guess there's no point, if everyone's about to wink out of existence."

"Relax, Robin. I know what I'm doing. I watch *Star Trek*. Everything should be fine if we put the diary back."

"I'm not so sure about that," Robin said slowly. "But let's do it. I'll put it back."

Margaret reluctantly returned the diary to her. It didn't take long for Jasper to boost Robin into the attic and moments later, she emerged from the closet empty-handed.

"I didn't memorize the exact position of the diary, so I did the best I could," Robin said, shrugging.

"It'll have to do." Pam walked toward the doorway and motioned for everyone to follow her. "Let's do this."

"I wasn't downstairs when it happened," Robin said. "I can't believe I'm actually saying this, but maybe I should be where I was when you . . . summoned them."

Pam grunted. "Good idea."

About to follow Pam, Margaret turned back toward Robin. "It was a pleasure."

"Yeah. With luck, we won't see each other again."

Margaret certainly hoped so!

Robin shrugged, almost apologetically. "But I think we will."

"Enough with the pessimism, Robin!" Pam hissed.

"I'm not being pessimistic. It's just—" She broke off. "It doesn't matter. Good luck."

"Good-bye, Robin," Jasper said.

Already in the hallway, Margaret didn't hear Robin's response, if there was one. She couldn't wait to return to the drawing room so Pam could return them to *her* drawing room. If Pam failed—Margaret couldn't bear to consider the end of everything she knew. Except Jasper. No matter what happened, she'd have him. She glanced over her shoulder. His smile reassured her.

When they reached the drawing room, Pam took charge. "All right, you two stand where you were when you arrived." She pointed to the appropriate spot and when they were in position, Pam plunked into the chair and snatched up the crystal. "Right, then." She moved the book onto her lap, opened it, and flipped to a page. "I was reading this rhyme, and I was holding the rose quartz in my left hand." She looked up at Margaret and Jasper. "Safe travels."

"It was a pleasure, Pam," Jasper said.

Margaret echoed him, then wanted to shake her head when Pam's eyes grew misty.

"Here we go, then." Pam took a deep breath, then read what sounded like a nonsensical rhyme. Nothing happened. "Oh, last time I read it to myself first. Let me try again." She was silent for a bit, then recited the rhyme aloud. Margaret wanted to cry out in frustration when they still stood in 2010.

"Robin!" Pam bellowed. "Are you sitting down?"

"Yes," came the shouted reply.

Pam switched the rose quartz to her other hand. She smiled sheepishly. "One more try." She lowered her head and, after a moment, said the rhyme again.

Margaret looked at Jasper, knew his resigned and sad eyes matched hers. Everyone—everything—they knew was gone. He reached for her hand and squeezed it. "We still have each other."

"Yes." She was grateful it was him, someone she cared for who was around her age.

Footsteps thudded down the stairs. Robin didn't seem surprised to see them. "Didn't work, then?"

Pam shook her head. "I'm sorry. This is all my fault."

Margaret didn't know at whom the apology was directed. And now what? Were they to start a new life here? How? What was outside the door? Where were they? In her home, or what used to be her home, but where? A lot could change in a hundred years. "Are we still in Toronto, in Canada?"

"What?" Pam said. Then, "Oh, yes, you are. Still Toronto, and still Canada, all ten provinces and three territories."

Margaret exchanged a glance with Jasper. Not quite the Canada they remembered, but at least they were in the same city and country.

Jasper pursed his lips. "We'll have to find lodging, though I don't know if the bills in my billfold are worth anything."

"Oh my god, you can't go out looking like that." Pam stood and tossed the book and crystal onto the chair. "You'll have to stay here until we figure out what to do." She thrust her chin out and looked at Robin, perhaps expecting defiance.

"What *are* we going to do?" Robin asked.

"There has to be a way to send them back. I have to talk to Jake."

Robin's eyes widened. "You can't tell him about them! We'll have every freaking reporter in the world here."

"I won't. I'll be careful."

"And if we can't figure out how to send them back?"

Pam swallowed. "Then we'll have to help them settle here."

Robin's hands went to her hips. "They don't even have ID!"

"First things first." Pam twisted to eye them up and down. "You have somewhere to stay, but you need clothes."

Margaret frowned down at herself. What was wrong with her dress?

"I'll have to measure you. And let's figure out sleeping arrangements."

Jasper pulled out his pocket watch. "It's only 4:15. Or rather, it was 4:15." He frowned. "My watch has stopped."

"Uh, it's almost nine." Robin leaned against the doorframe. "In the evening."

"Oh."

Pam smiled. "Not jet lag, time travel lag!" Her smile faded. "Doesn't matter. So, um, are you two together, or do you want separate bedrooms?"

Margaret's mouth dropped open; the tips of poor Jasper's ears turned red. "Separate bedrooms!" he sputtered. "How dare you suggest otherwise."

Margaret put her hand on his arm. "It's all right, Jasper. Perhaps the customs are different now."

"Still. Margaret and I, we're not married, we're . . ." He turned to her. She answered his unspoken question. "Engaged."

"Engaged," he repeated, beaming. "But wait." He glanced around, then his eyes searched the floor near his feet. "What happened to the ring?"

"What ring?" Pam asked.

"I was proposing when you brought us here. I was holding the ring." He fumbled in his jacket pockets, then shook his head.

"That's interesting," Robin said.

"That they were in the middle of getting engaged when I brought them here?" Pam clapped her hands. "I'll say."

"No, that the ring didn't come with them."

Margaret suddenly had a vision of Mother rushing into the drawing room, too impatient to wait for Margaret to emerge with the happy news, and finding nothing but the box with the ring lying on the floor.

Robin pushed herself away from the doorframe. "You'll need something to eat. While Pam sorts you out, I'll go get a pizza." She left without waiting for a reply.

A pizza?

"You'll like it," Pam said, noticing their puzzled faces. "All right, we only have three beds, so Jasper, take the guest room. You'll be more comfortable in there. Margaret, take Robin's room. Robin and I can sleep in my room."

"Are you sure Robin won't mind? I don't want to put her out of her own bedroom." It would likely antagonize the woman, the last thing Margaret wanted to do.

"She won't mind." Pam's eyes narrowed. "Okay, I'm going to make a wild guess here that the two of you don't want to sit and eat pizza in your underwear. So . . . we'll hold off on changing for bed. Jasper, would you mind coming upstairs with me? We've been using the guest room as a sort of storage area. Maybe you can help carry some boxes down to the basement."

"Of course." His hand brushed Margaret's elbow as he passed her. "I won't be long," he murmured.

And then she was alone. In her house, but not her house; her drawing room, but not her drawing room. The nearby window drew her eye, but she wouldn't dare lift the window covering, afraid of what she'd see. What would become of her and Jasper? They were nameless, homeless, and penniless, having no choice but to rely on two strange women either to send them home or help them adjust to their new circumstances. How could Pam have unintentionally brought them here? Were she and Robin practitioners of the dark arts, as Jasper had suggested? Would they gain Margaret and Jasper's trust, then sacrifice them as they lay sleeping in their beds?

Margaret shook herself. She was allowing fanciful thoughts to carry her away rather than facing an unbelievable truth: she and Jasper were now in the year 2010. Their families, friends, hopes, and dreams . . . gone. Dead. All of them, dead. Her eyes welled with tears.

"I forgot to ask what you—oh."

Margaret rubbed furiously at her eyes and kept one shoulder toward the door.

Robin approached, peered at her. "I'd feel overwhelmed, too," she said softly. Her eyes were kind, not mocking.

"I'm afraid to look out the window," Margaret admitted, surprising herself. But better for Robin to know about her fear than Jasper. She had to remain strong for him.

"Why don't you save that for tomorrow, when it's light? And why don't you sit down? You *can* sit down in that dress?"

Robin's absurd question brightened Margaret's mood. A giggle escaped her throat. "Of course I can sit down!" Perhaps she shouldn't be surprised that such a question had come from a woman who looked like a ruffian. "Don't women wear dresses anymore?"

Robin snorted. "I don't. Wouldn't be caught dead in one. But most women do. Not all the time, though. Sometimes."

"Oh." She had much to learn about 2010 women. Robin had shorter hair than some of the men Margaret knew. What about the men? Did they dress like women now and grow their hair long?

"Anyway, I forgot to ask what you and Jasper like to eat. I can choose what to put on the pizza. Ham, bacon, green pepper, mushrooms—"

Margaret didn't care; she wasn't hungry. "Anything. It doesn't matter."

Robin shrugged. "Okay. I'll go get dinner." She strode from the room.

Margaret chided herself. Where were her manners? Just because she'd been hurled into the future didn't mean she could behave like a lout. She should have thanked Robin, for her concern and for considering their basic needs. Because they were children here, incapable of taking care of themselves. Suddenly Margaret pinched the back of her hand, dug in her fingernails until the skin turned an angry red and droplets of blood formed. She looked around the room. No, she wasn't in her bed, dreaming. She was still here, in 2010.

Chapter Three

ROBIN LOWERED HER E-READER WHEN PAM came into the bedroom. "They all tucked in?"

Pam nodded. "I've stored Margaret's dress in your closet, so be careful with it."

Robin's brows shot up. "What do you think I'll do? Wear it?" She smiled at Pam's answering grin. "What are they sleeping in?"

"I didn't have anything for him, so I guess he's in his skivvies." Or nude. "I gave Margaret that nightie my mother gave me a few years ago, the one I've never worn. It's okay length-wise, but a little baggy. I tried to give her a t-shirt and sweats for tomorrow, but she wants a dress."

"She's going to sit around in a dress?"

Pam shrugged. "That's what she wants. I'll have to find her one that falls below the knee, so she won't be too scandalized. Jasper will have to wear the same clothes until I get home." She stuck her phone under Robin's nose.

"You took pictures?"

"I had to. Her hair won't stay like that. Somehow I'll have to recreate the style when we know how to send them back. Or take her to Steve's and show him this." She gasped. "I'm going to look them up on the Net, see if I can find anything."

Robin set her e-reader on the nightstand, rolled over, and propped herself up on one elbow. "Look for him. It sounds like he's some type of aristocrat."

Pam typed *Jasper Bainbridge* and waited for the search results. She scanned the list. Nothing jumped out at her, so she moved to the next page, and the next. "Oh my god, this could be something." She clicked and waited for the old newspaper article to appear on the display.

Halifax Social Pages, December 1910
Wilton-Bainbridge Wedding
The marriage of Miss Margaret Wilton, daughter of Mr. and Mrs. J.S. Wilton of Toronto, to Mr. Jasper Bainbridge, the eldest son of Mr. and Mrs. S.T. Bainbridge of Toronto, was solemnized on December 15, 1910 at St. Mark's Church. Mr. and Mrs. Bainbridge are honeymooning in New Brunswick. They will reside in Halifax.

Robin pointed. "Look at the date!"

"They certainly didn't waste any time. And they moved to Halifax." Excitement coursed through Pam. "And you know what this means? We figured out how to send them back! Or, rather, we will figure it out." This time travel stuff was confusing.

Robin rolled onto her back and threw her arm across her forehead. "So she married him."

"You sound surprised."

"She doesn't love him."

Pam snorted. "And you know that how?"

"From the last entry in her diary."

"Why? What did it say?" Pam gripped Robin's arm. "Tell me."

Robin shook her head. "It's bad enough that I read it. And because it *was* the last entry in her diary, I was pretty sure we wouldn't figure out how to send them back."

"No, don't you see? She didn't write in her diary again because she knew we'd eventually find it. And that's why she left it there. She knew she'd need it in 2010, to prove to us that they weren't lying."

Robin grunted.

"I wonder why she didn't write a message to us in the diary, though," Pam said. "Like, 'Dear Pam and Robin. You've just found this in the attic in 2010. A rhyme in a black book brought Jasper and me here. I hope this is enough proof for you, Robin.'"

"Maybe because she knew there wasn't a message when we found it," Robin said.

Pam had the feeling that if she thought too hard about Robin's answer, her brain would shut down. Time to move on. "So she doesn't love Jasper, eh? That sucks." She turned off her phone and put it on her nightstand, then climbed into bed. "Maybe that's why she quickly agreed that I could measure him. I told her she could do it, but she didn't want to."

"I don't think they're, uh . . . that familiar with each other." Robin's eyes glinted mischievously. "And maybe she wasn't sure what you wanted her to measure."

Pam barked a laugh, then covered her mouth and giggled into her hand. If she were Margaret, *she'd* certainly be more familiar with Jasper. When he'd removed his jacket before helping her move the boxes . . . well, his cotton shirt had barely restrained his biceps when he'd lifted two or three boxes at once, and she couldn't help admiring his ass as she'd followed him downstairs. His full head of sandy hair, neatly clipped moustache, and Roman nose contributed to his rugged handsomeness. And his red face when she'd measured his inseam had endeared him to her. Not wanting to embarrass him further, she hadn't voiced her observation that he hung to the right. If only he wasn't from 1910—and engaged. She felt a connection to him that ran deeper than physical attraction. It was his manner, his gentleness.

Out of all the people she could have summoned from the past, why them? Why him? Oh! She abruptly turned and grabbed Robin's arm again. "Maybe I was able to summon them because Jasper and I were lovers in a previous life!"

Robin snickered. "You wish! And not that I'm giving any credence to past lives, but wouldn't that mean you could have been Margaret?"

Pam grimaced. "Right. Scratch that theory." She let go of Robin. "Margaret's a lucky woman. What I wouldn't do for a man like Jasper." He was worth ten of the jerks like the one at dinner. "Anyway, no point drooling over what I can't have. Let's talk about tomorrow."

"What about tomorrow?" Robin asked, her brow furrowing.

"I have to go to work."

"And I have to go to class."

"We can't leave them here alone! How many classes do you have?"

"Two." Robin sighed. "But one's a lab. I guess I can skip them." She raised a finger. "But only this once. You have to figure out how to send them back."

"I will! You saw the marriage announcement. Have faith!" She blew out some air. "Look, I'll pick them up some clothes on my lunch hour. Saturday, we'll all go to Jake's."

"All of us? Are you sure that's a good idea? He can't know about them."

Pam held up her hand. "I know. But Jake's pretty intuitive." She lowered her voice. "And I've heard he can see auras. He's also a little psychic."

Robin's face screwed up. "How can he be a *little* psychic? He either is, or he isn't, and my money is on isn't. And I'm not going into that store. If anyone sees me there, I'll die."

"Fine, fine, I'll take them myself."

"Good. By Saturday I'll want some time alone, especially after babysitting all day Friday."

Pam reached over and turned off the lamp, so she could roll her eyes in the dark. She knew exactly what Robin would do when everyone else was at Jake's—sit on her ass in front of her computer and yell into her headset. So be it. They'd be better off without Robin along on their field trip. Pam wouldn't need Robin's skepticism rearing its head every five seconds, especially in front of Jake.

"Good night," she murmured, then closed her eyes and wondered if someone from the past could appear in her dreams. She hoped so.

WITH A MULTITUDE of bags hanging off her arms, Pam struggled to unlock the front door. She breathed a sigh of relief when the key finally turned in the lock. The TV was on. A peek into the living room located their two guests, or at least the backs of their heads. She dumped the bags on the hallway floor and inhaled the aroma of garlic and onions—Robin was probably in the kitchen. Pam strode up the hall, her heels clicking on the wooden floor.

"Do you think it's a good idea to let them watch TV?"

Robin looked up from the pot she was stirring. "What did you want me to do, lock them in a room all day? You're taking them out tomorrow."

Pam sighed and nodded. "I suppose we can't shelter them." She motioned for Robin to feed her a spoonful of the sauce. "Mmm. It's good," she said, savouring the sauce's zing. "So it went okay today?"

Robin nodded. "The TV? A godsend. They've been enraptured from the moment I turned it on. They did eat lunch, but then they wanted to go right back into the living room."

"Do they understand what it is?"

"Well, I explained it to them as best I could. They know about moving pictures, so it wasn't too much of a stretch to explain that we can broadcast them. And they love it!" She frowned. "They've been awfully quiet since the soap operas came on, though. I think they might have gone into some type of mental shock."

"Which you were happy to leave them in."

"What can I say?" Robin said with a shrug.

Pam sighed. "Did Mitzy come out?"

"I caught a glimpse of her a couple of hours ago, but no, she's still hiding."

"I'll try to find her later. Anyway, I'd better go see if they're all right."

Pam walked into the living room. "Good evening. How was your day?"

Two bleary-eyed faces turned to her. Jasper stood and extended his hand. After a moment of confusion, Pam held out hers. She grew weak at the knees when he kissed it. She would have giggled like a schoolgirl, if not for Margaret's presence. Looking at her made Pam want to call a chiropractor. "You can sit back, Margaret. You don't have to perch on the edge like that."

"I'm quite comfortable," Margaret said. "You look lovely, Pam."

"Oh." Pam felt herself blushing. "Thank you."

"Will Robin be dressing for dinner?"

"Dressing for dinner?" Pam sounded shrill. "No, Robin doesn't dress for dinner. I normally don't, either." She glanced at Jasper and cleared her throat. "But I will tonight." And Robin had better not say a damn thing about it. "Robin tells me you enjoy watching TV."

Jasper nodded. "We've been watching a rather melodramatic series of vignettes. I must say, I'm surprised at how many of them are of a carnal nature. I had to cover Margaret's eyes."

Pam raised her brows. "Did you? Well, whatever you think is appropriate." They *would* be going back to 1910, after all. Best not to corrupt the lady too much.

"What we're viewing now, though . . ." Margaret slowly shook her head. "The level of depravity, the greed, the self-absorption and complete lack of regard for others—it's shocking."

Curious, Pam turned to the TV, then chuckled. "Oh, don't worry about that, it's just the news."

Robin leaned around the archway. "Dinner's ready. We'll eat in the kitchen."

Jasper smiled. "Ladies." Pam jealously looked on as he offered Margaret his elbow.

"Aren't you changing?" Robin said when Pam reached the kitchen.

"No, I am *not*." She hoped her tone was enough to silence Robin.

Fortunately Robin took the hint, but her amused eyes spoke volumes. She lifted two plates. "Here, take these. They're all the same, so put them anywhere."

"All right." Pam carried them over to the table, in time to see Jasper pull out Margaret's chair for her. She set a plate down in front of Margaret. "Where are you sitting, Jasper? Next to Margaret?"

"Across from her."

Pam set the plate down on the other side of the table, then stifled a giggle when Jasper pulled out another chair. "Thank you." She grabbed the glass Robin had already filled with water and gulped some down. Now what was Jasper doing, standing behind his own chair?

Robin set the remaining plates on the table. "Sit, Jasper. We went through this at lunch. You don't have to stand at attention until I'm seated." He stepped to his right. "And don't pull out my chair. We went through that, too."

He stopped moving and met Margaret's eyes; she shrugged slightly and turned to Robin. "Let me help you with the meals tomorrow," she said.

"No, it's okay." Robin sat down. "I don't mind cooking."

"But I'd like to help. We're imposing."

"You're not responsible for that." Robin gave Pam a pointed look. "But if it'll make you feel better, okay, maybe we can cook dinner together tomorrow night."

Margaret nodded. "I would like that."

"Sounds like a plan, then." Pam eyed her food and reached for her napkin. Why was everyone just sitting there?

Jasper cleared his throat. "Would you like to say grace, Pam?"

"Huh?"

"Yes, would you like to say grace, Pam?" Robin's mouth twitched. "Just as we did at breakfast and lunch."

Oh, dear. Pam had run out that morning without eating breakfast. Usually she had at least a piece of toast, but between showing Margaret and Jasper how to work the shower and finding Margaret a dress, she'd barely made it out of the house on time and had picked up a coffee and muffin on the way to work. "Breakfast and lunch, eh? Jesus!" Two heads bowed. Oh, shit. "Yes, Jesus, uh, our Lord, we thank you for this, um, nourishment your humble servant Robin has prepared." She pressed her lips together to stop herself from laughing when Robin's shoulders shook. "Amen."

"Amen," Jasper and Margaret echoed.

"Let's eat," Pam announced, *before I get myself into more trouble.* She unfolded her napkin. "So, I picked up a few clothes for you. We'll have a little fashion show later. Margaret, I bought you a couple of dresses, but also casual wear. Just try everything on, all right? You might like the casual clothes."

"I'll have a look at them," Margaret said.

"Well, good. That's a start." Pam wound spaghetti around her fork.

Jasper had already sampled his plate. "It's very tasty. My compliments to the cook."

Margaret nodded. "Quite. But you're not Italian, are you? You're too fair. And Tillman isn't an Italian name."

"No, I just like Italian food," Robin said.

"You prepare it well."

"Thank you."

Pam lowered her head and smiled at Robin's flushed cheeks. It must be killing her to be so polite. Robin usually brushed aside compliments.

"So what's the plan for tomorrow, then?" Robin asked. "If we're lucky, Margaret and Jasper won't need most of the clothes you bought. Not that I'm anxious to see you go," she quickly added.

"After lunch, we'll go to Jake's, see what he has to say." Pam turned to Jasper. "I want you and Margaret to come with me."

"Who is Jake?" he asked.

"I bought the black book from his store. He's an expert in the area of the . . . uh, mystical arts."

Jasper's face clouded. "A practitioner of the dark arts?"

"No. It's a New Age store, selling spiritual books, and crystals, and relaxing music."

"And black books that tear people from their own time." He shook his head. "We won't go with you."

"You have to! Jake is . . . gifted." She ignored Robin's rolling eyes. "I need his advice, and having you and Margaret there will give him more to work with. He . . . senses things."

"I don't understand what he can learn from us. I gather it's prudent not to tell others who we are and where we're from."

"Oh, definitely. We can't breathe a word to anyone." Pam rested her fork on her plate so she could gesture with both hands. "But Jake . . . he can see auras." She touched her temples, rotated her hands. "He'll pick up any vibes you're emitting."

Jasper's brows rose. "It sounds like the dark arts to me. But if that's what brought us here and what has to send us back, and you think this man's knowledge can help—"

Pam nodded vigorously. "Oh, it can."

"Then I'll go with you, but not Margaret." He gazed across the table. "You shouldn't be exposed to such a man, or his establishment."

"I quite agree," Margaret said with a shudder.

Pam could hardly contain her glee. An afternoon out with Jasper! "Well, I suppose having one of you with me will do. Robin, you won't mind spending the afternoon in with Margaret, right?"

"No, of course not," Robin said. "Margaret can watch TV."

Margaret shook her head. "I've had quite enough of that."

Robin frowned. "Oh."

"I'm sure you'll find something to do." Pam smiled at her, hoping Robin would mask her displeasure by smiling in return. Robin did, but couldn't hide the resignation in her eyes.

Chapter Four

Pam held onto Jasper's arm so she wouldn't lose him. "Oops, don't cross on red, remember." She pulled him back from the curb.

"My apologies, Pam. I was looking at that silver motor over there and forgot to pay attention to the light."

So despite his charming manners, he wasn't so different from today's men, after all. Next he'd be scratching his crotch and demanding to watch hockey. "You have cars, don't you? The Model T or something like that?"

"I do have one, and they're becoming more popular. But I still prefer a horse and carriage when I'm out with a lady."

Ooh, lucky Margaret!

"Laurence—one of my friends—insists that everyone will eventually have a motor. He's a bit of a know-it-all, so I'm not about to tell him he's right." Jasper grinned.

Pam returned his smile and felt a lump in her throat. His confidence that he'd see his friend again was endearing. Feigned or genuine, she appreciated the support, and couldn't remember the last time she'd had so much fun on a man's arm. Jasper's almost running commentary had kept her entertained since they'd left the subway. He was so curious—and so brave! "Oh, green light. And the store we want is just around the corner."

They paused outside the window with *Mathers Mystic Marketplace* emblazoned across it.

"I didn't expect the shop to be in such a busy area. Quite brazen." Jasper peered through the window. "Are you sure this is necessary?"

"It's a perfectly respectable store, as I keep telling you. That's why it's not hidden down a back alley."

Jasper sniffed. "You wouldn't find an establishment like this on a busy road where I come from."

"Well, we're not there, are we? And if you want to go back to where you came from, I need to talk to Jake."

A man in a suit walked by them, pulled open the glass door, and disappeared into the store. Jasper pursed his lips. "He looked like a respectable gentleman and he went inside."

Slightly miffed that a stranger in a suit mattered to him more than her opinion, Pam tugged on his arm. "Come on." When he slipped his arm from hers, she opened her mouth to tell him to stay close, then realized he was opening the door for her. Her irritation with him fizzled. He was from 1910; it was only natural that a man's actions would sway him more than a woman's opinion, especially when it came from a strange woman from the future. She chuckled to herself and thanked him as she stepped into the store.

They entered an oasis from the hustle and bustle outside. The soothing music instantly relaxed her; she closed her eyes and quietly hummed, then almost yelped when Jasper's fingers dug into her arm. Her eyes snapped open. "What?"

"Evil!"

She followed his gaze. "They're tarot cards, Jasper. They're just a bit of fun."

"No respectable person would touch them!" His eyes focused on a point past the cards.

Crystal balls. Great. Before Jasper could open his mouth, she pulled him over to the *Angel* section. "Oh, look, angel meditations. You might like—" Shit! The *Angel* section was right next to the *Pagan* area. She'd browse another time. "Let's see if Jake's free."

The cashier directed them to the back room. Pam parted the strings of beads and knocked on the doorframe.

"Just a sec." Jake's eyes remained on the LCD as he tapped away at the keyboard. "There." He swung his chair around; his face lit up and he sprang to his feet. "Pamela! Why didn't you say it was you?"

She gave him a quick hug and offered her left cheek, then her right, for the obligatory air kisses.

Jake looked past her. "And I see you have a friend with you."

She noted the curiosity in his eyes with satisfaction. "Yes. This is Jasper. Jasper, Jake."

Jake lifted his hand to wave, then grasped the hand Jasper extended and pumped it. His attention shifted back to Pam. "So, what can I do for you, Pamela?"

"Ah, yes. Well." Time to tell him the story she'd concocted on the way. "Remember that book I bought on Thursday? The moon rhymes one?"

His brows drew together. "Of course. *Magical Moon Rhymes for All Times.* Is there a problem? I told you about the coffee stains. Even in its slightly damaged state, I let it go much too cheaply. There are some powerful rhymes in there."

No kidding. She put her hand on his arm. "No, no, I *love* the book, Jake. Love it! So much so that I wanted to learn more about moon rhymes. I came across an interesting site on the Net about people's experiences with them, and one . . . um, woman posted recently to the forum, saying she had a bit of a problem. I didn't know how to help her, but I thought, if anyone would know, it would be Jake."

He nodded. "What's the problem?"

"Well, you see, she was reading one of the rhymes, and all of a sudden a, uh . . . locket appeared on her lap. You can imagine how shocked she was. She figured it must have come from another time, so she desperately wanted to send it back to wherever it came from so that the, um, universal timeline wouldn't be affected. But she read the rhyme again, and nothing happened. It didn't go away, and she still has it. The poor woman is going out of her mind. Why isn't the rhyme working?" She gazed at him, hoping he knew the answer.

He stared at her, then burst out laughing. "Pamela, Pamela, Pamela. I'm so glad you came to me."

Her hopes rose. "Really?"

"Yes. You must be very careful when you're on the Internet. This poor woman is obviously deluded."

"What? No, she most certainly isn't deluded."

"You were there? You saw the locket appear?"

"Not exactly."

He lifted his hands, palms up. "See?"

Jasper folded his arms. "You just told the lady the book you sold her contains powerful rhymes."

Jake's eyes flicked to Jasper. "It does. But the rhymes affect the spiritual realm. I've never heard of a physical object travelling through time."

People were spiritual. "But you've heard of spirits travelling through time?" Pam asked.

"Of course. Spirits from the past grace us with their presence at séances."

But she'd thought spirits were outside time, in a different dimension. Wait—not when they were inside bodies! "Perhaps the locket contains spiritual energy!"

Jake shrugged. "It's possible, I suppose."

"Let's say it does. Why can't she send it back? Does she have to read another rhyme?" Oh! They hadn't tried that. Maybe she should read all the rhymes out loud.

"No. But you said she used a moon rhyme, correct?"

She nodded.

"When does she claim the locket arrived?"

Pam cleared her throat. "Oh, two or three days ago."

He sighed and rolled his eyes. "Ah, well, moon rhymes are obviously associated with the lunar cycle."

She waited for more. "So?"

"They only work once per cycle. Tell this woman she has to read the rhyme during the same phase of the next moon cycle."

"So, if she read the rhyme during a new moon, she has to wait for the next new moon to send the locket away?"

He nodded.

Yes! "Oh. Thank you."

"But, Pamela, the woman is putting you on. If she asks you for money, don't give her any."

"Don't worry, Jake. She won't." She turned to Jasper. "Shall we go?"

"Oh, before you do, I want to show you something." Jake motioned for her and Jasper to leave the back room, then led them to a display near the cash. "We received this new shipment of oils yesterday, and there's one that's just perfect for you." He scanned the stacked bottles, picked one up, and read from its label. "Protective Oil. Rub on forehead to protect against scammers and con artists."

"What does that mean?" Jasper murmured.

Pam turned to him. "It protects against, er, swindlers." She wasn't *that* gullible, but she didn't want to dismiss Jake's advice in front of Jasper. She turned back to Jake. "Is it scented?"

Jake nodded. "I suggest you apply it before you go on the Internet."

"Perhaps we should have rubbed some on our foreheads before coming into this shop," Jasper said.

Jake's eyes bulged. "Excuse me?"

Jasper tugged on Pam's arm. "You don't need that. Let's go."

"But—" Pam had no choice but to move or be dragged. "I'm sorry," she mouthed to Jake.

"Next time, leave the overprotective boyfriend at home," he snapped.

As soon as they were outside, she whirled. "What are you doing? Jake's a friend."

"You don't need those kind of friends."

"I'll decide what friends I need, not you!"

"He's a charlatan."

"Jasper!" She blew out an exasperated sigh. "I know the oil is useless. I was just being polite, showing some interest before I said no. It's a game."

"It's not just the oil." He jutted his chin toward the store. "It's the rest of it."

"You can't deny that the moon rhymes are powerful."

"I suppose I can't," he admitted.

"I thought you believed in the dark arts."

"I do. But perhaps their power has diminished over time, to the point that you people no longer take them seriously. Fun, indeed." His brow furrowed. "What's that aroma? It's quite appealing. It smells like coffee, but . . ."

Pam sniffed the air. "It is coffee. Flavoured. It's coming from the coffee shop on the corner."

Jasper glanced that way, then gazed at her and bit his lip. "Can I try one?"

Her irritation drained away. He looked like a little boy asking his mother if he could have an ice cream. Pam stifled a grin. "I could do with a coffee myself." She grabbed his arm. "And while we're out, let's do a bit of shopping. Since you won't be going home tonight, you'll need more clothes."

"I'm sorry if I upset you," he said as they strolled to the corner. "I only wanted to protect you."

"I know." She patted his arm, then let go of it. "And I'd much rather have *you* protect me than rub oil on my forehead." They grinned at each other. If he wanted to rub oil on her in more interesting places than her forehead, she'd be game. "Before we go in, let me call Robin, let her know what we're doing. Otherwise she'll worry." Pam pulled her phone from her purse and dialled their number. "Hi, it's me. We just left Jake's."

"And?"

"I've got good news! I think I know what to do."

"That's great!" Robin's elation strained her voice.

"Well, there is one slight catch."

"What is it?" Robin said quietly.

"The rhymes only work once per lunar cycle. So I can't send them back until the next, um . . . whatever phase the moon was in on Thursday."

"Are you serious?"

"It's not that bad. At least I know what to do now." She heard typing. "Robin?"

"I'm just looking up what phase the moon was in. Ha! Figures. It was a full moon." She sighed. "So you're telling me they'll live with us for a few more weeks? I can't skip classes again, Pam. I have to go in on Monday. Maybe we should find them somewhere else to stay."

Pam stepped away from Jasper and lowered her voice. "We can't. Nobody can know about them. I think we can trust them to be on their own while we're both out. We'll just make sure they know not to answer the door or the phone."

"I don't know. I'm still not convinced we don't have two sophisticated con artists on our hands."

"Robin, what will it take to convince you? The diary wasn't enough? How about my own eyes? They appeared right in front of me!"

"Don't take this the wrong way, but I'd have an easier time believing it if they'd appeared in front of *me*."

"I wish they had!" Pam forcefully exhaled. "Listen, what would they want from us? We're not rich. Okay, I have the house and Mom left me decent money, but I still have to work. And you make just enough to get by. What could they possibly want, that they'd go through this elaborate charade?" When Robin didn't reply, Pam interpreted her silence as acquiescence. "I'm calling because we won't be coming home right away. We're going to have a quick coffee and then pick up more clothes for them."

"How long do you think you'll be?"

"A couple of hours, maybe? What's Margaret doing? You'd better not be holed up in your bedroom."

"I'm in the study, working on an assignment. Margaret's reading downstairs."

Pam's heart pounded. "Downstairs! Have you been checking on her? To make sure she's okay, not to ensure that she hasn't absconded with the silver!"

Robin chuckled. "She's not a child."

"What's she reading?"

"Dickens."

"Why? She can read that anytime."

"Probably because it's familiar. I don't think she's very comfortable here."

No. Jasper was the more adventurous of the two. Pam admired his courage . . . and the way he carried himself. Nobody would ever guess that the relaxed, self-assured man watching the world go by was from 1910. And, ooh, she'd love to see him in a modern suit. If she could come up with a reason . . .

"Pam?"

She shook herself. "Why don't you spend some time with Margaret, talk to her?"

"I'm not sure she wants to talk."

"Then do something."

Robin snorted. "Like what, needlepoint? Oh, I know, we can do a jigsaw puzzle!"

Pam tutted. "If I were there, I'd slap you up the side of the head. All I'm asking you to do is keep her company until we come home."

"She might prefer to read." Robin paused. "But I'll go down and see how she's doing."

"Good. Anyway, I should go. Jasper's waiting."

They said good-bye. Pam shoved the phone into her purse and rejoined him. "Okay, Robin knows we'll be out for a while."

"Did you tell her what Jake said about the moon rhymes?" Jasper asked.

Pam nodded.

"I hope she wasn't upset."

"She wasn't." Not really. "Shall we go in?"

"Of course." He held the door open for her. As she brushed past him, she realized he hadn't asked about Margaret.

MARGARET SIGHED AND peered over the top of her book when footsteps thumped down the stairs. She'd only just stopped shaking after the telephone's shrill assault on her ears.

Robin bounded into the living room. "Still reading? Do you have enough light? This room doesn't get as much sun in the afternoon."

"Yes, I know," Margaret murmured. She tensed when Robin crossed to one of the windows and reached for the curtains.

Robin suddenly stopped and turned. "Have you looked out a window yet?"

Margaret swallowed. "No." The curtains had remained closed when they'd watched TV, she hadn't opened the blinds in Robin's bedroom, and she'd managed to avoid the large windows near the rear of the kitchen, though unless she were to renege on her offer to help Robin cook, she'd soon have to face them. Blood rushed to her cheeks when comprehension dawned in Robin's eyes.

"You'll strain your eyes, reading in this light. Why don't I open this curtain and then you can come over and have a look? There's nothing scary out there. Jasper's out with Pam."

And she was a coward who couldn't look out a window. Her thought; neither Robin's eyes nor her voice contained a hint of derision. "Open the curtain."

Light splashed onto the area rug. Margaret set the book on the coffee table and forced herself to stand.

Robin beckoned to her. "Come on."

Fighting the urge to close her eyes, Margaret tried not to cringe as she tentatively approached the window. Robin's presence bolstered her, gave her the impetus she needed to take the final few steps. And then she was there, surveying her road. The cobblestones were gone, and metal contraptions—motor cars?—lined the road, but she recognized the houses across the way. "Some of it is familiar." She pointed, then held her hand at shoulder height. "The last time I saw that tree, it was this tall."

"And now it's the tallest thing on the street."

"And those are motor cars?"

Robin nodded. "We just call them cars."

"Cars." Margaret turned away from the window, quite pleased with herself. "Thank you for the encouragement."

"Would you like something to drink? A coffee?"

Her throat felt dry, but she didn't want to trouble Robin. "No, I'm fine. Thank you."

"I feel like a cup of tea, so I'm going to put the kettle on."

"Tea?" Margaret blurted before she could stop herself.

"Would you like a cup?"

"Yes, please." She hesitated. "I prefer tea over coffee."

Robin's brows rose. "So do I. You should have said."

"I don't mind coffee. And you and Pam are being so kind."

"But you've seen me drink—" Robin shrugged. "Never mind." She looked past Margaret, then down. "You're barefoot."

She must have noticed the shoes near the sofa. "The shoes pinch. Don't tell Pam."

Robin sighed. "I'll at least get you a pair of socks. And don't be afraid to speak up. You'll be with us a while longer, so let us know what you need."

"What do you mean?"

"That was Pam on the phone. Apparently the rhyme she used to bring you here only works once per lunar cycle. So she can't send you back for a few weeks."

Margaret struggled to mask her dismay. Perhaps her hope that Pam would send them home today had been optimistic, but oh, how she'd wanted it to be true! "I'm sorry. Two strangers in your home must be the last thing you want."

"It's not your fault, Margaret. You didn't ask to come here." Robin smiled. "Why don't you come sit in the kitchen while I make the tea? If we get to know each other, we won't be strangers."

The prospect of conversing with Robin intimidated her, but to decline Robin's invitation would be rude. "Yes, let's do that." She followed Robin to the kitchen and settled into a chair that would allow her to watch Robin prepare the tea. If she and Jasper were to impose on their hosts for weeks, she had to make herself useful.

Robin filled the oddly-shaped kettle with water and pressed a button at its base. "I'll be back in a sec."

Margaret wondered if Robin had decided she didn't want to converse after all, but Robin was back a minute later, a pair of socks in hand.

"Thank you." She pulled them on. They looked ridiculous with her dress, but given Robin's . . . attire, Margaret wouldn't worry until Jasper and Pam returned. She'd squeeze back into the shoes then. "How long will it take for Jasper and Pam to return home?"

"Oh, sorry—Pam said that since you'll be here longer, they're going to shop for more clothes. They won't be home for a couple of hours."

Her feet appreciated the news. Jasper must be enjoying himself, or at least feeling comfortable enough in the city to want to experience more of it.

Robin had sat down. They stared at each other across the table. "It must be strange for you, being in this house," Robin finally said. "I suppose, to you, we're the ones out of place."

"No, too much has changed. Pam said this is her house?"

Robin nodded.

The same old questions ran through Margaret's mind. Why did Robin live here? Where were their families? Why weren't they married? Margaret was certain they were both older than her.

"Pam's grandparents bought the house in 1958, and Pam's parents took it over in 1985."

"Do you know who owned it before 1958?"

"No. Pam's lived here pretty much all her life. Unfortunately, her father was killed in a car accident when she was seventeen, and her mother passed away a couple of years ago."

"That's terrible!"

"Yeah." Robin heaved her shoulders. "She's an only child, so she inherited the house from her mother. She knows it's way too big for her, but she's emotionally attached to it. So she invited me to come live with her."

One question answered.

"I'm sure she'll eventually sell it. She'll get to the point where she's ready to move on. And she knows I can't live here forever."

"Why did she ask you to live with her?"

"We've been friends for years."

"I see. How old is Pam?" Margaret asked, hoping to learn Robin's age too.

"Twenty-six. How old are you?"

"Twenty-three," Margaret said absently, still absorbing Robin's shocking answer. Wasn't Pam worried that she'd never find a husband? Wasn't Robin?

"How old's Jasper?"

"Thirty."

"I'm the same age as Pam," Robin volunteered.

Twenty-six. Margaret's curiosity was too strong to quell. "Don't you want to get married?"

Robin shrugged. "Sure, one day."

But she was already twenty-six! Had she not found the right man? Who would be right for Robin? Margaret had a difficult time picturing her on a man's arm. "What type of man would you marry?"

Robin shifted in her chair and grimaced. "Um . . ." A click came from the direction of the kettle. "Water's boiled." She pushed away from the table. "How do you like your tea?"

"Just milk, please." Robin's discomfort when asked about the type of man she'd marry had piqued Margaret's interest. She wanted to ask Robin again, but didn't want to annoy her.

Robin carried two cups to the table and sat down. "So how did you and Jasper meet?"

The change of subject didn't surprise her. "Through mutual friends, I suppose. We would occasionally be invited to the same soirée and engage in conversation. And then he invited me to one of our annual balls." She remembered her elation when she'd received the invitation. Finally, a handsome man who didn't bore her. Surely she'd be swept off her feet; it would be her turn to entertain her friends with breathless accounts of the passionate kisses she and Jasper shared. But the stories she'd told them were just that—stories, with every passionate detail a lie. "We've dated since then."

"And from the sounds of it, you were in the middle of getting engaged when you were rudely brought here."

"Yes." And Robin had read the last page of her diary! Margaret felt her face flush; she picked up her tea and sipped it, even though it burned her tongue. If Robin were to ask how she felt about Jasper, if she loved him, what would she say? She gripped her cup with both hands.

"If Pam does succeed in sending you back, I wonder if you'll end up right where you left off, or a few weeks later, or . . ."

Margaret slowly let out the breath she was holding. "Arriving back in 1910 will be quite sufficient." She wanted to talk about something else. Perhaps there was another way to find out what type of men would attract Robin. For some reason, Margaret longed to know. "It's Saturday. Will you entertain callers this evening?"

Robin's brow furrowed. "Callers?"

"Gentlemen."

"Oh." Robin quickly lifted her cup to her mouth, but not in time to hide her amusement. "Saturday night is still a popular date night, but no, there won't be a line of gentlemen callers at our door. I suspect we'll watch one of Pam's old movies. I usually bow out, but since we have guests, I guess I'll make the popcorn and join you."

She made it sound as if she were facing a harrowing ordeal. From what Margaret had gathered, a movie was a long TV show. "You don't enjoy movies?"

"I don't really like the old ones. They're too traditional and sappy for me." Robin's eyes narrowed and she wagged her finger at Margaret. "But I'm thinking they'll be just your thing."

Margaret had the sneaking suspicion she'd just been insulted.

"Do you want biscuits?" Robin asked. "I should have offered before. Sorry."

"No, thank you." She searched for a way to bring the conversation back to gentlemen without being obvious, but couldn't think of one.

Robin leaned across the table. "I hope you won't be offended, but I have the impression that Jasper's family is quite well off."

Margaret nodded.

"And you're . . ."

"Upper middle class."

"So you won't have to work outside the home."

"No!"

"And you don't work now or go to university?"

"No." Women in her time did go to university or work, but reasonable and respectable women were content to take care of a husband and family. Margaret had no intention of shaming her parents.

"So what do you do with your time, then?" Robin smiled reassuringly, perhaps because she sensed Margaret's fear that anything she said would be mocked. "I'm just curious. Historians would kill for this opportunity. I mean, we know a lot about the early twentieth century, but that's no substitute for actually talking to someone like you."

Margaret lifted an eyebrow. "You're honestly curious?"

"Yes."

She hesitated, then decided there wouldn't be any harm in telling Robin about her hobbies, her afternoons out with her girlfriends, and her love of books. Robin peppered her with questions, wanting to know the tiniest details. It wasn't until after Jasper and Pam had returned and interrupted them that Margaret realized she'd spent the entire time talking about herself and had learned absolutely nothing about Robin. When conversing with someone she didn't entirely trust, Margaret would continuously ask questions so she wouldn't have to reveal anything about herself. Was that what Robin had been doing? She did seem the suspicious type, and perhaps still didn't believe that her guests were from 1910.

Next time Margaret had the opportunity to converse with Robin, *she* would ask the questions. And she dearly hoped there would be a next time, because Robin was different from any woman Margaret had ever met. Oh, Pam was too, by virtue of the hundred years that separated them. But Robin . . . she was both fascinating and frightening. Margaret felt drawn to her, in a way she never had to anyone else.

MARGARET STIFLED A yawn and tried to focus on the events unfolding on the TV. How Robin could ever have thought she'd be enthralled by this utter tripe was beyond her. From the corner of her eye, she glimpsed Pam reaching for another tissue. Margaret had used one earlier, and couldn't understand why anyone would prefer something that felt like paper to a soft handkerchief.

"It doesn't matter how many times I watch this scene," Pam sniffled. "It gets me every time."

Jasper turned away from the TV to murmur to Pam. Margaret had noticed how quickly Pam had claimed the place on the sofa to his left, leaving poor Robin with no choice but to squeeze in next to Margaret, probably the last person she wanted to sit next to. Robin had encouraged Margaret to sit back and relax. She had to admit, she was comfortable, especially since kicking off her shoes.

Robin was awfully still; she hadn't crunched on popcorn for ages. Margaret gave her a sidelong glance. Robin was asleep! Margaret wanted to elbow her awake, so she wouldn't have to suffer through this torture alone. Then she noticed that the half-full popcorn bowl on Robin's lap had tipped to one side. She carefully reached for it and tried to right it without disturbing Robin, but Robin's eyes snapped open. "Sorry," Margaret mouthed.

Pam chose that moment to groan at whatever was happening in the movie. "Oh, the poor man. I almost can't bear to watch this part," she said with a sob.

Robin caught Margaret's eye; her mouth twitched. Laughter bubbled up within Margaret. She pressed her lips together, covered her mouth, and leaned forward.

"It's all right, Margaret," Jasper murmured. "Would you like a tissue?"

His misguided concern almost had her in stitches. She could feel Robin shaking and didn't dare look at her. Jasper interpreted her silence as affirmation and snapped a tissue from the box. Margaret accepted it with her free hand, keeping her other hand firmly over her mouth. The dam still threatened to burst. She squeezed the tissue until she'd mastered herself, then leaned back and dabbed at her moist eyes.

Robin nudged her arm and tilted the popcorn bowl toward her. Margaret scooped out several kernels. She popped one into her mouth and tried to pay attention to the movie, but a heightened awareness of Robin kept intruding. Margaret noticed every time Robin shifted, reached for popcorn with her long fingers, yawned, breathed! It was as if Robin's senses were connected to her own.

Chapter Five

MARGARET PUSHED A BOOK INTO THE bookcase and pulled out another one. At this rate, she'd finish rereading all of Dickens' work before Pam sent them home. Normally she read in bed, not in the afternoons, when she'd be out with friends or entertaining guests with Mother. She wasn't used to spending so much time alone.

Yesterday had begun with a bizarre church service she and Jasper watched on TV. What was the point? Wasn't church about community? She'd expected Pam and Robin to watch the service with them, but they'd both insisted that they had things to do that couldn't wait. After lunch, Pam had monopolized almost all of Jasper's time, though she wasn't entirely at fault. Jasper had offered to fix a loose door knob here and a wobbly chair there, and Pam hadn't dissuaded him. Margaret could have spent time with them after supper, but they'd both wanted to watch another one of those horrid movies, so she'd decided to read in the kitchen instead.

If Robin would have been there to silently laugh with her, maybe she would have joined them, but Robin had passed most of the day behind a closed study door, and the evening shut away in her bedroom. "She's in elf-land," Pam had said when Margaret inquired about the occasional muffled shouts. "It's a game people play over the computer. She's yelling at her teammates. Don't worry if you don't understand it. I don't, either."

When Robin had finally emerged from the bedroom and come downstairs, all she'd said was that the room was free for Margaret and good night, much to Margaret's disappointment. Robin didn't want much to do with her and Jasper; she was polite but mainly kept to herself. Pam, on the other hand, appeared eager to play the host, especially with Jasper. It had crossed Margaret's mind that Pam might have a special interest in him, but what if she did? They were engaged. Jasper was an honourable man. This morning he'd reminded her that they would spend time alone under the same roof, which would be inappropriate back home, and that they must observe the proprieties of their time—as if she'd intended to behave any differently. Margaret only had reason to worry if Pam couldn't send them back, but she refused to consider that awful possibility.

Would she and Jasper arrive back in 1910 on the same day and at the same time they'd left, or was the time they were passing here also passing in 1910? If the latter, what did people think had happened? Had she and Jasper seemingly disappeared into thin air? Had her parents called in the police? Did people think they'd eloped? What if they arrived back in a different year? What if they ended up further into the future, with people not as hospitable as Robin and Pam? What a ridiculous situation! She'd be certain it was a dream, if everything didn't feel real and events since they'd arrived here weren't so coherent.

Jasper came into the living room, wiping his forehead with his arm. "I've finished sanding that old chair. I hope Pam brings home the right stain."

"I'm sure she will." And Margaret would spend another day reading while Jasper laboured in the basement. But if it wasn't the chair, it would be something else. He clearly wanted to make himself useful, and his idea of observing proprieties meant avoiding being in the same room with her, though he'd sat with her to eat the sandwiches she'd made them for lunch. "What time is it?"

He pulled out his pocket watch. "Just after five."

"I'd better start preparing dinner. You should wash up."

"Yes." He hovered a moment longer, then cleared his throat and went upstairs. She couldn't blame him for feeling uncomfortable. At home, they'd see each other perhaps once or twice a week. Jasper would be busy working with his father, spending time at his gentlemen's club, and engaging in sports activities with his brothers and friends. Here, they were in each other's pockets and slept only a room apart. Under any other circumstances, their behaviour would be scandalous. Perhaps it was best to limit their time together when they could. After all, familiarity sometimes bred contempt. Best to save that until after they were married.

Margaret busied herself in the kitchen, and had just finished setting the table when Pam strode in, her heels clicking on the linoleum floor. "Oh, the table looks lovely. But we only need three places."

"Three?"

Pam nodded. "Robin won't be joining us for dinner. She's out with a friend."

"Oh." Margaret's disappointment and curiosity surprised her. Was Robin dining with a gentleman? It shouldn't matter to her, but it did, perhaps because Robin hadn't answered the question about the type of man who attracted her.

Margaret was rather proud that she'd managed to prepare dinner on her own, and graciously accepted Pam and Jasper's praise. As they ate, Pam described her day, and told them more about her job in human resources. Her complaints about her duties and her superior, and the "bitch sessions" she apparently frequently had with her colleagues, reinforced Margaret's conviction that women should only work if they had to. Pam should find herself a husband and be done with it.

After helping Pam load the dishwasher—Margaret could understand the machine's popularity—they decided to play cards, much to her relief. They'd been playing for about an hour when Robin came home. "What, no movie?"

Pam shook her head. "We can watch a movie tomorrow night."

Margaret could hardly wait.

Robin picked up the kettle and carried it to the sink. "Anyone want tea? Margaret?"

"No, thank you." She restrained herself from asking about Robin's evening; it was none of her business.

"Can you put coffee on?" Pam asked.

"Sure," Robin said. "I heard it's going to pour tomorrow."

Pam nodded. "Sue's pissed because she'd booked the day off to play golf."

"Golf?" Jasper said. "I love golf."

"Do you?" Pam picked up a card from the stack in the middle of the table and slid it into her hand. "So do I. We should go." She glanced at Margaret. "All of us. Robin, check the weather for Friday. I could take the day off, have a long weekend."

"I'll check, but I'm not going. I can't just book the day off." Robin leaned against the counter near the kettle and peered at her phone. "It's supposed to be nice, but that could change."

"I'll book Friday off anyway. If we don't golf, we can do something else."

"That sounds like a wonderful idea!" Jasper smiled broadly. "I hope we *can* golf. Are the rules different? The equipment? I'm looking forward to finding out."

Pam twisted in her chair. "What about you, Margaret? Do you play?"

"I tried it once. I didn't enjoy it," she admitted. And she wasn't sure she wanted to leave the house and be swallowed up by 2010. She already knew too much about the future. Nothing she'd learned had diminished her longing to return home, or caused her to question the norms of her day, but what if she learned something that did? She had to return to 1910; the less she knew about 2010, the better. Frankly, she felt that Jasper should shelter himself as well, but it wasn't her place to question him. "Why don't you go with Pam, Jasper? I don't mind staying here."

"No, Margaret," Jasper said as Pam shook her head. "You can't stay here alone."

"Someone might come to the door," Pam said.

Someone could come to the door while she and Jasper were here alone. What did it matter if one or both of them were inside? "I know not to answer it."

"Why don't you come with us?" Pam said. "You don't have to play."

"What will she do while you're playing?" Robin asked. "You can't leave her to fend for herself while you and Jasper are out on the course."

"And I don't think Margaret should go," Jasper said. "Some of the sights I saw on Saturday aren't suitable for a lady's eyes."

Pam's brows shot up.

"A lady of 1910," he quickly clarified.

"That's better," Pam murmured. "Oh well, maybe we can go another time, when Robin will be around." She sighed. "Of course, the weather's only going to get worse."

Margaret held her cards in front of her face and blinked back tears. Why didn't they trust her to stay here by herself? She wouldn't mind if Jasper and Pam went off to play golf; she would be perfectly fine on her own. They were treating her like a child! And yet she felt guilty because they refused to golf with her but wouldn't golf without her!

"If I could swing most of Friday afternoon off—no pun intended— would that help?" Robin asked.

"You just said you can't book the day off," Pam said as Margaret slowly lowered her cards to peek at Robin.

"Well, I can't be home the *entire* day. I have a class at 11:00 and a lab at 1:00. But if I sit in on Thursday's lab instead, I could be home around 12:45."

Pam's face lit up. "That would work! Are you sure?"

Robin dropped a teabag into a mug. "It means I'll be home a little later on Thursday, but yeah. I'm sure."

"And you don't mind staying here with Margaret?"

"No."

"All right, then. I'll book Friday off. I'm glad it worked out."

It had worked out for Pam and Jasper. Robin had only offered to rearrange her schedule when it had become clear that they needed a child-minder. Margaret wished she were home. Here, everyone seemed more sophisticated, including Jasper. She didn't belong.

"Your turn," Jasper murmured.

She slid a card from her hand and tossed it onto the table, but her heart was no longer in the game. Robin quietly left after making her tea, and when Pam won the game and got up to make coffee, Margaret seized the opportunity to retire early. She picked up her Dickens book from the living room and trudged up the stairs.

On the landing, she could see Robin working in the study. Margaret hesitated, then walked to the open door and knocked on it. Robin looked up. "Thank you for agreeing to stay with me on Friday," Margaret said.

"Sure."

"I'm sorry that you'll have to rearrange your schedule."

"No, it's fine, really. I don't mind."

Margaret's grip tightened on the book. "Are you working on something for your class?"

Robin nodded. "I'm reading a scientific paper. I have to critique it."

"Oh." Margaret swallowed. "I won't keep you. And I'll try not to disturb you on Friday. Good night." She turned away.

"Margaret."

Margaret turned back.

"Let's do something on Friday." Robin smiled. "Not a movie. I'm sure we can find something else to do."

"But your work . . ."

Robin shrugged. "I'd normally be in a lab, and I'll have the weekend to do homework. So let's spend the afternoon together. Even if we just talk."

"I would like that." Margaret's heart was pounding so fast that she barely got the words out. Robin wanting to pass the time with her was the last thing she'd expected—a wonderful surprise!

"I'll look forward to it. Good night." Robin's head bowed.

"Good night." Margaret's step was light as she walked to the bedroom. The heavy spirit she'd dragged up the stairs now soared.

FROM A WINDOW, Margaret watched Jasper and Pam walk down the front path. When she could no longer see them, she let the curtain go and turned to the empty living room. Her heart sank. When Robin had come home, she'd eaten a quick lunch, said good-bye to Pam and Jasper, and gone upstairs. No mention of spending the afternoon together, just a wave as she'd passed the living room on her way to the kitchen.

Margaret fought her disappointment. She and Jasper were imposing. Robin and Pam led busy lives, though Pam seemed eager to make time for Jasper, who would never golf alone with another woman if they were in 1910, not after their engagement was announced. Margaret should be upset, but she wasn't. Since Pam would send them back to their own time in mere weeks, nothing would come of her friendship with Jasper. But if Pam failed and they were doomed to remain in the future—no, Margaret refused to entertain that possibility. Pam would succeed. They would return to 1910, announce their engagement, marry, and eventually wonder if this interlude had been a dream, a shared temporary madness.

Margaret was almost grateful for Pam's willingness to occupy Jasper's time. He was running out of ways to busy himself and they both felt awkward, residing under the same roof and becoming too familiar with each other's habits before God had joined them together. When they returned home, they must never breathe a word of this time to anyone, not only because nobody would believe them, but because Jasper's family might refuse to accept her, even though she'd committed no impropriety. Oh, why couldn't it be a full moon tonight?

With a sigh, she went over to the bookcase, and was debating whether to try someone other than Dickens when footsteps thumped down the stairs. "They gone?" Robin asked.

Hope rising within her, Margaret nodded.

"I just wanted to get a few emails—letters—out of the way, so my afternoon would be clear."

Pam had explained how people could instantly send letters from one place to another. Margaret could appreciate the efficiency of the method, but not its impersonal nature. When she wrote a letter, she always selected the stationery with great care. Each letter she sent was personal, and she always valued the ones she received, viewed them as keepsakes.

Robin went to the window and gazed out. "They certainly couldn't have asked for better weather." She spun around. "Would you consider going for a walk?"

Margaret gulped. "I—I shouldn't. I know Jasper wants to experience . . . the present, but I feel I should remained sheltered, so it won't be such a shock when I go home." Nor potentially disappointing.

Robin folded her arms. "That's prudent of you. But I'm not suggesting we go downtown or anything like that. We're not that far from the lake."

"I know." She often strolled along the boardwalk with her friends.

"Of course you do," Robin said sheepishly. "So you know we can walk there. You won't see anything spectacular. You've seen cars. Um . . . people will be dressed differently to what you're used to. Signs, maybe? But that's all. So what do you say?"

She wanted to please Robin, and couldn't deny the excitement that mingled with her fear of stepping out into the future.

"You've been here a week. You must be tired of being cooped up inside."

She wanted to—but no, she couldn't. "You can go for a walk, if you like. I'll be all right here on my own."

Robin shook her head. "Pam and Jasper would kill me if they found out. And I'd like your company." She dropped her arms to her sides. "But if you don't want to go, I'll understand."

And be disappointed, no doubt. Margaret swallowed. "Jasper wouldn't want me to go."

Robin lifted an eyebrow. "Who said anything about telling Jasper? He's out playing golf. What's good for the goose is good for the gander."

Dare she? She wanted to. She was tired of her own company and would feel guilty if Robin had to share her confinement on such a beautiful day.

"I promise I'll stay right next to you," Robin said. "I won't let you out of my sight."

Her desire to not disappoint Robin was too strong to resist. "All right."

Robin smiled. "Great! Do you want to change into the pants Pam bought you? Okay, maybe that's asking too much," she said with a laugh; Margaret's horror at the thought of wearing trousers must have shown on her face. "But put on running shoes, at least."

Running shoes?

"Shoes like mine."

Margaret looked down at Robin's feet.

"You can't go out barefoot."

Robin must think her vain for wearing shoes that hurt when Jasper was here.

"You can wear Pam's old pair. They're on the mat. I'll get you a pair of socks." Robin bounded up the stairs.

Margaret went into the hallway and peered at Pam's running shoes. Perhaps she should reconsider leaving the house, but what would Robin think? If Margaret changed her mind, Robin would never offer to pass the time with her again.

"Thank you," she murmured when Robin returned and handed her the socks. While Margaret pulled them on and squeezed her feet into the running shoes, she could see Robin hunched over one of the end tables in the living room, writing on a piece of paper.

"A map from the boardwalk to the house," Robin announced. "In case we do get separated and the route isn't the same as it was in 1910." She inspected Margaret; her mouth turned up at the corners. "All you need is a coat. Take one of Pam's. It'll be a little big, but who cares?"

Margaret wouldn't. The running shoes already made her feel mannish.

Robin rummaged through the coat closet, pulled out a full-length fall coat, and held it out to Margaret. She slipped into it and hoped she didn't look ridiculous.

"Put the map in your pocket," Robin said. "And I'm giving you my phone. If we do get separated, don't talk to anyone, and don't go anywhere with anyone. I don't care how nice they look or sound. Either follow the map, or phone here. I'll come back here and wait for your call."

Margaret quaked inside. This would be her last opportunity to do the sensible thing and stay here. But she wanted to go with Robin. "How do I—"

"Here." Robin showed her how to use the phone, then had her practice a few times. "Ready?" When Margaret nodded, Robin threw on a black leather waist-length coat. "Let's go."

She followed Robin outside and paused on the doorstep to get her bearings. As she'd discovered the first time she gazed out the window, the surroundings were strange, yet familiar. If the cars weren't there, the road cobbled, and the trees not so tall, she'd almost believe that the front door led to 1910. Her eyes settled on Robin. Except women dressed like women, where she came from.

Robin walked to the end of the path and beckoned to her. Encouraged, Margaret walked down the steps. "You all right?" Robin asked when Margaret reached her.

"Yes." She fell into step with Robin. The warmth of the sun on her face and the light breeze in her hair were welcome sensations; she felt more alive than she had in days. Her decision to accompany Robin was reckless, but the alternative would have been to pass yet another afternoon reading by herself. She was outside and not alone! Robin's desire for her company was rooted in politeness, but Margaret was grateful for her thoughtfulness and would tell her so later. She didn't mind that Robin shoved her hands into her jacket pockets and only spoke when they had to cross a road. For now, she wanted to stroll next to her and imagine that she was out with one of her girlfriends.

A wave of melancholy washed over her when she spotted the lake. If she blocked out the people, the strange noises, and the storefronts, she would forgive herself for believing she was home.

Robin's hands came out of her pockets. "I was thinking we could pick up a couple of teas and then find somewhere to sit. It's breezier here, but if we get chilly, we can walk."

Margaret readily agreed, and stayed close to Robin in what appeared to be a café—once again strange, yet familiar, though her eyes nearly popped out of her head when she read the price list. Inflation, indeed. "Can I see that?" she asked when Robin pulled out a bill from what looked like a man's billfold.

Robin handed her the five-dollar bill. "That's Sir Wilfrid Laurier," Margaret said. "He's the prime minister."

"Not anymore," Robin said with a chuckle.

Of course. How silly of her! But . . . "I saw him not too long ago. We were in Ottawa for the weekend."

"Your family?"

"Yes! Not me and Jasper."

Robin took the bill from her and used it to pay for their teas. She pressed a hot paper cup into Margaret's hand and they found a place to sit, on a bench facing the boardwalk. A woman sat reading a newspaper at one end. Robin motioned for Margaret to sit at the other end and settled in next to her.

"Has it changed much?" Robin asked.

"The lake looks the same." Had it only been last week that she'd walked down to the lake with Mother? To her, yes, yet it had been a century ago! Mother was dead! Father, her brothers, everyone. Intellectually she understood that, but she couldn't accept it. They were very much alive; she thought of them in the present tense. She could remember every detail of her walk with Mother. They'd spoken of Jasper, of what a suitable husband he'd make. Jasper had visited Father the very next day. Had Mother suspected that Jasper intended to ask Father's permission for her hand? Father and the Bainbridges belonged to the same gentlemen's club. So had Victor Tillman, until he'd been tossed out on his ear for defaulting on his dues.

She gave Robin a sidelong glance. Was she related to *that* Tillman family? The Tillmans had been quite respectable, until Leo Tillman died. His sons were all misfits, especially Victor, the eldest. It hadn't taken him long to gamble away his inheritance. From a stately home on a respectable road to a working class townhouse—what a comedown! Pam had been quick to say that Robin wasn't related to Victor Tillman, but was she sure, or had she been worried that Margaret's comment would cause offence? Normally Margaret wouldn't dream of blurting out something so crass, but normally she wasn't dropped into the middle of a conversation with two strangers from the future, either. "Do you mind if I ask you about your family?" she said to Robin. "We spoke about mine last time we took tea together."

"There's not much to know." Robin sipped her tea. "My parents are divorced, and I have an older brother."

Divorce? That must have been difficult for Robin's mother. How had she managed? "That's unfortunate about your parents."

Robin shrugged. "They divorced when I was fourteen."

"Are your grandparents alive?" Margaret asked, seeking a piece of information that would either connect her to Victor Tillman, or eliminate him as an ancestor. She didn't want to remind Robin of her crass comment by asking outright.

"My mom's mom is still alive and kicking. My father's parents are both around too, but I haven't seen them in years. I'm not close to my father."

"Oh?"

"He travels a lot. Me and Chris—my brother—we have dinner with him occasionally, when he passes through town. As a matter of fact, we'll be meeting up with him in a couple of weeks."

Margaret wondered why Robin didn't sound too happy about it. "You must be looking forward to seeing him."

Robin's mouth tightened. "We don't have a lot in common."

"Do you see your mother often?"

"I try to drop in at least once a week, mainly to see my brother. They don't live far from the university."

Why would Robin live with Pam when her family lived closer to the university? And how odd that Robin lived outside the home and her brother didn't. "Why don't you live with them?"

Robin lifted her cup to her lips. "Boy, you don't mess around with the questions, do you?" Margaret drew breath to apologize, but Robin shook her head and, after gulping down tea, tossed her cup into a nearby wastebasket. "It's only fair. I asked you a lot of questions the other day." She sighed heavily. "It's easier living with Pam than living at home. And cheaper. Since Pam owns the house outright, she doesn't charge me room and board. I couldn't go to university when I was living at home. I had to work, to help out. That's why I'm only in my second year, even though I'm twenty-six."

"What about your brother? Wasn't he supporting you?"

Robin snorted. "No."

"Why not?"

"It doesn't work that way now, Margaret. And even if it did, he wouldn't be able to support me." Robin twisted to face her. "Do you know what schizophrenia is?"

"No."

"It's a mental illness. Chris is schizophrenic."

"You mean he's retarded?"

Robin stared at her for a moment. "If you were anyone else—" She sighed. "No, he's not retarded. It's an illness, like any other illness. As long as he stays on his medication, he's okay. And he does occasionally manage to hold down a job for a while, but the sort of job that pays him barely enough to support himself, let alone me. Mom doesn't work, either. She's an alcoholic, and not very good at hiding it. She was fired from one too many jobs."

Margaret hoped her dismay didn't show on her face. Robin's family sounded just like the 1910 Tillmans!

"So after I graduated from high school, I worked. They're on social assistance, but that's barely enough to get by."

"What about your father? He should be caring for his family."

To Margaret's surprise, Robin barked a laugh. "It didn't take long for Mom to drink her way through her divorce settlement, and Dad's," she wiggled her fingers in the air, "obligation to me and Chris ended the second we turned eighteen. He remarried and had two more kids, so he has another family to worry about now." She examined her fingernails. "Doesn't matter. We've managed okay without him."

But Margaret could see that it did matter. Up to that point, she'd thought Robin unflappable. "You stepped into his shoes, tried to care for everyone."

"You sound like Pam." Robin gazed out at the lake. "If you ask her about our living arrangement, she'll make it sound like I'm doing her a favour, when it's really the other way around. If it wasn't for her, I'd still be working two jobs and dreaming about going to university."

As far as Margaret knew, Robin no longer worked at all. "Does Pam pay your tuition?"

Robin shook her head. "I have a student loan. And I make pocket change on the Internet. I'm willing to work part-time, so I can pay Pam rent, but she won't let me. She said we'll talk about rent after I graduate." Robin smiled. "And she's been very stubborn about sticking to that." Her smile faded. "I wish we could have gone through university together. And I wish I could have gone to university while living at home. It's not that I don't like living with Pam, I do. But I worry about Mom and Chris."

Confused, Margaret opened her mouth to ask a question, then realized she hadn't drank any tea. She took a sip, felt the still-warm liquid run down her throat. "I don't understand. If you wanted to stay home to help your family, couldn't you have worked part-time and gone to university? Forgive me if that doesn't make sense."

"If I'd still managed to get a student loan, yeah, that might have worked."

"Then why didn't you do that?"

Robin avoided Margaret's eyes. "I couldn't," she said quietly. "Please don't ask me why."

Margaret nearly burst with curiosity but didn't want to pry, especially when Robin shoved her hands back into her pockets and blinked out at the lake. She drank more tea and waited for Robin to speak.

"Anyway, enough talk about me." Robin straightened. "You must be sick of Dickens by now."

So Robin had noticed.

"I could bring the newspaper home for you to read."

"No, thank you. I want to remain sheltered."

"Right. But you did watch TV that day."

"I wish I hadn't. I mainly did because Jasper liked it."

"Okay." Robin pursed her lips. "Last time we talked—" her mouth turned up at the corners "—last time we took tea together, you said you like to knit. Why don't we see if we can find a craft shop? We can pick up whatever you need to make something."

The idea appealed, but . . . Margaret eyed Robin's clothing: the leather jacket with its worn elbows and sleeves, the faded and frayed trousers, and running shoes that had clearly walked miles. How much of that pocket change ended up in her mother and brother's pockets? "No, that's all right. But thank you for offering."

"Oh, come on. You must want something else to do. It sounded like you really enjoy knitting."

She did; it soothed her.

"Let me buy what you need."

Margaret could see that Robin wouldn't allow her to decline the offer without an explanation, one Margaret didn't want to give. "All right. But . . . would you let me knit something for you?"

"You don't have to."

"I would like to." Earnestly.

Robin hesitated. "Okay."

"I'll knit something for Pam, too." Margaret pondered a moment. "Perhaps a shawl." She cocked her head, felt the beginnings of a giggle. "Would you like a shawl?" She wanted to laugh when Robin started to stammer a response, and controlled her mirth with difficulty. "No, I don't suppose you would."

Robin's eyes narrowed. "Are you teasing me, Margaret?"

"Perhaps."

They gazed at each other, Robin's amused expression mirroring Margaret's. "Winter's coming. What about a tuque and mittens?" Or a sweater, scarf, or nice warm socks. "I'm sure I can knit something that will meet with your approval."

A smile spread across Robin's face. "I'm sure you can."

Warmth flooded through Margaret, and it wasn't from the tea; the cup was now cold to the touch. She could grow fond of this odd woman from the future and wished they could be friends, a prospect she never would have imagined when she'd first set eyes on her.

"Shall we walk a little?" Robin asked.

"Yes." Margaret stood and deposited her cup in the wastebasket. They strolled along the boardwalk in companionable silence. More people walked, cycled, and ran along it than before, out enjoying the afternoon sun. A woman with two dogs straining against their leashes hurried past; Margaret wasn't sure who was walking who. She glanced over her shoulder and watched the woman's receding back, then faced forward and stopped. A young man was heading toward her, but he wasn't walking, he was standing on a board . . . with wheels? One of his feet left the board; he pushed it against the boardwalk, then stood on the board again. Margaret watched him race past, then followed him with her eyes as he wove around people. She suspected it took some skill, but he made it look effortless.

When she could no longer see him, she turned to Robin to ask—Robin! Where was Robin? Frantic, Margaret searched for her, but found only strange faces. Her heart pounded. Recalling Robin's instructions, she dug her hands into the coat pocket, feeling for the map and phone.

"Margaret!"

She shook with relief when Robin was suddenly there, and resisted the urge to grab onto her. "I—I'm sorry. I stopped to look—" Her voice choked off.

"No, I should have noticed you weren't next to me. As soon as I did, I backtracked." Robin peered at her. "Are you okay? Do you want to go home?"

Yes! Home! To 1910! She closed her eyes, took a deep breath, exhaled slowly. "I'm all right."

"You sure?"

She nodded. "Let's continue our walk." It really was a beautiful day and, quite taken with the idea of knitting something for Robin, she wanted to visit a craft shop. "I've learned my lesson. I won't stop again."

"Well, that's no fun. Why shouldn't you stop if you see something interesting?" Robin shoved her hands into her pockets and extended her right elbow. "Here, take my arm and don't let go of it. If something catches your eye, I'll know right away."

Margaret slipped her arm through Robin's and rested her hand on Robin's leather sleeve. Her breath quickened; her free hand went to her throat. They walked, but Margaret no longer took heed of her surroundings. She couldn't, not when all she could think about was Robin next to her, the warmth of Robin's arm, her body . . . good Lord, what was wrong with her? Margaret's face burned. Her heart raced. She felt as if she might crumple to the ground at any second.

"I could hardly breathe! I felt as if I was dying! If a doctor had taken my temperature, he would have rushed me to the hospital!" All her friends had squealed and nodded, and so had Margaret, even though she'd never reacted that way when strolling with Jasper, or any other suitor. She hadn't related at all to what her friends described, had never experienced it . . . until now. But—it didn't make sense! Robin was—she— Margaret should let go of her arm—immediately! But she didn't want to, and not only because she was afraid they'd be separated. Dear Jesus in heaven, she was attracted to Robin.

But this wasn't the first time she'd slipped her arm through a girlfriend's when out for a stroll, yet she'd never, *ever* felt like this. Something terrible must have happened to her when she was pulled through time! She wasn't one of those wicked people she'd heard whispers about. Depraved, sinful creatures! She wasn't one of *them*! Back in 1910, she'd be normal again.

Robin pressed against Margaret when she sidestepped to avoid bumping into someone. Heat flared in Margaret's chest. She tightened her grip on Robin's arm.

Chapter Six

PAM GROANED WHEN HER BALL LANDED far short of the target green. "I told you, I'm terrible at this."

"That's why I suggested we end the afternoon on the driving range." Jasper leaned on his club. "It's your posture."

"My posture?"

He nodded. "Your back isn't straight. Look." Jasper slipped his club behind him and held it with both hands just underneath his bum, parallel to the ground. "Now if I hang onto the club and then lean forward, my back will remain straight." He demonstrated. "Do you see?"

She lifted her sunglasses and eyed his firm ass. "Uh-huh." It looked damn good, considering it was technically 130 years old.

"This is the position you want. You want to bend from the hips, and you don't want to be back on your heels. If your posture is right, everything else will follow." Pam sighed in disappointment when he slid the club from behind him. "If you have the right posture, just let your arms hang and that's exactly where you should grip the club." He assumed a golf stance and smiled at her. "Do you want to try again?"

"Only if you won't be disappointed when I hit the ball exactly where it just landed."

He frowned. "You have to have more confidence, or you'll never improve."

"You're right." She teed up another ball, then felt a bit silly as she mimicked Jasper's demonstration by holding the club under her ass and bending forward. Since she couldn't hold the club in that position when she entered her stance, she didn't see much point—except to please him. "I think I understand." *All right, pretend I'm hanging onto a club under my ass.* She assumed her stance, hoped her arms were hanging right, then swung.

Jasper shielded his eyes. "It looks good."

Did it? She watched in disbelief as the ball arced through the air and landed on the edge of the target green. "I did it! I did it! Oh my god!" She dropped the driver, leaped into Jasper, and hugged him. *Oh shit!* She pulled back. Wait, his arms were around her too, and he didn't seem in a hurry to let her go. She reluctantly pushed away from him. "Sorry. I didn't mean to get carried away." But given half the chance, she'd be in his arms again.

His eyes met hers. He looked . . . pensive. Confused. The moment passed. He tore his eyes from hers and stooped to pick up his club.

Pam cleared her throat. "I think we should call it a day." But she didn't feel like going home to play cards or watch a movie. Okay, maybe she wanted Jasper to herself for a while longer. "Do you want to have dinner out? There's a decent pub nearby. We can eat and then play pool, or darts."

"Pool? You play billiards?"

"Uh, yeah."

"I've never played with a woman before."

She lifted an eyebrow. "Then I'll warn you that I'm better at pool than I am at golf. If you can't handle being beaten by a woman, maybe you should pass."

He scoffed. "I'm not worried about being beaten."

"We'll see, won't we?" she said with a wink, thrilled that he was interested in playing.

"But what about Margaret and Robin? We said we'd only be out for the afternoon."

So they had. "I'll call Robin. I don't think she has any plans for tonight, so she probably won't mind. Let's take these clubs back."

Fifteen minutes later, she dug her phone out of her purse and dialled home while Jasper visited the men's room. Funny, nobody was answering. "Hi, you've reached Pam and Robin. We can't—" Pam hung up. Robin had better not be sitting upstairs with her damn headset on. She'd said she was going to spend time with Margaret.

Pam called Robin's cell, and was about to hang up after eight rings—why wasn't it going through to voice mail?—when Robin said, "Hello."

"Why aren't you answering the damn phone? I tried home first."

"Oh, was that you? I was, uh, in the bathroom. I only heard the cell when I came out."

Pam could hardly hear her. "What's that in the background?"

"What?"

She sighed. "Never mind. Listen, Jasper and I have finished golfing, but we want to go to the pub, have something to eat and play pool. You're not going out tonight, right?"

"Nope."

"Do you mind if we stay out, then?"

"Just a second." Pam heard muffled voices but couldn't make out any words. She waited for Robin to remove her hand from the phone. The background noise returned. "Margaret says she doesn't mind."

"Great, we'll see you later, then." Pam quickly rang off, guilt snaking through her for not considering how Margaret would feel about it. But it wasn't as if she and Jasper were going on a date, and Margaret had him to herself while Pam was at work. She was probably grateful for the break.

Pam looked in the direction of the men's room and waved when Jasper emerged. As she watched him approach, she felt herself smile. Margaret was one lucky woman. If not for Jasper's engagement and that little "from 1910" thing, Pam would be working her charms on him. They had so much in common, more than he did with Margaret. And they weren't doing anything wrong by enjoying each other's company for a day. No harm would come from it. According to the announcement she'd found on the Internet, Jasper and Margaret wouldn't waste any time getting married once they returned to their own time.

Hmm . . . did their brief trip into the future have anything to do with their quickie wedding? Pam wouldn't dare tell Jasper about the historical record; who knew how the universe would be affected? But curiosity drove her to dance around the subject as they enjoyed a beer after stuffing themselves on wings. "So have you and Margaret set a wedding date?"

Jasper shook his head. "We didn't have an opportunity to do so. I was in the middle of asking for her hand when . . ." He looked pointedly at her.

"When I rudely interrupted," Pam finished for him. "I didn't mean to, honest." Despite the music and the myriad of chattering voices, she lowered her voice and leaned over the table. "I had no idea the rhyme had the power to transport people through time."

"I wonder why it chose us."

"Probably because you were in the same house, the same room."

"But why not someone from another time period?"

Pam shuddered. What if a younger version of her parents had appeared in front of her—or herself as a child? No, her gut told her that only one of her could exist in the universe at a time. But seeing her parents? As much as she missed them . . . creepy! "Maybe the one hundred year gap is significant. Jake might know."

Jasper's grimace clearly conveyed his opinion of Jake. "He belittled you, Pam. He doesn't believe the rhyme holds any power, certainly not the power to move objects—or people—through time."

"But he told me about the rhyme only working once per lunar cycle."

"To humour you." Jasper glanced down at his beer, then reached across the table and touched Pam's arm. She swallowed, fighting the desire to cover his hand with hers. "Don't be upset with me, but I've—" His lifted his shoulders. "I've considered the possibility that Margaret and I may be here for good."

"No, Jasper. I'll send you back."

"I know you believe you can, and it's not you I doubt. You're a formidable woman. If anyone can send us back, you can." His gentle tone, the warmth of his touch . . . if he didn't move his hand away soon, she wouldn't be responsible for her actions. "But I have to consider the possibility that whatever happened when you read the rhyme was a fluke that won't be repeated."

"I'll send you back," she said firmly. "The rhyme will work." The historical record proved it.

Jasper's fingers tightened around her arm. "I admire your conviction."

Since she couldn't grab him, she grabbed her beer and gulped some down. When he finally lifted his hand from her arm and leaned back, the sensation of his touch lingered. If the rhyme's effectiveness depended on how strongly its reader wanted it to work, they could be in trouble! But no, it couldn't. She'd unwittingly brought them here, so her emotional state and desires weren't a factor.

"You and Margaret will return." They *would* marry. And Pam would continue to search for a decent, considerate man who could appreciate an independent woman and be gracious. Unfortunately she'd measure everyone against the man across from her, and probably find them falling short. She inwardly sighed. No point wanting what she couldn't have. Yep, Margaret was one lucky woman. "And you'll get married!" She forced a smile. "I know you didn't have a chance to set a date back in 1910, but I thought maybe you'd talked about it here."

"No. Neither of us has broached the subject. I suppose we want to see what happens."

She knew he meant whether they'd make it back to their own time. "Assuming you do return, when do you think you'll marry?"

"I'd like a summer wedding, and I'm sure the idea will appeal to Margaret, as well. So perhaps July or August."

"July or August 1911?"

He nodded.

But . . . "Where do you think you'll live?"

"Toronto, of course. Both our families are here."

But . . . "Is there any reason you wouldn't live in Toronto?"

His brows drew together. "No. Why would we live elsewhere? We both like the city, and we wouldn't want to leave our families. I'll eventually take over the business from Father. That's years away, I hope, but I need to be here."

Maybe the marriage announcement she'd found wasn't Jasper and Margaret's. No, it had to be them. How many Jasper Bainbridges and Margaret Wiltons would there be in 1910 . . . and married to each other? "So there's absolutely, positively, no reason you and Margaret would move away from Toronto?"

"Why do you ask?"

"I'm just trying to, uh, learn about the customs of your time." She swilled around the remains of her beer and downed it.

"I can't see any reason why we'd move. As for customs, generally speaking, people move for all sorts of reasons."

"Is there anything that would make people move in a hurry?"

Jasper drained his beer as he pondered the question. He set his empty glass on the table. "A scandal can sometimes force people to another city, so they can get a fresh start where tongues aren't wagging."

A scandal? God, Margaret wasn't pregnant, was she? Pam dismissed the thought when she remembered how they'd reacted to the notion of sharing a bedroom. But now they were alone together all day. What if . . . even if they were, Margaret wouldn't be showing in December. She wouldn't even be sure she was pregnant. Did they have pregnancy kits in those days?

"Of course, *we'd* never be involved in a scandal. I would never dishonour my family, and I chose Margaret because she has an excellent reputation."

"And you love her."

He cocked his head. "I have great affection for her."

That didn't sound like love. "But you don't love her?"

"You sound surprised."

"Why would you marry someone you don't love?" If Robin had accurately interpreted the last entry in Margaret's diary, Margaret was in the same boat.

"Because I want a good wife, and Margaret will be a wonderful wife and mother to our children."

"But what about love?"

Jasper picked up his glass, even though it was empty. "Father says the ideal wife will put me and the children first, that it's not necessary that I love her, only that I respect her." He stared into the glass; his voice grew wistful. "That affection will always outlast passion. That marrying for love is a mistake."

The way he suddenly aged before Pam's eyes, the longing in his voice . . . "You wanted to marry someone else, but your father disapproved of her," she stated.

He put the glass down. "Yes."

She gasped. "Who? When? Why didn't he like her? Does Margaret know?"

Jasper shook his head. "I shouldn't speak of this."

"Why not? Come on, Jasper, you can tell me. Who am I going to tell that matters?" She leaned across the table. "I won't breathe a word to Margaret, I swear. What was her name?"

She watched his face as he struggled with himself. His shoulders slumped. "Emily." His eyes grew distant for a minute, then brightened. "I met her at a baseball match. I couldn't help but notice her. She sat right behind me and kept shouting at the players. I managed to ignore her, until she spilled lemonade on my shoulder. I turned around to express my displeasure . . . and fell in love."

Pam hated her already.

"She insisted on having my jacket cleaned, I insisted on buying her another lemonade, and we were soon inseparable. Oh, she was wonderful, Pam. The spirited discussions we had, the matches we watched together, the rides around the park. She golfed, swam, shared so many of my interests, and never let me get away with underestimating her because she was a woman." He met Pam's eyes. "You remind me of her."

Blood rushed to her cheeks. She was sure he meant it as a compliment. "So what happened? Why didn't your father approve of her?"

His face slackened. "Because she was too independent-minded, as he put it. Emily and I discussed marriage. She wanted to marry, but not then. She'd just started university. Father said she'd always put herself before me. And he'd noticed that I was questioning my role in the family business. He blamed her for that."

"Why?"

"Because I told her that investments aren't my passion. She encouraged me to do what I really wanted to do."

"Which is?" Pam blurted when it looked as if Jasper wasn't going to tell her.

"Carpentry. More specifically, cabinetmaking."

His answer failed to surprise her. "Then do that! You did a beautiful job on our chairs, and the doorframe."

"I can't. Father would be incensed if I backed out of the family business to be a lowly tradesman."

Father sounded like a bastard who had his son desperate for his approval. Jasper wasn't the first man she'd met who wanted to please daddy; it certainly wasn't a condition limited to early twentieth century men.

"Emily said the money, my position in society—it didn't matter to her."

Okay, maybe Pam liked her a teensy little bit.

"I told her I would be satisfied working with my father, especially if she was my wife. I would have married her. I would have waited. But . . ." He blinked rapidly.

"But what?" Pam asked quietly, wanting to reach out and comfort him.

"Father told me to get rid of her. I told him I wanted to marry her, but he said she wouldn't make a suitable wife. He spoke to her father, told him we were . . ." he shifted in his chair " . . . having carnal relations."

Carnal relations? Pam coughed into her hand, then cleared her throat. "Of course, you weren't."

He didn't reply.

"You were!" Maybe Margaret *was* pregnant. "You and Margaret, are you, um—"

Jasper's eyes widened. "No! Absolutely not. Margaret will be my wife."

"You wanted to marry Emily, but that didn't stop you," Pam pointed out.

"We loved each other. I don't regret a second we had together, but we were reckless. I didn't consider her reputation. I should have. We were discreet, but foolish."

No wonder he didn't want Margaret's stay in 2010 to tarnish her. "How did your father find out?"

"He didn't. He said whatever he thought it would take for Emily's father to put an end to our relationship. It worked. She transferred to a university in the United States."

"When did all this happen?"

"When I was twenty-four."

"And Margaret doesn't know?"

He shook his head. "And she will never know."

Message received, not that Pam would have said anything. "Has there been anyone since then—apart from Margaret?"

"A few dalliances here and there." Jasper's Adam's apple bobbed. "Last year, Father left a newspaper clipping near my breakfast plate. Emily married an American." The muscle near his right eye jumped.

"I'm sorry." This time Pam patted his hand, and refrained from asking if he'd thought of going after Emily when she'd left for the

States. Defying daddy would have been beyond him, so why twist the knife of regret deeper?

"A couple of weeks later, Father had a talk with me. Said it was time to settle down, that I was almost thirty. He suggested several suitable women, Margaret among them. I eventually met them all. I liked Margaret the most."

Cripes, it sounded like an episode of that silly reality TV show in which a bachelor chose who to marry.

"I know you probably think badly of me, but I am fond of Margaret, and I'll take good care of her. What I'm doing isn't unusual, especially for a man in my position. And Margaret belongs to a respectable middle class family. I doubt love was her primary concern when she considered who would make a suitable husband."

Apparently not. "I don't think badly of you, Jasper. I'm sad for you. Your father's approval, your position . . . money. It isn't everything. Don't you want to be happy?"

"I will be happy."

"No, really happy. Fulfilled—work you enjoy, and a wife you love, truly love, with passion. The universe wants you to be happy. It doesn't want you to settle." And so she wouldn't, no matter how many jerks she had to go through before she met Mr. Right.

Jasper gazed at her. "You sound like you believe that."

"I do."

"Are you happy, Pam?"

His question caught her off guard. "Well, yes, for the most part. I admit, I'd be happier with a man in my life. If I didn't have Robin, I'd be lonely. But I haven't settled for someone I don't love just so I won't be alone when Robin moves out. I'd rather be lonely than settle."

"But you want to marry."

"Oh, yes. Definitely."

Jasper grunted. "Robin's a queer woman, isn't she?"

Shock made her voice shrill. "What makes you say that?" Wait. "Oh, you mean odd." When he nodded, her heart stopped pounding.

"She's not . . . feminine," Jasper said.

"Why, because she wears her hair short and prefers pants to dresses? That's not unusual today, Jasper. Okay, she doesn't wear makeup or jewelry either, but so what? She's her own person."

"I didn't mean to criticize her," Jasper said, motioning for Pam to calm down.

"Then don't judge her by how she looks!" Pam took a deep breath, reminded herself that she was sitting with someone from another time. "Listen, I can see how she might seem unusual to you. But I love her to bits. I know we're not blood-related, but she's family, the only family I've got. I'd do anything for her, and I know she'd do the same for me. So I can get a little defensive about her."

"I apologize. Robin is a most gracious host. And so are you."

Flattery would get him everywhere. "Apology accepted."

"Do you think she'll marry?"

"I hope she does." Robin would probably marry before Pam did—if she stopped worrying about her useless family and started living for herself. Jasper's lost love, his future tepid marriage to Margaret, Robin eventually meeting a nice woman and moving out . . . what a depressing conversation! "But enough chit-chat. Let's shoot some pool. Or are you afraid of losing?"

He snorted and pushed back his chair.

Pam's phone rang. She lifted it from her purse and glanced at the display. "I should take this. Hi," she said to Brenda, a co-worker and drinking buddy. "What's up? Did something happen at the office today?"

"No, I'm calling about my party. I need to know how many are coming. You said you'd let me know by today."

"Oh, right." Damn, she'd forgotten about the party. Jasper and Margaret would still be here; it was on October 16th, the weekend before she'd be trying to send them back. If she didn't attend, she'd miss too much gossip and appear antisocial, especially since she'd skipped Sue's party last month. "Yeah, I'll be there."

"Great! Will you be bringing someone?"

She eyed Jasper, and ignored the rational voice that always insisted on butting in at times like this. "Yes," she said, "I probably will."

MARGARET RAISED HER hand to pull a pin from her hair, then stopped when someone knocked at the closed bedroom door. "Margaret, are you decent?" Pam bellowed.

Of course she was decent! What kind of question was that?

"Margaret? Can I come in?"

"Just a minute." She glanced at the dresser to make sure Robin had hidden all the wool in its bottom drawer. Pam couldn't know about the wool until Robin had told her about their outing. "Yes, come in."

The door swung open. Pam stepped into the room. "Oh good, I'm glad I caught you before you went to bed. Did you enjoy your day today?"

"Very much." What did Pam want? She hadn't stepped foot in the bedroom since she'd helped Margaret the evening they'd arrived. "I gather you and Jasper also had an enjoyable day." Upon their return home, Margaret had shared a coffee with them and listened to their spirited banter about their golf game and billiard matches. They'd included her in the conversation, but she'd felt like the odd one out. Constantly wondering what Robin was doing hadn't helped.

"Yes, we did." Pam's smile was fixed. She shifted her weight. "Um, I want to ask you something. A favour. And don't feel you have to agree to it."

"All right," Margaret said, her curiosity piqued.

"You see, one of my work colleagues is having a party in a couple of weeks. I missed the last one, so I don't want to miss this one, too. It would be nice if I didn't have to go alone, because everyone else will be there with someone. I was wondering if . . . well, I thought it might make sense if . . ."

"You want Jasper to escort you."

Pam nodded. "But only if you agree."

Why was Pam asking for permission now? She hadn't asked for permission to spend today with him, or to monopolize his time every evening. Perhaps the difference was that their attendance at the party would be more like a date.

She should refuse Pam's request. She'd seen the way Jasper and Pam looked at each other, had sensed the attraction between them. If they were all in 1910, she'd worry that Jasper might call off their engagement. But if they were all in 1910, he never would have met Pam, and even if he had, they wouldn't be spending so much time together. They certainly wouldn't be living under the same roof! "Have you spoken to him about it?"

"Not yet. I thought I'd ask you first. There's no point asking him if you don't want him to go with me."

Did she have a choice? Pam said she wasn't obliged to agree, but she was living in the woman's house, eating the woman's food, and wearing clothes the woman had bought for her. Refusing her could cause tension between them. Margaret didn't want that, not when they still had to live together.

"And if you agree, I'll have to talk to Robin, see if she'll be around that night."

As much as she wanted to, Margaret couldn't deny that she'd look forward to an evening alone with Robin. What was wrong with her? Could whatever was affecting her also be affecting Jasper? Was that why he was attracted to Pam? If Robin was a man, would Margaret be stepping out with him right under Jasper's nose? She shook herself and tried to focus on Pam's request. "Are you sure it will be prudent to take Jasper with you? I assume he'll have to converse with the other guests."

"Yes, but what's the worst that can happen? They might think he's a little strange, but nobody's going to think, 'Oh my, he must be from 1910.'"

No, she supposed not.

"I'll be at his side all evening."

Of that, Margaret had no doubt. Oh, what harm would one evening do? She and Jasper would return to 1910 and their time here would feel as if it had been a dream. "Then I agree. When you speak to Jasper about it, please tell him that I don't mind." If he asked.

Pam's face lit up. "Thank you, Margaret. I'll take good care of him and have him back before he turns into a pumpkin, I promise. Good night."

"Good night."

The door clicked shut. Troubled, Margaret sank onto the edge of the bed. She should be jealous of Pam, but she wasn't. She should be furious with Jasper if he readily agreed to escort Pam, but she wouldn't be. She shouldn't hope that Robin would be free and that they'd pass the evening of the party together, but she did.

Pam would send them home on October 23rd, and it couldn't come fast enough. If they didn't return . . . Margaret couldn't bear to consider the consequences! She wanted everything back to normal again, including herself. That rhyme had better work.

Chapter Seven

Pam tossed her last card onto the pile, whooped, and thrust her fist into the air. "I win!"

Jasper added the remaining cards in his hand to the pile, facedown. "Good game."

"Yes, good game," Margaret murmured, hoping they wouldn't want to play again. Aware of Robin upstairs, she couldn't focus. Her mind was too busy trying to come up with an excuse to speak to Robin, but at the same time, Margaret didn't want to disturb her. Perhaps a quick question was the answer? She'd knitted that afternoon, while Pam was at work, and would like to do so this evening, especially since Pam had already suggested a movie. Robin must have told Pam about the wool and their outing by now—she'd had ample opportunity—but it wouldn't hurt to check with her to make sure. If Margaret were to start a sweater, she'd also need an idea of Robin's size.

"So, movie?" Pam said cheerfully.

Jasper nodded. "How many movies do you have?"

"Enough that you won't see them all before you go back."

Margaret stifled a snort. How disappointing!

"You watching with us tonight, Margaret?" Pam asked.

"No, thank you." She knew she wouldn't be missed.

Pam pushed herself up from the table. "I'll put the coffee on, then we'll choose a movie," she said to Jasper.

Margaret helped Jasper collect the cards, then gathered her courage and went upstairs. Oh, the study door was ajar, not open. Robin probably didn't want to be interrupted, but the compulsion to see her was too strong for Margaret to resist, and she only wanted to ask a simple question. She tapped at the door.

"Come in," Robin called.

Margaret pushed the door open. "I'm sorry if I'm disturbing you, but I was wondering if you've told Pam about Friday. I'd like to knit tonight, if I can."

Robin dragged what appeared to be a thick pen across a line in the book she was reading, colouring the line yellow. She looked up. "Sorry, I should have mentioned it to you. Yes, I told her." Her mouth turned up at the corners. "She wasn't exactly happy about it, but what could she say, given that she'd spent almost the entire day out with Jasper? So go ahead and knit. She won't ask you where the wool came from."

"Thank you." Margaret hovered, reluctant to leave. Oh . . . "I want to start knitting your sweater, but I don't know what size you are. Can I show you the pattern? It lists all the measurements."

"Sure. And you can always measure me."

Her breath quickened. "Let's try the pattern first," she said faintly. "I'll fetch it." Were her cheeks as red as they felt? The thought of wrapping a measuring tape around Robin had her all aflutter! She hurried into the bedroom, snatched the pattern from Robin's desk, and returned to the study.

Robin took it from her and studied it. "I remember this one, it's the last one we printed."

On Friday night, they'd sat in front of Robin's computer, searching for and printing out patterns. Margaret had marvelled at how one could instantly obtain patterns, just like that! "You said you like it," she reminded Robin.

"I do. And . . . I'm a medium."

"Medium," Margaret repeated, disappointed that she wouldn't need the measuring tape, but certain it was for the best.

Robin handed back the pattern. "Are you sure you want to knit me a sweater? You don't have to."

"I'd like to, very much."

"Then, thank you." Robin touched Margaret's arm.

Margaret swallowed. "It will be my pleasure." She didn't want to leave. "Would you like a cup of tea?" At least that would give her a reason to come up and see Robin again.

"I'd love one. But only if you're having one, as well. In fact, why don't you have your tea with me up here? I could use a break." Robin cupped her hand around her ear. "And is that a movie I hear starting downstairs?"

She didn't need to be asked twice! "I would like to have tea with you, as long as it doesn't interfere with your work."

Robin shook her head. "Like I said, I need a break. By the time you've made the tea, I'll have finished this chapter."

"I'll go put the kettle on, then." Now eager to leave before Robin changed her mind, Margaret returned the pattern to the bedroom and went down to the kitchen.

The sensations she felt around Robin were most pleasant . . . and wrong. Now she understood why her friends swooned, yearned to see their suitors, and struggled to retain their innocence. But *their* feelings were normal. Hers weren't. If she could feel half as drawn to Jasper as she was to Robin, their marriage would be filled with passion. Perhaps returning to 1910 would redirect her attraction to him, where it belonged.

For now, she should avoid Robin, not indulge the . . . longing for her. But it was as if someone had cast a spell over Margaret, making it impossible to resist her desire. And so here she was, willing the kettle to boil so she could make the tea and hurry back upstairs. She must be careful to never let a hint of her feelings for Robin show. If Robin even suspected, she and Pam would throw Margaret out onto the street, and deservedly so. The most generous of hosts would refuse to harbour a deviant.

MARGARET RESTED HER knitting on her lap and glanced at the time on the machine Pam used to play her movies. *10:45.* Would Robin be home soon from the late dinner with her father? Margaret had missed their nightly ritual this evening. The tea she'd taken up to Robin last week had been the first of many. She'd easily fallen into the habit of sipping tea with her for fifteen or twenty minutes, then settling into the comfy armchair in the study and knitting while Robin worked. Tonight she'd knit in the study alone, only coming downstairs when Jasper and Pam had retired. She should be in bed too, but knew she wouldn't sleep until Robin was home. Her feelings were a curse! Yet she couldn't resist them.

She picked up her knitting, then froze when a key turned in the front door lock and the door opened and closed. Margaret expected Robin to come into the living room when she saw the light on, but Robin strode past the living room archway and down the hallway, still wearing her jacket. She didn't go upstairs, though; it sounded as if she'd gone into the kitchen.

Margaret dithered over what to do—whether to remain in the living room and hope Robin noticed the light when she left the kitchen, or go into the kitchen under the pretense of wanting a glass of water. No, she wouldn't force her company on Robin. There was always tomorrow. But when Robin was still in the kitchen ten minutes later and the house sounded completely silent, Margaret's curiosity got the better of her. She left her knitting on the coffee table and went to the kitchen. Odd, the kitchen light wasn't on. Had Robin quietly gone to bed?

Disappointed, Margaret turned to go upstairs, then decided that she actually wouldn't mind a glass of water. She flicked on the kitchen light. The unexpected sight of someone sitting at the table made her gasp in fright. "Oh my goodness, I'm sorry!"

She stared in astonishment as Robin quickly dabbed at her eyes with a tissue. "It's all right. You didn't know I was here."

Again, Margaret dithered. She'd intruded on a private moment and should leave Robin in peace, but she couldn't pretend she hadn't noticed Robin's distress and walk away as if she didn't care. Concern and curiosity propelled her farther into the kitchen. When Robin didn't shoo her away, Margaret pulled out a chair and sat down. Her heart ached at Robin's hunched shoulders, her hands clenched around the tissue, and her downcast eyes. This wasn't the confident, assured woman she was used to.

The urge to comfort Robin by touching her was overwhelming. Margaret tucked her hands underneath the table and gripped her dress for good measure. "Did the dinner with your father not go well?" she asked gently. Robin hadn't seemed enthusiastic about seeing her father, both the first time she'd mentioned it and when she'd reminded Margaret about it last night.

To her surprise, Robin smiled. "Well, you could say that, but then, it never does." She drew a shaky breath. "I don't know why he bothers. I guess he just can't pass up any opportunity to tell us how perfect his second family is." The bitterness in her voice was unmistakable.

"Why would he want to do that?"

"I guess he's glad to be rid of the drunk and the schizo." Robin sighed. "And me. Though he likes to see me and Chris every once in a while, just to make sure we don't forget what a wonderful life he has now."

He sounded like a horrid man! But something Robin had said bothered her. She could understand, though not condone, his abandonment of his wife and son. Life with an alcoholic wife and ill son must have been difficult, and perhaps he was unable to overcome a lingering resentment toward them. But why hurt Robin? Why resent her? "Why is he glad to be rid of you?" Margaret blurted before she could change her mind. She shouldn't ask, but she wanted—needed—to know. "He should be proud of you," she said when Robin didn't answer. "You're in university, you're kind-hearted." Margaret swallowed. "You're a lovely woman. Why would he—"

Robin abruptly pushed back her chair and stood. "I appreciate your concern, Margaret, I really do. But you'll be gone next week. You don't need to get mixed up with my problems." She shoved the tissue into her jacket pocket. "I'm going to bed."

"I'm sorry if I offended you," Margaret quickly said, not wanting them to part on a bad note.

"You didn't, not at all. It's my fault. For some reason I feel comfortable talking to you about personal stuff, maybe because I know you won't be here for long. I don't know." Robin shrugged. "I just know I shouldn't take advantage and whine to you. I'm sorry." She pressed her hand against her chest. "I hope you'll still bring me tea tomorrow."

Margaret's throat tightened. "Of course I will." She wouldn't miss her time with Robin for the world.

"I'd miss it, if you didn't." Robin walked toward the hallway and stopped when she reached it. "I'd miss you, too. Good night."

She was gone before Margaret had a chance to respond—not that she would have said anything. She was too busy reeling over Robin's parting words. Was Robin being polite, or had she meant it? For the first time, Margaret realized that returning to 1910 would bring her sadness as well as joy. She would spend the rest of her life missing someone who hadn't been born.

PAM JUMPED WHEN the bedroom door swung open; when Robin strode in she lowered her book and tried not to wince at Robin's red eyes. "Another wonderful dinner with daddy dearest?"

"I don't know why I bother." Robin shut the door, then sat at the end of the bed and pulled off her shoes.

"Neither do I. Next time he wants to grace you with his presence as an afterthought as he's passing through town, tell him to fuck off."

Robin twisted around. "He's my father."

"So what? All he does is tell you what a disappointment you are because you're gay. And did he tell Chris to dump his meds again, that all they are is a crutch and he needs to man up and make something of himself?" Robin's silence answered the question. "The man's a complete ass. I'm sorry, I know he's your father, but he is." Was it wrong to wish that he'd died in a fiery crash instead of *her* father? The world would have been better off, especially Robin and Chris. "So honestly, I don't get these dinners. He's not going to suddenly turn around and tell you and Chris that he loves you just as you are. So forget about him already. Stop hoping the next dinner will be the one when he admits that he has two damn good kids, and I'm not talking about the brats." She could tell from Robin's face that her words weren't making any difference. "My god, what is it with grown adults wanting the approval of their parents? Jasper's the same way. The two people I care—" Her brain overruled her tongue.

Robin pointed at her. "You were going to say the two people you care about most."

Pam cursed herself. "No, I wasn't."

"Yes, you were."

"Stop trying to change the subject. How is Chris, anyway?" Pam said, changing the subject.

"He's good."

"I hope he's not going to listen to your father."

Robin shook her head. "I think he tunes Dad out now."

"Good. You should do the same."

"He has a girlfriend."

"I hope you mean Chris." She wouldn't put it past Robin's father to have a mistress and brag about it.

Robin nodded. "I met her a couple of weeks ago. She seems nice. He met her at group. She's schizophrenic, too."

"Oh god, let's hope they don't both hear voices at the same time, or things could get interesting. Imagine the arguments."

Robin chuckled. "I've been meaning to mention her to you." She paused. "But you're always busy."

Was Robin scolding her?

"Are you sure it's a good idea to take Jasper to the party with you?"

So Robin *was* upset about Jasper. "I asked Margaret and she doesn't mind."

"That's not what I meant. But now that you've mentioned Margaret, they *are* engaged."

"And they'll get married and live happily ever after," Pam snapped. "You saw the marriage announcement. Oh, and I've found something else on the Net since then."

Robin's brow furrowed. "What did you find?"

"A graduation announcement for one Elizabeth Margaret Bainbridge, parents Jasper and Margaret Bainbridge. Look." Pam grabbed her phone from the nightstand and brought up the historical newspaper website she'd found. "And she graduated from Dalhousie, so I guess they were still living in Halifax." Robin rounded the bed to sit nearer to Pam and peered at the phone's display. "You see?" Pam said. "They get married, they have a family, everything's hunky-dory. Remember you said that Margaret doesn't love him?"

Her attention still on the phone, Robin nodded.

"Well, Jasper doesn't exactly love her, either. It's sort of like an arranged marriage, except they arranged it themselves." With their fathers' help. "So who cares if Jasper has one last hurrah before he plays the dutiful husband for the rest of his life? It's not as if I'll come out of the woodwork later and destroy their marriage."

Robin looked up at her. "Just what type of hurrah are we talking about?"

"Going out for an evening with someone other than Margaret, that's all." And with a woman who truly felt for him, and, if Pam's reading of the situation was correct, a woman he truly felt for.

"I'm not going to tell you what to do," Robin said.

"But?"

Robin was silent for a moment. "They're going back in just over a week. Don't get too attached."

Yeah, she was painfully aware of when they were going back. Robin's advice was too late.

"And they might not love each other now, but I'm sure they're hoping love will grow over time. Don't make that more difficult by being the perfect woman he'll measure Margaret against. It'll be hard to compete against a woman he was sort of on vacation with for a month, too short a time to see her bad side."

"Well, thank you very much!"

"You know what I mean."

Pam stuck out her tongue.

"Did you find anything else?" Robin asked.

"No. I could poke around on one of the genealogy sites, but you have to pay for those to see anything interesting. And, uh . . ." Pam cleared her throat. "I could search cemetery records."

Robin grimaced. "God, no. I don't think I could deal with that. Maybe after they've been gone for a while, but now? No."

"Yeah, the thought made me shudder too, so I haven't. I figure it's best not to know." She set the phone back on the nightstand. "I didn't tell Jasper about the marriage announcement—I wouldn't," she quickly added when Robin gave her a look, "but I asked him a few questions, like where they'd live, that sort of thing. They're not planning a move to Halifax. He made it sound like something unusual would have to happen to make them move, like a scandal of some sort."

"It would have to happen pretty quickly, given when they got married. I hope it has nothing to do with them being here." Robin pressed her lips together. "Nah, if they went around telling people they'd visited 2010, they'd end up in a lunatic asylum. And whatever they do here, stays here. Something unexpected must happen."

But what? Maybe after they'd returned, Pam would really dig around and see what she could find out, even if she had to shell out a few bucks to access records or slog herself down to a library to view microfilm reels.

"Do you ever wonder if this is actually happening?" Robin asked. "Maybe this is one long dream, something our brains are cooking up to comfort us as we're slowly dying from carbon monoxide poisoning."

"And we're both in the same dream, talking to each other and going about our daily lives? It feels too real and too rational."

Robin snorted. "Except for the 'we believe we're living with two people from 1910' part."

"Yes, but the fact that we occasionally think we're nuts means we're not, right? If we were really nuts, we wouldn't think we were nuts."

"Or maybe that's what we want to believe. Sometimes I wonder if this is how it is for Chris." Robin stood. "Anyway, I should get ready for bed." She lifted her pyjamas from the top of the dresser and left for the bathroom.

Pam was certain her life for the past few weeks wasn't a delusion. If her brain had built this world, Jasper would be sharing her bed, not Robin.

Chapter Eight

P AM SIPPED HER WINE AND WATCHED Jasper fill his plate
with goodies available at the snack table. When another party
guest approached him, she didn't rush to his side. Not only did the
Bainbridge family often host soirées, they were on everyone's guest
list—and it showed in the skill with which Jasper worked a room,
even here in 2010. If he didn't get a joke, he laughed anyway. If he
didn't understand a cultural reference or question, he pretended he
hadn't heard and deftly steered the conversation back to the other
person. People loved to talk about themselves, and Jasper had little
trouble encouraging them to do so. The guest who'd joined him near
the table was already happily chattering away while Jasper nodded
and stuffed his face.

She turned to her left when someone nudged her arm. "So where
did you find him?" Brenda asked. "He's so charming." Her eyes narrowed. "You've never mentioned him before."

"Oh, he's one of my mother's friend's sons, in town visiting. It was
a last minute thing. I said I'd show him around."

"I can see the sparks flying."

Pam leaned closer and dropped her voice. "It's too bad he'll be
leaving next week."

"It's nothing to hop on a plane these days. If you don't mind a
long-distance relationship," Brenda said from the corner of her mouth.

"Unfortunately, he's spoken for. Engaged."

"Oh," Brenda mouthed. "Too bad."

Pam loved how she could tell the truth and make perfect sense as
long as she didn't mention 1910.

Another guest joined them. "Brenda, I just *love* the chocolate cake. Did you make it?"

Pam lightly touched Brenda's arm and murmured, "I'll talk to you later," then hovered near Jasper until he noticed her and politely ended his conversation. "Enjoying yourself?" she asked.

Chewing on something, he said, "Mmm," and held out his plate. She chose one of the two remaining sugar cookies. Jasper made fast work of the other one. "Conversations haven't changed much. Work, people, hobbies. Same old thing. Oh, the military came up. I didn't quite understand what was being said, but I gathered that we were involved in an overseas campaign in Europe at some point."

He didn't know about the world wars, and she wasn't about to tell him. When selecting movies to watch, she'd passed over those that made mention of them. The First World War would start a mere four years after he returned. If he enlisted, did he survive? Maybe finding out what had happened to Jasper after he returned wasn't such a good idea. She'd rather imagine him happy, raising children with Margaret and then enjoying his grandchildren, not dead on a battlefield, and Margaret a war widow with young children to care for. "It's best you not know."

He accepted her answer with a nod, as he had the handful of other times she'd decided to withhold information. Out of the corner of her eye she glimpsed Mike and Angela, two of the few guests who smoked, coming back into the living room from the balcony. She grabbed Jasper's arm. "Come on, I want to show you something." She allowed him time to set his plate atop the dirty stack at the end of the snack table before dragging him outside, and grinned from ear to ear when his mouth dropped open.

Jasper went to the railing and looked down. Pam remained a few steps behind him, her stomach flip-flopping. She wasn't terrified of heights—she was out here—but she wasn't brave enough to stand at the railing. "Quite the sight, eh? We're up thirty-five floors."

"It's magnificent. The lights . . . everything looks so small . . ." He was silent for a moment, then turned around. "Don't you want to see?"

"Uh, well, I'm okay here." She smiled sheepishly.

He held out his hand.

Oh god. Not wanting him to think her a coward, she forced herself to take it and walk to his side, her insides quaking. *Don't look down, don't look down!* She gripped the railing with her free hand and clung to Jasper with her other. The warmth of his hand reassured her and she felt safe, but if the light breeze suddenly gusted, she was outta here. His hand wasn't enough to keep her warm, though. Her thin blouse didn't stand a chance against the chill. Shivering, she wanted to rub the goose bumps from her arms, but she wasn't about to let go of the railing and Jasper's hand!

"You're cold."

When Jasper loosened his hold on her hand, she tightened her grip. "No! Don't let go."

"I want to give you my jacket. Look at me."

"I'll look at you from over here." She moved away from the railing, clinging to it until she had to let go, and stopped where she was sure a strong wind couldn't blow her off the balcony. Only then did she let go of Jasper's hand.

She chuckled to herself as he removed his jacket. She'd had a hell of a time persuading him to forgo a tie and not button his shirt up to his chin. They'd sounded like her parents when Mom was dressing Dad for an evening out—an old married couple, affectionately bickering.

A lump rose in her throat when Jasper placed his jacket around her shoulders. She hugged it to herself. "Thank you."

"My pleasure."

Their eyes met. "You can look out a bit more, if you like. I'll just stand here," Pam said.

He didn't move. Did he feel it too, the yearning to close the short distance between them? She tried to tear her eyes away from his, but couldn't.

"I'm starting to wonder how it will feel, to be back home," he said quietly. "I've seen wondrous sights, glimpsed how inventions from my time shaped things to come, and seen machines that even my children will probably never have the opportunity to use. I've lived the future! But the sights, the machines, the changes—they're not what I'll remember the most." Pam couldn't breathe when he gently ran his finger down her cheek and cupped her chin. "I'll miss you."

Unable to resist any longer, she let his jacket fall to the ground and threw her arms around his neck, then closed her eyes when she felt his arms tighten around her. Relief, sorrow, and lust mingled together as she pressed her cheek against his. God, she'd miss him too. It was a good thing she couldn't control what would happen when she read the rhyme; otherwise she'd be tempted to send Margaret back and keep him, marry him and raise a family, argue with him about stupid ties, and want to bash her head against the dashboard while teaching him how to drive in 2010.

"Pam—"

No, she didn't want to talk, not anymore, when they had so little time left. She pressed her lips against his neck, his jaw, moved to his mouth when she felt him respond. But the second her lips touched his, they both pulled back and stared at each other, the heat between them still raging. "We can't do this." She swallowed and relaxed into him, but pressed her right hand against his shoulder, ready to push away if she felt herself weakening. "As much as I'd like to, we can't," she whispered.

His chest heaved against hers. "I know," he said huskily. "If we were both from the same time . . ."

Her heart ached; their lips were almost touching. "But we're not. So when you're back, forget about me. You have Margaret, and I want you to take care of her and be a good husband to her, you understand? I'll be watching you," her lips trembled, "from wherever we are before we're born."

If she looked at him any longer, her actions would belie her words. Pam patted his chest, then stooped to pick up his jacket. She didn't protest when he took it from her and draped it around her shoulders, or when he put his arm around her and pulled her into him. She slipped her arm around his waist, laid her head on his shoulder, and blinked out at the blurred lights.

MARGARET STROKED MITZY's head and cooed at her when she purred. For the first couple of weeks, Mitzy had wanted nothing to do with her. Now she leaped onto Margaret's lap at every opportunity. Margaret was especially grateful for Mitzy's company now, and kept her attention on the purring cat while Robin pulled on the knitted sweater. When Robin said, "It fits," Margaret lifted her head.

Robin stood with her hands on her hips. "What do you think?"

That Robin looked gorgeous in the snug sweater that accentuated her small breasts and matched her blue eyes. "Is it too tight?"

"No. It's perfect. Thank you."

"Try on the tuque and mitts."

Robin picked them up from the coffee table and pulled on the tuque, then the mitts. She flexed her hands in front of her. "Wow, I'm actually colour coordinated," she said with a laugh. "I love them. I'm not usually big on hats, but I might actually wear this one. Wise decision, not adding a pom-pom."

Margaret inwardly smiled. If she'd knitted the tuque for anyone else, it would have a pom-pom. But Robin? No. "There will be a scarf and socks to go with them by the time I leave." To her dismay, Robin's smile wilted. "If you don't want them—"

"I do want them. I know I'll love them. It's just that . . ." Robin rounded the coffee table, plunked down on the sofa, and shifted position to face Margaret. "Well, I have to admit, I'll feel a bit sad whenever I wear anything you knit. You *are* leaving, and you're going somewhere I won't be able to email or phone you." She paused a second. "I bet you're eager to get back."

For the most part. Her family and friends—her life—were in the past. Margaret dearly missed them and looked forward to seeing everyone again. Jasper was here, but though they'd lived under the same roof for weeks, she felt less close to him than she had in their own time. But with Pam and Robin no longer in their lives to distract and occupy them, Margaret was confident they'd easily resume their socializing and comfortable friendship, especially with all the fuss their engagement would bring. Jasper's . . . dalliance with Pam, Margaret's . . . fascination with Robin—both would soon be in *their* pasts, despite having taken place in the future. Their brief stay here would forever bind them together, and perhaps infuse their relationship with the passion it had thus far lacked for her. She fervently hoped so. If she could feel for Jasper what she felt for Robin . . .

She believed that returning to 1910 would remedy her abnormal feelings for Robin, but couldn't deny that, right now, those abnormal feelings made the thought of returning home almost unbearable. She'd worry about Robin, someone who hadn't been born, and wonder how her life would turn out. Would she finish her degree, marry, have children, work out her problems with her family? When the items Margaret had knitted wore out, would Robin keep them or toss them aside, her visitors from the past a distant memory, or perhaps forgotten? Margaret hoped Robin would always remember her, as she would always remember Robin.

She shook herself. No, when she returned to 1910, she'd be normal again, remember? She'd never forget Robin and Pam and her time here, but Robin wouldn't monopolize her thoughts, as she did now. Jasper and their impending marriage would.

The motion of Robin's hand stroking Mitzy brought Margaret back to the conversation. "I am looking forward to returning. But I'll miss the two friends I made here." She wanted to add, "I won't forget you," but didn't want to sound sentimental.

"I'll have all these beautiful things you've knitted to remember you," Robin said, making Margaret wonder if she could read minds. "If you could take something back with you to remember me by, what would you want?"

You. Margaret pushed the inappropriate and impetuous response from her mind. Robin in 1910 was the last thing she'd want. "A photograph of you and Pam." As long as it was a good photograph of Robin. No, that wasn't fair. Pam had been a gracious host and, despite her friendship with Jasper that was stretching the bounds of propriety, Margaret liked her. But a photograph of the two of them still wouldn't be her first choice.

"Really? That's what you'd want?"

No, it was her polite answer, and one that wouldn't betray her feelings. If she could, she'd have a more personal item of Robin's.

"Is there anything else you'd want? You've practically made me a whole outfit, here."

Dare she? It could be a way of expressing how she felt without explicitly saying it, and would be obscure enough that she could deny her feelings, if Robin somehow guessed at her true motivation for wanting the items. Margaret stroked Mitzy for moral support, then plunged

ahead. "I'd want a page of your study notes. One that's handwritten."
When Robin didn't react, she continued. "And your leather jacket."

Incredulity was written all over Robin's face. "My jacket? That's
the last thing I expected you to say. Why would you want that?"

Because she'd never forget the moment she'd slipped her arm
through Robin's—the delicious sensations that had stirred when she'd
felt the warmth of Robin's body, and the smoothness of the leather
under her hand as it had rested on Robin's sleeve. Nor the way her
heart leaped every time Robin came through the front door, waved
hello, and took off her jacket, and the longing she felt after Robin had
slipped on her jacket and left for a day at university. Margaret would
cherish that jacket until the day she died. "You said something to
remember you by," she said, sure that poor Mitzy must feel harassed by
her incessant stroking. "Your jacket would certainly remind me of you."

She held her breath when Robin stared at her, worried that she'd
revealed too much. Then Robin smiled. "My lack of fashion sense, I
suppose."

Relieved, Margaret slowly exhaled and chided herself for losing
her head. She must be mad!

"And considering you sit with me most nights, I can understand
why you'd want a page of my notes." She frowned in thought. "I'd
gladly give you one, but I'm wondering if we should risk it. It might
interfere with sending you back."

"You're right," Margaret quickly said, hoping Robin would drop
the subject.

Robin's brow furrowed. "I wonder if your memory of being here
will be wiped out."

She hoped not. Her feelings for Robin were wrong, but not remembering them . . . that would be wrong, too. She didn't want to lose a
month of her life and what she'd learned. Now she understood the
conversations with her friends and knew what she'd eventually feel
for Jasper. Being in 2010 had somehow twisted the experience—she
wished those feelings had first stirred for Jasper, or another man. But
no matter. Once home, everything would return to normal, and it was
best that she not have anything of Robin's with her. She'd probably
wonder why on earth she'd asked for the items, then remind herself that
her "2010 self" would have cherished them, but her "1910 self" didn't.

Robin pushed herself away from the back of the sofa. "Well, thank you for your wonderful knitting. I really appreciate it. I think I'll keep the sweater on for now." She pulled off the tuque and mitts. "Do you want a cup of tea?"

"Yes, please."

"I'll put the kettle on."

Margaret watched her walk from the living room. She couldn't believe that in a mere week, she'd never see her again, that it would be as if Robin had never existed. How could feelings so wrong be so precious?

CONCERNED THAT SHE'D missed a couple of stitches, Margaret double-checked the sock pattern on her lap and groaned. If she wasn't rushing, she wouldn't make such stupid mistakes. She could afford to slow down; she'd already finished one sock and had the rest of the morning and the entire afternoon to finish this one.

A knock at the study door startled her. She jerked her head up. "Oh, is it time for lunch already?" she asked Jasper.

"Not quite." He hovered a moment longer, then came into the study. Margaret's mouth tightened when he sat in Robin's habitual spot. She put down her knitting and waited while he cleared his throat and studied his hands. "We're going back tomorrow," he said, finally looking at her. Did her eyes look as sad as his? "I thought we should talk about that."

"What would you like to talk about?" Was he going to call off their engagement because of Pam? That wouldn't make sense.

"We should prepare ourselves for the possibility that nothing happens when Pam reads the rhyme."

Margaret didn't want to entertain the frightening possibility that she could be trapped here in her abnormal state, nor her suspicion that, should the future become their permanent home, Jasper would cast her aside for Pam. "Perhaps we should save that conversation until we need it, Jasper. It's one we should have with Pam and Robin. We would need their advice." And their help.

When Jasper slowly nodded, his ready agreement to drop the subject made Margaret wonder if he really wanted to talk about something else. "I think we did right, not spending every moment together," he said, deepening her suspicion, especially when his attention shifted to his hands again. "I know I've spent quite a bit of time with Pam—"

"We've been caught up in unusual circumstances." How could she resent the attention he'd paid to Pam? At least his feelings for her were normal! Being in the future had obviously affected them both. It *was* good that they'd limited their time alone together—their moral fibre was obviously distorted, so who knew what might have happened? She wished Jasper had isolated himself more from 2010, rather than stepping out with Pam and watching TV and movies, but it was too late to do anything about that now.

"I'd rather talk about what will happen when we do return. What if we suddenly appear in the middle of the drawing room and there are others present? What if we've been missing? What if we return in 1911 or 1912?" Sudden panic drove her to her feet. Her knitting slid to the floor. Jasper came over and put his arms around her. She leaned into him, but felt nothing—and thought of Robin. If Robin's arms were around her, Margaret would be a puddle on the floor. Lord have mercy on her!

"Just as you didn't want to have the conversation about what we'll do if nothing happens, let's wait and see where we end up," Jasper murmured.

"But what if we end up somewhere with people who aren't as hospitable as Pam and Robin? What if Pam sends us further into the future?"

"Let's assume we'll arrive back when we left, or very close to it." Jasper stepped back and smiled reassuringly. "No matter what happens, we'll announce our engagement immediately, of course."

She nodded, grateful, but not surprised, that he'd stand by her. If they didn't arrive back exactly when they'd left, everyone would assume they'd been away together. Her parents would insist on a hasty wedding, and Jasper would have to defend her when his family questioned whether she'd still make a suitable wife. And what explanation would they give for running away together the moment they got engaged and then returning unmarried? It would be an absolutely rash and stupid thing to do. If they hadn't eloped, why on earth had they run away? Or was that the answer? If they discovered that time had elapsed in 1910 while they were in 2010, why not marry before facing their families? They could then explain their absence in a way that made sense and preserved their moral character. To add authenticity to their story and account for the fact that nobody had seen them around town, they'd also have to leave Toronto and marry elsewhere, before returning home

Oh, what would tomorrow bring? If fortune smiled upon them, they'd end up in the drawing room in 1910, with Jasper on his knee proposing. And when she thought of Robin and he thought of Pam, it would be with innocent affection and the wistfulness one feels when missing friends, nothing more.

PAM KICKED OFF her slippers and climbed into bed, but didn't turn off the bedside lamp. Robin was lying on her back with her hands behind her head, staring into space. She'd been unusually quiet during supper, too—not that Robin was ever a chatterbox, but she usually threw more than a couple of words into the conversation. "Okay, I knew I'd feel like shit." Pam rolled onto her side and propped herself up on one elbow. "But I thought you'd be dancing around with joy. This time tomorrow, they'll be gone."

Robin sighed. "It'll be nice not having to make up excuses anymore about why I can't go out. Everyone's convinced I've fallen in love with someone online and I'm spending all my time chatting with them. And I'm sure my guild thinks I've quit the game." She paused. "And yeah, when they first arrived, I couldn't wait for them to go back."

"But they grew on you?"

Robin hesitated a beat. "It feels like they've always been here, and now, poof, they'll be gone. I'll miss the nightly ritual with Margaret. It'll be funny, not hearing the clicking of her knitting needles."

"I can always bring you tea," Pam said with a chuckle. "But don't expect me to knit. Anyway, I'm surprised you've tolerated that while you're working."

"She's wanted company while you and Jasper are cuddling on the sofa, watching your movies."

"We don't cuddle!" Pam said indignantly.

"You don't, huh?" Robin snorted. "Well, while you've been busy doing whatever it is you're not doing, it's been lonely for her. I haven't minded keeping her company."

"You were taking care of her, like you take care of everyone else? You know, children of alcoholics have a tendency to do that."

Robin glared at her. "You know I hate it when you do that. You've been taking care of Jasper."

Point taken.

"It's good they're going back tomorrow. Any more time here and we'd have a mess on our hands," Robin said.

"What mess?"

"You know what mess. I hope you haven't done too much damage already."

Pam opened her mouth to protest, then shut it. Guilty as charged. If she hadn't known that Jasper and Margaret didn't love each other—yet—would she have still spent so much time with him? Allowed herself to fall for him? Taken advantage of his fiancée's predicament? She'd like to think not, and it took two. Maybe she should think less of him for not discouraging her, but he'd play the dutiful husband for the rest of his life. As she'd previously said to Robin, what was wrong with one last quasi-fling, one that couldn't hurt him or Margaret in their own time? "Okay, I admit it, I really like him, I've enjoyed every moment with him, and yeah, I didn't think much about Margaret."

Robin's eyebrows shot up. "At least you're honest."

"It doesn't matter. They're going back tomorrow."

"You sound confident about that."

"I am! You read the marriage announcement. Not only that, they had a daughter, and probably other children. What I'm hoping doesn't happen is that they leave and others arrive." She gripped Robin's arm. "If my parents show up, I'm running out of the house screaming. You'll have to deal with them."

"If your parents show up, *I'm* running out of the house screaming and staying with my mom until you send them back. They wouldn't need us to take care of them. Even if they arrived from 1985, they could take care of themselves in 2010."

Oh my god! "Mom couldn't go out. Half the freaking street was at her funeral! Imagine the headlines," Pam wailed.

Robin slid one of her hands from behind her head and patted Pam's arm. "Don't panic. I doubt your parents will show up. Margaret and

Jasper will go back, and we'll carry on with our lives."

Pam closed her eyes and took deep breaths to calm herself. If she'd kept up her nightly meditation time, maybe she wouldn't fly into a tizzy at the slightest provocation. But that would have meant time away from Jasper. She let out her last deep breath with a groan and opened her eyes.

Robin stared at her. "You okay?"

She nodded. "I've been thinking about tomorrow," she said briskly. "I think we should try to create the same circumstances as when they arrived, so you should be in your bedroom."

"Okay."

"And let's do it around 9:00. We'll have to have an early dinner, because I need time to do Margaret's hair. It won't be perfect, but good enough. And hey, if they arrive back when they left, everyone will probably assume they sealed their engagement with a passionate kiss and her hair got mussed up." Her smile felt fake, and was. "The pictures I took of her will come in handy. Oh, will you take one of me and Jasper before they go? And let's take a few of him and Margaret in their old clothes."

"I don't think that's a good idea. The less of them left here, the better."

"I'm not dumping the shawl Margaret knitted for me. It's beautiful."

"I'm not suggesting you do. But pictures?" Robin frowned. "I don't know. What would we say if someone else saw them? That they're photos of long dead relatives? In colour?"

Pam swallowed. She'd been trying to avoid the reality that the moment Jasper disappeared tomorrow, he'd literally be dead to her. "Do you want to do something on Sunday? We haven't spent a day just hanging out together in a while. Let's go out, stroll, have a coffee and tea somewhere and talk."

Robin blinked at her. "Grieve together?"

Her eyes welled up. "Yes. And don't laugh at me if I cry tomorrow."

"I won't!" Robin's voice softened. "I'll be missing them too."

Her throat tight, Pam nodded. Afraid of blubbering right there and then, she twisted and turned out the light.

"Good night," Robin murmured.

Pam silently thanked her and said, "Night." She lay down and closed her eyes, expecting sleep to elude her for a while and then to toss and turn all night. Yep, tomorrow she'd ball her eyes out. She knew Jasper had to go back—that he did go back. But if the historical record was wrong and the rhyme somehow failed? That was one outcome she wouldn't cry about.

Chapter Nine

Pam waited in the hallway as Jasper said good-bye to Robin, then beckoned for him to follow her. She glanced at her closed bedroom door as she passed it, to reassure herself that Margaret was still inside making last minute adjustments to her hair. "We don't have much time," she whispered to Jasper when they were both inside the guest room.

She almost couldn't bear to look at him. The sight of him in his old-fashioned clothing reminded her of the shock and confusion she'd felt when he and Margaret had suddenly appeared right in front of her eyes. In a few short weeks, one of those potentially menacing strangers had become the man she'd always dreamed of meeting and spending the rest of her life with. And now he was leaving, to marry someone else, have children, and die, all in the blink of an eye. That she was about to lose him—the horror of it—paralyzed her.

His face more drawn than usual, Jasper stepped toward her. "There won't be a day that goes by when I won't think of you," he said quietly.

A million responses raced through her mind. *To hell with them!* She threw herself into his arms and hugged him so tightly that he probably couldn't breathe. "I'll always cherish the time we had together," she murmured into his ear. "I wish we'd had more."

Her eyes closed when he said, "Me too," and his cheek flexed against hers.

They held each other, both fighting for composure. If Pam knew how to manipulate time, instead of being at the mercy of a rhyme, she'd stop time right now, keep him here, never let him go. Life wasn't fair!

She heard the door to her bedroom opening down the hall, and pecked Jasper on the cheek, then quickly stepped back. She met Margaret in the hallway. "Ready?" Her voice sounded too cheerful and shrill.

Margaret nodded, then looked past Pam. She couldn't have helped but notice that Pam and Jasper had both emerged from the guest bedroom, but her expression remained neutral. Her eyes settled on Pam's face. "Thank you for your hospitality and kindness."

"Oh, you're welcome. I'm the one who brought you here, and I'm sorry about that." She hesitated, then forced out polite words. "I hope you and Jasper have a lovely life together."

"Thank you." Margaret paused. "That's very generous of you."

Blood rushed to Pam's cheeks. She could really like the woman, if she wasn't resentful that Margaret would have Jasper for the rest of her life. "Shall we go?"

"If you don't mind, I'd like to take a minute to say good-bye to Robin."

Mind? She'd relish a few more minutes alone with Jasper. "Sure, we'll meet you downstairs." When Margaret moved aside, Pam brushed by her, trusting that Jasper was right behind her.

As she descended the stairs, everything felt surreal. She'd entered that defensive zone the body created to cushion the psyche from the trauma of a dreaded event, otherwise known as the *I can't believe this is happening* zone. At the bottom of the stairs, safely away from Margaret's eyes, Pam took Jasper's hand. They walked to the exercise room in silence. She avoided looking at the book and rose quartz she'd placed on the chair earlier. She wanted to gaze at *him*, and took his face in her hands, determined to commit every detail to memory. This was the man who'd forever changed her life. Everyone else would be measured against Jasper and fail to impress. Life wasn't fair.

Tears threatened. Nope, not allowed, not when Margaret could come downstairs at any moment. Plus, Pam wanted to read the rhyme in a clear and steady voice. Blubbering through it might hamper its effectiveness. She steeled herself and nodded, then drew strength from Jasper's answering nod and the trust he was placing in her. She lifted her hands from his face. The book and the rose quartz beckoned.

With a heavy heart, Pam settled herself into the chair, flipped to the rhyme, and held the rose quartz in her hand.

MARGARET REMAINED IN the hallway until Jasper and Pam reached the bottom of the stairs. Only then did she gather her resolve and walk into Robin's bedroom.

Robin stood near her computer, facing the door with her hands in her pockets. Her eyes widened. "Wow, I'd forgotten how you looked. Sort of drives it home, you know? You're really going."

Margaret's heart ached. "Yes."

"I heard you say you were going to say good-bye to me. I would have come out, otherwise." She twisted toward her chair. "I was sitting down when you arrived, so Pam said to make sure I'm sitting when she reads the rhyme, not that I'm convinced it matters."

"I imagine you'll be pleased to have your bedroom back."

"I was starting to think of it as your bedroom." Robin chuckled. "And I guess it truly will be in a few minutes."

A few minutes. To be among her family and friends again, and in *her* house, would bring Margaret much joy . . . and much sorrow. No, she had to believe that travelling through time again would return her to normal. But at this moment, knowing that she would no longer bring Robin tea, that she couldn't offer support regarding Robin's family, and that she'd never know what happened to her, grieved Margaret almost more than she could bear. While in Pam's bedroom, she'd thought about what her parting words to Robin would be, but her carefully crafted, cautious remarks fled her mind. "I'll miss you. I hope you'll think of me on occasion."

"Of course I will." Robin pulled her hands from her pockets and pointed to her right. "I'll think of you every time I'm in the study and every time I wear one of the lovely things you knitted for me." She smiled, but was the bleakness in her eyes genuine, or what Margaret wanted to see? "I'm glad I met you, Margaret. I didn't think I'd say that when you first arrived, but I am. You became a good friend. I'll miss you very much."

Oh, if only she could tell Robin what was in her heart! But what good would that do, except to ruin Robin's memories of her? Margaret wanted to leave Robin as a good friend, not as a deviant. To ensure that would be the case, she spoke the most difficult words she'd ever said. "They're waiting. I should go."

Robin held out her arms. "Can I hug you good-bye? I promise not to mess up your hair."

Desire and politeness overruled better judgement. Margaret willingly went to her, intending to lean in and give her a quick embrace—the type of impersonal hug she shared when greeting a friend, but this time meaning so much more. But when she touched Robin, felt the warmth and pressure of Robin's hands against her back . . . Robin . . . she would never see her again . . . Margaret pressed against her and held her closer than she'd ever wanted to hold anyone. She felt so at home, so alive, in Robin's arms; if only she could remain here and hold her forever. Robin's neck was so soft and warm, so tantalizingly close to Margaret's lips. She swallowed, and—*No!* What was she doing?

It took every ounce of willpower to slide her arms from around Robin's neck, determined to end their embrace before she betrayed herself further. But as she stepped back, her lips brushed Robin's cheek . . . and Robin chose that moment to turn her head . . . and Margaret couldn't stop herself. Her last rational thought was about how delicate Robin's lips felt compared to Jasper's, then she utterly lost herself to that blissful state she'd never before experienced—until Robin's fingers dug into her shoulders.

God, forgive me! Margaret pushed herself away from Robin and stared in horror at her shocked face. "I'm—I'm sorry," she stammered. "Oh, Robin, I'm so sorry." On the verge of tears, she wheeled and fled the bedroom.

"Margaret!"

No, she had to run, get away, escape back to 1910 where she'd fall in love with Jasper, marry him, and forget about her time here and the corruption it had wrought. As she raced down the stairs as quickly as she could without tripping over her dress, she wished she could take the kiss back, not because she regretted committing such a despicable and morally bankrupt act, but because Robin would forever remember her as a deviant. What was wrong with her? She should be concerned about her moral character, not with what Robin thought of her!

Pam and Jasper looked at her when she hurried into the drawing room. She rushed over to Jasper and clung to his arm, taking solace in the familiar. *Please, please, Robin, don't come down. Please allow me to go back to my life—my normal life—without humiliating me and forever turning Jasper against me.* After what she'd just done, she had no right to ask for or expect such kindness. All the same, she was relieved to hear no footsteps pounding down the stairs.

"Margaret, you're trembling!" Jasper peered at her. "Are you all right?"

Pam leaned forward. "You okay?"

"Yes, I'm fine. Just anxious to get home."

"Robin, you ready?" Pam shouted.

"Yes," Robin shouted in reply.

Thank you, Robin.

Pam sat back, appeared about to say something, then nodded and looked down at the open book on her lap.

Hurry!

Pam read aloud:

> *when in the wrong time*
> *universe will not be kind*
> *until you align*
> *with swapping souls*

A loud rushing sound filled Margaret's ears. Nausea suddenly wracked her; she clutched her stomach, doubled over, squeezed her eyes shut at the incessant noise—and then as quickly as it had started, the nausea passed. The deafening noise ceased. Margaret slowly straightened and forced her eyes open.

Jasper was on his knee, staring up at her and holding out a box with a ring. The clock on the mantel said *4:15*! The newspaper on the table was dated September 19, 1910! She was standing in *her* drawing room! "We're exactly where we were when we left," she breathed.

"Holy shit!"

She twisted toward the voice. Pam sat on the floor near the piano, her mouth agape. Margaret met Jasper's startled eyes, then quickly went to the door and pushed it shut. When she turned around, Jasper was helping Pam to her feet.

"I don't freaking believe it!" Pam cried. "Why am I here? Only you two were supposed to come back."

Hoping against all hope, Margaret said, "Since you'd be reading the rhyme in a different time, perhaps you don't have to wait for the next lunar cycle. You could try reading it again right now."

Pam nodded. "There's only one problem."

"What?"

"I don't have the book."

No! Margaret frantically searched the area around Pam, to no avail. "Do you remember the rhyme?"

"Only bits of it. And who knows what will happen if I say it wrong?"

"We can't risk it," Jasper said.

Was it that he didn't want to risk it, or that he didn't want Pam to go back? Margaret's engagement could be the shortest one on record, and not because the future bride and groom couldn't wait for their wedding day.

Pam clutched the sides of her head and screwed up her face. "I'm pretty sure the book was published in the 1800s, and in Toronto. If we can find a copy here . . ."

"What about the rose quartz?" Jasper asked.

"To be honest, I doubt we need it. That was just my own little improvisation I threw in."

"Then let's find a copy of the book, though it may take time. We'll have to look in the . . . seedier areas of town."

"You can't stay here," Margaret said. "I would gladly host you, if I could. But I doubt my family will be as understanding as Robin was." Robin. Margaret was horrified when she felt a pang of longing. Those feelings weren't supposed to have travelled to 1910!

"I'll put her up in one of the guest houses on the estate," Jasper said. "But she can't go out looking like this. Margaret!"

She shook herself. "I'll go fetch a dress for her. Pam, somehow you'll have to leave the house without—"

Someone rapped sharply at the door. "Margaret? Is everything all right in there?"

Mother! She crossed to the door and opened it a crack. Mother hovered anxiously outside. "Yes, Mother. I'll be out in a moment." She lowered her voice. "Jasper asked me to shut the door. I believe he's about to propose."

Mother's eyes lit up. "I'll just sneak away, then."

An idea struck her. "Why don't you gather everyone in the back garden? We'll come out and tell everyone the good news."

"I'll have Sally bring up a bottle of champagne."

"Yes, do that." Her heart racing, Margaret waited until Mother was out of sight. "I'll be back in a minute," she said over her shoulder. She pulled the door closed behind her and headed for the stairs. Sally was coming down them. "Mother's looking for you in the kitchen," Margaret said. "Mr. Bainbridge and I are about to make an announcement in the back garden."

"Oh, I see," Sally said with a knowing smile. "I'll go see what she wants." She scurried off.

Margaret blew out a relieved sigh. She carried on up the stairs, swung her bedroom door open, walked to the closet, and froze. She could have sworn . . . She slowly turned toward the figure she'd glimpsed from the corner of her eye.

Robin stood near the vanity with her arms folded. "Am I where I think I am?" she said flatly.

"Yes. Pam is here too." Margaret shut the door. "She's in the drawing room."

Robin's eyes briefly closed. "Thank god. She can get us back."

"The book didn't come with her." Margaret flinched at the fear in Robin's eyes. "But we're going to try to find a copy here. Until then, you'll stay in a guest house on the Bainbridge Estate. I came up to get Pam a dress." Wanting to hide, she opened the closet door and stepped inside, burning with shame. She had no doubt that once Robin recovered from the initial shock of being in 1910, she'd warn Jasper about the deviant nature of his future wife. She was surprised Robin could bear to be in the same room with her; under any other circumstances, Robin would probably refuse to speak with her. Perhaps travelling to the past had somehow cleansed Robin's memory of her last terrible moments in 2010, though Margaret remembered every luscious detail.

She forced herself to focus on the task at hand and selected a dress for Pam. What about Robin? Despite the certainty that her life was ruined, Margaret felt like giggling. If not for the rift that now surely existed between them, she'd tease Robin by asking which dress she'd like. But if the goal was to not draw attention to the two visitors from 2010 as they travelled to the Bainbridge Estate, putting Robin in a dress wouldn't do; she probably wouldn't make it down the front path without the neighbours pointing!

Margaret laid the dress she'd chosen for Pam on the bed. "I'll be back in a minute," she said without looking at Robin, and true to her word, returned a minute later with one of her brother's jackets and a cap. "Here, put these on." She cursed the feelings that stirred as Robin silently complied. Oh, what about a hat for Pam? No, Mother would notice if one went missing from the hall tree, and Pam only had to walk to the motor car.

Picking up the dress, Margaret said, "Follow me." Aware of Robin behind her, she opened the door and peered into the hallway. Empty, and the house sounded quiet, too. "Come on." They made it to the drawing room without running into anyone.

"Robin! Oh my god, not you too." Pam hugged her, the sort of hug Margaret had intended to give her when saying good-bye. "Oh, is that my dress?"

Margaret nodded and draped it over Pam's outstretched arm. "Just wear it over your clothes. By the time you're ready, it will be safe for you to leave."

"My motor is right outside," Jasper said. "Wait for me on the veranda. I shouldn't be long."

Robin remained silent, her rigid posture and tight face making Margaret wonder if she was angry, and why. Was she upset at being in 1910, in the same room as a deviant, or both? "We should go," she said to Jasper, worried that Robin might divulge her secret right there and then.

"We know where the front door is," Pam said. Her attention shifted to the dress.

Outside the drawing room, Jasper said, "We're forgetting something."

Margaret frowned. "What?"

He dug the ring box from his pocket, opened it, and lifted out the ring. "This."

She held out her hand, feeling as if she were performing a role in a play. As he slipped the ring on her finger, she tried to muster excitement, but failed. "Everyone's waiting," she said, to spare them both the indignity of pretending to be happy.

Nodding, Jasper returned the empty box to his pocket and offered Margaret his arm. "That was a good idea, sending everyone out into the garden," he said as she took it.

"Thank you," she murmured, not looking forward to the excited and happy faces that would greet them when they stepped into the back garden. When Robin finally spoke about what had happened and Jasper explained to Father why he was breaking their engagement, those faces would become shocked and angry. What would happen to her? Would Father put her on a train to relatives in another city? After word got around, no family here would have her, and a scandal of this magnitude would spread like wildfire. Or would Father commit her to one of those awful lunatic hospitals? For a moment, she wanted to go back to the drawing room and beg Robin not to tell anyone, but it was too late for that. Jasper was already opening the back door; rushing back now would be as good as telling him.

Margaret pasted a smile on her face. She might as well try to enjoy what could be her last champagne. Then she'd wait for the inevitable to happen and face a life in tatters.

Chapter Ten

Pam pressed her hand against the car door to steady herself as Jasper made a sharp turn onto a dirt road. As they'd driven to the Bainbridge Estate, she'd felt as if she were in a movie about the early twentieth century. She and Robin had an advantage over Jasper and Margaret; travelling to the past wasn't as disorienting as travelling to the future. Okay, if she and Robin had arrived in ancient Rome, she'd probably be freaking, but here? They'd seen photos of this time period, watched the documentaries, visited the museums, read the prominent writers and sat through the plays. That wasn't to say that she could sashay into town, blend in, and fend for herself, but she wouldn't have to contend with an overwhelming number of unfamiliar sights, sounds, and objects. She'd cope.

She gave Robin a sidelong glance. Oh boy. Robin was still sitting as if she had a stick up her ass; Pam could almost see the smoke coming out of her ears. She hadn't said a word since they'd left Margaret's. If Pam discounted Robin's terse one-word responses and grunts out on the veranda, she hadn't said anything since coming down to the exerci—drawing room.

Jasper pulled up outside what Pam assumed was the guest house, though it looked more like a cottage. Her exit from the car was far from graceful, despite Jasper opening the door and offering a supportive hand. She tripped over Margaret's beautiful long dress, and would have to practice walking in it if she were to venture out dressed like a lady. Ever the gentleman, Jasper pretended she hadn't almost ended up with her face in the dirt and walked her to the cottage's entrance. Robin waited near the front door, still looking pissed.

They followed Jasper into the small living room. "Here we are," he said. "It's not as modern as you're used to." Pam chuckled along with him, but Robin remained stone-faced. "But there are two bedrooms, and a fire to keep you warm. Oh, but I don't think the pantry is stocked. I'll bring round a hamper from the house, but I might not be back for a couple of hours. I'll have to dine first."

Not wanting to appear uncomfortable, Pam resisted the urge to rub her arms and chase away the chill. "Don't worry, Jasper, we'll be fine."

His forehead creased. "Will you? I wish I could be here for you, like you were for us. I feel awful, running out on you, but I'm expected for dinner."

She smiled reassuringly. "We'll manage, won't we, Robin?"

Robin grunted.

"It'll be like staying in a cottage out on the lake. We used to do that all the time when I was younger. Robin used to come with us occasionally. You always enjoyed yourself, didn't you, Robin?"

Another grunt.

Pam inwardly sighed. "I guess I'd be optimistic if I looked for light switches."

Jasper nodded. "You'll have to light the lamps. The main house is connected, but not this one. I chose this house because it's in the farthest corner of the estate. Nobody should bother you here. You can even go for a walk, if you want to."

"I'm tired," Pam said, then covered her mouth when her words evoked a yawn. "It's night for us. And you'll be having a second supper."

"So I will." He clasped his hands in front of him. "All right, I'll bring you round a hamper in a little while. Tomorrow we'll start searching for the book. We'll go, Pam. I'll send a note to Margaret tonight, see if she'll come keep Robin company and bring you more clothes."

"What about Robin?"

"Oh yes, I'll have Margaret bring her clothes, too."

Pam quickly spoke up when Robin's face grew darker than it already was. "Um, didn't you say you have a younger brother? Maybe when you drop off that hamper, you can bring a couple of his shirts and pants for Robin, if you think they'll fit."

Appearing nonplussed, Jasper hesitated.

"Please, Jasper."

"All right. But she can't go out dressed like a boy."

"I'm not dressed like a boy, I'm dressed like me," Robin snapped.

"When we were in your time, we had to dress in accordance with the norms of your time," Jasper said. "Now that you're here—"

"We'll worry about that if Robin has to go out," Pam said, hoping to head off a heated discussion. "Maybe she won't. Assuming it doesn't take us too long to find the book, when's the earliest we can go back? The rhyme seems attuned to the full moon." Oh my god. "When's the next full moon? What phase of the moon are we in? There's no Internet here," Pam wailed.

"You could always try looking outside later on," Jasper said.

"Of course! We'll look outside!" She felt like a complete ass.

Jasper grinned, felt inside his pocket, and pulled out his pocket watch, which he'd set in the drawing room. He frowned at the time. "I have to go. Oh, let me light the fire." He also lit the lamps in the living room. "Make yourselves at home. I'll be back as soon as I can."

When he reached the front door, Robin said, "Jasper."

He turned.

Pam expected her to apologize, but she said, "Can you tell Margaret I'm looking forward to seeing her?"

He nodded. "I'll tell her." Then he left.

When she could no longer hear the car, Pam took a deep breath and faced Robin. "Okay, I've got us into a bit of a pickle."

Robin gaped. "A bit of a pickle? That's what you call this?" She whipped the cap off her head and threw it onto a chair. "We could be stuck here for the rest of our fucking lives!"

"We won't be. We'll find the book and get ourselves back." She wandered into one of the bedrooms.

Robin followed her. "And what if we don't find the book? What then?"

Pam caught a glimpse of herself in the antique full-length mirror. She turned sideways and sucked in her stomach. She looked rather fetching in Margaret's—

"Will you stop admiring yourself in the goddamn mirror, already? Jesus, Pam! Maybe this is a big adventure for you, but for me it's a nightmare! I don't belong here. I've got to get back."

"We both have to get back," Pam said calmly. "And we will." She gasped. "Mitzy! Oh my god! Nobody will be feeding her. Oh my god!" She covered her mouth with both hands as she imagined returning to a skeletal mummy near the food bowl.

"Don't worry about Mitzy. She won't even exist for another . . ." Robin scrunched up her face " . . . ninety-seven years. Worry about us. Please!"

Robin's pleading tone finally brought Pam to reality. She couldn't deny that spending time in 1910—on Jasper's arm and dressed to the hilt—appealed, but once the novelty wore off, she'd miss the comforts of home, probably when she caught her first cold or had a toothache. And Robin . . . my god, Robin couldn't stay here. She'd have to constantly deny herself. What sort of life would she have? If they were trapped in 1910, Pam could and would eventually adjust, but Robin . . . to adjust would likely mean living a celibate and lonely life on the fringes of society. And it would be all Pam's fault. She met Robin's eyes. "No matter how long we have to search, we'll find the book and go home."

"I hope so, because staying here won't just be a problem for me and you. We have Margaret and Jasper to consider."

"You think I'll break them up." Pam put her hands on her hips. "They get married, remember?"

"Yeah, in Halifax. They *leave* Toronto. We didn't think it was because of us, but now that we're here . . ."

"You don't think they leave because they need to get us out of Toronto, do you?"

"Maybe they leave to get away from us," Robin suggested.

"Why would they do that?" She expected Robin to say, *Because you're coming between them.*

But after a moment, Robin shrugged. "I don't know, I'm just thinking out loud. Do you want to check out the other bedroom and decide which one you want?"

"Sure," Pam said, happy to drop the subject and counting the minutes until Jasper returned.

MARGARET SPOONED THE last of her pudding into her mouth and dropped the spoon into the dish. Its clang drowned out Mother's voice. "Pardon."

"I said, we'll have to set the date and visit the dressmaker's." Since Mother hadn't stopped talking since they'd sat down for lunch, she'd hardly touched her pudding.

"I expect we'll have a summer wedding," Margaret said, suspecting there wouldn't be a wedding at all. Her life, ruined for committing a single indiscretion—a moment's insanity! Despite the anxiety that had unsettled her since returning home, she stifled a yawn. She hadn't slept a wink last night; she kept reliving the kiss over and over again, perhaps trying to figure out whether she'd imagined it. When the note had arrived from Jasper, who still stubbornly refused to use the telephone, she'd cringed as she'd slipped the paper out of the envelope, sure it would convey harsh, shocked words and a warning that he would be paying a visit to Father. But it had simply said:

Dear Margaret,
My guests have settled into one of the guest houses. I would be obliged if you would lend Pamela clothing, as the railway has misplaced her trunk. I would also be obliged if you would call on Robin tomorrow afternoon while Pamela and I go into town. I will come for you at two o'clock.
J.B.

Either Robin hadn't told him about the kiss, or it hadn't happened. Could Margaret's desire have somehow possessed her mind as she'd travelled from 2010 to 1910? No, the kiss, Robin's lips, the delicious sensation of their bodies pressed together—Margaret grabbed her water glass and gulped the cool liquid down.

"Are you listening to me?" Mother barked.

"I'm sorry, Mother." She set the glass on the table.

"You're still all aflutter about yesterday, I suppose." Mother smiled indulgently.

Margaret smiled in return. Mother had spoken the truth—in a way—but she wouldn't smile when Robin finally broke her silence. Was Robin planning to tell everyone this afternoon, so Margaret would be forced to watch the horror on Pam and Jasper's faces as comprehension dawned?

The prospect of seeing Robin excited and terrified her. Her lapse of judgement had ripped away her mask. Robin knew her exactly for what she was—could be—no, she wasn't one of *those* depraved people. Robin was an exception; Margaret's attraction to her a warped representation of normal attraction, perhaps born of the unusual circumstances in which they'd lived for almost a month. Once Robin was gone, Margaret's feelings would subside and she would never feel that way for another woman again.

Mother's eyes brightened. "Oh, in all the excitement, I forgot to tell you what happened when I was out strolling with Violet a couple of days ago."

"What happened?" Margaret asked, grateful for the potential distraction.

"You'll never guess who accosted us, demanding that we speak to him. Victor Tillman!" Mother thundered. "Bold as brass and stinking like a distillery. At eleven in the morning! Wanted to walk with us. Can you imagine?"

Margaret felt strangely defensive on Tillman's behalf. "You used to be friends." Until everyone in his former social circle had dropped him the moment his financial woes became common knowledge.

"Used to be, Margaret. The man is a disgrace! The whole family is a disgrace!" Mother picked up her spoon and gestured with it. "There's only one way to deal with a Tillman, and that's to carry on as if they're not there. Do you hear me? If Victor Tillman, or any other Tillman, approaches you, walk the other way. You don't want the Bainbridges to think that you socialize with rabble. Victor and his ilk should stick to their own kind, and their own neighbourhood."

Oh, how she'd love to tell Mother that a Tillman was currently staying on the Bainbridge Estate, albeit covertly. Margaret glanced at the time on the grandfather clock ticking away in the corner. "I must go, Mother." She dabbed at her mouth with a napkin and hoped her churning stomach wouldn't bring up her lunch. "I'd like to freshen up before Jasper arrives."

"The poor man can't bear to be a day without you."

No, that would be Pam. "Fortunately Helena wasn't too put out when I cancelled our afternoon tea." Margaret had cursed at her busy appointment book, then had laughed at herself for thinking that she could otherwise have spent more time with Robin. She would soon be sent away, and Robin wouldn't want anything to do with her. Why *was* Robin keeping her silence?

Margaret was still turning that question over in her mind when Jasper arrived. Her heart in her mouth, she went down to the drawing room to greet him. She relaxed slightly when he smiled and kissed her hand. So Robin still hadn't said anything. "How are your guests?"

"In fair spirits. I lunched with them."

"Did you discuss anything interesting?" she asked as casually as she could.

"Nothing you'd consider remarkable. Questions about the guest house, the estate—oh, they might stay almost a month. It will depend on the weather."

If she understood him correctly, they had almost a month to find the book before the next full moon; otherwise Robin and Pam would be trapped here for another month. It would be easier if they could speak plainly, but Mother sometimes hovered outside when callers were in the drawing room.

"Have you selected the clothing you'll lend to Pamela?" Jasper asked.

"Yes." Margaret saw herself walking into the guest house carrying several dresses and then dropping them when Robin and Pam pointed at her and shouted *deviant!* "Are you sure Pamela should go with you? Perhaps we should go. You can take the clothing to Pamela when you call on them later."

"You're not a book collector, Margaret, and our search may take us into the less desirable neighbourhoods, ones in which you don't belong."

He wouldn't feel that way when Robin finally spoke up.

Jasper shifted his weight. "Don't you want to call on Robin? I had the impression the two of you are friendly."

Startled, she searched his face and concluded the remark was innocent.

"Robin is expecting you," Jasper said. "She said to tell you she looks forward to seeing you. I forgot to include that in my note."

"Robin said that? That she's looking forward to seeing me?"

He nodded.

Margaret didn't know what to make of it. *Had* she imagined the kiss?

"Shall we go?"

"Yes. I'll fetch the clothing. Why don't you come to the bottom of the stairs? I'll bring down the dresses and then go back for the other items."

Twenty minutes later they drove into the Bainbridge Estate. Margaret had sat quietly on the way, revelling in the familiar surroundings, but unable to ignore the nagging apprehension that now gripped her. She held the dresses in front of her as she stepped into the guest house's living room, wishing she could hide her face behind them. When she glimpsed Robin and Pam, she swallowed and tried to smile.

"You're back!" Pam declared, shooting up from one of the wooden chairs near the fire. Her eyes widened. "Oh, those dresses look beautiful. Will you help me dress, Margaret, so I can get the look right? I may actually speak with people today." She reached out and fingered one of the dresses.

Robin stood behind Pam. "When they're gone, I'll make us tea."

Bewildered, Margaret struggled to find her voice. Not brave enough to speak to Robin, she gave Pam her attention. "Shall we go into the bedroom?"

"Yes, let's."

Margaret followed Pam into "her" bedroom and listened to her chatter as she helped her dress, grateful that Pam was practically holding the conversation on her own. To delay her time alone with Robin, she fussed over every detail, only relenting when Pam grew restless.

Pam gasped when she saw herself in the mirror. "Look at me! You don't have a fan and a parasol, do you?" She giggled. "You know, when I first saw this mirror, I thought it was an antique, but it's not, not here."

"Do the shoes feel comfortable?"

Pam lifted the dress and stuck one foot out. "They remind me of my grandmother." Her hand went to her mouth. "Oh, sorry. I forgot. I mean—"

Margaret waved away her apology. "It doesn't matter."

"They're a tad big." Still hitching the dress up, Pam swung her leg. "But they won't fall off, and I'm planning to take it slow." She let the dress fall, then glided into the living room when Margaret, who didn't want to go first, stood aside and motioned for her to pass.

"Wow. I'd almost believe you've lived here all your life," Robin said.

Jasper appeared struck dumb, and stared at Pam with an intensity Margaret had never witnessed. "You look—"

Beautiful, Margaret thought, finishing the sentence for him.

"—authentic."

"Authentic?" Pam lifted an eyebrow.

"Time to find the book," Robin said, perhaps feeling, as Margaret did, that Pam and Jasper would rather be alone. Margaret should care, but she was more worried about being alone with Robin than about any juicy conversation her fiancé might have with another woman.

"Do you remember anything about the publisher or printer?" Jasper asked.

Pam shook her head. "I read the copyright page once. I only remember the year because it was published in Toronto, and I thought that was interesting."

Jasper shrugged. "Then we'll start near the docks. Shall we?"

"See you later, girls," Pam cheerfully said.

Her heart pounding, Margaret went to the window and watched as Jasper helped Pam into the motor. Even though she knew they wouldn't notice, she waved as they drove off, and continued to stare out the window, only turning when the clink of a cup meeting a saucer told her that Robin had gone into the kitchen. Torn between avoiding Robin as long as possible and wanting to be with her, she compromised and walked nearer to the fire, but was too agitated to sit down. Would they pass the afternoon with no mention of her transgression? Had the experience been so traumatic for Robin that she'd blocked it from her mind, wanting to pretend it had never happened?

When she heard the sound of tea being stirred, she forced herself to face the kitchen. Continuously having her back to Robin would be rude and impractical. Robin strolled into the living room. "Do you want to sit in the kitchen," she smiled, "or is that not done?"

Focusing on her for the first time, Margaret realized that Robin was wearing a man's shirt, probably on loan from Jasper or one of his brothers. On any other woman, it would have looked ridiculous and bordering on indecent, but Margaret couldn't imagine her in anything else. "The kitchen will be fine. Usually we don't have, um, tables to eat on in the kitchen, but this house is too small to have a dining room."

"It's warmer in here," Robin said over her shoulder as Margaret settled into a chair. Robin set a cup of tea in front of her. "I hope

it tastes all right. The tea here is a little stronger than I'm used to. I
don't know if I've compensated correctly."

Margaret lifted her cup and took a tentative sip, surprised at her
steady hands. She said what she would have said whether the tea had
tasted delightful or horrid. "Thank you. It tastes fine." She expected
Robin to sit across from her, but Robin set her tea down at the place
to Margaret's right and pulled out the chair.

Suddenly feeling self-conscious, Margaret sipped her tea again,
even though it was still too hot to comfortably drink. "Jasper showed
you how to operate the stove?"

Robin nodded. "We sort of already knew. I think this is less jarring
for us than it was for you and Jasper. In some ways." She paused. "At
least we have some knowledge of this time period."

"Yes." They lapsed into silence, but not the companionable silence
they'd enjoyed the evenings Margaret had knitted while Robin worked.
This silence was uncomfortable, fraught with tension and unsaid words.
Why had she kissed Robin? Why hadn't she had the strength to deny
herself? Margaret stared miserably at her tea.

"Do you want to talk about it or forget about it?" Robin asked softly.

Feeling as if her heart were leaping from her chest, Margaret lifted
her head. Robin's eyes contained only sympathy, not the condemnation
Margaret had expected to see. "I owe you an apology," she stammered.
"I don't understand what came over me. I—when you—I couldn't
help—" Her voice choked off as the shame of it overwhelmed her.
She buried her face in her hands.

"It sounds like you want to talk about it." Silence. "Margaret?"

Still covering her face, Margaret nodded. The conversation would
be excruciating, but she desperately wanted what she didn't deserve:
Robin's forgiveness. "I know what you must think of me," she said, re-
moving her hands from her face but avoiding Robin's eyes. "I would—"

Robin cut across her. "If we're going to have an honest conversation about it, let me say something first."

Certain that she was about to hear exactly what Robin thought
of her, Margaret clenched her hands on her lap and braced herself.
"All right."

"Okay, bear with me, because I don't know what words you're using
right now for people who are attracted to members of their own sex."

"I am not a deviant!" Anger, shock, and a touch of fear had Margaret quaking inside.

"I am," Robin said.

Flabbergasted, Margaret gaped at her. How could she sit there and admit it so calmly and unapologetically? *Robin?* No, she couldn't be. Margaret had lived with her for a month. She would have known, spotted signs of Robin's sickness. Robin was normal—but did dress like a man. Then again, so did Pam at times, and so had many of the women strolling along the boardwalk and shopping in the crafts store. "You're lying! Why? Are you trying to provoke me into saying that I am? I'm not! Something happened to me when I travelled through time. I—" She hesitated. "I have never felt for a woman what . . ." Oh, what was the point of denying her feelings for Robin? The kiss had already betrayed her. "What I feel for you. It won't happen again."

"I'll go back to 2010 and you'll go back to normal? For your sake, I wish that were true."

"It is!"

"So up to this point, you've only ever been attracted to men?"

A reflexive and vehement *yes!* died on her tongue as the many times she'd sat bewildered and confused during those conversations with her friends came rushing back. She'd never experienced what they described—until Robin. If she *was* a deviant—she wasn't, but if she entertained the hypothetical notion for a minute—why had she never been attracted to any of her girlfriends?

She balled a handful of her dress within her hands as another memory surfaced: her loneliness and despair when Ruth's family had moved to Montreal. Mother had chided her, told her that she had plenty of other friends and that she and Ruth could write to each other. But as Ruth quickly forged new friendships, her letters became few and far between, then stopped altogether. Hurt that Ruth had so easily cast her aside, Margaret's longing had turned to resentment. She'd rashly cut up Ruth's letters and thrown them into the trash, only to regret it later. But when she and Ruth had sometimes linked arms when out for a walk, Margaret hadn't reacted in the same way she had with Robin. Had she been too young? Or had she not allowed herself those feelings in her time, but had in 2010, where she'd expected—wrongly—that anything she felt and did would have no bearing on her real life back in 1910.

"I read the last entry in your diary. I know you don't feel anything for Jasper. Well, not anything you should feel for the man you're engaged to, anyway." Robin sipped her tea.

How could Robin sit there and drink tea as if they were discussing the weather? The conversation was tying Margaret in knots. "If you were a man, I would feel the same way about you. I'm—I'm attracted to you, not your—" Margaret hunched her shoulders "—body."

"I told myself that at first, too. But when I kept being attracted to only, uh, women-persons, I had to admit that the woman part was important. And if what you're saying is true, wouldn't you be attracted to Jasper? You seem to like him and enjoy yourself when you're out with him, so if it's all about the person and not whether they're a man or a woman, why aren't you attracted to Jasper?"

"Why aren't I attracted to everybody whose company I enjoy, then?" Margaret snapped. "I should be in love with half of Toronto!" Her face flushed. She'd said too much!

Robin held up her hands. "Hey, you're the one who's claiming you're attracted to the inner person, not me."

"And you claim you're a—" No, she wouldn't use such a disparaging term for Robin. "One of those people, yet you told me you want to get married."

"I do, eventually. To a woman."

"Now you're being ridiculous!" Tears sprang to Margaret's eyes. "Think what you will, but don't laugh at me. I am sorry, I truly am. I don't know why I feel what I feel for you, just that I do. I'll understand if you never wish to see me again, but I . . ." She swallowed. "I would ask your forgiveness. If you could extend me that one kindness. I wish I hadn't revealed how I feel because I'd hoped you'd remember our time together fondly, but I suppose that's no longer possible. Please, forgive me, and then I'll leave you alone. You can tell Jasper and Pam that I wasn't feeling well and went to the main house."

Her soul bared, Margaret stared at her teacup and waited for Robin to absolve her of her sin and ask her to leave. Either way, she'd have to live with her indiscretion for the rest of her life. Most people regretted transgressions in their pasts. She'd regret a transgression that had taken place in the future, and one for which she could never make amends. Years after her body had been returned to the earth, Robin would think ill of her. The clothing Margaret had lovingly knitted for her wouldn't be worn and evoke cherished memories, but be discarded, an unpleasant reminder of a kiss Robin would rather forget.

When Robin leaned forward and rested her elbows on the table, Margaret wanted to flee the house so she wouldn't have to listen to words that would cut. But this may be the last time they spoke, and her desire to remain with Robin was too strong. She was truly lost.

"You don't need my forgiveness, Margaret. You didn't do anything wrong. You surprised me when you kissed me, but that's not a cardinal sin." Robin raised her hand when Margaret twisted toward her. "And I wasn't being facetious when I said I'd marry a woman. A lot's changed—will change over the next hundred years. I can marry a woman, back in 2010. And if I do get married, that's exactly what I'll do. It's also why I need to get back. Here, I'm a deviant and would constantly have to hide who I really am. At home, I can be me. Sure, there are still those who wish we'd go away, but there will always be idiots." Her face lit up with amusement. "That hasn't changed, and probably never will."

It was as if Robin were speaking a foreign language. She could marry a woman? She didn't have to hide her deviance? But she had. "If that's true, why didn't you tell Jasper and I about yourself?"

"There was no need—or at least, I thought there wasn't. If everything went according to plan, you were only going to be with us for a short time. I honestly didn't have to hide anything. I don't conduct secret rituals in the study every night or anything like that. I didn't volunteer the information, that's all." Robin shrugged. "I had the advantage of knowing about your time, about what the attitudes are toward so called sexual deviance. I figured you and Jasper wouldn't be comfortable sharing a home with a, uh, deviant. I didn't want to create a tense atmosphere."

Margaret admitted that if Robin had told them when they'd first arrived, they probably would have treated her rudely.

"Unfortunately you're a deviant in your time, though I wouldn't call you that."

"What would you call me?" Margaret asked. She understood why Robin raised her eyebrows. While Margaret couldn't suddenly embrace her deviance, she wouldn't deny it, either, especially when this could be her only opportunity to have a truly honest conversation about a part of herself that nobody else would ever understand or accept. She didn't want to squander it.

"A lesbian."

How queer! "The meaning of the word must have changed. We don't use it that way. Lesbianism, yes, but we don't refer to such women as lesbians."

Robin's mouth twitched. "Women like me, you mean?" Her brow furrowed. "I read about the history of the word once. Give it a few more years."

Yes, to Robin, this was history. Yet it wasn't, because the future hadn't happened yet. Was Margaret wrong for wishing that Robin's history would ultimately become Robin's present? Her conscience shouted, *Yes!* It was the height of selfishness to wish such a thing for Robin, to want her trapped in a time when her kind—their kind—were, at best, mentally ill, and at worst, filthy sinners whom God and respectable folk rejected. Jasper and Pam had better find that book, and soon. "Does Pam know about you?"

"Of course."

They'd shared a bed! Was Pam feigning her attraction to Jasper, perhaps to protect herself and Robin? "Is Pam . . . like you?"

"No! Pam's as straight as they come."

"What do you mean?"

"Heterosexual." Then, when Margaret shook her head, Robin added, "Attracted to men and only men."

Oh. "Does your family know?"

Robin's face grew wary. "Yes."

Margaret recalled Robin's distress after the dinner with her father. "Is that why you and your father don't get along?"

Robin heaved her shoulders. "One of the reasons, yes."

"But you said things have changed."

"I also said there are still idiots." She waved a dismissive hand. "But if it weren't that, he'd find something else to criticize."

"What about your mother?"

"She doesn't care."

Robin sounded so bleak that Margaret wasn't sure if she meant that her mother didn't care about her deviance or her in general. When Robin drank some tea, Margaret did the same, wanting to finish it before it grew cold. She set the cup back in its saucer and tried to sort out the multitude of questions running through her mind. One in particular begged to be asked: how did Robin feel about her? Dare Margaret ask it?

Robin eyed Margaret's empty cup. "If we're to do the sensible thing, you'll go to the main house, as you said, and then never come to see me again."

Shocked and wounded, Margaret stiffened and blinked back tears. Robin would send her away? Then . . . she must not feel the same way, and Margaret was a fool. It was too late to mask her distress, but she lowered her head anyway and wiped her eyes with her hand.

"I'm thinking about what's best for you," Robin said softly.

A glimmer of hope welled within her. "Then answer one question, and answer it honestly. Do you want me to leave and never come back?" Not brave enough to face Robin, she kept her head down. But when no answer came, she looked up.

Robin stared at her, chewing her lip. Was she searching for more diplomatic words than a simple *yes*? Perhaps she was weighing the merits of lying to avoid hurting Margaret's feelings—after all, assuming they found the book, she'd soon be gone. Or did she want Margaret to stay, but was struggling to put aside her desire for what she believed would be best for Margaret? "Answer me honestly," Margaret said again, in case her latter guess was correct.

After what felt like an eternity, Robin sighed. "I don't want you to leave."

Margaret sagged with relief, but one burning question remained unanswered, and she might as well ask it. If she horribly embarrassed herself or the air grew too awkward between them, she could still do the sensible thing and flee the guest house for good. "If I—" She faltered. Perhaps she should be grateful that Robin still wanted to see her, and leave things as they were. *Courage!* If she didn't ask, she'd only wonder. She gulped and forged ahead. "If I were from your time—living in your time—would you call on me?"

Robin's brows drew together. "Take you out, you mean? Like, on a date?"

Margaret nodded and held her breath. Once again, the silence stretched as Robin fought an inner battle. She grimaced, downed the remains of her tea, and blew out yet another sigh. "Yes."

The word had never sounded so beautiful to Margaret's ears, nor had her smile ever been wider. "Then don't ask me to leave and never see you again. Assuming they find the book, that awful time will come soon enough. If I could, I'd come see you every day. Unfortunately my engagement book is full, and I can't offer excuses for everything without causing a fuss. But I'll reschedule what I can. I know that once the search for the book has successfully concluded, we won't have an opportunity to be alone."

Disappointing, yet in a way, she was relieved. According to the standards of her time, she'd already behaved scandalously and recklessly by admitting to and openly discussing her feelings for Robin. She couldn't deny her elation—but to go further, to act on those feelings in a physical manner . . . She no longer regretted the kiss and would kiss Robin again in a heartbeat. But to do more . . . as much as she might desire it, turning her back on the norms of her society would be difficult, despite her love for Robin. Even if that weren't so, the possibility of Jasper and Pam coming back at any moment would deter her. Robin would return to 2010—oh Lord, Margaret's heart ached—and when she did, Margaret would desperately need a semblance of a life to return to, her reputation intact, if she weren't to hopelessly despair for the rest of her life. "It will be enough to be in your company." She moistened her lips. "I'm not sure we should risk acting upon our—I would want to, but—"

"As you said, it will be enough to be together." Robin hesitated. "But when we're alone, like we are now, maybe you'll let me hold your hand while we talk." She smiled, her eyes bright. "If we stick to that, I won't have to worry about messing up your hair."

Thoughts of how Robin might mess up her hair intrigued and excited her. "I would like that," Margaret said faintly, then felt a rush of heat as Robin's fingers touched, then curled around hers, under the table. Yes, best not to do anything beyond this, or her reputation, be damned!

"This is a little strange for me," Robin said.

"Holding hands?" What did women normally do together in Robin's time?

"No, having to worry about it. I hope knowing that people like you—like us—will be accepted in the future will help you accept yourself. But I guess knowing that we can live openly as lesbians in the future will be small comfort to you."

Margaret silently agreed. What type of life would she have? She'd never feel for Jasper what she felt for Robin. She'd hoped—assumed—that, over time, love would grow between them. It still might, but for her, it would be the love she might feel for a cherished friend, not a lover. She had no choice but to marry him, though. Not true, she told herself. She could break off their engagement, defy her parents, and have all her friends believing she'd lost her mind. But to what end? To spend her life alone instead of marrying a decent man and a good friend? Things had been distant between her and Jasper lately, but that would change when Robin and Pam were gone. Not only would they be planning their wedding together, but who else could they talk to about the two people who'd so touched their lives in such a brief time?

Theirs would be a marriage between two friends, and under other circumstances could have served them quite well, especially Jasper. Perhaps if he hadn't met Pam, he would have fallen in love with Margaret eventually, but not now. Any happiness they might manage would always be marred by his longing for Pam and her longing for Robin. She wouldn't be the only one settling for someone she'd never love.

Robin was correct. The knowledge that people like them didn't have to hide their preferences in the future wouldn't do her much good. "I suppose since you can marry, you *can* truly be yourself. How did that come about?"

Robin pursed her lips. "There's no harm in telling you, I guess. But would you like me to make more tea first?"

"Only if you'll take my hand again when it's ready," Margaret quickly said, bringing a grin to Robin's face.

"I most certainly will."

Margaret spent the rest of the afternoon listening in fascination to Robin and peppering her with questions. When the sound of a motor reached her ears, she reluctantly let go of Robin's hand. They both went into the living room.

Pam stumbled inside and plopped into a chair. "My poor feet," she moaned.

"Did you find the book?" Robin asked.

She shook her head.

"Damn it, Pam!"

Jasper leaped to Pam's defence. "We've only just begun our search. I said this could take a while."

Pam kicked off her shoes and massaged one of her ankles. "We spoke to a printer who suggested a couple of places we might find it."

"We'll go out again tomorrow," Jasper added.

"I won't be able to keep you company tomorrow," Margaret said to Robin. "But I'll see you soon." Her heart fluttered at Robin's answering nod.

"If we don't find it tomorrow, we'll have to wait until Friday," Jasper said to her. "We have that tea at the McManuses' on Thursday afternoon."

"Oh, yes." She would do everything in her power to reschedule whatever was in her book for Friday afternoon, especially since they wouldn't search for the rhyme book over the weekend. Margaret would visit Robin and Pam with Jasper on Saturday or Sunday, but she didn't want to wait a whole week before she could hold Robin's hand again. If they found the book tomorrow, she'd persuade Jasper to take Pam out for a drive on Friday. She doubted it would take much coaxing.

Jasper stood near the open front door. "I'll drive Margaret home and then drop in again, to make sure you have everything you need for dinner."

"Maybe I'll be able to walk again by then," Pam mumbled.

"Good-bye," Margaret said.

Still focused on her feet, Pam waved.

"I enjoyed the afternoon," Robin said.

Margaret inclined her head. "As did I." She left the guest house in front of Jasper, feeling as if she were walking on air.

Chapter Eleven

Pam stifled a groan as she and Jasper approached the dilapidated shack a woman had pointed to from the corner. This was worse than the last one, where the proprietor should have handed out hardhats at the door, along with a map that directed customers around the maze of junk piles. "Should we even go in?" she said to Jasper. "What are the chances he'll have the book?"

"We're running out of places," Jasper pointed out.

Two weeks of slogging from half-decent shops to market stalls to hovels like the last "store," and still no book. If Robin didn't kill her, her feet would. "Lead the way," she murmured, knowing he'd open the door for her and she'd have to be the one to step inside and wrinkle her nose first. She could barely read the handwritten sign hanging in one of the grimy windows: *Balms and Powders.* "It doesn't say anything about books."

"It will only take a minute to ask." Jasper turned the handle, pushed the door open, and waved her through.

Cringing, she stepped through the doorway and . . . wow, she could see the wooden counter from here, and the inventory was neatly stacked on shelves. Her nose wasn't convulsing as it tried to keep out the stench, either. Only mothballs, incense, and smoke assaulted it, not the usual odour that told her rodents called the place home. The proprietor, however . . . he stooped behind the counter, his face gaunt, gray hair thinning, and skeletal fingers clutching a lit pipe. Oh, god. If Jasper bellowed, he'd blow the poor man over. As she walked with Jasper to the counter, she glanced around for any sign of books, but found none. Why had that woman directed them here?

The proprietor warily eyed them. Pam pasted a smile on her face. Jasper would do the talking. She was here to look pretty.

"Good afternoon," Jasper said.

"Afternoon, sir," the proprietor said around his pipe. "Nicholas Stone at your service. What can I do for you?"

"A woman suggested your shop to us, but we're looking for a book, not medical aid."

"I have a few books in the back, sir."

"I see. Would you have a book called *Magical Moon Rhymes for All Times*?"

Stone's eyes narrowed. He removed the pipe from his mouth. "Now why would you be looking for a book like that?"

Excitement coursed through Pam. "You know of it?" Jasper said evenly.

"I might. But if you'll pardon me, sir, you don't look like the sort of folk who dabble in such activities."

Not the stupid black magic thing again. Pam groaned inwardly. The book was merely a collection of rhymes that didn't even make sense. Okay, one had the power to hurtle unsuspecting people through time, but that didn't make it *bad*.

"We're the sort of folk who spend good money when we want something," Jasper said.

"And we really want that book." Pam broadened her smile and batted her eyelashes.

Stone's eyes flicked from Pam to Jasper, then back to Pam. "Let me have a look in the back." He shuffled into an area that doubled as a storage room and bedroom, from what Pam could glimpse through the doorway. Her breath caught in her throat when he returned with a black book and set it on the counter. Shit. There it was. *MAGICAL MOON RHYMES FOR ALL TIMES.*

"May I look at it?" Jasper asked, following the script they'd agreed upon if they found the book.

Stone nodded.

Pam leaned in as Jasper lifted the cover. This book was in much better shape than the one she had in 2010—duh. Cripes, it wasn't the same book, was it? It could be! She wanted to grab it and flip to page 17, but had to restrain herself as Jasper turned each pristine page.

Pages 12 and 13, 14 and 15—she held her breath—16 and 17 . . . *For those who were born before or after their time.* Holy shit. Their ticket home. "This seems to be what we're looking for," she said.

Jasper closed the book. "How much are you asking for it?"

Stone stuck his pipe back into his mouth and chewed on it. "Are you sure you want it? Not many printed, and even fewer survive. Book's cursed."

"And yet you have it."

"A friend wanted to burn it, but burning books . . . I couldn't go along with that, so I took it off his hands, said I'd take care of it. I've never opened it, though. It's sat back there for near on twenty years. I'd forgotten about it—until today."

"Why do you think it's cursed?" Pam asked.

Stone shifted his attention to her. "Well, I'm not sure it is cursed, Miss, but I thought I'd better warn you, in case the stories were true."

"What stories?"

"They might be tall tales." Stone leaned over the counter and lowered his voice. "But apparently some who came into possession of this book disappeared. Gone, just like that, into thin air. Never heard from again. Happened to a man and his wife, right in this very neighbourhood." He shrugged. "Now, I'm sure they just ran from their troubles—if they disappeared at all. I'm just repeating what I heard."

Pam almost blurted, "They must have read page 17!" but stifled it by covering her mouth.

Jasper guffawed. "Tall tales, indeed. Stop frightening the lady."

"Oh, but that's not all," Stone said. "Around the same time, a couple of strangers appeared in the neighbourhood. That's not unusual, of course, but these strangers . . . they didn't last here long. They're either dead or still shut away in the lunatic asylum, shouting about how they're from the nineteenth century and don't know how they got here. Poor sods." He suddenly barked a laugh, making Pam jump. "Never saw them myself, of course. The gentleman is right, they're only tall tales, and I have no use for the book."

"Then you'll sell it to us?" Jasper asked.

"That I will. My friend, God bless him, passed away last year, so he won't have anything to say about it." Stone rubbed his chin. "A dollar."

"A dollar!" Jasper shook his head. "That's highway robbery! I'll give you twenty cents, which is still more than you deserve, but since not many were printed . . ."

"Eighty cents."

"Thirty."

"Fifty."

"Done!" Jasper fished several coins from his pocket. "A pleasure doing business with you." He hesitated, then picked up the book. Pam couldn't blame him. There was no way she would open the book and read anything in it until it was time for them to go back. Who knew what would happen?

Outside, she gulped down the fresh air. Jasper tucked the book under his arm. "Don't lose it," Pam said. "It could be the only copy in existence." She sighed. "I guess we should go tell the girls the good news."

"I suppose we should."

His voice lacked enthusiasm, and so did she. For a split second, she wanted to suggest that they throw the book into the lake and forget about it. They'd tell Robin and Margaret that they'd spent another fruitless afternoon searching for a book they weren't likely to find, and that it was time to accept that 1910 had two new permanent inhabitants. And then what? Did she expect Jasper to break his engagement with Margaret and marry her? Was she that selfish that she'd condemn Robin to life here, just so she and Jasper could be together? The fairy-tale life she envisioned would elude her, eclipsed by guilt and the horrible secret that would forever hang over her and Jasper.

She wanted to cry. Having a conscience could really suck, but she wouldn't have it any other way. "Do you think Margaret would mind if we were to go for a drive or a stroll before Robin and I leave? By ourselves, I mean. Not today. When it's closer."

"I'll ask her." He paused. "She's been very kind to us."

"I know. I should probably feel guilty for hogging you, but she'll have you for the rest of her life. I have to give her credit for being secure enough to let us . . . see each other. I can't help but resent her a little, though. I know that sounds terrible."

He smiled ruefully. "I envy Robin. She'll be a lifelong friend and know what happens to you. I'll always wonder." His eyes grew sad as his smile faded. "If things were different . . . if I'd met you in this time . . ."

"I know." She briefly closed her eyes, then tried to muster enthusiasm. "Anyway, let's go back. And don't forget to ask Margaret about giving us one more afternoon together." So they could say good-bye.

WITH A HEAVY heart, Margaret only half listened to Jasper as he drove her home, laughing when he did and hoping the one or two words she uttered now and then were satisfactory. Earlier, when Jasper and Pam had returned to the guest house and he'd held up the book with a triumphant, albeit strained, smile, Margaret had tried, oh so hard, to be happy for Robin, despite the instant death of the fantasies she'd entertained about building a life with the woman she shouldn't love. She'd not only imagined them running away together here, but had considered the possibility that the rhyme would send them all back to 2010, where she and Robin could marry. Impossible, foolish, sinful fantasies, but ones that represented what she truly wanted—and could never have.

Robin's relief had been apparent; if she'd tried not to appear too pleased, she'd failed. Given what Margaret now knew about what life was like for . . . lesbians in 2010, she couldn't blame her, but understanding how imperative it was for Robin to return to her own time didn't prevent Margaret from feeling hurt that Robin looked forward to going home. Her reaction was unfair; in Robin's shoes, she'd feel the same way. But knowing that didn't help.

Jasper pulled up outside the Wilton home. She waited while he rounded the car, opened her door, and offered a steadying hand. She expected him to walk her up the path and give her a parting peck on the lips, but he stood rooted next to the car. "Would you mind if I came in for a moment?" he asked, to her amazement. He'd never invited himself in before. "I'd like to speak with you about something."

"Of course. Let's go into the drawing room." She quickly discarded the panicked notion that he might suspect her true feelings for Robin. If that were so, he wouldn't want to touch her, and he certainly wouldn't politely ask to discuss the matter privately. He'd storm through the front door, shouting for Father.

"Would you like a drink?" she asked when they reached the drawing room.

"No, thank you." He glanced toward the open door.

She shut it, and patiently waited for him to conquer whatever apprehension was causing him to clear his throat and straighten his jacket. "We found the book," he finally said.

"Yes."

"Pam and I no longer have a reason to go out."

Margaret waited.

"On our own." He swallowed. "We thought perhaps we might go out for a drive, before they go back. You and Robin are welcome to—"

She raised her hand. "Jasper." She should make him squirm. If she were another woman and under any other circumstances, she would. But she was hardly in a position to have her nose out of joint. "If you're asking if I would object to you and Pam going out on a drive by yourselves, the answer is no." She decided to speak plainly. "I know you and Pam are fond of each other. I haven't objected to your friendship because I know she'll soon be out of our lives." Well, she hadn't been sure until they'd found the book, but she was lying about why his relationship with Pam didn't matter to her. "So have your drive with Pam. Several, if that's what you want. But do Robin the courtesy of arranging a meeting with Pam at a time when I can keep her company."

"Perhaps you and Robin can go for a walk," Jasper suggested. "She must be growing tired of being cooped up."

Margaret shook her head. "Robin would refuse to wear a dress." And seemed afraid to venture out in case something happened that would prevent her from returning home.

"I have to admit, I'm surprised the two of you get along so well. You seem so different."

They were more alike than he'd ever suspect. "When I first met her, I thought the same. But I enjoy her conversation." She paused. "Robin does walk on the estate in the early morning and late evening."

"Does she?"

"Yes, near the guest house. With Pam." Perhaps she shouldn't have said anything, in case Jasper took it upon himself to intrude. "Let me get my engagement book." Without waiting for a reply, she left the drawing room, went to her bedroom, and slid the engagement book from a cubbyhole in her vanity. She opened it and frowned at the numerous entries between now and October 18th, the date they expected a full moon. What could she reschedule? Her hair could wait. Tea with Aunt Grace could be postponed—all she talked about was her late husband. Margaret's eyes fell on the entry for Saturday, October 15th. Hmm.

She returned to the drawing room and, supporting the open book with one hand, she tapped at an entry with her other. "I could call on Robin the afternoons of the ninth and twelfth."

"What days of the week are they?"

"Sunday and Wednesday."

Jasper frowned. "I can definitely manage the Sunday, but Father's already angry with me for being scarce around the office lately. I'll have to see about the Wednesday."

Not wanting the ninth to be the last time she could be alone with Robin, Margaret made what Jasper might view as an outlandish suggestion. "The Halloween Ball is on the fifteenth. Why don't you escort Pam?"

His face slackened. "What?"

"Escort Pam. I'll take her out, buy her a lovely hat, dress, and shoes. She'll love the experience, both the shopping and the ball."

"But—what will people think? And what about you? Don't you want to go to the ball?"

"There will be plenty of balls in our future, Jasper. As for others, make something up. I can be under the weather, and Pam can be a visiting distant cousin who graciously agreed to step in and take my place."

"Our families will be there!"

"All right, an old friend, then," Margaret said, thinking quickly. "I can pretend I have a bad tummy. I'll find my way to the estate once everyone else has gone. Mother will be beside herself—" not because her daughter was ill, but because Margaret wouldn't be on Jasper's arm for the first major social event since their engagement was announced "—but I'll deal with Mother."

Jasper stepped toward her. "Margaret, you don't have to be so generous."

"I want you to give her a good send-off, Jasper. It will perhaps help you to refocus on us and our relationship, once she's gone." *Our relationship?* Margaret suddenly felt sick.

"Thank you," Jasper murmured.

"You'll escort her?"

"Yes."

She looked down at her engagement book again and pursed her lips. "Tell her we'll go shopping on Friday morning." Margaret closed the book.

"I'll let her know." He stared at her for a moment, then swept out his arm. "After you."

Not surprisingly, Mother hovered in the hallway. "Oh! I was wondering if you two were in there."

Margaret restrained herself from rolling her eyes.

"Would you like to stay for dinner, Jasper?"

Jasper hesitated, then smiled. "I'd be delighted."

"Wonderful! I'll have Sally set another place." Mother clapped her hands together. "Oh, look at the two of you! Such a handsome pair. I expect you'll be a familiar face at the dinner table from now on, Jasper. Oh, Sally!" She raced up the hallway, waving at the housemaid.

Margaret returned the engagement book to her bedroom and gathered with the rest of her family and Jasper in the living room to make small talk. She was fine until everyone proceeded to the dining room and Jasper pulled out her chair, then sat next to her. Though he'd dined with them before, his presence at the table as her fiancé was a novelty. Her parents and brothers kept glancing at them: Margaret and her future husband.

She wanted to bolt from the table. Sitting here next to Jasper, seeing everyone already clothing her in the role of the loving wife, had brought to the surface a certainty she'd sensed, but feared. She could never fill that role. If she hadn't been transported into the future, hadn't met Robin and been introduced to herself, she wouldn't see marrying Jasper as settling, not only for her, but for him. Her confusion over why she didn't feel for him what her friends felt for their husbands would have deepened, especially when her expectation that those feelings would come later proved false. But she would have tried to be the wife he wanted, and perhaps Jasper wouldn't have noticed that his wife lacked passion. Perhaps he wouldn't have minded a supportive woman at his side who held him in genuine affection. But not anymore. Any woman at his side would be in Pam's shadow, but at least others would love him. She couldn't, not as a wife should love him. Margaret had no hope of living up to Pam, nor did she want to.

She couldn't marry Jasper. She wouldn't marry him.

MARGARET KNOCKED ON the guest house door and opened it in response to a muffled invitation to enter. Pam looked past her. "Jasper not with you?"

"No, I came on my own." This wasn't her first visit of the day, despite the morning hour. She caught Robin's eye and nodded, then refocused on Pam. "You look ready to go."

"I am." Pam turned to Robin. "Are you sure you don't want to come with us? I doubt we'll be back for lunch. It won't take me long to get you into a dress." Smiling mischievously, she ran her fingers through Robin's short locks. "And do your hair."

Robin slapped Pam's hand away. "I hate shopping at home. Do you think I want to shop all day here—for clothes? And in a dress?" She grimaced. "And I don't want to take any chances."

Pam tutted. "What do you think will happen, you'll get trampled by a horse and carriage?"

Robin folded her arms. "No, more like I'll end up in jail for ripping the balls off the first guy that treats me like an idiot woman."

"On second thought, you're better off here," Pam said with a laugh. She patted Robin's shoulder. "Not that I expected you to come."

"If you don't mind, I'll have tea with you when we return," Margaret said, wishing she could run her fingers through Robin's hair.

Robin's mouth turned up at the corners and she dropped her arms to her sides. "I'd like that."

Her response gave Margaret a much needed energy boost. She'd felt as if she were swaying on her feet. Since her epiphany while at the dinner table that night with Jasper, she'd barely slept. How would she extricate herself from their engagement without embarrassing him, provoking her parents' wrath, and making everyone close to her believe that she'd lost her mind? Ruminating about that would have been enough to deprive her of sleep, but there was also Robin's imminent departure from her life. Consoling herself with platitudes—that at least she'd experienced love, truly knew herself, wouldn't be trapped in a loveless marriage—did little to stem the darkness that eclipsed more of her soul each day.

However, she *had* come up with a plan to break her engagement, and had taken her first concrete step toward that end with her earlier visit that morning. It wouldn't banish her sleepless nights—she still faced living out her life without the woman she loved—but it was a start.

Chapter Twelve

Pam lifted a glass of wine from the tray a white-gloved waiter extended and clinked glasses with Jasper before taking a sip. "I feel like I'm in a movie," she squealed. Everyone was dressed to the nines, and oh-so polite. She waved away the smoke blown her way by a gentleman puffing on a cigarette. Okay, there were downsides, like everyone's apparent wish to die of cancer. But she felt more comfortable here than she ever had in chic nightclubs with their flashing lights and too-loud-to-talk music. Not worrying about anyone spiking her drink when she wasn't looking was a bonus.

This time period must have its share of noisy clubs and obnoxious patrons, but not here, among society's elite. If she'd belonged to this time, she was sure she would have been in the upper classes. Was it surprising that, back in 2010, she lived in a home that formerly belonged to an upper middle class family? And the book had summoned two refined residents of 1910, not foul-mouthed sailors off the docks. Though she had no idea why the rhyme had brought Jasper and Margaret into her life. Why tease her with Jasper? Why give her the knowledge of what she could never have?

Jasper nudged her arm. "Margaret's parents," he murmured.

She tensed and gulped down more wine. They'd practised what to say to the Wiltons, but she was still nervous. Since arriving, she'd feared that someone might ask her a question that she didn't understand or would inadvertently answer in a way that only made sense in her time. Her appreciation for how well Jasper had handled himself at Brenda's party deepened. He'd carried on conversations without her at his side, something she wasn't brave enough to do. When he visited the men's room, she'd hide, despite not having committed any gaffes thus far.

A couple that looked to be in their late forties approached. "Jasper," the woman crowed.

Pam resisted the urge to hang onto him. Not a good idea when Margaret's parents were standing right in front of them. If Jasper hadn't warned her, she would have known anyway; Margaret was the spitting image of her mother.

"I'm so sorry Margaret left you in the lurch. What a time for her tummy to act up! Oh, but where are my manners? Mr. and Mrs. James Wilton," Margaret's mother announced.

Pam inclined her head. "Miss Pamela Holden. A pleasure to meet you."

"Likewise," Mr. Wilton said.

"Margaret said you and Jasper are old friends?" Mrs. Wilton's eyes were alight with curiosity.

Jasper stepped in. "Not exactly. Miss Holden is the daughter of a longstanding client of mine. I was lunching with him when Margaret telephoned about her condition. I intended to send my regrets to the host committee, but Gerald asked if I'd consider escorting his daughter."

Mrs. Wilton's brows lifted. "I don't know a Gerald Holden."

"We're from Kingston," Pam said. "My father has investments here."

"I see. So you're visiting?"

"Yes. I suppose my father didn't want to see me cooped up in a hotel room for another night, but it's unfortunate that I'm here because your daughter is ill."

"Girl's too fragile," Mr. Wilton growled. "This is one of the premiere balls of the year, and she's at home in bed."

Not if Margaret had gone to the guest house as she'd intended. What did she and Robin spend all their time talking about? Robin didn't open up to people easily, and Pam wouldn't have pegged Margaret as someone with whom Robin would forge a close bond. Of course, Margaret hadn't faked a bad stomach so she could spend time with Robin; she'd done it for Jasper. Once Pam was out of the picture, Margaret would have Jasper to herself and in her debt. Bravo, Margaret. Well played.

"A bit of fresh air and dancing would have done her a world of good," Mr. Wilton continued. "Once she was here, she would have forgotten about her tummy ache."

"I'm sure Margaret would have come, if she was able," Jasper said.

Mrs. Wilton's attention remained on Pam. "When will you return to Kingston?"

"This week," Pam said. If the rhyme worked, they'd be gone Tuesday night. She inwardly, then visibly, sighed. "I miss my fiancé. Jasper's a lovely man, but we're both acting as poor substitutes for others."

A relieved smile spread across Mrs. Wilton's face. Apparently Pam had said the magic words that translated to, "I won't steal your daughter's betrothed."

"Well, we won't keep you," Mrs. Wilton said. "Shall I tell Margaret to expect a visit from you tomorrow, Jasper?"

He nodded. "I'm sure her condition will have improved by then."

Pam stifled a giggle, then exhaled slowly as she watched the Wiltons walk over to another couple. "Glad that's done." Now she'd met both sets of parents. Jasper's father had been nothing like she'd imagined. Based on the story Jasper had told about his lost love, she'd expected an overbearing, gruff man, not the mild-mannered gentleman who'd let his wife do all the talking. One could never tell what went on behind closed doors.

"Poor substitutes?" Jasper said with feigned indignation.

"It just popped into my head, and it worked. She's not worried about me now."

"She'd have reason to worry, if circumstances were different."

That was the third time he'd implied as much since they'd arrived, but with Tuesday night looming, his repeated referrals to what could have been didn't warm her heart. She appreciated what he was trying to tell her, but she wished he'd stop, so she could forget, just for to-night, that the fairy tale was almost at its end. Her irritation with him quickly died. Tuesday night was hanging over him too; he probably kept reminding her because he couldn't stop thinking about it. She lightly touched his arm, but only for a second, aware of Margaret's parents nearby. "Jasper—"

A loud crash and the sound of shattering glass drowned out her words. A collective gasp rose around her. The music petered out. Pam jerked her head in the direction of the ruckus. A waiter lay sprawled on his back in the middle of broken glasses and spilled wine; an overturned silver tray lay next to him. A dishevelled man with an unkempt beard peered down at the waiter, then raised a glass and smiled toothily. "My invitation must have been lost in the post!" He downed the wine in one go and plunked the empty glass on a table, then glanced around, probably looking for another waiter.

The man in coattails who'd greeted Pam and Jasper when they'd arrived at the ball glared at him, his hands clenched at his sides. "Tillman! I swear—"

"Victor, what in the hell are you doing?" a woman shouted, striding up to him. Her thin coat, threadbare stockings, and worn boots clearly labelled her as another interloper.

"For god's sake, Elenora, get him out of here," someone said.

Pam's hand went to her mouth. *Oh. My. God.* "Robin's great-grandparents," she hissed to Jasper, then pulled him away from the crowd until they were behind a pillar. "I can't go anywhere near them. I don't even want them to see me." She wasn't supposed to be here and didn't want to risk altering future events. What if Robin winked out of existence because Pam's presence delayed the Tillmans from leaving the building and they were run down by a crazed runaway horse, as a result?

When she whispered her fear to Jasper, he shook his head. "Whatever is happening now had already happened in 2010, and Robin existed then."

Yes, but they hadn't travelled to 1910 yet. Or had they? She rubbed her temples. This time travel stuff gave her a headache.

"So they're Robin's ancestors on her father's side," Jasper murmured.

"No, her mother's. When she was nineteen, she changed her last name to her mother's maiden name." And her father hadn't cared. Bastard.

The crowd had closed in around the Tillmans; Pam could no longer see them from her vantage point. After a great deal more shouting and the sounds of scuffling, several backs parted to allow those in the middle of the throng to leave. "Just throw him onto the pavement," Elenora bellowed, her face hard. As several men dragged Victor toward the hall's entrance, she turned to those gawking. "Oh, what are you all looking at? Thank the Lord I no longer have to suffer through these parties. They always bored me to tears!" She whipped around and stomped after her husband.

Pam chuckled. Fortunately Robin didn't closely resemble either of them, or the entire incident would have felt surreal. Everyone drifted back to wherever they'd rushed from. Music filled the hall again. The man in coattails fussed around the mess, waving his arms and barking orders to his underlings, while the poor waiter who'd ended up on the floor retrieved the tray and did his best to make a dignified exit, despite his wine-soaked ass and back. He'd probably have to pick glass shards out of his trousers, too.

Jasper lifted Pam's empty glass from her hand. "Let's dance."

"Are you sure? I won't know what I'm doing."

"Nobody will notice. Just follow me."

He'd meant on the dance floor, but she trailed after him as he carried their glasses to a table and set them down. Only when he offered her his arm did she step to his side. Feeling like the princess at the ball, she swept onto the dance floor, and smiled up at him as he gently positioned her hands. If she could find that elusive rhyme that could stop time, she'd use it now to freeze this moment and remain in this blissful state forever. Returning to 2010 would be hard to take; the future would be a bleak and lonely place. If only her future could be here, in the past, with Jasper.

When the morning sun once again held promise and she could laugh at a joke, she'd find out what had happened to the vibrant man holding her, visit his gravesite, and weep for what could never have been.

MARGARET STARED MISERABLY into the fire and marvelled at how naive she'd been to expect her last evening with Robin to be anything but depressing. They'd pushed the two chairs together and sat with their shoulders touching, their interlocked hands resting on the chair arms that formed a barrier between them. To Margaret, their physical arrangement mirrored her inner state. She wanted to be close to Robin, but there were lines she wouldn't cross, not when Robin would soon be gone and with years of religious and moral teachings to overcome. If they had more time . . . Margaret bowed her head, brought Robin's hand to her lips, and kissed it. If she could, she'd never let her go.

She'd be quite happy to spend her life gazing into the fire with Robin at her side. "What will you do first when you return?" she asked, to fill the dull silence and dispel the fantasy.

"Take a long shower," Robin said.

Margaret had enjoyed her morning showers, one of the more practical improvements in 2010. "To wash away the dust and grime of 1910, I suppose."

"No. So I can have a nice, long, private cry and maybe not look like I've been beaten up afterward." She snorted softly. "I expect I'll be taking quite a few long showers, actually."

"I will weep too," Margaret said mournfully. How would she fulfill all those engagements she'd rescheduled without anyone sensing her grief? What would Mother think if she spent all her time shut away in her bedroom?

"Be careful," Robin said, as if reading Margaret's mind. "You just got engaged, remember."

Yes, and rather than hiding her distress, perhaps allowing her family and friends to see it would work in her favour when it came time to put her plan into motion. "Oh, now we know why she was upset," they'd say. It might help them to more readily accept what would initially sound like madness, or at least to believe that she was sincere. Margaret had vacillated between telling Robin that she would break her engagement with Jasper, and allowing Robin to imagine that she'd married him and built some semblance of a happy life. But did she want Robin to believe a lie? What if Robin decided to find out what had happened to her? Would she look for the record of their marriage and try to find their descendants? What if she discovered that Margaret had died as Margaret Wilton, not Margaret Bainbridge? Would she wonder if Margaret had changed her mind at the last minute or known all along? Would she ask why, knowing the question could never be answered?

Well, it could be answered, but only if Margaret explained herself now, not only for Robin's sake, but so she could receive Robin's blessing. As she lived out her life, she'd feel closer to her, knowing that Robin knew the truth. It shouldn't matter; Margaret could never stop what she was doing and imagine Robin thinking of her at that moment, since she'd be long dead in Robin's time. But somehow, the knowledge that Robin knew the truth and would look back in honesty would comfort Margaret when she despaired. She tightened her grip on Robin's hand. "I'm not going to marry Jasper."

Robin whipped toward her. "What?"

"I'm not marrying him."

"No!" Robin pulled her hand from Margaret's and leaped to her feet. "You have to marry him!"

Shocked, Margaret looked up at her. "You don't care that I'll marry him?"

"I'm not thrilled by the idea, but I understand this is a different time. I don't want you to throw your life away."

"I won't."

"No? What will happen when you break the engagement? What will Jasper think, and your family? People will want to know why."

"And I'll tell them," Margaret said evenly.

Robin gaped at her.

"I'll tell them I want to become a nun."

"What?" Robin shrieked. Her hands went to her hips. "No! No way! I won't let you do it. I don't want this responsibility hanging over me."

Margaret pushed herself up from the chair so she could more easily meet Robin's eyes. "What responsibility?"

Robin thrust out her hands. "Ruining your life!"

"So you'd rather I enter a loveless marriage? You'd condemn both Jasper and I to that?"

"At least you'd be free to have a life."

"A lie, Robin! I'd have a lie."

Robin glared at her. Margaret could sense the turmoil seething beneath the surface and wouldn't have been surprised if Robin suddenly picked up the nearby vase and threw it against the wall. "Would you marry a man?" she asked, hoping her quiet voice would calm Robin.

Robin's nostrils flared. "No."

"Then don't make me do what you wouldn't do."

"But—"

"And don't tell me I have no choice. I do have a choice, and I've made it."

They stared at each other. Robin raised her hands in surrender. "Okay. But a religious order? You're not even Catholic!"

"There are Anglican nuns. I've already made inquiries."

"What will your family think?"

"They'll be upset, but it's difficult to argue against God's will."

"But it's not God's will. It's *yours*."

Margaret clenched her hands and strove to keep her irritation from her voice. "My will is not to lie, not to trap myself and someone else in a bad marriage, but to live my life in honesty. In this case, I'd say my will coincides with His."

Robin groaned. "I can't go back, then. I'll have to stay here."

"What? Why on earth would you do that?"

"So you won't have to become a nun. Our life won't be a bed of roses, but it has to be better than that. I have no idea what we'll do, just that I'll be here to support you when you break your engagement and everyone freaks out."

Margaret had never felt so mortified. "No, Robin. Don't you *dare* stay here." She'd once entertained that fantasy, but no longer. "You said you don't want the responsibility of ruining my life. *I* don't want to ruin yours. If you stayed here, I could never live with myself, never look at you without feeling guilty for what I'd denied you. I do not want you here. If you stay, I'll never speak to you again. You don't belong here."

Robin's face crumpled. She sank into her chair and buried her face in her hands.

Trembling, Margaret knelt in front of her. "Robin," she murmured. When Robin didn't respond, Margaret used Robin's lap for support as she leaned into her, stopping when her lips were mere inches away from Robin's hands. "I want you to go back to 2010. I want you to finish university. I want you to find a nice woman, someone you can love, and marry her. Can you do that for me?"

Robin's shoulders shook. She sobbed into her hands.

"Please, Robin. The knowledge that you went back and lived your life the way it's meant to be lived will be the greatest gift you can give me. So, please, do this for me. You can't do anything for me here." She winced when Robin dropped her hands, and reached out to help dry her tears.

Robin drew a shaky breath. "I wish Pam had never bought that stupid book."

"I'm glad she did. Otherwise I always would have thought there was something wrong with me. And I never would have met you. I never would have truly loved."

"And been loved," Robin whispered.

Margaret's vision blurred.

"You'll always be loved, Margaret. As long as I'm alive, you'll be alive, and loved."

Overcome by sorrow, Margaret closed her eyes, then opened them in confusion when Robin gently pushed her away. She struggled to her feet at the same time Robin rose, and didn't protest when Robin pulled her into her arms. Oh, it felt so natural to embrace Robin and rest her head against Robin's shoulder! She would hold this moment in her heart forever, savour it, draw on it to banish the coming loneliness.

"I will stay, if you want me to." Robin's breath warmed Margaret's ear.

"I know, and that humbles me more than I can say. But no, I couldn't bear it." Margaret plunged ahead, not willing to waste what could be her final opportunity to convey the depth of her love. "If we were in your time . . . if you were willing to be patient, to give me time to fully accept my true nature . . . I would marry you, Robin Tillman—if you'd have me."

Robin drew back. "You'd marry me?"

Margaret nodded and wiped away a tear. "But we can't be together here. You have to go back, and you have to believe me when I tell you that with what I know now, I'll live a much more fulfilling life inside a religious order than inside a marriage."

"I'll worry."

"That would be a waste of time. The moment you're back, I'll have already lived my life, so worrying would be for naught."

"I'll worry about how it was for you."

If only she could somehow reassure Robin that everything would be all right. "When you retrieved my diary from the attic, was there anything else there?"

Robin's brow furrowed. "What do you mean?"

"Other papers. Letters, perhaps?"

"I don't know. As soon as I lifted the floorboard and saw the diary, I took it. I didn't check for anything else."

Then perhaps she *could* put Robin's mind at ease. "There's room for more. I'll write to you about how it went when I told Jasper and my family about my plans. I'll tuck any letters farther back under the floorboard, somewhere you wouldn't see them unless you knew to look." Funny how she hadn't known about any letters when she was in 2010, even though she'd come from the past. But then, she hadn't lived this part of her life yet. "Check the attic when you get back. I can't write to you once I'm in the order, but at least you'll know how I fared before then."

Robin lifted an eyebrow. "I guess taking a long shower will be the second thing I'll do when I get back, not the first."

Margaret smiled through her tears. She gazed at Robin, lightly tracing her nose, lips, and chin with her fingers. Never had a face been so precious. The desire to kiss Robin was overpowering, but so was the fear that if she touched her lips to Robin's and melted into her, she'd commit acts that she'd later come to regret. Rushing herself when she wasn't ready would only mar cherished memories. If only they had more time.

She tore her gaze away and murmured, "I'm sorry." Over Robin's shoulder, she glimpsed the clock on the mantel. Her heart sank. Had they sat for that long? "Come, let's dry our eyes and sit together again. We don't have much time."

Robin gripped her shoulders. "Margaret."

She swallowed and forced her eyes back to Robin's.

"I would be patient."

Margaret nodded. "I know." If only Robin would have the opportunity. With a heavy spirit, Margaret pulled a handkerchief from under her sleeve and dabbed at her eyes as Robin rubbed at hers. Back in their chairs, they laced fingers, stared into the fire, and occasionally said a word or two to chase away the oppressive silence that would soon be all they had.

Chapter Thirteen

P AM YAWNED AND STRETCHED AS SHE padded into the kitchen, and wasn't surprised to see Robin already sitting at the table, nursing a cup of tea. "Excited? If everything goes as expected, you'll have your morning tea in our kitchen tomorrow." She walked over to the tea tin—bring on decent coffee in 2010—but twisted around when Robin didn't respond. Robin looked like hell. Pam had assumed that excitement had prevented Robin from sleeping more than a few hours the past couple of nights, but— "You all right?"

Robin shrugged. "I never thought I'd say this, but I'm not entirely looking forward to going back," she said dully.

That was the last thing Pam expected her to say. "Are you serious? Why wouldn't you want to go back? Besides the obvious, you've been cooped up in here for almost a month. You must be chomping at the bit to go home."

Robin remained silent.

"Robin?"

She sighed. "I'm not looking forward to going back for the same reason you aren't."

That didn't make sense. Robin knew she dreaded leaving Jasper and would probably spend the next year on the sofa, clutching tissues and moaning Jasper's name as she tore through her movie collection for the umpteenth time. Robin didn't care about Jasper, not in that way. So why—whoa! The tea could wait.

Pam pulled out a chair and plunked into it. "You're not saying you've fallen for Margaret? God, Robin, I know the two of you have spent a lot of time together, but she's straight. You usually don't fall into that trap. Maybe you're experiencing the same thing hostages do for their captors. What's it called? Oh, I know—Stockholm syndrome."

Robin rolled her eyes. "We're not hostages, for god's sake." She lowered her voice. "And Margaret isn't straight. We're sorta, kinda involved."

"What? You and Margaret?"

Robin nodded.

"What the hell did you do?"

"Nothing! She made the first move, not me."

Margaret? "Spill it, girl."

Robin lifted her cup to her lips, then noticed it was empty and put it down. "She kissed me when she came to say good-bye."

"When? Just the other night?"

"No, at home, in 2010. I offered to hug her, expecting a quick hug and that's all."

Pam could hardly contain herself. "And?"

"I got the full body treatment. I thought, okay, maybe she always hugs her friends this way. But then she kissed me, and it was more than a friendly kiss."

Margaret?

"To make a long story short, we've grown closer here. I would have been okay with going back—though I would have missed her—until she told me she's not going to marry Jasper."

Cripes, this was going from bad to worse, though Pam couldn't deny feeling a teeny-weeny bit pleased. "You're not thinking of staying here and running away with her? Your life would be hell."

"No, I'm not. She doesn't want me to."

So they'd discussed it. Jesus.

"She's going to become a nun."

"A nun? A freaking *nun*?"

"Yeah, a freaking nun. And I feel like it's my fault. I mean, god, Pam, what sort of life will she have?"

"She'll marry Jasper."

Robin shook her head. "No, she—"

"I don't care what she's planning to do. The marriage announcement, remember? They get married. They have a daughter."

"That was before we arrived here."

"No. I mean, yes, but that doesn't matter. We looked up the past when we were in 2010. We'd already been here at that point, even though we hadn't been." She sympathized when Robin groaned. "So she doesn't go through with the nun thing."

"But why would she change her mind? She seems dead set against marrying him."

Pam straightened. "I'll tell you what I think happens. She has to tell Jasper she doesn't want to marry him, and why. I bet he talks her out of it. She might even end up telling him the truth about herself."

Robin frowned. "I can't see that."

"Jasper's not an unreasonable man. If she's really upset when she tells him, I can see that happening, and I can believe he'd still marry her."

"I don't know, Pam, he still might marry her, but I honestly don't believe she'd marry him. She doesn't want to live a lie. She doesn't want to condemn him to a loveless marriage."

"I wonder if this has anything to do with why they ended up in Halifax and married so quickly?" Pam mused. "Anyway, she probably feels very brave and determined right now, while you're still here. Wait until reality sinks in and she has to face breaking her engagement and the shit that'll hit the fan. Maybe she decides on her own not to go through with it. And that doesn't mean she doesn't care about you," Pam added when Robin's shoulders hunched. "It means she's being realistic and accepting that you're gone and that Jasper is still here and does care about her." But why Halifax, then? She leaned back. "You and Margaret—I can't believe it! Margaret doesn't seem your type." She paused. "You know, we don't *have* to go back."

"Yes, we do," Robin said firmly. "Margaret wants me to go back." She tapped one of her temples. "And I know up here that I have to go back, not only for me, but for Mom and Chris. I'm just not completely happy about it. And since you believe the marriage announcement, there's no point you staying here, either."

"I kind of like it here," Pam said. "I feel like I fit in. But you're right, Jasper is the big draw. And this will sound arrogant, but the fact that he married Margaret means I didn't stay."

Robin barked a laugh. "You're right, it does sound arrogant."

"What can I say?" Pam said unapologetically. "It also means the rhyme will work tonight. We're checking out."

"You know, I won't be surprised if I wake up to see a doctor hovering over me and I discover I've been in a coma for months."

Pam reached out and pinched Robin's arm—hard.

Robin yelped. "What was that for?"

"I'm real, not some figment of your imagination." Pam clasped her hands on the table as Robin rubbed her arm. "You know what I don't understand?"

Robin looked at her expectantly.

"Won't we keep living this over and over again now?"

"What do you mean?"

"Well, we're in 1910, right? Time will march on here, and eventually we'll be born again and grow up again and end up in 2010. Jasper and Margaret will arrive again, we'll be sucked back here, rinse and repeat."

"I've had time to think about this, all those afternoons you were out and Margaret wasn't here." Robin stabbed her finger on the table. "I figure each life is a thread. You're born at one end of the thread and die at the other. You can only move forward along the thread, not backward. But the thread can be woven through time. Somehow that rhyme allowed the needle to be pushed in at 2010 and lifted out in 1910. Tonight, if all goes to plan, it will be pushed in again today and lifted out at 2010, and we'll continue to move forward along the thread. We can't go backward and be born a second time. Margaret and Jasper won't be resurrected over and over again."

"A sewing analogy? Margaret's rubbing off on you." And Pam's head hurt. "Wouldn't that mean our presence here *could* change history?" Such as scuttle Jasper and Margaret's engagement? "If you're right, we hadn't already been here when we found the marriage announcement in 2010."

"No, we had, because although we can only move forward on our threads, the threads themselves can be threaded backward and forward. So even though each moment in our lives can only be lived once, they don't have to be lived chronologically." Robin closed her eyes and buried her head in her hands.

"Robin?"

After a moment, Robin dropped her hands and met Pam's gaze. "I think I've just convinced myself that you're right. She does marry him."

"Disappointed?" Pam asked softly.

"I'm not crazy about the idea—"

"Join the club."

"—but I understand why she does it."

"I guess we'll never know what made her give up on the nun idea or why they went to Halifax," Pam said.

"We might. She said she'll write to me."

"How?"

"The attic. It's possible other papers were there. I didn't look."

"Ooh, maybe she'll write you love letters." Pam sighed. "Are we pathetic, or what? We can't find people in our own time?"

"Let's hope we get back to our own time."

She frowned at Robin. "What do you mean?"

"We know *they're* fine because of the marriage announcement. But who knows where *we'll* end up? You can't control where we go, and so far, we've never tried sending people forward, only back."

"Jasper and Margaret went forward," Pam pointed out.

"Yes, but you read the book in their future. Maybe I'm worrying about nothing, but we know the rhyme works both ways. I'm hoping we don't end up in 1810, or worse."

"You know what would be really interesting? If we *all* end up in 2010. I know, I know, it won't happen. They get married here in 1910 and live happily ever after." Or make a damn good show of it, anyway. "But would you be crushed if Margaret arrived back in 2010 with us?" She batted her eyelashes at Robin. To her delight, Robin smiled.

"I think I'd be frightened."

"Why?"

"She'd want to marry me."

"And you wouldn't want that," Pam said slowly.

"She's not ready for that."

Was Robin?

"I'd like to think I'd have the patience to wait, but what if she's never ready? What if it takes her years? And I'm not sure I'd want the responsibility of compensating for the loss of almost every other freaking person she's ever known in her life, including her entire family. That would be a huge burden to bear. How could I ever live up to that, especially once she met my family?"

Pam chuckled. "It wouldn't be only you, Robin. She'd also benefit from all the changes between now and then."

"That might not be enough. Though she wouldn't be the first lesbian forced to turn her back on her family and friends to be who she is." Robin's eyes narrowed. "What about you and Jasper? Do you think you'd ride off into the sunset together?"

God, she wished! "I'd like to think we would, but you're right. He'd have to leave everyone behind. He might be okay with that at first, but when we reach the point where I'm yelling at him for throwing his dirty underwear on the floor, he might wish he was back here and wonder why he gave it all up. So yeah, they'd probably stay for a month again, we'd read the damn rhyme, and we'd all end up back here. Instead of spending summers at home and winters in Florida, the four of us would spend odd months in 2010 and even months in 1910."

Robin threw back her head and laughed. "And we'd seem to grow older twice as fast as everyone else, which would be really, really freaky."

"Yeah, so if the four of us do somehow end up in 2010 tonight, screw the rhyme. We'd have to put roots down in one time period, and they'd have an easier time in 2010 than you'd have here." Pam slapped the table. "But it won't happen. They get married. We end up at home, we hope. We'll feel like shit for a while, but somehow we'll get through it." Her throat felt dry; it was time for that tea. She pushed back her chair and rose, slipped her arm around Robin's shoulders, and squeezed her. "But we can dream, eh? We can dream."

"And we'll destroy the book, right? Otherwise it'll taunt us."

"Yeah, we will. I'm with you there." She shuffled over to the tea tin and spooned tea leaves into the strainer. "Jasper said he'll have dinner with us and then we'll head to Margaret's." So it was only a matter of time. Regardless of how she and Robin kept themselves busy until then, Pam would feel like a condemned woman waiting for the hangman to arrive.

PAM DIDN'T DARE look at Jasper or Robin as they trudged up the path to Margaret's house. If someone jumped out, stuck a gun to their heads, and demanded that they smile, they'd all be dead. She could almost touch the waves of dread and sorrow emanating from them. It was incomprehensible. They were about to die—she and Robin to

Jasper and Margaret, and Jasper and Margaret to them. This was it, really it. Even Margaret's letters in the attic, if there were any, would be a relic from the past, the writer long returned to dust—nothing but a brutal reminder of people who'd touched their hearts and left them weeping.

Margaret was waiting for them at the bottom of the stairs, her hands clenched in front of her. She wordlessly motioned for Pam and Jasper to go to the drawing room. Pam glanced over her shoulder and saw Robin and Margaret ever so briefly squeeze each other's hands. A lump rose in her throat. She turned away and continued down the hallway as Robin quietly climbed the stairs.

"I'll sit on the floor near the piano." Pam stepped out of Margaret's loaned dress and laid it across the piano bench. She'd imagined this moment so many times. In her mind, she'd seen herself embracing Jasper, passionately kissing him, promising to hold him in her heart forever. Fantasies always conveniently overlooked how shitty one would actually feel at a time like this. She couldn't muster a passionate kiss if she tried, and there was nothing more to say that wouldn't sound trite or make them want to kill themselves.

As Pam sat on the floor, an anemic-looking Margaret came into the drawing room and closed the door. "We don't have much time," she said urgently. "Everyone's in the dining room, playing cards."

So her plan had worked. Plan B had been to "call" on Margaret and hope they could have the drawing room to themselves. If not, they would have tried again the next evening.

"I excused myself to make tea and warm the scones. They'll expect me back soon."

Margaret looked so fragile and on the verge of tears that Pam wanted to jump up and hug the poor woman. Time to get on with it, for all their sakes. "Then let's not drag it out." She held out her hand. "Jasper."

He hesitated a beat, then handed her the book he'd had tucked under his arm. Margaret went to his side. Pam peered up at them through moist eyes. "Have a good life, you two," she managed to whisper, then quickly lowered her head and struggled with her composure. Lucky Robin, up in Margaret's room by herself. It didn't matter if she cried or her lips were trembling. *Come on, Pam, hold it together long enough to read the rhyme!* She shifted position so she could rest the book on her crossed legs. The desire to look at Jasper one last time was strong, but all she'd see was pain, so she kept her head down and flipped to page 17. She stared at the rhyme. *Do it!*

She drew a quavering breath and read the rhyme to herself once. *Do it!* "All right. Here we go . . ."

> *when in the wrong time*
> *universe will not be kind*
> *until you align*
> *by swapping souls*

Shit! No obnoxious noise, no nausea, and she could still feel the hard floor under her bum. "Let me try again."

> *when in the wrong time*
> *universe will not be—*

"Pam," Jasper said.

She held up her hand. "I know, I know. I'm trying again."

> *when in the wrong time—*

"Pam!"

She jerked her head up. "What?"

"Margaret's gone."

"Where is she?" Pam snapped, unable to keep her irritation from her voice. Had Margaret run upstairs to give Robin a good-bye kiss?

Jasper's face was ashen. "She disappeared, Pam. When you read the rhyme."

"What?" *Oh my god.* "Are you sure?" She glanced at the door. Still closed, and Pam hadn't heard the rustle of Margaret's dress, though she'd been focused on the rhyme.

"Yes." He stared at where Margaret had been standing just a minute ago and waved his arms through nothingness. "She just . . . disappeared. Right before my eyes."

Holy shit! "We'd better go find out if Robin's still here."

"I can't go into Margaret's bedroom."

"I'm not going alone, Jasper, and we know Margaret's not there. You won't be caught in a compromising position, so come on." Trusting him to follow, Pam grabbed the dress from the piano bench, went to the door, and opened it a crack. It sounded as if everyone was still in the dining room. They crept down the hallway and up the stairs.

Pam opened Margaret's bedroom door. "Robin!" she whispered as she stepped into the dim room. Silence. "Robin!" She waved Jasper inside and shut the door, then glanced around. The only traces of Robin were the cap and jacket she'd left on Margaret's bed. "She's gone." And Pam immediately grasped the implications. She laid the dress and book on the bed. "They're in 2010, and they're not coming back."

"What? No, Pam. They'll read the rhyme next lunar cycle. Or you will. Margaret will want to come back."

She shook her head. "They don't read the rhyme, Jasper. Don't you see? If they did, Margaret would already be back. She would have returned to the exact same time she left. To us, it would look as if she'd never gone, except she'd start babbling about how she'd just spent another month in 2010. She's not coming back."

Jasper's brows drew together. "But why? Why would she want to stay? Everyone she loves is here."

Not everyone.

"What will Margaret do? She's all alone!"

"No, she isn't. She's with Robin. I know you think Robin's . . . queer, but trust me, she'll take care of Margaret."

"Perhaps the rhyme didn't work. Perhaps Margaret is trapped!" Jasper said, wild-eyed.

"I doubt it. The rhyme has always worked when we've read it at the right time."

"Then you can read the rhyme next lunar cycle, bring Margaret back, and go home. Don't you want to return to your own time?"

"Margaret doesn't want to come back, Jasper." And Pam had no intention of inadvertently sucking Robin back to 1910. "She made her decision, and I've made mine. I'm staying."

He gaped at her. "What will you do?"

The moment of truth had arrived. "I think that's up to you." Hoping to calm her shaking hands, she shoved them into her pockets and met his eyes.

His Adam's apple bobbed, but he didn't dither. "If we're to marry, you'll need a birth certificate."

Pam wanted to leap into the air and whoop, but the celebration would have to wait. She glanced around the bedroom, then went to the vanity in the corner and pulled open a drawer.

"What are you doing?" Jasper asked.

"Looking for Margaret's birth certificate. She doesn't need it anymore."

"See if you can find something in her handwriting, too."

Pam rummaged through the drawer. "Why?"

"So we can try to forge a letter to her parents that explains why she ran away."

She chuckled. "We'll say she's eloped with a Tillman."

Jasper snorted. "We can't say that! Margaret would never elope with a Tillman."

Wanna bet? "Aha! Here it is. There's nothing in here with her handwriting, though." She twisted to give the birth certificate to Jasper.

He pointed at the vanity. "I think that's her engagement book. We'll take that." He slid it from the cubbyhole and slipped the birth certificate inside its front cover.

As Pam pushed the drawer shut, her gaze fell on the three boxes of stationery stacked on the vanity. *The attic. It's possible other papers were there. I didn't look.* She flipped the lid off the top box and pulled out a sheet of paper, then opened the drawer again and reached for the fountain pen she'd spotted inside.

"Pam, we have to go, before someone finds us here," Jasper said.

"Just give me a minute. I won't be long." What to say to Robin? Unless they could somehow get into Margaret's bedroom again, this would be her last chance to say anything, and the time pressure didn't help. She took a deep breath and tried to sort through her thoughts. So much to say, so little time to say it! *Oh god, Robin. I'm going to miss you so much.* A wave of melancholy washed over her. No, just like the celebration, the tears would have to wait.

"Pam!"

She hastily scribbled a note, silently cursing at her bad writing. Fountain pens! She'd have no choice but to use them now. She paused to read what she'd written:

Girls,
I don't have much time, so I'll be brief and practical, otherwise I'll dissolve into a flood of tears.
1. Margaret, you have my blessing. I'll be fine here. I want to stay with Jasper.
2. Robin, be patient. Don't blow it.
3. I'm not sure how you'll do it, but have Margaret be me until you sell the house and get your paws on every last dime I have. I don't need it.
4. My PIN number is 5598. For everything. I know, I know.
5. Tell everyone I eloped with the guy at Brenda's party and I'm in Mexico sipping tequilas by the pool.
God, I'll miss you. I already do. Robin, what can I say? You know what you are to me. Okay, that flood is threatening. I'm outta here.
Have a great life, girls. You'll have years of positive thoughts coming your way.
Love, Pam.

Pam folded the paper, slipped it into an envelope, and sealed it. "Jasper, put this in the attic near Margaret's diary. Make sure it's not easy to see without someone having to get on their hands and knees and really look. It's for Robin and Margaret."

Clearly anxious to leave the bedroom and the house, Jasper did what Pam asked without arguing while she climbed back into Margaret's dress. She grabbed the book from the bed and followed Jasper into the upstairs hallway. They tiptoed along the hall, silently descended the stairs, and escaped out the front door.

"We'll have to leave Toronto," Jasper said as they raced down the path. "You can't be Margaret Wilton here. Too many people know her."

"But what about your father? The business?"

He shook his head. "I'm not making the same mistake twice. I want to marry you, and I want to make furniture. Father be damned!"

She couldn't wait until they were alone, so she could tell him how proud she was and give him that passionate kiss, and more. Perhaps they could manage one blissful hour, before they mourned lost friends. "Where should we go?"

Jasper pursed his lips. "I have an old school friend who probably wouldn't mind putting us up while we get our bearings."

Pam touched his arm. "Does this old school friend live in Halifax?"

His eyes lit up with surprise. "Yes! How did you know?"

"Lucky guess."

THREADED THROUGH TIME

BOOK TWO

For the lesbians who couldn't escape.

Chapter One

MARGARET STIFLED AN IMPATIENT SIGH AND willed Mother to draw a card from her hand. She glanced at the grandfather clock again. Dear God in heaven, it was almost 8:00! Robin was about to be torn away from her! Margaret held her cards in front of her face to hide her panic. Could she calmly return to the dining room and continue to play cards after losing the woman she loved? Somehow she must, unless she could use Jasper as a reason to excuse herself from the game. Would he desire her company, or would he want to return home and grieve for Pam in private? *Her* first choice would be to run into her bedroom, throw herself onto the bed, and weep, but that would raise eyebrows and invite questions. Since she couldn't be alone, she'd rather be with Jasper. He'd at least understand why she was upset, even if he didn't know the depth of her loss.

"I think I might have won this hand," Mother murmured when she finally placed a card on the table.

Father peered at the card through his glasses. "I believe you have."

Margaret quickly seized the opportunity. "I feel a bit peckish," she said, tossing her cards down. "I think I'll warm some scones. Anyone want tea?"

"Yes, please," Mother said. Father and Hubert nodded.

"Play the next hand without me." She pushed back her chair and escaped, making sure to close the door behind her. Should she start the tea and scones? No. She'd wait until after . . . oh, she couldn't bear to think of it! Yes, wait until afterward; she'd need every precious minute to compose herself before facing her family.

To her dismay, the front door opened the moment she reached the bottom of the stairs. She clenched her hands in front of her as Pam stepped into the house, followed by Robin and Jasper. Margaret motioned for Jasper and Pam to continue down the hallway to the drawing room. Then she braced herself and forced her eyes to Robin's.

Cold fingers grasped hers and squeezed. Robin nodded, and then she was gone. Margaret turned and watched her climb the stairs. They had agreed to the quick farewell, knowing that anything else would be agonizing, but perhaps they should have embraced one last time. That they'd die to each other like this . . .

Robin had already reached the landing. Margaret drew a deep breath, then went into the drawing room and shut the door. "We don't have much time," she said urgently. "Everyone's in the dining room, playing cards. I excused myself to make tea and warm the scones. They'll expect me back soon."

Sitting on the floor near the piano, Pam looked up at her. Margaret trembled at the sight of Pam in her modern clothes. It was really happening. Robin and Pam were returning to 2010, and Margaret would break her engagement with Jasper and enter a nunnery. *Lord, help me!*

"Then let's not drag it out." Pam held out her hand. "Jasper."

He hesitated, then handed her the book he'd tucked under his arm. Feeling light-headed, Margaret went to his side and fought tears.

Pam peered up at them, her eyes moist. "Have a good life, you two," she whispered. She lowered her head, crossed her legs, and rested the book on her lap.

Margaret could hardly breathe as Pam turned to the rhyme that would return her and Robin to their own time. *Good-bye, Robin. I'll always love you.*

Pam drew a shaky breath and sat silent for a moment. Then she said, "All right. Here we go . . ."

when in the wrong time
universe will not be kind
until you align
by swapping souls

Nausea doubled Margaret over. A shrill noise assaulted her ears. She squeezed her eyes shut, clutched her stomach, felt torn ten different ways . . . and then, as usual, the world stabilized. The noise ceased. Her stomach suddenly settled. She slowly straightened, opened her eyes a crack, and recognized the wallpaper and the rug. At least this time she knew what had happened and where she was. "I wonder why we all keep travelling together. Only Jasper and I were affected the first time."

Silence greeted her remark. Her heart pounded; her eyes snapped fully open. The chair Pam had sat in was empty, save for the rose quartz crystal. The black rhyme book lay open and facedown on the rug near the chair. Margaret whipped to her left. Jasper wasn't there! Good Lord, she was alone! In 2010! Where were the others? In a panic, she ran into the hallway, then stopped when footsteps pounded down the stairs. *Robin.*

"We made it!" Robin was shouting as she descended. She came into the hallway and stopped, her eyes wide. "Margaret! Oh my god, we all came back. Pam and I didn't think that would happen." She frowned. "What's wrong? Apart from being in 2010 again."

Margaret swallowed. "We didn't all come back."

Robin walked up the hallway, her eyes on Margaret's. "What do you mean?"

"Jasper and Pam aren't here."

"What? No—they have to be." She brushed past Margaret and went into the drawing room. "Pam? Pam!" Margaret followed her and paused in the doorway. Robin stood with her hands on her hips, staring at the empty chair. "I don't understand. Why didn't they come back with us?"

"Perhaps Pam's desire to be with Jasper and my—my desire to be with you somehow influenced the rhyme's effect."

Robin turned to her. "Then why didn't we all come back? Or why didn't I stay in 1910 with you? Or why didn't Jasper come here with Pam?" She shook her head. "I don't know, we didn't even know each other the first time Pam read the rhyme. And I had the impression you wanted to get away from me the second time she read it."

Blood rushed to Margaret's face. "You're right. It was a silly thought."

"No. You could be right. We've never understood how this rhyme works." They both eyed the book lying on the floor. "It could just be chance. Read the rhyme and whoever travels is random, though it's always an even number of travellers," Robin said.

"What should we do?" Margaret asked from the doorway. "Should we read the rhyme?"

Robin appeared lost in thought. Not wanting to break her concentration, Margaret waited and tried not to think about her predicament and whether Robin was pleased or dismayed by her presence in 2010.

"Something's wrong," Robin finally said. "Whoever's travelled has always returned to the exact same time they left. We did." She pointed up. "When Pam read the rhyme, I was sitting at my computer and I just happened to look at the time before I suddenly found myself in your bedroom. When I just found myself back in my chair, the time hadn't changed. My screen looked exactly the same. It's as if we never left."

"It was the same for Jasper and me when we returned."

"Yes. So Pam should already be here. Don't you see? At this point, she can't return to the time she left. It's too late."

"Perhaps she can return at a later date."

"But when? And how old will she be?" Robin's brows drew together. "Unless she suddenly appears before the next full moon, she'll have skipped over at least a month in her own time."

"She has to return sometime." When Robin paled and covered her mouth with her hands, fear tightened Margaret's throat. "You don't think . . ." No, she couldn't voice such a thought.

Robin dropped her hands to her sides. "We should check the attic," she said quietly. "I doubt there will be a message there, but you never know."

Was it only two months ago that they'd all stood in this room and discussed the attic? It felt like a lifetime. Her mind racing, Margaret followed Robin upstairs. How would they rectify this situation? As Robin had said, the rhyme always affected an even number of people. If Pam didn't travel again, how would Margaret return to 1910 without dragging Robin back with her? What if they read the rhyme, Robin went back, and Jasper came forward?

On the landing, Robin murmured, "I'll get the stepladder. I think the flashlight's still in my bedroom." Margaret knew where it was: standing on the floor near the closet.

Entering Robin's bedroom again felt surreal. Everything was where Margaret had left it. Her 2010 clothes were neatly folded at the end of the bed, the last pair of shoes she'd worn was tucked underneath it, and the wool she hadn't used was sitting on top of the dresser, along with the needles and patterns. Her eyes moved to the splash of colour on the wall. Now she knew what it was: a rainbow flag. Yes, here, in this time, she wasn't a deviant. She was nobody. She didn't exist.

She picked up the flashlight, and moved away from the closet when Robin carried the stepladder into the room. "I'll need you to boost me," Robin said as she opened the ladder inside the closet. She accepted the flashlight from Margaret, climbed to the trapdoor, and pushed it open. "Now," she said a moment later.

Unsure of what to do, Margaret placed her hands underneath one of Robin's feet and stood on her tip-toes, throwing her weight upward. It worked; Robin managed to hoist herself into the attic. "Don't bring down my letters!" Margaret shouted, wondering if Robin could hear her. She didn't want to know how many letters she'd written to Robin about breaking her engagement and preparing to enter the nunnery, and she certainly didn't want to know what was in them. Best not to know anything about her future.

The ceiling creaked overhead. Robin's feet and legs appeared. "Just guide my feet to the stepladder if it looks like I'm going to miss," Margaret heard her say. She stood poised, ready to help, but Robin's feet landed on the top step without aid. To give her room, Margaret moved away and waited near Robin's desk. A moment later, Robin emerged from the closet and held up an envelope. "I found this."

Margaret peered at it. "That's my stationery, but I didn't put it there. I would have written your name on the envelope."

"Pam or Jasper did."

"How can you tell?"

"I had to really look for it. Whoever put it there knew we were going to look for your diary." Robin turned the envelope over in her hands. Her reluctance to open it sent a chill up Margaret's spine. "Well, I guess we should read it." Robin chuckled nervously and sat on the bed. She ripped the envelope open with her thumb, drew out a single sheet of paper, and unfolded it. "It's addressed to Girls, which I assume means us. Why don't you come sit over here? We'll read it together."

Margaret hesitated, then crossed to the bed and settled next to Robin, who held the letter where they both could read it:

Girls,

I don't have much time, so I'll be brief and practical, otherwise I'll dissolve into a flood of tears.

1. Margaret, you have my blessing. I'll be fine here. I want to stay with Jasper.

2. Robin, be patient. Don't blow it.

3. I'm not sure how you'll do it, but have Margaret be me until you sell the house and get your paws on every last dime I have. I don't need it.

4. My PIN number is 5598. For everything. I know, I know.

5. Tell everyone I eloped with the guy at Brenda's party and I'm in Mexico sipping tequilas by the pool.

God, I'll miss you. I already do. Robin, what can I say? You know what you are to me. Okay, that flood is threatening. I'm outta here.

Have a great life, girls. You'll have years of positive thoughts coming your way.

Love, Pam.

Margaret didn't understand all of it, but what she did comprehend shocked her to her core. Pam sounded as if she wasn't coming back, and . . . No, it couldn't be. Margaret's hand went to her throat. Her life. Her family. Fear drove her to her feet. She walked over to the desk and kept her back to Robin as she tried to calm her breathing. "Were there any letters from me in the attic?" she asked. When Robin's answer didn't immediately come, she closed her eyes.

"No."

Her voice shook. "I would have written to you." Oh, Lord. Her knees buckled. Robin was suddenly there, supporting her elbow and steering her back to the bed. They both sank onto it. When Robin slipped her arm around Margaret's shoulders, Margaret leaned into her and fought tears. She had to keep her wits about her!

Robin squeezed her. "It'll be all right."

Would it? Her life had just been torn away!

With her free hand, Robin picked up Pam's letter from the bed and read it again. She pursed her lips. "Let's think this through. When Pam read the rhyme, you and I disappeared. For some reason, Pam thought you'd decided not to return to 1910, probably because you didn't return when you were supposed to."

"How did she get back into the house and put the letter in the attic?" Margaret asked dully.

"She probably put it there on the same night she read the rhyme. I'm speculating here, but she must have concluded that you didn't return because you wanted to stay here, in this time." Robin fell silent for a moment, then sighed. "I guess it doesn't matter what ran through her mind. All that matters is that she isn't here. She loves Jasper. She must have decided right there and then to stay. She's not . . . she's not coming back."

Robin's distressed expression reminded Margaret that she wasn't the only one facing a tremendous loss. Robin's theory also troubled her. Why had Pam quickly jumped to the conclusion that she'd chosen to remain in the future? She tucked the question away to talk about later.

"She was wrong. You hadn't decided to stay—or rather, her letter might be what led to your decision. God, I hate time travel," Robin groaned, then looked at the letter again. "Then again, nothing's stopping *us* from reading the rhyme. But we have no idea where—well, what date and time—you'll end up."

"I would have written to you. Since there aren't any letters from me, I never stepped foot back inside this house in my time."

Robin lifted her eyes from the letter. "Margaret, I know what you staying here means, what you'd be giving up," she said solemnly. "We *can* read the rhyme next month. Maybe you'll return a month after you left. That wouldn't be so bad."

"You're not listening to me, Robin," Margaret said, frustration straining her voice. "I would have written to you. I didn't. So, no, I didn't return only a month later. If we read the rhyme, we have no idea what will happen to me, or you, or Pam, or Jasper, or anyone!" She brushed aside new tears and bit her lip, determined not to lose her composure.

When Robin lifted her arm, Margaret worried that she'd spoken too harshly. But Robin twisted toward her and took both her hands. "Don't get angry with me, but I thought that maybe after I'd left, you'd give up on your plan to enter the order, that you'd go ahead and marry Jasper."

"No! Perhaps you think me weak-minded, but I'm not. It would have been difficult, but I wouldn't have married Jasper, not—" she gulped "—not after you."

"I don't think you're weak-minded. Not at all. I asked because the historical record shows that you married Jasper and had at least one child."

"What? No!"

"Then Pam must have, acting as you. That's why the marriage took place in Halifax. We wondered why you'd left Toronto and married so soon after visiting our time."

A multitude of questions raced through Margaret's mind, but again, she'd save them for later. "You never told us."

"We didn't think it would be a good idea for you to know your future." Robin's grip on Margaret's hands tightened. "We didn't know it was actually Pam's future."

"Did you find anything else out about us? Perhaps something that might tell us if—what happened to me?"

Robin shook her head. "We did think about searching cemetery records—"

Margaret shuddered.

"—but we couldn't do it, not while you were still here. If we had, I doubt we would have found one for you—not for a Margaret Wilton who never married. You haven't died yet." Robin hesitated. "For the same reason I haven't. Our deaths are in the future."

How could this be? Two months ago she'd stood in her bedroom worrying about marrying a man she didn't love. Now she faced a life one hundred years in the future with a woman she did love. She couldn't grasp it. When would it seem real? Next week? Next month, when the full moon came and went? Next year? How did Robin feel about it? Two months ago Robin had shared a house with Pam, not expecting two people from the past to appear out of nowhere. Now Pam was gone, and Margaret would depend on Robin until she could independently navigate this time. Robin was in university, had a family, friends, a life that didn't include Margaret.

She looked into Robin's eyes. "This will not only be trying for me, but also for you. Please tell me how you feel about it. I don't want to be a burden for you. I know what we said to each other in 1910, but you didn't expect this. If you want me to, I'll read the rhyme." Her throat tightened. "I'll understand."

Robin blinked at her, then let out a long, heartfelt sigh. "It's going to be rough, really rough, without Pam, but you can't read the rhyme, and I wouldn't want you to. Not only because I care about you, but because it's too risky, for all of us." Her face darkened. "If Pam wants to come back, she has the book. Her copy didn't come with us." Robin almost sounded angry. "But don't worry about Pam, or me. It's your decision. You stand to lose the most."

"That isn't true," Margaret said quietly. "Pam is dear to you."

Robin bit her lip and nodded.

"In all honesty, my mind is bursting right now. I'm torn between you and my family, knowing that if I were to go back, my life would never be the same—and not knowing if I would ever see my family again anyway, because I didn't return when expected, and there aren't any letters in the attic." But she knew. Deep down, she knew. She gathered her courage and resolve. "What I know in my heart, above all, is that I won't risk taking you back to my time, or any time when you would be scorned."

"Margaret—"

"No, Robin. You said I have the most to lose, but I don't. I grant you my losses will be dire, but I was prepared to leave my family and friends so I could live an honest life. I am making the same choice now." For both of them. "If I read that rhyme and you return to 1910, I could never live with myself for taking away from you what I wanted so much, I was prepared to turn my life upside down for it. So unless you tell me that you want me to go, that you couldn't bear it if I stay, I will not read the rhyme." She waited, suddenly appreciating what the bride and groom must feel when the minister asks that anyone who knows a reason why the two shouldn't marry should speak now.

"Like I said, I don't want you to read the rhyme. I just wanted to make sure that you . . ." Robin snorted. "Well, of course you understand what it means."

"It means I will need your help." Now that Margaret had voiced her desire to remain in this time, she couldn't hold back her panic. "You're all I have. I'm nobody here. I don't have a name!"

Robin pulled her hands away and grasped Margaret's shoulders. "You're Margaret Wilton. You'll adapt to living here. And I'll always be here for you. No matter what happens—between us—I promise you that. I'll always be here. I'm your family now."

Margaret's vision blurred. "I meant everything I said to you in 1910."

Robin smiled. "So did I."

She didn't protest when Robin pulled her into an embrace, but though her eyes were moist, she was too numb to cry. A flood of tears would come later, when she truly understood that her family and friends were all gone. Dead.

"Now we have the time we never thought we'd have," Robin murmured into Margaret's ear. "That's one bright spot. Right?"

Did she still not believe that Margaret truly loved her? "Yes. I'm glad we do." She'd fantasized about living out her life with Robin, never dreaming that her flight of fancy would become a potential reality. Robin understood that she needed time to fully accept her true nature. Margaret had thought to bury that part of herself in a nunnery. Now she'd try to overcome her fear and embrace it, while trying to adjust to the loss of almost everyone she loved, and to a familiar yet alien world. It would be easier to close her eyes and remain in Robin's arms forever, but the time for fantasy was over.

She drew back, and accepted one of those horrible tissues Robin snapped from the box on the night stand. "What should I do now?" she asked as she dabbed at one eye.

Robin frowned. "I don't know about you, but I doubt I'll be able to sleep for a while. It's early anyway."

Margaret nodded.

"Why don't you change, and then we'll have tea and try to relax for a bit?" Robin picked up Pam's letter. "I think I'll change, too. Sort of a symbolic act, you know? I'll meet you in the kitchen."

Margaret managed a small smile. "All right." But after the door clicked shut behind Robin, she couldn't bring herself to undress right away. She had nothing but the clothes on her back, the only vestige of her life in 1910. Shedding them would be shedding that life—and then what? The rest of her life stretched before her, a dark and perilous unknown, with Robin the only light to guide her. Margaret stared down at her hands, and only then noticed that her engagement ring was no longer on her finger.

ROBIN SHUT THE door to Pam's bedroom and leaned against it. *Jesus, Pam. Jesus!* She lifted the letter and read it again. *Oh, sure, Margaret will take your identity, just like that. No problem. Shit!* Pam had really dropped her in it this time—her, and Margaret. Robin understood that Pam loved—had loved? *Shit!*—Jasper, but giving up life here to stay with him in 1910? This wasn't a fucking movie. *God, Pam. You would have found someone here eventually.* But she loved Jasper, just as Robin loved Margaret. She *was* glad that Margaret was here—and freaking terrified. It would be so much easier if Pam had returned too. How would she explain Pam's disappearance into thin air? How would she get Margaret into the system? How would Margaret cope, once the shock wore off?

The trusting look in Margaret's eyes when she'd asked, *What should I do now* . . . Robin had answered as if Margaret meant, "What should I do in the next five minutes?" But the question was applicable to the rest of her life. What *would* she do? Robin wanted to cry.

Nope, she couldn't lose it, not when she was Margaret's only lifeline. *She* was home. She had her life and was in her own time. If anyone had freak-out rights, Margaret did. Robin's gaze settled on the bed, then on Pam's phone, resting on the night stand next to the photo of her parents; on her sweats draped over the back of the chair; on the tanzanite crystal from Jake's on top of the dresser. She raised a trembling hand to cover her mouth and heaved a shuddering sigh. Then she steeled herself. Margaret shouldn't have to wait in an empty kitchen while she blubbered upstairs.

She didn't really need to change; she'd used it as an excuse to give herself a few minutes to hyperventilate in private. *Time's up.* Dropping the letter next to the tanzanite, Robin pulled open the drawer Pam had temporarily assigned to her, which would now be hers for longer than she'd expected. She'd try not to cry herself to sleep tonight—she'd be surprised if she slept at all. Tomorrow morning she'd let a long shower wash away her tears, then try to figure out how best to help Margaret pick up the pieces.

Chapter Two

Pam sipped her coffee and grimaced. Okay, so the coffee available in the guest house wasn't all that great, but that didn't mean there wasn't good coffee to be had in this time period. She took another bite of her toast and leaned back in her chair. If only she could be a fly on the wall in one hundred years, when Robin and Margaret found themselves back in 2010—together! The surprise, the widening eyes and smouldering looks as they realized they could be together forever, and then the embrace and the passionate kiss . . . Pam clasped her hand over her heart. It would be just like an old movie—if they'd made old movies in which the lesbians didn't die horrible deaths in the end, or be locked up in lunatic asylums or prisons, or commit suicide. Would Robin and Margaret enjoy a night of passion? Probably not. They weren't ready for that yet, unlike her and Jasper.

She glanced at the rumpled bedclothes visible through the open bedroom doorway. Jasper had left only an hour ago, but it already felt like a lifetime. When she told Robin about— Pam blinked rapidly and swallowed her mouthful of toast. Robin couldn't have stayed here, but Pam didn't know yet whether all of them returning to 2010 would have been a better scenario. Maybe by this time next year she'd be wondering what the hell she'd been thinking, and fighting the desire to get back to her own time. But right now, being here felt pretty damn good—except that Robin was gone. *Damn it, woman, you'd better have a wonderful life.* Pam certainly intended to, so she wouldn't start her first day as a permanent resident in 1910 getting all maudlin. *Think about the positives: you're with Jasper. Robin's back in 2010 where she belongs, and Margaret . . . oh Margaret, your life will be so much better than it could have been here.* Cripes, wait until she saw the Gay Pride parade! Just that would make it all worth it. The woman had made a wise choice when she'd decided to stay in the future.

She ate the last of her toast, then tidied up the guest house to keep herself occupied. Should she dress to go out? Jasper had gone to the main house to phone his friend in Halifax; he thought that they should leave Toronto as soon as possible. Pam was supposed to be practising Margaret's handwriting, so she could write the sayonara note to her parents. She opened the engagement book on the kitchen table and skimmed the entries. Margaret had been quite the social butterfly, but with no TV or Internet, what else was there to do except hang out with friends?

Shit! She'd only just picked up the fountain pen and it was already leaking all over her fingers. She wiped them on a handkerchief she'd found in one of the dresser drawers, then tensed when she heard a car pull up to the house. It would be Jasper, but just in case, she hovered outside the bedroom, prepared to duck into hiding. The front door swung open. When Jasper stepped into the living room, Pam blew out a relieved sigh. "Did you phone Oliver?"

He nodded. She stared at him for a moment, then went to him and threw her arms around his neck. After restraining herself for so long, not having to worry about embracing him and kissing him and wanting to drag him into the bedroom to mess up the bedclothes again was liberating. The quick kiss she'd intended to give him left them breathless when they finally drew apart five minutes later.

"There's definitely something to be said for passion in a relationship," Jasper said hoarsely. He led her by the hand to the two chairs near the fire. "Oliver is expecting us."

"What did you tell him?"

"That my father and I had an argument about my desire to leave the family business and that I want to leave Toronto to start fresh elsewhere."

Pam leaned forward. "What about me?"

"I'd already told him that I'm engaged to you—Margaret. I said that you wanted to come with me and that we'd marry after we'd found somewhere to live. He'll be able to accommodate us in a fashion that won't raise eyebrows."

"You mean separate bedrooms, right?"

"Not quite. I'll stay with him. You'll stay with his parents, though they're currently touring Europe." He smiled when Pam groaned. "Oliver lives on the same estate, so we won't be far from each other. His sister Doris is around your age. She can introduce you to her friends and help you with the wedding. She's also engaged, but they're not marrying until the summer."

The wedding. It sounded surreal.

"I'll go to the train station this afternoon and purchase our tickets. I'm hoping we can be on a train tomorrow."

"I need clothes! I have a couple of dresses and the items that Margaret lent me, but—"

Jasper raised his hand. "We'll worry about that when we're there. The less we're seen here, the better." He paused. "I've been thinking about the Wiltons. We need to explain why Margaret and I fled to Halifax."

"You—we—eloped because we couldn't wait to get married."

He shook his head. "Nothing is preventing us from having a quick wedding here."

"We'll tell them the same thing you told Oliver."

"Why would Margaret leave without telling them? We have to explain why she left without saying good-bye." He heaved his shoulders. "I've come up with a possible reason. As much as it pains me—"

The sound of another car had them both on their feet. Jasper glanced out the window and paled. "The Wiltons!" he hissed.

Holy shit!

"Hide!"

Pam didn't have to be told twice. Blood pounding in her ears, she darted into the bedroom Robin had used and shut the door, but she felt exposed. If anyone came in . . . She went to the tall dresser against the same wall as the door and crouched next to it. As long as nobody walked into the room and turned around, she should be all right.

"The butler told us you'd gone for a drive around the estate." The deep voice was audible through the paper-thin wall. Margaret's father?

"Where's Margaret?" *Mrs. Wilton.* "Last night she went to make tea and never came back. One of the neighbours told us he saw your motor outside the house."

Shit. If they'd known how things would turn out, they would have been more careful not to be seen.

"Let me handle this, May. Perhaps you should wait outside."

"No! I'm not naive, James. I knew what was going on as soon as we saw Jasper's motor outside this house. No, I knew when we spoke to the neighbours last night. So did you. Otherwise we would have had the police out looking for her!"

Shit!

"Where is she?" Mrs. Wilton cried. "Is she here? Margaret? Margaret!"

Pam jumped and held her breath when the door suddenly swung open. "Margaret?" Mrs. Wilton said loudly. The door swung shut. Pam slowly exhaled. Jesus, she was shaking. She heard the door to the other bedroom open. "Margaret? Oh my Lord!"

"What?" Mr. Wilton barked.

"One of Margaret's dresses. Oh, James. And here's her engagement book." Footsteps thumped back into the living room. "Where is she?"

"Where's my daughter?" Mr. Wilton asked.

"She's gone," Jasper said.

"Gone? What do you mean, gone?"

Pam's brow furrowed. Yes, what did he mean?

"She's on her way to Halifax."

Silence, then, "Why? And why are her things still here?"

"She's with child," Jasper said.

Pam gaped, then winced when she heard a loud slap. Ouch, that must have hurt. Jasper's ears were probably ringing.

"You bastard!" Mrs. Wilton shouted. "You take advantage of my daughter and then send her away to have a baby? You're going to wash your hands of the entire affair and marry someone else?"

"Mrs. Wilton—"

"Oh my Lord. Oh James. No wonder she hasn't been herself lately. Oh, and remember the Halloween Ball? Her tricky tummy? Oh my Lord."

"I trusted you," Mr. Wilton growled. "I thought you'd make a worthy husband."

"I will," Jasper said. "I still intend to marry Margaret."

"Then why have you sent her away to Halifax?"

"Even though I'll marry Margaret, my parents will always consider our child illegitimate. My family will never accept Margaret now. They'll look down on the child. We need a fresh start somewhere else. Margaret's already ashamed—"

"As she should be!" Mrs. Wilton thundered. "Stupid, stupid girl!"

Pam rolled her eyes. *Jesus, lady, get a grip.* They'd had a roll in the hay, not murdered anyone. She looked down at her stomach. *Shit!* Hopefully *she* wasn't pregnant. That daughter of theirs had better not make her entrance into the world nine months from now. She stifled a gasp with her hand. Did they have epidurals here? She'd always known that, when the time came, she wouldn't want any part of that natural childbirth crap.

"We knew we had to leave, but she couldn't face you and tell you about her predicament," Jasper said.

"So you decided to run away like cowards!" Mr. Wilton said. "I knew something was brewing last night. Margaret was nervous and kept looking at the clock."

"I would have left with her, but I have some business to conclude here. Margaret will send you a letter—"

"Tell her not to bother!" Mrs. Wilton shrieked. "And tell her all her belongings are going to the poor!"

"May!"

"No, James, I won't have this. She's no better than a—a Tillman! She lied to us! Tea and scones, indeed."

Mr. Wilton wasn't so eager to be rid of his daughter. "They can move up the wedding, get married next week."

"A quick wedding won't fool anyone. All it will do is set tongues wagging, and when the baby arrives in . . ."

"Five months," Jasper said.

"Five months. Oh my Lord." Pam could imagine the stunned expression on Mrs. Wilton's face. "Idiot girl! Tell her to enjoy her new life in Halifax! And tell her not to come crawling back. I won't have a harlot under my roof!"

A moment later, the front door slammed shut. A motor roared to life. When Pam could no longer hear the car, she left her hiding place and opened the door a crack. Jasper was slumped forward in one of the chairs near the fire, rubbing his forehead. "I should see Father before the Wiltons speak to him," he murmured. "When he hears that I'm leaving the family business and about Margaret's pregnancy, he'll help the Wiltons drag my name through the mud." His shoulders stiffened. "And Margaret's."

Pam rounded the chair to peer at him, and cringed at the red welt across one cheek. She bit her lip. "Regrets?"

Jasper looked up and shook his head. "No. I would have preferred not to destroy Margaret's reputation, but there wasn't any other way. When people find out that we've left the city together, they'll jump to the conclusion that she's pregnant, so I thought I might as well use it." He sighed. "But what if Margaret comes back?"

"She won't." She'd better not. *Note to Margaret: I'd stay where you are, sweetie, unless you won't mind being the town slut.*

"I still don't understand it. When we were in 2010, she was so adamant about sheltering herself. Why would she choose to remain in the future?"

Pam considered telling him the truth, but only for a second. Unmarried sex and pregnancy threw everyone into a tizzy; imagine what an unabashed lesbian relationship would do. It would probably induce mass hysteria—and perhaps turn Jasper against her. She'd lived with Robin; because of that, he might question her own moral character. Ridiculous, but he was a product of his time—though apparently not above a little fornicating now and then. But homosexuality? Better left unsaid. *Sorry, Robin, but I know you'd understand. You kept your mouth shut in 2010 for the same reason.*

Would she carry on conversations with Robin and Margaret in her head for the rest of her life? Probably. It was her way of keeping them with her. Tears suddenly sprang to her eyes. *Cripes.* She lowered her head and brushed them away before Jasper noticed.

"Why would she give up everything she knows?" Jasper said.

Pam focused on him. "She might have done it for us, and for Robin. She knew we were in love. She knew Robin hated it here. We don't know how the rhyme works. She knows that reading it could bring Robin back to 1910, or separate us."

His voice softened. "Margaret always thought of others before herself. She was so generous when we were all together, and then to give up her life here so we can spend the rest of our lives with each other . . . what a sacrifice."

Pam stifled a snort. Saint Margaret was getting a brand new life out of the deal. She cleared her throat. "Well, I guess I don't have to practice her handwriting now. What's the plan?"

Jasper brightened. "After I've spoken to Father, I'll go to the train station. Then we'll have an early supper together."

"Um, this may be a long shot, but do you know what a condom is?" She gasped when he reddened. "You do! Can you, uh, get your hands on a couple . . . a few . . . enough to last us to Halifax?"

He raised his eyebrows. "I doubt we'll have much opportunity to, uh, be together in private in Halifax."

Oh my god, their wedding wouldn't take place until December. "Then you'd better get a move on, so you can hurry back and spend the rest of the day with me."

He reached out and caught her hand. "I have the feeling that sharing my life with a twenty-first-century woman is going to be quite the experience."

Pam winked at him.

Chapter Three

MARGARET OPENED HER EYES AND STRETCHED, then sat up with a start. The sunlight—*what time is it?* She glanced at the clock on the night table. Almost 10:00! Good Lord, she never slept this late, but she'd fallen asleep after three in the morning and then tossed and turned all night. Her eyes settled on the rainbow flag on the wall. She'd awakened to it for a month without understanding what it represented, but it was familiar, and hence comforting. She'd offered to sleep in Pam's bedroom or the guest room, so that Robin could have her own bedroom back. But Robin had rightly guessed that Margaret would feel more at ease in the room that had been "hers" in 2010. She had so few anchors here: Robin, this room, the chair in the study, the spot on the sofa where she'd sat and read Dickens. One foot felt warmer than the other. Margaret reached out and stroked Mitzy. "And you."

Mitzy ignored her, only stirring when Margaret carefully slid her foot from underneath her and swung her legs off the bed. But how did Mitzy get into the bedroom? She looked to the door, which stood ajar; Margaret was sure she'd closed it. Crossing to it, she peered out into the hallway. The house was quiet. Was Robin still asleep after a restless night, or was she in the study or downstairs?

Except for her first morning in 2010, Margaret had always awakened to the alarm she'd set for 6:00. She'd showered before anyone else rose, and by the time she was ready to go downstairs, everyone was already up and dressed. She would have been horrified if Jasper had seen her in her nightgown, and seeing him in his nightclothes would have embarrassed them both. But was that the custom of this time? Would it be improper for Robin to see her in her nightgown, or for her to see Robin in her . . . did Robin wear a nightgown?

Margaret had no intention of going downstairs before dressing, but she wanted to shower. She shut the door, threw on a dress, and quickly pinned up her hair. At least she'd look presentable if she bumped into Robin on her way to the bathroom.

By the time Margaret stepped into the empty study, it was after 11:00. Her heart pounding, she descended the stairs, and let out a quiet sigh of relief when she entered the kitchen and saw Robin sitting at the table, hunched over a sheet of paper.

Robin looked up and smiled. "Good morning." She pointed to a mug on the table. "Tea. I would have made you toast, but it's so close to lunchtime, I wasn't sure if you'd rather have a sandwich."

Blood rushed to Margaret's cheeks. "I'm sorry. I—"

"No! No, no. I wasn't criticizing. You can sleep in as long as you like, though I did look in on you, to make sure you were all right. Mitzy darted into the room. I didn't want to risk waking you up by shooing her out. I hope she didn't bother you."

What? Robin had seen her as she slept, with her hair in disarray and . . . Margaret hoped the blanket had been pulled up to her chin! "No, she didn't," she mumbled, then pulled out the chair in front of the mug and sat down. "Have you been up long?"

"A few hours. I came down and had a tea, then went back upstairs and showered."

But had she been dressed when she came downstairs? Margaret sipped her tea. Despite how silly she'd feel, it would be better to ask than wonder. "I expect I'll ask you many stupid questions in the coming months."

Robin frowned. "Margaret, you're missing a hundred years. Of course you'll ask questions, and they won't be stupid."

"When you came down for your tea, were you dressed?" When Robin's brows drew together, she added, "I don't know if it would be improper for you to see me in my nightgown, and for me to see you in your . . ."

"Pyjamas," Robin said, her eyes bright. "No, it wouldn't be improper. On the weekends, I sometimes don't get dressed until after lunch."

"But—"

"I know, the month you and Jasper were here. We didn't want to make you uncomfortable, and frankly, I didn't want to lounge around in my PJs in front of Jasper. I won't mind with just you." She raised her hand. "But I don't want you to be uncomfortable."

"No, I . . . I wouldn't mind."

"Don't feel you have to waltz around in your nightie, though. If you want to dress before coming down, that's fine. If not, you can always wear Pam's robe. Well, I guess it'll be yours now." Robin paused. "We'll have to go through her clothes, see what fits."

Margaret could tell that Robin wasn't looking forward to it, and neither was she. "I've often seen my girlfriends in their nightclothes. I only asked because we're . . . we . . ."

"We're involved?" Robin chuckled. "This is a bit strange, living together when we haven't even gone on a date. Talk about putting the cart before the horse. It's one of the first things I'll do when you're comfortable going out."

"What?"

"Take you on a date."

The prospect thrilled and frightened her. To step out with Robin . . . Where would they go?

"Talking about being more comfortable, I've been writing down a list of what we need to do."

Margaret tilted her head so she could read it:

Pam—resign
Birth certificate—find it
Photo ID
Evening class
Newspapers
Friends

"It's not comprehensive," Robin said. "I just wanted to write down some thoughts I had last night before I forgot them."

While she was lying awake in bed, no doubt.

"Our main problem right now is Pam, or rather, her disappearance. Our second problem is getting you into the system. I know Pam said to be her, but it's not that easy."

Robin's comment reminded Margaret of Pam's letter and the questions she'd tucked away. "Why do you think Pam jumped to the conclusion that I'd decided to remain here? There could have been any number of reasons why I didn't reappear."

Robin pressed her lips together and avoided Margaret's eyes. "This is my fault."

"How can it be your fault?"

"I told her. About you and me. I only told her the morning we were—*yesterday* morning, for god's sake." Robin shook her head. "I'm sorry. I knew I had to come back to 2010, but I still felt torn, you know? I needed to talk about it. But I had no right to tell her about you."

Margaret wanted to touch her. She reached for her mug instead, then stopped herself. Why shouldn't she comfort Robin? Her heart leaped in her chest as she grasped Robin's fingers and squeezed them, then her breath quickened when Robin's face relaxed and her fingers interlocked with Margaret's. These were the moments Margaret would cling to when grief intruded; the moments she never could have experienced in her own time. "You and Pam were almost like sisters," she said quietly. "Of course you would talk to her. I'm sure you talked about Jasper. She would have talked your ear off about him here, had you both returned."

"That would have been different. If I'd told her here instead of in 1910, you wouldn't have been forced into this situation by having the decision taken away from you."

"The decision wasn't taken away from me," Margaret said. "Her letter merely lent support to the only choice that makes sense."

Robin studied her. "You're just saying that."

"No, I'm not. I would never risk taking you back to 1910." She raised her free hand when Robin's mouth opened. "But that's not the only reason. What do I have to go back to? A broken engagement, a disappointed family, life as a nun? I had already made the decision to give up my family and friends so I wouldn't have to live a lie."

"They would have visited you."

"That's true. But when I weigh the occasional social hour against living as myself, fully myself, all the time, the choice is clear, though still a painful one. I will miss them." Terribly. "I wonder what they thought became of me."

Robin pursed her lips. "Well, Pam and Jasper probably took off to Halifax pretty quickly. Perhaps they wrote a letter. Perhaps Jasper went to see them, to explain why you'd left so suddenly."

Margaret lifted her brows. "What would he say?"

"I don't know." Robin squeezed Margaret's hand. "But I'm sure they explained your abrupt departure in a way that offered comfort to your family. They would have been kind."

"I know." Not wanting to exacerbate Robin's guilt after she'd just soothed it, Margaret looked away when her eyes grew misty. "Tell me about your list," she said, hoping a change of subject would allow her to master her composure.

Robin picked up the pen lying next to the paper and pointed to the first item. "We have to explain why Pam isn't here anymore, otherwise someone will report her missing, and that's the last thing we want. I'm mainly worried about her work. She's obviously not going to be there tomorrow."

It was Sunday! She'd missed watching her church service, but perhaps God would forgive her this once. Surely He'd take into account her sudden change of circumstances. "What are we going to do?" she asked Robin.

"I'm going to email—write a letter—to Pam's manager, telling her that I'm not back from a weekend getaway."

"Why would you tell Pam's manager about you?" Margaret asked, confused.

"Sorry. I'll send the email from Pam's account. It'll be like I'm signing the letter as Pam," Robin clarified, probably seeing Margaret's incomprehension on her face. "I'll start with the weekend getaway so Pam's manager won't be completely surprised when I drop off a resignation letter from Pam."

"You'll forge her handwriting."

"No, you'll forge her signature. We'll type the letter, so all we have to worry about is her signature."

Fear snaked through Margaret at the prospect of committing a criminal act. "Why me?" she breathed.

"To get you into the system as you, you'll have to be Pam for a while. Once we have ID with your photo and you've transferred ownership of the house to me, you can change your name. Points two and three on my list are about that." Robin tapped the two lines with her pen. "The first step is being able to sign Pam's name, so your task for today is to start practising. After lunch, I'll find something with her signature on it."

Learning how to write Pam's signature shouldn't excite her, but it did, perhaps because she'd be doing something useful.

"Point four, evening class. I'm going to pick up the schedules for a couple of the colleges and school boards. I'll also check online—on the computer. Many of them have, uh, hobby classes in the evenings. I thought we could find one for you that starts in January."

Margaret gaped. "What?"

Robin smiled. "Don't panic. We'll find something you're comfortable with, and by January, the thought won't be so intimidating."

"But—"

"Just one class, Margaret. There are classes about cooking and crafts. Or maybe you'll try a beginner's computer course, though I'll teach you the basics—and more, if you're interested."

Margaret's mind raced. In 1910—until recently—she'd seen herself living out her life as a wife, mother, and, if God blessed her with longevity, a grandmother. She would support her husband, raise children, call on friends, and become involved in charitable works. That was the life she'd fully expected to live ever since she was a little girl.

Last night, as she'd lain awake, she'd wondered what Robin would expect of her here. She'd still seen herself in the role of a wife. She was a woman—but then, so was Robin, and Margaret couldn't see *her* at home in an apron all day. But what if Margaret *wanted* to be a wife, to stay home and take care of Robin? Would Robin allow it? Would it disappoint her? What was acceptable in this time? Were all women expected to work? Did lesbians have wives? Perhaps they were both expected to behave like husbands. Margaret wanted to cry out in frustration. Perhaps she shouldn't have sheltered herself so much when she was here before, but she'd never dreamed that this time would become *her* time, and that her friendship with Robin would grow into something more.

She could no longer rely on anything she believed or knew. She was a child again, trying to understand the world in which she lived.

"It's overwhelming." She hadn't meant to say the words aloud, but when Robin's forehead puckered, she realized that she had.

"I can't imagine it." Robin's eyes were sympathetic. "You're like an immigrant to a strange new country. But you speak the language. You have some familiarity with the neighbourhood." Her voice softened. "And you have me."

A lump rose in Margaret's throat.

"You also have time. I'm only suggesting a class because it will get you out there doing something, where you can interact with other people. It will only be one night a week, and hopefully you'll enjoy it. I think you'll be ready for that by January, but I don't want to rush you. We can always enrol you and then cancel, if need be." Robin jutted her chin toward Margaret's mug. "Drink your tea before it gets cold."

Margaret had forgotten about it. The warm liquid calmed her nerves somewhat.

"Point five, newspapers. I'll bring one home every night for you to read. We can have a little question and answer period in the study, while we're having our tea."

She relaxed further. The thought of tea with Robin in the study every night warmed her more than the tea had.

Robin waved the pen at Margaret. "I'll expect you to read the previous day's newspaper every day while I'm in class. No lying around watching TV or Pam's movies all day." Her amused eyes mirrored Margaret's opinion of that. "Okay, point six, friends. Namely, mine. You'll have to meet them. They're already wondering why I've been a hermit for a month." Robin's brows lifted. "Of course, it's been *two* months, but they don't know that. When I turn twenty-seven, I'll actually be—" Her brow furrowed. "When's your birthday?"

"May 12th. I was born in 1887."

Robin stared at her. "You can't go around saying *that*! In fact, you can't even say the May 12th part. From now on, your birthday is January 18th and you were born in 1984."

"Pam's birthday?" When Robin nodded, Margaret's heart sank. Would there be any trace of her left in the end?

Robin wrote *May 12th* on the sheet of paper, then looked up. Margaret closed her eyes when Robin let go of her hand and caressed her cheek. "You'll be lucky," Robin said softly. "You'll have two birthday celebrations every year, one public and one private."

Margaret gulped down her sorrow and opened moist eyes. "When is your birthday?"

Robin lowered her hand and rested it on Margaret's arm. "November 20th. I'm a couple of months older than Pam."

"You were born in . . ."

"Ninety-six years after you, in 1983. But I'm still older than you. Don't try to tell me otherwise."

Margaret wouldn't dare; next to Robin, she felt like a newborn babe. "Your birthday is soon. What are the customs now? Do you still give presents?" She wouldn't have anything to give her! "I don't—"

Robin's fingers tightened around her arm. "We'll talk about birthdays later. Let's get back to the list. You're not ready to meet my friends yet, but we can't leave it too long. I think the best way to explain the past month is to tell them about you."

Blood pounded in Margaret's ears. "What do you mean? You're going to tell them I'm from the past?" When Robin patted Margaret's arm and lifted her hand, Margaret wanted to grab and cling to it.

Robin scratched her head, then dropped her hand to her lap, much to Margaret's disappointment. "No! I'm going to tell them I have a girlfriend—with a big G."

Then they'd know! But Robin had said things were different now. "All your friends know about you."

Robin smiled. "Margaret, most of my friends are lesbians, and the ones who aren't don't care about my sexual orientation. I wouldn't want friends who don't accept me for who I am." She peered at Margaret's face. "They won't think any less of you, and we'll already be hiding enough without hiding something we don't have to hide. Let's only lie when we have to, okay?"

She nodded, but she wouldn't believe that Robin's friends would accept their relationship until she witnessed it with her own eyes. Surely those who weren't like them would look down their noses.

"Telling them we're together will explain why you're living here, too."

"We're not married!" Margaret hissed.

"It doesn't matter. Tons of couples who aren't married live together. Some raise families."

And nobody cared? Considering that deviants were accepted, she shouldn't be surprised.

"Anyway, I'll start talking about you this week, but I'll hold off on introducing you to anyone until at least next week."

Next week!

Robin scribbled *Cathy* on the paper. "I'll start with Cathy. Next to Pam, she's my closest friend, and she's been worried. We'll have to come up with answers to the inevitable questions and make sure our stories are straight."

"What sorts of questions?"

"When one of your friends told you she was seeing a new, uh, gentleman, what would you ask her?"

Margaret frowned in thought. "Where they met. His profession. Where he lives."

Robin nodded. "Well, that hasn't changed. Before you meet anyone, we have to come up with answers for all of those questions and anything else we think we'll be asked."

Fear gripped her. "What if they ask questions of me, ones I don't understand?"

"I'll be with you. That's another good thing about introducing you as my girlfriend. It'll allow me to support you in ways that would seem odd if you were just a friend. Friends normally don't answer questions for each other, but couples sometimes do."

"Will you introduce me as Pam?"

"No. Most of them have met Pam." Robin suddenly barked a laugh. "And they'd be *flabbergasted* if I told them Pam and I are girlfriends. You only have to be Pam Holden when we're doing something, um, legal or official, and hopefully we won't have to do much. Otherwise, you're Margaret Wilton."

I don't know if I can do this!

"Anyway, that's it for my list," Robin finished.

"What about your family? Won't you introduce me to them?" She would have thought they'd be at the top of Robin's list.

Robin cleared her throat. "Yeah . . . um, as far as my family goes, let's wait until you're a little more adjusted to your, uh, new situation."

"But—"

"You'll want to put your best foot forward with them, right?"

Of course. If she and Robin were to eventually marry . . .

"If we leave it for a bit, you'll be less stressed out about it. As for today, all you have to do is practice Pam's signature. My task will be to send Pam's manager an email." Robin set down the pen and sighed. "Pam and I had planned to relax together today, go to a café and drown our sorrows in tea and coffee. We thought we'd be missing you and Jasper." Her eyes grew distant. "Things didn't turn out that way."

Margaret swallowed. Would Robin come to wish that Pam had returned and she'd stayed behind?

"Oh, wait!" Robin picked up the pen again. "I forgot something." She wrote *Go on a date!* "I'm looking forward to that one!"

Despite her inner turmoil, Margaret smiled. She had no idea what a date would entail, but she did know that an afternoon or evening out with Robin would be lovely. The evenings she'd sat at this table, wondering what Robin was doing upstairs, and sure that Robin would hate her if she knew . . . She'd never considered the possibility that Robin felt the same. But had she? When Robin had held out her arms to say good-bye, had she intended an innocent hug that would have meant more in her heart? Perhaps Margaret would ask her someday, when their future felt more secure than it did now.

"Are you ready for a sandwich?" Robin asked.

"I'll make it. What would you like?"

"I think there's ham. But I can make them."

"No." Margaret pushed back her chair. "I have to do something."

"Okay. If you think you'll be all right on your own, I'll go get today's newspaper from the corner store. It will only take me five minutes."

Margaret's stomach fluttered. Heavens, if being alone for five minutes frightened her, how would she cope when Robin was at university all day! She forced a smile. "I'll be all right."

Robin stood and walked toward the hallway, then spun around. "Oh, there is one other thing." Motioning for Margaret to follow her, she led her to the drawing room. "What are we going to do with that?" She pointed at the rhyme book, which still lay on the rug. "Pam and I planned to destroy it." She paused. "But maybe we should hang onto it for a couple of full moons, in case you change your mind. Once you're sure, we'll burn it."

Margaret imagined the book screaming. She shuddered and gripped Robin's arm. "Can you think of a reason we shouldn't destroy it?"

Robin blew out some air. "Well . . ."

"What?"

"We don't know if you'll suffer any ill effects from being in this time for months—years. We might want to try to send you back, if you do."

Margaret leaned into her and impetuously kissed her cheek. She'd learned that Robin saw a potential disaster around every corner, to the point that she'd been terrified of straying far from the guest house in 1910. "If that happens, I would rather suffer here with you, than return to a life without you." Her resolve hardened when she felt Robin's arm slip around her shoulders. "Let's destroy the book today."

Robin twisted toward her. "Are you sure?"

Yes. Otherwise every setback, every tear shed in grief for her family and friends, every moment of frustration, could have her turning the pages to that wretched rhyme. Oh, how she'd regret reading it when she arrived back in 1910, even if Robin returned with her. Robin's place—their place—was here. "Yes, Robin. I'm sure."

MARGARET STOOD IN front of the drawing room's fireplace and listened to the fire roar and pop as its flames leaped higher. She twisted to reach for the poker, then tutted. Robin was holding it, and it wouldn't have been where Margaret expected it to be, anyway. This wasn't *her* drawing room—yet. "May I have the poker," she murmured.

Gazing into the fire, Robin held it out to her.

Margaret took it and poked at the wood. "We can do it now."

Robin lifted the moon rhymes book from the chair and turned to Margaret. "Are you absolutely sure? You're probably in shock. You've lost so much. Maybe we should wait."

She met Robin's eyes. "I know what I'm losing. I've explained why I won't read the rhyme." When Robin didn't move, Margaret reminded herself that she wasn't the only one affected by this decision. Was she urging Robin to burn the book to remove the choice of sending her back to 1910? "If you'd rather wait . . . if you'd feel more comfortable knowing we can use the rhyme, then we'll wait."

"I'm thinking about why we might want to try to send you back. What if something goes wrong when you try to act as Pam? What if you find it too difficult to adjust?" Robin swallowed. "What if you decide you don't want to be with me?"

Margaret couldn't imagine being without Robin. Recklessly kissing her before they were all sent to 1910, meeting with Robin at the guest house, planning to break her engagement and enter a nunnery . . . A woman of her time, Robin couldn't appreciate the depth of the love that had compelled Margaret to turn her back on the norms of *her* time, risk ruin, and plan to bitterly disappoint her family. If anything, Robin would decide that she'd rather marry a woman from this time period. "You said you would be my family, no matter what happens between us."

Robin nodded. "I promise."

Then she would always be a part of Robin's life; Robin took her responsibilities seriously and would never renege on such a vow. Margaret watched the dancing flames reflected in Robin's eyes. "I don't want to go back. From what you've told me about Pam and Jasper's life, I doubt Pam wants to come back, and she has the book, if that's not the case. If we're truly committed to a life together, then no matter what happens, we'll never have need of the rhyme. The book in your hands is dangerous. We should destroy it. I want us to destroy it. But I will leave the timing to you."

Robin blinked at her, then looked down at the book. Margaret watched her face and wondered what was running through her mind, then stepped back when Robin suddenly opened the book and tossed it facedown onto the flames. The fire hissed; the book's cover curled; the rhyme's words travelled up the chimney and into the sky, forever lost.

They stood in silence until only black ashes remained, then turned to each other and embraced. Margaret rested her head on the shoulder of the woman she loved, the woman she now depended on for everything.

What have I done?

Chapter Four

ROBIN PULLED HER PHONE FROM HER jacket pocket as she strode from the classroom. Last night she'd phoned the landline from her cell several times so Margaret could see its number and *Robin* on the display. She should pick up.

After three rings, she did. "Hello?"

"It's me. How are you? Is everything all right?"

"Yes," Margaret replied. "I'm reading."

"Not Dickens, I hope." Robin smiled when Margaret chuckled.

"No. Yesterday's newspaper." She paused. "I have questions."

"I'd be very surprised if you didn't. Do you want to tell me one or two, just to give me an idea of how difficult they'll be?"

"I don't have the list with me. Let me see . . . sunscreen, HST, airports, dog fashion shows, blogs, international space station, hacker, colon cleansing—"

"Um, we might not get to everything tonight. We'll have to prioritize. You can put that last one at the bottom of the list."

"All right. There's more, but that's all I remember."

Jesus, how many were there? "You can keep a running list. We'll work our way through everything eventually." Though if they never reached colon cleansing, oh well. "We have time."

"Yes, we do."

Robin's eyes filled with tears. God, she was an emotional wreck. She'd almost broken down in class when she'd thought about phoning Pam at work to see if she could remember whether they needed bread. "I don't suppose you know if we need bread."

"Yes, we do. I had a look in the pantry and all the kitchen cupboards when I was deciding what to make us for dinner."

"You don't have to make dinner."

"I want to. Will you still be home around 4:30?"

"Yes, but—" No, she'd let Margaret do it. If she were in Margaret's shoes, she'd want to feel useful and keep herself busy to hold the panic at bay. "I have to go. I want to go to the library before my next class. I'll look forward to dinner, and seeing you. You know how to phone me, right?"

"Yes. But I'll be all right. I'll look forward to seeing you, too."

Robin's throat tightened. Jesus! "Bye, Margaret."

"Good-bye."

Blinking back tears, Robin hung up and checked Pam's email. Her heart pounded. Pam's manager had replied to the email Robin had sent yesterday afternoon. She held her breath as she pulled it up:

My god, Pam, talk about leaving me in the lurch. I'm peeved and envious! I thought the guy at Brenda's party was engaged, but I'm not surprised. The two of you were obviously smitten with each other. His fiancée (I guess that's ex-fiancée now LOL) must hate your guts—nope, Margaret didn't—but when she calms down, she'll probably be grateful they didn't make it to the altar. Anyway, things are slow, so I can't be too miffed, especially since you hardly ever take vacation. See you in a few days. Sue.

Robin slowly exhaled. So far, so good. But how would the resignation letter go down, especially when Pam didn't deliver it in person and couldn't be reached? If someone reported her missing, she and Margaret would be in deep trouble. They shouldn't have burned the book. Then again, they couldn't have risked using it, not when they had no idea where Margaret—maybe both of them—would end up. If only Pam had returned with them!

Hmm, maybe she'd send another email before the resignation letter. The photos of Jasper she'd found on Pam's phone might come in handy. Apparently Pam hadn't been able to resist taking them that day they'd golfed, and had failed to mention them to Robin when they'd discussed taking photos of Margaret and Jasper in their period clothing. She'd tease Pam about it, if Pam were here. *Jesus!* Robin blinked away another tear.

"Robin!"

She spun around and saw Cathy striding toward her.

"I feel like I haven't seen you in a month! What are you doing later?" Cathy frowned. "Did you do something to your hair?"

Robin's hand came up to touch her hair. "Nope." When she had a minute, she'd have to call Steve and see if he could squeeze her in later in the week for a haircut.

"It's just that—your hair's growing awfully fast." Cathy's eyes narrowed. "Or maybe it isn't. Like I said, I haven't seen you for a while, have I?" She sounded accusatory. "When's your last class? Let's grab a tea."

"I can't." Robin turned off her phone and slid it into her pocket.

"Robin! What the fuck is going on with you?"

She shrugged. "I have things to do."

Cathy gave her a long look. "Don't bullshit me. What's going on? If I didn't see you around here occasionally, I'd wonder if you'd dropped off the face of the earth. When's the last time we got together? Are you pissed at me or something?"

Robin's mind raced. Maybe now would be a good time to start spinning the yarns. "Okay, okay," she sighed, "I'm seeing someone."

"I knew it!" Cathy smiled as her hands went to her hips. "Who is she? When do I get to meet her?"

"Her name's Margaret. You'll meet her soon."

"Did you meet her on the Net?"

"No."

Cathy's brow furrowed. "Oh. I figured you were holed up at home chatting with someone. Where did you meet?"

"Why don't we tell you when we see you?" After they'd worked out that part of their story. Time to change the subject. "Margaret's not the only reason I've been distracted. Pam ran off with some guy."

Cathy's mouth dropped open. "What? What do you mean?"

"She took some guy to a party a couple of weeks ago, one of her mother's friend's sons, I think. They hit it off—in a big way. When he went back to, um . . ." she hadn't specified a location in her email to Pam's manager " . . . BC, she went with him, planning to stay for a few days. But I got an email from her last night, and it sounds like she's not coming back."

"Are you serious?"

"You want to hear the worst part? He was engaged."

"Holy shit!" Cathy chortled. "What are you going to do? It's her house."

"Yeah," Robin said with a sigh. "I don't know yet. I mean, she's not kicking me out or anything, but he's in . . ." Jesus, what did he say at the party? Pam had said they'd told the truth when it made sense. " . . . investments, and he's leaving for a job in, um . . ." *Think!* " . . . London—London, England—and it sounds like she's going with him. So I don't think she'll be coming back anytime soon."

Cathy shook her head. "You know, I'm not really surprised."

"No?"

"Come on, it's Pam. She's always been into that 'Prince Charming will come and sweep me off my feet one day' bullshit. And this is happening more and more these days. One of my sister's friends flew to Calgary to meet someone she'd chatted with on the Net. They got married while she was out there and she never came back! At least Pam had actually met the guy before she fell for him."

This was turning out to be easier than Robin had expected, but Cathy wouldn't have reported Pam missing, anyway. Pam's employer was the real problem.

"You can't go back to your mom's," Cathy said.

"I know. I'm hoping she won't want to sell the house right away."

"I guess she wasn't thinking about you when she decided to run off—not that I'd expect her to."

Tears threatened. Robin clenched her hands and dug her fingernails into her palms. Pam *had* thought of her, and Margaret. She'd dropped them in it, but she'd given them a priceless gift: the chance at a life together, and so much more for Margaret. God, she hoped Pam hadn't regretted her decision to stay, that she'd been happy with Jasper and felt it all worth it in the end. Robin would try to find out what had happened to her, when she could think of Pam without dissolving into tears. *Shit!*

"Hey." Cathy rubbed her arm. "This is why you need to talk to your friends, not hide from them."

Robin wiped her eyes and forced a smile. "I'll be okay. It just came out of the blue, that's all. I know I'm worrying for nothing. Pam will do right by me. She got me out of my mom's place. She won't do anything that'll force me back."

"You can't go back," Cathy said sternly. "And I agree about Pam. She'll probably hold off on selling the house until you've graduated, or at least until you've found somewhere else to live that doesn't include your mother. So stop being a worrywart. You always expect the worst."

"I'll miss her."

Cathy's voice softened. "I know. I'm sure she'll miss you, too. When I said she wasn't thinking of you, I didn't mean because she doesn't care. I meant that she's focused on the boyfriend." She nudged Robin's arm. "And *you* have a girlfriend, so it's not all doom and gloom. When did you say I'd get to meet her?"

"I don't know, um—"

"Friday?"

"No."

"Next week, then! Otherwise I'll start to wonder if she's a blow-up doll."

Despite her melancholy, Robin laughed. "Jesus, Cathy."

"Well, come on. You've hibernated enough. Time to get some air. Next Friday."

Would Margaret be ready by then? If she wasn't, the worst that could happen was that Cathy would think her weird. Nobody would ever wonder if Margaret was from the past. "Okay."

Cathy smiled. "Great! Let's invite Debbie and Francine along. They've also been wondering what the hell's happened to you."

"No, let's keep it to just us. Margaret's shy. I don't want her to be uncomfortable."

"Okay." Cathy's eyes glinted mischievously. "I'll try not to interrogate her."

"You'd better not."

"Ooh. Protective."

Yes. Very. "What about you? Anyone on your radar?"

Cathy's eyes grew wary. "I'm still not ready after Jan. Don't say anything."

Like, Jan was a jerk and good riddance? "I won't. Anyway, I should get to the library."

"I'm glad I ran into you. I know we've chatted on the phone, but it's not the same, and with Pam taking off on you . . . don't try to deal with everything yourself like you usually do, okay?"

Okay . . . um, I need to get someone from 1910 into the system. Can you help with that? Robin chuckled to herself. "I'll try not to."

So, Margaret wasn't a secret anymore, Robin mused as they said good-bye and parted ways. The year 2010—the present—was beginning to claim her.

PAM TRIED NOT to gape as she accepted Jasper's supporting hand and climbed off the carriage. She'd gathered that Oliver's family was well off, but hadn't expected the perfectly landscaped and expansive grounds—the ride from the gates to the house had taken forever, and "house" was inadequate. She was standing in front of a freaking mansion! But—she wrinkled her nose. Would she eventually grow used to the smell? At least horse manure didn't blacken her lungs.

A young man in a dark suit descended the front steps and nodded to Oliver. "The black trunk should go into the guest room nearest to Doris's," Oliver said. He turned to Pam and Jasper. "Shall we?"

Pam almost gasped when she stepped into the entrance hall. The chandelier, the winding staircase leading to the second floor, the beautiful mirrors . . . she needed a fan!

Another man in a dark suit accepted their hats with a murmured, "Thank you," then Oliver led them into a drawing room about four times the size of Margaret's. In one corner, a woman sat absorbed in a book, her brow furrowed. Oliver's lips compressed into a thin line. "Get your nose out of that book, Doris! We have guests!"

Doris jumped and looked up with an abrupt, "Oh!" She snapped the book shut and set it on the small round table next to her, then stood and smoothed her skirt.

"Jasper, you've met my sister, I believe."

"I've only had the pleasure once." Jasper accepted Doris's hand and brushed it with his lips.

"And this is Miss Margaret Wilton." Oliver turned to Pam and beckoned her forward. "My sister, Miss Doris Pembleton."

Pam inclined her head. "Pleased to meet you."

Doris shifted her attention to Pam. Her brows drew together. After a moment's hesitation, she mumbled, "And you."

Hmm, was Doris not pleased to be saddled with the runaway fiancée of her brother's friend? Maybe she'd relished having the house to herself—with who knew how many servants—while her parents were away.

"Doris fancies herself something of an intellectual," Oliver said with an indulgent smile.

Doris's face flushed. God, Pam hoped Oliver wasn't a chauvinistic asshole. She could take men treating her as if she was wrapped in cotton wool—in fact, she quite liked it—and she wouldn't mind playing the good little housewife to Jasper and maybe going to university to get a degree she'd never use. But she wouldn't be able to bear the company of a man who talked down to her because she was a woman.

"Would you like tea?" Doris asked.

Pam nodded. "That would be lovely."

"I'll ask Bella for sandwiches and cake, too." Doris strode from the room.

Oliver stared after her and shook his head. "She could have rung for Bella."

Pam had the distinct impression that Doris had wanted to get away before she said something she'd regret.

"Please sit down, Margaret."

Huh? Oh, Margaret! "Thank you." Pam lowered herself into a chair.

"I must say, I wasn't entirely surprised when you told me about your decision, or your father's reaction to it." Oliver dropped into the chair vacated by Doris; Jasper followed his lead and sat in the chair next to Pam. "You spoke about cabinetmaking back in our schooldays, but when you went into investments, I thought you'd abandoned the idea. I'm glad to see that you hadn't. And you, Margaret, leaving your family to support Jasper." He formed a steeple with his fingers and studied Pam. "I can understand why Jasper wants you as his wife. You're as beautiful as Jasper described you. In fact, he didn't do you justice."

Pam giggled. "Thank you, Oliver." That crack about Doris? Forgiven!

"What are your plans, Jasper? You and Margaret are welcome to stay with us as long as you like, but I assume you're eager to find a home and marry."

Jasper nodded. Pam listened while he and Oliver discussed the real estate market and suitable neighbourhoods, noting with interest that Jasper's flight from Toronto hadn't left him destitute—far from it. He may not have wanted to be an investment banker for life, but it sounded as if he had a flair for it. Would they end up living on an estate like this one? Pam would be happy with a house connected to an electrical grid. If she had to guess, this room was illuminated by gaslights.

A servant—Bella, Pam presumed—carried in a tray laden with tea, sandwiches, and cakes. Pam felt like royalty when Bella poured her tea and served her sandwiches on a china plate. She laid the starched cloth napkin Bella offered her on her lap, and reminded herself that a lady wouldn't suck down her sandwiches like a Hoover.

Doris returned and accepted tea and sandwiches from Bella. Jasper and Oliver did the same, then resumed their conversation. Pam smiled when she caught Doris looking at her, then frowned when Doris quickly looked away. A minute later, Pam caught Doris eyeing her again. Freaking hell, Doris wasn't another closet lesbian, was she? Were they everywhere in this time period? No, Doris looked pissed, not interested.

After polishing off two pieces of cake and sitting quietly for half an hour while Jasper and Oliver chatted—Doris was sitting too far away to converse with her—Pam's eyelids drooped; sleep hadn't come easily on the train. She snapped awake when Jasper patted her arm.

"Perhaps it's time to let the ladies become better acquainted," he said. "Will we dine together tonight?"

Oliver turned to Doris. "Why don't you and Margaret come round to us about 6:30? That will give Margaret time to settle in. Hortense is eager to meet her, and assumed we'd host dinner tonight."

Hortense? He'd married a woman named Hortense? Pam imagined a very long face and blinkers.

Doris nodded. "We'll do that, Oliver."

Jasper and Oliver rose. Since Doris remained seated, Pam did too. "See you later," Jasper murmured to Pam. Oliver nodded as he passed her.

The room was suddenly quiet. Bella hovered in the doorway. "Would you like more tea?"

"No, thank you," Pam said.

"Why don't you show Miss Wilton to her room?" Doris suggested. "You have time for a short nap," she said to Pam.

So much for getting acquainted. "I would like to freshen up and unpack a few items," Pam admitted.

"If you'll follow me," Bella said.

As she left the drawing room, Pam could feel Doris's eyes on her. She followed Bella up the winding staircase and into a bright and spacious room that instantly perked her up.

"I hope this is satisfactory."

"What?" Pam turned to Bella. "Oh, yes, quite satisfactory. Thank you."

Bella nodded, turned away, and strode down the hall. Pam waited until Bella started down the stairs, then walked to the middle of the room and twirled once. She loved the feel of the old house. The panelling, the richly coloured rug, the antique furnishings, the quilt covering the bed—even the air felt different. It had a stillness, or perhaps quietness, that one could never experience in a modern city. She was bound to miss the comforts of home, but despite the conveniences that eased daily life and having everything at her fingertips, she'd never felt at peace. Her harried life had led to her frequent trips to Jake's and consequently to this time period, where she wouldn't have to consciously slow down the day's pace through meditation.

At home, she'd be at work bitching about something or someone, rushing around doing errands on her lunch hour, racing home to do her share of the housework, squeezing in a friend for coffee, dragging herself out on the weekend to do groceries and other scintillating activities, feeling guilty for not exercising, and writing cheques to charities because she couldn't donate time. She had no idea how her friends with kids coped—on three hours of sleep, maybe? They'd want to kill her if they could see her standing in the middle of this bedroom, contemplating lying down for an hour or two before climbing into a carriage and riding off for a god-knows-how-many course meal. Moving to the window, Pam gazed at the manicured lawn that stretched out as far as she could see. Of course, being loaded helped.

She turned away from the window and eyed the black trunk on the floor near what she presumed was the closet door. Was she expected to change for dinner? Her time in the Bainbridge guest house and on the train hadn't taught her the rules. She and Jasper had focused on rehearsing her background as Margaret Wilton. She hadn't thought to ask him about life as a cultured lady. If she was expected to arrive at Oliver's in a different dress, she didn't have many to choose from. If Margaret hadn't taken her out shopping for a dress for the Halloween Ball, she'd have only the dress on her back and the one that Jasper had bought that sorta, kinda fit her. She planned to wear the latter one tomorrow, when she'd venture into town to shop for more clothes.

Crouching in front of the trunk, she lifted its lid. Even though she'd pilfered several items from the guest house, such as the hairbrush Margaret had left behind after helping Pam dress for her first day out in 1910, the trunk was only half full. Pam rummaged around inside it. Now where was that—

She tensed when moving aside one of the folded dresses revealed the moon rhymes book. Was this the same book that had made its way to Mathers Mystic Marketplace in 2010? If so, had one of her descendants carried it to Toronto? What would happen if Pam were to write a note next to the rhyme on page 17? Had one of those coffee stains obscured the words, *To myself in 2010: make up the guest bedroom*?

If she were to write a note, what would she say? Would she warn against reading the rhyme? No! So there was no point in writing anything, and she wouldn't dare turn to page 17, anyway. The only reason she was hanging onto the book, rather than destroying it, was because it *could* be the book she'd held in 2010. Oh god, she felt the onset of one of those "Am I not doing something because I know it didn't happen that way in the future, or because I wouldn't have done it anyway and that's why it didn't happen in the future?" headaches.

Had Robin and Margaret destroyed their book—or rather, would they? Where were they now? Suspended in time? Pam could only think of them in the present tense. She couldn't grasp that Robin hadn't been born yet, and didn't even want to contemplate what state Margaret might be in. Nope, as far as she was concerned, they were in Toronto—its 2010 incarnation—and she'd moved to Halifax to be with her future husband. Someday the fact that she'd never see

Robin again would catch up to her, when she was settled enough, and felt safe enough, to let her guard down and have one of those gut-wrenching cries that made her look as if she'd just had plastic surgery.

Okay, she'd better hang the dress Jasper had bought her. If she didn't have to wear it later, she'd need it tomorrow. She removed it from the trunk, draped it over her arm, turned and—gasped. The dress slid to the floor.

Doris stared at her from the doorway. "I'm sorry. I didn't mean to frighten you."

Pam took a moment to calm herself. "It's all right. You surprised me, that's all." How long had she been there?

Doris strode in and picked up the dress. "I thought I'd make sure Bella had put you into the right room." She opened the closet, drew out a hanger, and hung the dress. As she moved away from the closet, she glanced down at the trunk. "You didn't bring much with you."

Could she see the book? Not that it mattered; Doris wouldn't know the power of page 17. "I left in a bit of a hurry," Pam said.

"I can imagine. Oliver didn't tell me much. He never does. But I gathered that Jasper's announcement that he was turning his back on the family business wasn't well received."

"No."

"I wonder why he didn't wait until after you were married. Surely he must have known what an awkward position his father's wrath would place you in—having to choose between him and remaining in Toronto." Doris studied Pam with unreadable eyes. "Was the situation so bad that he couldn't have kept his secret until the summer? Why did you decide to come here, rather than marrying sooner in Toronto?"

The hairs on the back of Pam's neck stood up. Was Doris merely curious? Fortunately she had a story ready. "I encouraged Jasper to speak to his father." Pam forced a smile she hoped looked genuine. "Truth be told, he didn't need much encouragement. Once he knew he had my support, he did something he should have done years ago, and I was happy for him! I want him to be himself, to do what the universe—" Oops, she didn't want Doris to search the trunk for voodoo dolls. "What God wants him to do." Jesus. "What we didn't anticipate was his father's reaction. We knew he'd be upset, but we didn't expect him to spread vicious rumours about us that would leave us no choice *but* to say good-bye to Toronto."

Doris's eyes widened. "What types of rumours?" she breathed.

Pam cleared her throat. "Rumours I wouldn't dare repeat." She lowered her voice and leaned forward. "They involve a future child."

Doris's brows shot up.

"Of course, the rumours aren't true." Pam straightened and clasped her hands across her stomach, trying to appear virtuous. Unfortunately, her position drew Doris's eyes to her hands.

"You don't have an engagement ring."

"I do. A beautiful diamond ring that's being adjusted at the jewellers—in Toronto." She sighed. "So you can appreciate how quickly we wanted to leave the vicious rumours behind us. Jasper said the first thing he'll do is buy me another one." Time to change the subject. "As you've noticed, the ring isn't the only item we left behind. I have three dresses with me, and one is only suitable for formal occasions. If I'm expected to change for dinner—"

Doris shook her head. "Oh no, don't worry about that. We're only going to Oliver's. But we must remedy the state of your wardrobe as quickly as we can. Let's go into town tomorrow. I'll introduce you to my dressmaker and take you to the best shops."

So, the ice queen was melting. "That would be lovely." But she had no money! She'd have to get Jasper alone at Oliver's and ask him to fork over some cash. The prospect of having to ask Jasper for money every time she needed something didn't sit well with Pam. She was used to taking care of herself. Would Margaret have had money of her own? Had she received an allowance from her father? If Pam decided that she wanted to work, would Jasper protest? What careers would be open to her—truly open, not grudgingly open? The 1910 fairy tale suddenly lost some of its sparkle. She hadn't thought much about life here beyond being with Jasper. What would she do with herself?

"We can make a day of it," Doris said. "I'll have Robert bring the carriage around about 9:00. I'll show you some of the city in the morning. After lunch we'll visit the shops." She pressed her hands together. "Oh, and you'll want to meet the neighbourhood wives and other young ladies. I'll see who's available for tea the day after next."

Pam nodded. "Thank you."

"Anyway, I'll leave you to your nap. Ring for Bella if you need anything."

"Thank you," Pam said again. With a sinking heart, she watched Doris leave. She was grateful that Doris was willing to take her under her wing, but when would she see Jasper?

Chapter Five

ROBIN INHALED AS SHE SHRUGGED OFF her jacket and hung it in the closet. God, she wasn't used to this, coming home to a cooked meal and a table laid as if they'd be dining with guests. She left her knapsack on the floor near the boot mat and went into the kitchen.

Margaret was leaning against the kitchen counter; she lowered the newspaper and smiled, and Robin's heart leaped. As she had every time she'd stepped into the kitchen this week upon returning home, she wanted to go to Margaret and kiss her full on the lips. But how would Margaret react? *Robin, be patient. Don't blow it.* Sage advice, but she'd have to risk a passionate kiss sometime. "Sorry I'm a little late. Steve was running behind."

Margaret lifted an eyebrow. "You must be relieved that your hair is now a quarter of an inch long, rather than half an inch."

Robin opened her mouth to retort, then noticed Margaret's bright eyes. Two could play at this game. "I've scheduled you an appointment. He'll cut your hair on Saturday."

Margaret gaped. "What?"

"Trust me, you'll feel much better without all that hair."

"But—my hair—" Margaret sputtered. Then her eyes narrowed. "You're teasing."

"Guilty as charged," Robin admitted, not wanting to unduly alarm her. Margaret seemed in good spirits now, but that hadn't been the case last night, when she'd read a newspaper article about a man who reminded her of her father. Again, Robin fought the desire to sweep Margaret into her arms and give her much more than a friendly and supportive hug. "You have beautiful hair, Margaret."

Margaret's face flushed. "Thank you."

Not wanting to offend, Robin carefully chose her next words. "Not many of today's women wear their hair as long as you do. If you ever decide that you do want to cut your hair—not as short as mine," she said with a laugh, "but shorter—just say."

"The thought has crossed my mind," Margaret said, to Robin's surprise. "When I read the Fashion section of the newspaper, I take note of the hairstyles women wear in the advertisements and photos. Perhaps I will consider cutting mine."

Women actually paid attention to that stuff? Wow.

"And I neglected to say that I quite like your hairstyle—on you." Margaret folded the newspaper and handed it to Robin. "Dinner will be ready soon. I've made spaghetti. I hope it's up to your standards."

"The sauce smells great."

"Thank you," Margaret murmured again. "I've signed the resignation letter. Do you want to see?"

Robin's stomach fluttered as she nodded. Tomorrow she'd personally hand the letter to Pam's manager. She wanted to see Sue's reaction, not try to divine it from an email, though if Sue appeared suspicious, Robin didn't know what she'd do. Suddenly leaving Toronto with Margaret would make them look guilty. She lifted the newspaper. "Have you finished with this?" At Margaret's answering nod, she added the newspaper to the recycling pile, then followed her up to the study.

Margaret lifted a paper from the desk. "I hope it's adequate. I had to try a few times." She tipped her head toward the crumpled papers she'd tossed into the waste bin.

"We can always print off more." Robin peered at the signature, then placed the resignation letter on the desk, next to the copy of a bank deposit record that contained Pam's signature. She looked from one to the other. "That's pretty damn good. Sue's not going to examine the signature with a magnifying glass."

Margaret stood next to her and stared down at the two documents. "Is there no other way? I feel as if we're doing something criminal."

She'd said the same when Robin had shown her the photos of Pam and Jasper out golfing—altered, of course, to make it appear that they were at a resort, not a city golf course. "I know how you feel. I'll probably look guilty as sin when I drop in at Pam's work tomorrow. But we have to do this, otherwise her work will probably report her missing and we'll have police poking around here. That's the last thing we want."

"Perhaps we shouldn't have burned the book," Margaret said quietly.

"Are you saying that because you want to return to your time, or—"

"No. I don't want you to be in trouble with the police."

Robin slipped her arm around Margaret's shoulders, squeezed her, and kissed her cheek. "Don't worry about me." She was more worried about Margaret and her lack of an official identity. Robin smiled when she felt Margaret's arm around her waist. "How many topics did you add to your list today?"

"Mmm, around seventeen."

"Only seventeen? Soon you'll be down to one or two. I have to work on an assignment tonight, but we'll try to get through a couple more. Did you look at the course schedules I brought home, or the ones I printed last night?"

Margaret shook her head.

"Maybe you can have a look at them tomorrow."

"I'll try," Margaret said, but her voice lacked enthusiasm. She was probably worried about participating in a class on her own.

Robin twisted to look at her. "I know taking a class feels daunting, but it won't feel as intimidating in two months." Her heart skipped a beat when she met Margaret's gorgeous eyes. How would Margaret react if she leaned in and kissed her right now?

When Margaret leaned into *her*, Robin thought *she* was about to be kissed, but Margaret murmured, "I should check the sauce," and fled the room.

Robin stared after her. Margaret had wanted to kiss her; she'd stake her life on it! *Be patient. Don't blow it.* Margaret had managed to kiss her in the bedroom that night, but she'd thought they'd never see each other again. Still, she had it in her to initiate a kiss; it was just a matter of time. Pam was right. Patience. Margaret was worth it.

ROBIN FORCED A smile when Sue strode into the reception area and shook her head. "Oh god, do I want to know?" She beckoned for Robin to follow her and led her into an office with a *Susan Burke* nameplate to the right of its door. "Sit down," Sue said, plunking into her own chair.

"It's okay, I'm not staying long," Robin said, too keyed up to sit. She swung her knapsack off her back, unzipped a side pocket, and pulled out the resignation letter.

Sue accepted it with a sigh. "I've been half expecting this." Robin held her breath as Sue tore open the envelope, unfolded the letter, and read it. "When did you get this?" she asked, her eyes still on the letter. "Why didn't Pam bring it?"

"She's already in England. I had to meet her at Pearson last night to pick up the letter and talk about the house and stuff. They only had a couple of hours before their connecting flight."

"Christ." Sue dropped the letter onto her desk. "Like I said, I half expected it. The moment I got that first email, I—" She waved in the direction of the door. "Brenda! Get in here!"

Brenda stepped into the office. Sue held up the letter. "You were right. She's not coming back."

"I told you! I knew at my party the two of them were meant for each other. Fiancée, schmiancée. That marriage was doomed to never take place."

"She's in England."

"England!" Brenda squealed. "Lucky bitch!" She turned to Robin. "When's she coming back?"

Robin had met Brenda several times, at the house and the odd time Pam had dragged her to a social event with her work colleagues. She'd also talked to Sue at a couple of those. "She's not. Jasper's starting a job there, and she decided to go with him. Forget *her* job." Robin frowned. "Forget her friends."

The other two women shook their heads and tutted. "Trust Pam," Sue muttered.

"But can you blame her?" Brenda pressed her hand against her chest. "I can't. I'd probably do the same in her position."

"I'm not sure I'd be so quick to throw my life away for someone else's," Sue said.

"You saw them at the party. They couldn't keep their hands off each other on the balcony."

Really? Pam had apparently left out an important detail when she'd told Robin about the party.

"Not that I was spying on them or anything. I just happened to be passing by the balcony doors when—well, anyway. Robin, what's going to happen to you?" Brenda asked.

Robin knew she meant the house. "Well, she's not selling the house immediately, so maybe she is hedging her bets a little."

"Tell her that if she changes her mind in the next month or so, she can have her job back." Sue waved a finger. "After that, no guarantees."

"I'll tell her."

"And tell her to email us now and then." Brenda's eyes grew misty. "I'll miss her."

Sue barked a laugh. "I'm sure she's not missing us. She's too busy with Mr. Right."

Robin smiled and shrugged on her knapsack. "Well, I should go. Sorry to be the bearer of bad news."

"Hey, it's not your fault," Sue said. "Take care."

"Bye," Brenda murmured as Robin left the office.

"Bye," Robin said over her shoulder. Brenda and Sue had already forgotten about her; they were chattering about Pam's resignation and her new life in England. Fighting the urge to run, Robin strode down the corridor, waved good-bye to the receptionist, and swung open the company's glass door. Fortunately the elevator didn't take long to arrive.

A minute later, she stood on the sidewalk. Her heart thumped when a police cruiser drove past. As Margaret had said when she'd forged Pam's signature, Robin felt like a criminal. Strictly speaking, she and Margaret *were* criminals. They hadn't done away with Pam, but they were impersonating her, right?

At least Pam's employer was satisfied for now, and it would probably remain that way. When Robin had left her jobs, everyone had always tearfully promised to stay in touch, but that was the last she'd spoken to any of them. For all she knew, they were all dead. So, okay, she mentally ticked off *Pam's work*, but that had been the easy part. Now the hard part: getting Margaret out into 2010. Then the really hard part: introducing Margaret to her family. Maybe Robin shouldn't even consider passionately kissing Margaret. After

Margaret met her mother, she'd want nothing more to do with her. She'd spend all her time searching for a copy of the rhyme book, as Pam and Jasper had in 1910.

Chapter Six

LOOKING FORWARD TO AN ENTIRE DAY with Robin, Margaret examined herself in the bathroom mirror one last time. As she was brushing her hair in the bedroom after showering and dressing, she'd heard Robin rise, and a peek into Robin's bedroom—or was it still Pam's?—on her way to the bathroom had confirmed that Robin was up. She wished Robin's bedroom had a mirror, but what would Robin use it for? She didn't wear makeup, and a shake of her head after showering was the only attention her hair required.

Margaret descended the stairs, strode into the kitchen, and—oh! Robin was walking to the kitchen counter, and she wasn't dressed. She wore a t-shirt that came down past her hips, sweat pants, and . . . Margaret looked down . . . thick, fuzzy socks. When she lifted her head, Robin was leaning against the counter and staring at her with amused eyes. "They're more comfortable than slippers. Comfort's important. I'm glad you no longer wear those silly shoes that are too tight."

Her cheeks grew warm. She'd taken to padding around in a pair of old slippers Robin had handed to her one morning. Pam's, she presumed, and because they'd been worn many times, she didn't have to squeeze her feet into them. It wasn't that she didn't want to dress nicely for Robin, but she'd quickly learned that vain gestures, such as hobbling around in too-small pretty shoes, didn't impress her.

Robin turned back to the counter. "Tea?"

"Yes, please. Have you eaten?"

"No. I—"

Margaret moved to the pantry. "I'll—"

"No, sit. I can make my own breakfast, and yours. What would you like?"

"You've been at school all week."

"And you've been hard at work reading newspapers and cooking dinner." Robin chuckled. "And forging Pam's signature." She switched on the kettle and turned to Margaret. "You're almost through your first week here as a permanent resident. Given what you left behind, I wouldn't have been surprised if you'd spent the week moping. I'm proud of you."

Margaret swallowed. Robin's praise meant more to her than she could express. "I've had a few weepy moments," she felt compelled to confess. "Not because I don't want to be here. For those who aren't with me." Her voice quavered. When Robin held out her arms and stepped forward, Margaret didn't hesitate to meet her halfway. She wrapped her arms around Robin's neck and clung to her.

Robin's breasts pressed against her through the thin t-shirt; Margaret's fingers rested on skin, rather than on a shirt collar or sweatshirt. Despite her sudden bout of melancholy, desire stirred. She resisted the impulse to pull away, not wanting to deny herself for the sake of what was proper. Holding Robin like this, feeling Robin's arms around her and the warmth of her cheek, was most pleasant, evoking sensations she wanted to savour, not end. Her eyelids slid shut. "Did you sleep in these clothes?" she murmured dreamily.

Robin's cheek pushed against Margaret's; her chuckle vibrated under Margaret's fingers. Good Lord! What an impolite and—and improper question to ask! Where was her head? She tried to draw back and apologize, but Robin's arms wouldn't give an inch. "I don't wear the socks to bed." Robin paused. "Or the pants. I put the pants on for you."

"That was thoughtful of you," Margaret said faintly. Could Robin feel her racing heart? "You said you wear pyjamas."

"Sorry, I can see why I confused you. To me, 'pyjamas' means 'not a nightie.' When it's not too cold, I usually just sleep in a t-shirt and my undies. I wear proper pyjamas during winter. I wore them when I was sharing the bedroom with Pam, too."

"I see," Margaret breathed, sure her cheek must be scorching Robin's. Robin without pants . . . She'd seen her girlfriends in various

states of undress, but she'd never needed a fan. Robin, though . . .
If—when—if they decided to consummate their love, Margaret hoped
she wouldn't scuttle the experience by passing out when she beheld Robin's
nude . . . Oh, Lord! If Robin were to scoop her up into her arms and
carry her upstairs right now, Margaret's protests would be feeble.

"I should start breakfast," Robin said, to Margaret's relief—and
disappointment. "What do you want?"

Margaret opened her mouth to reply; it hung open when Robin's
lips pressed against her cheek and lingered. Robin finally stepped
back, then turned to the counter and lifted the lid from the teabag
jar. Margaret understood why: that moment in the study a few nights
ago when she'd fled the room. By immediately turning away, Robin
hadn't put her into the position of facing the same decision again.
She wanted to kiss Robin, but she was afraid of where it might lead.
Perhaps she was worrying for nothing and should trust herself more.
Robin's touch did have a way of banishing rational thought, but
Margaret fervently believed that she must be sure, must be ready,
or regret would win the day. "An egg, and a piece of toast with jam,
would be welcome."

Robin turned to her and smiled. "I'll miss that when you start
sounding like a 2010 native."

Margaret had no idea what she meant, but the remark didn't
sound derogatory.

"Do you want some hash browns? I'm making some for me."

She'd learned what those were during her first month in this time
period. "Since you're preparing them anyway, yes, please." Feeling
a bit at a loose end, Margaret sat at the kitchen table and graciously
accepted a cup of tea and her breakfast, even though she would have
preferred to cook her own breakfast, and Robin's. She silently said grace.

Robin sprinkled salt on her hash browns and forked a few into
her mouth. "Did you have a chance to look at the course schedules?"

Margaret nodded. "I've chosen a course."

Robin's eyes lit up. "Really?"

"Yes. Beginner sewing."

"Beginner sewing," Robin drawled. "Okay. It's a start."

Margaret's heart sank. "Do you want me to choose another one?"

"No, no. You're taking it to get yourself out there. It doesn't have to be anything serious."

Sewing *was* serious. "Do you know how to sew?"

"I can sew a button on, in a pinch. It wouldn't be pretty, but it would stay on."

"I can make clothes!"

Robin's brow furrowed. "Then why beginner sewing?"

"Because I'm familiar with it. I'm following your advice." But apparently she'd disappointed Robin. Not serious, indeed. Margaret's desire to take care of Robin was wrong-headed. Robin would rather she be out in the world participating in—what had Pam called them?—bitch sessions.

"You're right." Robin patted Margaret's hand. "I didn't mean to belittle you and your talents. I couldn't knit the clothes you made for me. I'll enjoy wearing them even more, now that you'll be here to see me in them."

Margaret grinned. Robin certainly knew how to appease!

"Don't be offended, but I hope you didn't choose the sewing course only because you're familiar with it. I suggested doing that so you won't be learning something completely new when you're worrying about interacting with people, but I'm probably being overprotective. If there was something else that appealed, but you decided against it because of what I said . . ."

Margaret shook her head. "I haven't used a modern sewing machine, so I will learn something new. Your advice was sound. I will feel more confident in a sewing class than I would in a computer class."

Robin sipped her tea. "You might not feel that way in a couple of months. I thought we'd spend some time in front of the computer tomorrow. I'd like to start teaching you how to use one."

"I would like that." While she'd gathered that workers often used computers to perform their duties, she also knew that people used them to accomplish household tasks, such as sending letters, conversing, and shopping. "But what about your schoolwork?"

"I can do homework later. We have to go grocery shopping, first. I say 'we,' because you're going with me."

A shiver of excitement ran up Margaret's spine. She dipped her toast in her egg's yolk and took a bite.

"The grocery store isn't far, so we'll walk there. I'll give you my phone again, but when we get there, we'll choose a spot to meet, in case we do get separated."

"May I draw up a list of items for dinners I'd like to prepare?"

"Sure."

She was quite looking forward to the outing. "Is it a big shop?"

"Yeah. It's a superstore. But don't panic. Like I said, we'll choose a meeting spot. It's a contained space, so as long as you don't leave the store without me, I'll eventually find you."

Then Margaret had nothing to worry about. She wouldn't dare step outside by herself, not yet.

"We should take our time walking the aisles. It will be a good learning experience." Robin popped the last of her toast into her mouth and chewed. "I usually hate grocery shopping, but this is going to be fun."

Wouldn't people wonder why Robin had to explain to a grown woman what should be common knowledge? "Will it be safe to speak freely?"

"We won't be shouting. And people are usually distracted, pushing their carts around and talking on their phones. Then there's the music . . ."

Carts? Music? It sounded like a carnival.

An hour later, she gazed in amazement at the large building Robin pointed to as they stood waiting for a light to change.

"You all right?" Robin asked.

Margaret nodded. Her second outing into 2010 hadn't intimidated her as much as the first, perhaps because she knew she was here to stay and was paying more attention to her surroundings. Rather than being frightened, she'd discovered that, while the illusion of change was great, not much was actually new. Strolling along a sidewalk in 2010 wasn't very different from strolling along one in 1910. Everything looked more modern, but was still recognizable, though occasionally a sight did surprise and bewilder her, such as the woman they'd passed with blue hair and a cattle nose ring.

The light changed and she crossed the road with Robin, her curiosity growing as she spotted people pushing metal carts—the grocery carts Robin had described, she presumed—into the building, which seemed to swallow them up behind a pair of glass windows. "They're doors,"

Robin said as they approached them. "They'll open automatically." And so they did! Worried that they'd squash her, Margaret hurried through them, then felt foolish when Robin chuckled. "They won't close on you," Robin said. "And if they do for some reason, they'll quickly open as soon as they touch you."

She'd rather not find out what they'd do, thank you very much! She glanced around and gathered that they were in some type of lobby area, not in the shop itself. Margaret watched as Robin pulled a cart from a long chain of them and dropped the bags she'd carried from home into the basket, then walked behind her as Robin steered the cart into the shop. The lights, music, clattering carts, people . . . no wonder Pam had resorted to meditation!

For the first fifteen minutes, Margaret followed Robin around in a daze, overwhelmed by the number of choices that faced them. There were dozens of varieties of something as simple as a potato. "What's an organic potato?" she murmured.

"Um, a potato that's been grown naturally," Robin replied.

How else would they be grown?

"Without pesticides."

That, she understood.

"And they're not genetically modified, but we haven't talked about genetics yet. I'll add it to our list."

Lord, even the potatoes were more sophisticated here. Her wonder at the number of choices only increased as Robin pushed the cart through the aisles. How did people decide what to buy? She felt paralyzed when Robin asked if she wanted biscuits and swept her arm toward the cookie and biscuit section that stretched from one end of an aisle to the other. There weren't just different flavours; there were twenty different choices for the exact same type of biscuit! Similar foods were often priced differently, and Margaret cringed at the prices. How could Robin afford to eat and feed *her*? "I can do without biscuits."

Robin frowned. "You snack on biscuits all the time, and you haven't said no to chocolate chip cookies."

"We have to talk about money." A topic that weighed on Margaret's mind as she ate Robin's food, wore Pam's clothes, and slept in Pam's house. Back in 1910, that would have been expected, if Robin was her husband. Here, women depending on their husbands seemed to be frowned upon, and Robin wasn't her husband. Margaret didn't know what Robin was—just that she loved her and hoped to eventually marry her. But Robin wouldn't be a husband, and Margaret didn't want to ask what Robin would expect of her. She was afraid of the answer.

"Don't worry about money," Robin said.

"You're taking care of me."

"Because I want to. And I'm not doing it alone." She smiled at Margaret's confusion. "You'll see. Now, what biscuits do you want?"

She chose the same ones they already had; perhaps that was how everyone did it. But how had they known what to choose the very first time? "I always buy what my mother did," Robin said when Margaret voiced the question. But how had her mother known? Something to ponder when she contemplated similar mysteries, such as "Who created God?"

By the time they reached the last aisle and Robin placed the final item in the cart, Margaret was exhausted. The number of cashiers amazed her, and she noted the modern cash registers with their computer screens—no surprise there. As Robin unloaded the cart by placing items on a moving belt, Margaret stayed out of the way and observed. Automation seemed to be the way of life here. God forbid that anyone had to push items along using their arms!

She almost slapped her ears when the cashier announced the total. It was half of what some people made in a year—where she came from. Robin pulled out her billfold and handed the cashier a plastic card, then hunched over a small machine and looked as if she were punching in a phone number, though Margaret knew she wasn't. She added another question to the ever-growing, seemingly endless list.

"Why did you bring bags when they have them here?" she asked Robin as they carried their groceries from the store.

"You have to pay for plastic bags. Remember we talked about the environment and landfill?"

"Oh, yes."

Robin turned to her. "So, what did you think about the store?"

"What surprises me most is that nobody talks to each other." It was the same out here. People strode by without so much as a glance. No smile, no, "Good morning," or, "Hello." Heads down, hands in pockets or holding a phone, and when someone did meet her eyes, they quickly looked away as if they'd committed a social gaffe.

"That's the big city for you. Nobody trusts anybody."

It must be lonely. How would she make friends when she felt brave enough to take that step? She whipped to her left when Robin grasped her arm. "Let me get some money," Robin said, pulling open a door and entering a small lobby. She stepped up to a machine—Margaret should have guessed—and plopped her bags on the floor. "This is an ATM. It pretty much does what a bank teller does."

Margaret's bags joined Robin's as she leaned in for a closer look. "This," Robin said, pulling a plastic card from her billfold, "is Pam's bank card. I used it to pay for the groceries, too. See? I'm not the only one taking care of you." She inserted the card into a slot, and it disappeared.

Margaret's hand went to her throat. "Oh my goodness!"

Robin's mouth turned up at the corners. "It's okay. That's supposed to happen."

"Why are you pressing those numbers? You did the same thing in the grocery shop."

"I'm entering what's called a PIN. Remember Pam's letter?"

She vaguely recalled mention of a number.

"You need the card and the PIN to access the bank account. Otherwise if you lose your card and someone finds it, they could use it to dip into your funds."

Dealing with an actual teller who knew you would solve that problem, she thought as she watched Robin grab the bills that emerged from the machine, then the card that slid back out. "Is everything automated?" Margaret asked. "Do you ever have to speak to another person?"

Robin chuckled. "Yes, you do, though I bet you could survive without ever having to deal with anyone in person—for the most part. I wonder if anyone's tried it." She bent down to pick up her bags.

"If everyone did it, that would be a quick end to the human race," Margaret pointed out as she slipped her fingers through her bags' handles.

Robin pushed the door open with her shoulder. "I don't know. You'd be surprised what you can order online."

Oh, dear. Margaret didn't want to think about it.

Chapter Seven

PAM MOISTENED HER DRY THROAT WITH some tea and surveyed the curious faces peering at her. Now she knew how prisoners must feel under the bright interrogation light. The well-to-do neighbourhood ladies, whom she now knew as Abigail, Rosalie, Charlotte, and Clara, had peppered her with questions, pausing only to daintily bite into finger sandwiches and sip their tea. Since they'd mainly asked about her and Jasper's flight from Toronto, their engagement, and their future plans, Pam had managed to flub her way through the answers. If they'd grilled her about her background, she might have confused the details she and Jasper had rehearsed. As it was, she'd almost had a heart attack when Rosalie said, "You must know my uncle." Then Rosalie's brow had furrowed and she'd added, "Oh, but he's been in England for several years now, so perhaps you don't." Pam's heart had stopped racing.

Doris had remained silent, not asking a single question, but every time Pam glanced her way, Doris was staring at her. Pam couldn't figure her out; Doris ran hot and cold. Yesterday they'd spent a lovely day shopping and chatting, but today Pam seemed to be *persona non grata* again. At first she'd thought Doris wanted to give everyone else a chance to get to know the new kid on the block, but those intense eyes . . .

Charlotte clapped her hands together. "Well, I just want to say that you've chosen right, coming to Halifax. We're glad to have you." Everyone smiled and nodded in agreement. "Now, how about a bit of embroidery?"

What?

"Oh, yes, that sounds lovely." Abigail lifted a burlap bag onto her lap, pulled out a wooden hoop, and handed it to Charlotte. "Here's yours."

"Thank you," Charlotte said.

Pam had wondered what was in the bag Abigail had carried into the drawing room. Out came more wooden hoops, fabric, cotton, scissors . . . Abigail must be the official carrier of the embroidery supplies.

Doris rose. "Mine's upstairs." She turned to Pam. "I'll bring down a hoop for you. But I don't think I have any fabric with the pattern traced—"

"I have plenty extra." Abigail beamed as she held out a piece of fabric to Pam. "Use this, Margaret. It's probably easier than you're used to, but I traced it for my daughter."

"I don't want to take your daughter's fabric." She didn't want any fabric! She hadn't embroidered since . . . ever!

"Nonsense. Take it. Take it!" Abigail thrust it toward her. "Go on, take it!"

Pam accepted it, worried that behind Abigail's smile was a crazed embroidery enthusiast who'd go berserk if Pam refused to participate. She examined the pattern of a dog, then lifted her head and watched closely as the other women mounted their fabric in their hoops. Okay, embroidery was sort of like sewing, right? All she had to do was follow the pattern. Cripes, she'd seen a man walk on the moon and knew about DNA. Surely she could embroider. How hard could it be?

She managed a sick smile when Doris returned and handed her a hoop, then congratulated herself for being an observant and quick learner when she attached her fabric to it without much trouble. Oh, wait. Where was the pattern? Shit. Fortunately everyone else was focused on their hoops, including laser-eyed Doris. Pam quickly loosened the hoop and shifted the fabric until the pattern was in the middle.

Clara had pushed a small round table to within everyone's reach and unrolled a cloth on it. Yikes, those needles looked big! Pam had never thought of embroidery needles as deadly weapons before, and patted herself on the back for not refusing Abigail's offer. She pulled one of the needles from the cloth and picked up some thread. Charlotte had split her thread, but Pam wasn't about to get fancy. She threaded the needle, grasped the hoop, pushed the needle through, and—*Fuck! Get your goddamn finger out of the way, already!* She curled the fingers on her left hand so they weren't dangling underneath the fabric and tried again. Okay, not bad, she'd done a stitch. Oh look, another one. She could get the hang of this!

Proud of herself, she managed to stitch what appeared to be part of the dog's ear. Maybe purple hadn't been the best colour choice. She stuck her needle through a point outside the pattern, then lifted her head to see if there was any brown thread, and caught Doris staring at her—again. Pam ignored her, but couldn't help glancing at her after she'd lifted brown thread from the table. Doris's eyes bored into her—again. Jesus. Pam sighed and looked down at her fabric. Okay, what was she supposed to do with the purple thread? Tie it off? She unthreaded the needle and tried, but . . . Oh, Charlotte was tying her thread using the needle. Pam decided to just let hers hang loose. She wasn't embroidering for a competition or a crafts shop or anything.

She started to stitch the outline of the dog's head, and after ten minutes of intense concentration, she surveyed her handiwork. Were the stitches supposed to zigzag like that? She snuck a peek at Abigail's work, and frowned at the elegant and smooth arcs. And the stitching . . . she wasn't simply sticking her needle in and pulling it out. Sometimes she wrapped the thread around the needle several times, or pushed the needle in underneath the fabric, or inserted it where it had just come out. Deflated, Pam gazed at her work with a critical eye and knew Abigail's daughter would embroider the skirt off her.

Charlotte and Clara chattered away as they stitched. Pam would have gladly joined in—if she could talk and embroider at the same time. Twenty minutes later, her heart leaped into her mouth when Abigail tucked her hoop down the side of her chair cushion, rose, and peered at Charlotte's work. "Lovely, dear," she murmured, and moved on to Clara's. Freaking hell! Inspection time. Pam gulped and tried not to cringe as she viewed the beginnings of a pathetic dog that looked in dire need of a vet. If she didn't know it was supposed to be a dog . . .

She tensed when Abigail stopped in front of her. Abigail's smile wilted. "Oh, that's, um . . . well, it's not quite what I had in mind when I traced the dog."

The others curiously looked on. Doris was probably staring at her; Pam didn't dare glance her way. She cleared her throat. "I'm not used to embroidering, uh, real objects."

"What do you mean?" Abigail asked.

"Objects you can recognize. Over the past few years, I've been quite taken with, uh, abstract embroidery."

"Abstract embroidery?" Charlotte said excitedly. Rosalie and Clara leaned forward.

"Yes. This is my, um, interpretation of this particular dog. Don't you have that here? It's all the rage in Toronto."

"Really?" Charlotte squealed. "Did you hear that, Clara? All the rage in Toronto!"

"Trust Toronto," Rosalie muttered. "They can't just do what the rest of us do, they have to make it all hoity-toity and la-di-da-like."

"Oh, hush, Rosie," Abigail said. "We must try it. Evelyn and Victoria would love this. Let's arrange an afternoon. Would you be so kind as to guide us, Margaret?"

Pam stifled a snort.

"Guide us?" Rosalie waved a dismissive hand. "From the looks of it, all you have to do is ignore the pattern. Stick your needle in wherever you want and don't bother to worry about your stitching."

"Rosie!" Abigail hissed.

Rosalie was starting to seriously get on Pam's nerves. "Rosalie's right," she said, hoping that pandering to the woman would shut her up. "Expert embroiderers like yourselves don't need guidance. In fact, guiding you would run counter to what abstract embroidery is all about. When you're given a pattern, you can either follow that pattern, or you can expand your mind." Gaining steam, Pam swept her hands through the air. "You can embroider the abstract representation of the pattern that's uniquely and utterly *you*, a one of a kind creation that represents your inner self."

"Oh, I suppose I can give it a try," Rosalie said, "though I don't see the point of creating something that nobody can recognize."

"It's for you, Rosalie," Charlotte said. "Didn't you hear what Margaret said? Uniquely and utterly you."

Abigail clasped her hands against her chest. "It's almost spiritual, isn't it? Let's try it. New patterns, everyone. We'll work on these another time. You continue what you're doing, Margaret."

Pam had every intention of doing so, and watched the other women crowd around Abigail's bag and choose new patterns. All except Doris. Her face lacked the animation that lit everyone else's, and she remained seated, her mouth pinched and her eyes hard.

MARGARET WAS SO tense that she almost cried out when Robin grasped her arm outside the café where they were to meet her friend, Cathy.

"Now remember, no matter what you say, Cathy will never guess that you're from the past," Robin said.

"She may think me simple."

Robin smiled. "I'll be right next to you. If I think you're in trouble, I'll help. You ready?"

Margaret nodded, hoping the details she and Robin had discussed wouldn't elude her at the worst moment.

"All right, here we go." Robin pulled the door open and ushered Margaret into the café. "She's here." Robin waved; Margaret followed her gaze. A woman sitting alone nodded, then shook her head when Robin pointed at the mug that sat on the table in front of her. "Come on, let's get our teas," Robin murmured.

Too soon, Margaret had a tea and two large cookies in hand. Breathing rapidly, she followed Robin to the table and tried not to stare at the woman who peered curiously at her. Good Lord, was that a tattoo on Cathy's forearm? Her hair was barely longer than Robin's, and a leather jacket was slung over the back of her chair. Did all lesbians wear leather jackets, jeans, and t-shirts? No, Margaret recalled seeing a photo of one in a dress in the newspaper, and her shock at the accompanying article's casual and brazen discussion of the woman's lesbianism. Robin hadn't been lying when she'd stated that things had changed over the past one hundred years.

Unlike Robin, Cathy wore earrings, which also suggested that not all lesbians were alike. Margaret had gathered that individuality was important in 2010, so she shouldn't be surprised.

"Hey," Robin said. Cathy smiled, but her attention remained on Margaret, who felt Robin's hand on her back. "This is Margaret. Margaret, Cathy."

"Pleased to meet you," Cathy said, apparently taking the introduction as permission to openly study her. Her brows lifted when her gaze settled on Margaret's hair.

"And you," Margaret said. Following Robin's lead, she set her tea on the table, shrugged off Pam's fall coat and hung it over the back of the chair, and sat down.

Cathy's eyes narrowed. "Robin's been very coy about you. I'm glad you're the reason she's been in hermit mode for the past month." Her gaze shifted to Robin. "Mike said you haven't grouped with him for a few weeks." She winked. "You must have it bad."

Robin chuckled. "Stop it."

Already lost, Margaret remained silent as one of the tactics she and Robin had discussed ran through her mind: *Only speak when I understand the conversation.*

Cathy leaned forward and curled both her hands around her mug. "So how did you meet? When did you meet?"

"Through Pam, believe it or not," Robin said. *Only lie when we have to.* "Margaret stopped by the house to see her, and we got talking."

"It must have been some conversation. So you're a friend of Pam's?" Cathy asked Margaret.

Despite Margaret's nerves, the story she'd rehearsed was at her fingertips. "Yes. I stopped by the house to drop off a book."

"Pam wasn't home," Robin said, smoothly picking up the story. "But she was on her way home from work, so I offered Margaret a tea, and—"

"The rest is herstory!" Cathy stated. She waggled her eyebrows at Margaret. "You could have just left the book. But you wanted to have that tea with Robin."

Margaret felt herself blush. The prospect of taking tea with Robin had intimidated her, but she hadn't wanted to be rude. By the time Jasper and Pam had returned from their outing into town, Margaret had hoped for more conversations with Robin. Attraction had stirred then, but Margaret hadn't recognized it for what it was until she'd slipped her arm through Robin's that fateful afternoon.

A sly smile spread across Cathy's face. "Did Pam forget the book somewhere? Maybe she deliberately left it and then made sure she wouldn't be home when Margaret brought it by, if you know what I mean."

Robin shook her head. "Pam didn't intend to bring us together. It just happened."

Margaret smiled down at her lap, then lifted her head. "How did the two of you meet?" Asking questions was a safe way to engage in the conversation—especially when Margaret already knew the answer.

"As long as it's about Cathy, not about something general that you 'should' already know," Robin had added.

Robin and Cathy both spoke at once, then stopped. "You go," Robin said.

"At university," Cathy said. "As you might have figured out, I'm an older student, too. So when I showed up for my Intro to Programming course and spotted Robin slouched in the back, I made a beeline for her, especially since she looked like a dyke."

Margaret sipped her tea to cover her confusion. Why would Cathy think that Robin looked like a dam?

"You know when you meet someone, and you can talk to them as if you've known each other for years?" Apparently not expecting a reply, Cathy carried on, wagging her finger between Robin and herself. "That's how it felt when we started talking. It's hard to believe we've only known each other for just over a year."

It sounded like Margaret's friendship with Helena. From the day they'd met four years ago, conversation had come easily between them, though they'd seen less of each other since Helena's courtship with, and then engagement to, Teddy. Margaret shook herself. Helena was dead. So was Teddy. What had Helena thought when "Margaret" ran away to Halifax without saying good-bye, never to be heard from again? She'd probably been beside herself. *I'm sorry, Helena. It wasn't me.*

"We really hit it off! As friends," Cathy quickly added. "I was seeing someone at the time. The less said about her, the better."

Margaret wouldn't have dared to pry anyway, and gave Robin a sidelong glance. Would it be rude to ask Robin about her former girlfriends? Not here; when they were alone.

"So you guys have been seeing each other for . . ."

"A couple of months," Robin said, stretching the truth a little.

"A couple of months? I guess things suddenly grew serious over the past month, when you disappeared."

Oh, if only Cathy knew the truth of her words!

"What do you do, Margaret?"

"I'm trying to figure that out," she said, dutifully regurgitating the words Robin had told her to say. She'd thought the answer inadequate, but Cathy said, "So many people are doing that now, what with the economy and layoffs and all that."

Due to Margaret's newspaper education and subsequent chats with Robin, she understood every word and felt quite proud of herself.

"Do you live in the same neighbourhood as Robin?"

Margaret sensed Robin tense.

"Did I say something wrong?" Cathy asked when Robin shifted in her chair.

"We're living together," Robin mumbled.

"Living together?" Cathy's wide eyes and sharp tone conveyed her surprise. "The old U-haul on the second date, eh? And with Pam gone now, things must be cozy."

Blood rushed to Margaret's cheeks. Cathy assumed they were sharing a bed! Fortunately Cathy's attention was still on Robin. Margaret lifted her mug, hoping that Cathy would attribute her beet-red face to the hot tea.

"Funny how things always work out like that, isn't it?" Cathy said. "Margaret came along just as Pam left. And I'm glad you did." Her smile appeared genuine. "It's about time Robin had someone special in her life. I think she'd convinced herself that—"

"Okay, enough, enough," Robin said, much to Margaret's chagrin. "Can we talk about something else, like—why don't you tell Margaret about your singing?"

Cathy's face lit up. "Sure!"

Margaret nibbled on a cookie as she listened to Cathy describe her practices and concerts with a local choir. When the conversation turned to local news, Margaret was able to throw in a word here and there; in fact, she held her own for the rest of the evening, thanks in large part to Robin, who always deftly steered the conversation onto more general topics whenever Cathy tried to uncover more details about Margaret and her relationship with Robin.

"You guys are coming to the women's dance at the Y, right?" Cathy asked as she pushed back her chair and grabbed her jacket.

"We haven't talked about it," Robin said.

"Come on, you can come out of your cocoon for one night."

"We'll think about it." Robin ignored Cathy's pointed look.

They walked together to the streetcar stop, where they said goodbye to Cathy. Margaret had ridden a streetcar in *her* Toronto, albeit in an earlier model, so climbing aboard at the stop near the house earlier that evening had evoked a feeling of déjà vu. Now, when the streetcar arrived, she boarded first and dropped the token Robin had given her into the slot. The driver grunted. In her time, she would have exchanged a few words with him, but not here. She slid into a seat and smiled when Robin sat next to her.

Margaret had several questions for Robin regarding the conversation with Cathy, but they'd have to wait until nobody could overhear them. She gazed out the window, wondering if the feeling that she and Robin were engaged in nefarious activities would ever go away. It was the secretiveness, and the knowledge that, should she ever speak of her background to anyone other than Robin, people would think her mad, or a liar. Although she was sitting in plain sight, she was hiding—a time intruder. Would she feel the same way in five years? Ten? Twenty?

Based on what she'd experienced so far, the chances of tripping herself up with a stranger were slim. People kept to themselves. When she ventured outside the house with Robin, she worried about getting lost, not about inadvertently alerting others to her background. She was an anonymous woman among a mass of anonymous people. The population must have grown ten times since 1910, yet she would be hard-pressed to make friends, were she ready to do so. Then again, walking about the neighbourhood and riding the streetcar would be less intimidating because she wouldn't have to worry about strangers striking up a conversation with her.

Not long later, she relaxed when they stepped into the house. Margaret hung her coat and turned to Robin, who was locking the front door. Robin grinned at her. "You did great. You've definitely been paying attention to the newspapers. And you're very brave. I don't know if I could do it."

Margaret flushed at Robin's praise. "I can only do it because you're with me."

"Soon you won't need me."

"I will always need you." She wanted to touch her. She hesitated, then reached for Robin, and closed her eyes when Robin's arms slipped around her waist. Oh, how she'd longed to hold Robin in her jacket. She ran her hand up Robin's back, revelling in the sensation of the smooth, cool leather underneath her fingers. "You were wearing this jacket when I realized I . . . felt more for you than I should," she murmured.

"When?" Robin asked, her breath tickling Margaret's ear. "Here, in the hallway?"

"No. Walking along the boardwalk." She'd never imagined then that she'd act on her feelings, partly because she'd considered them perverted, and partly because she'd assumed that Robin would be revolted by any display of affection.

"Is that why you wanted this jacket? Remember when I asked what you'd want?" Robin said.

"Yes. And yes." Dare she ask a question that had teased her ever since their first conversation in the Bainbridge guest house? "When did you know that you cared for me?" She regretted the question when Robin drew back, then held her breath as Robin's fingers traced her lips.

"Well, it's probably more a question of when I admitted it," Robin said softly. "I think I fell in love with you during those nights in the study. But I couldn't let myself go there. I didn't let myself think about it. I told myself I was keeping you company while Pam and Jasper were, um, occupied. After all, you were straight. And engaged."

Now she was neither. She would never be "straight" again. But engaged? She hoped so, if Robin would accept her as she was, with her old-fashioned ways.

Robin met Margaret's eyes. "I'm glad you kissed me. May I kiss you?" Her mouth turned up at the corners. "I might mess up your hair."

"That's all right," Margaret said faintly. "We'll be going to bed soon, anyway." She sucked in her breath. "Alone. I didn't mean—"

Robin's face was alight with amusement. "I know what you meant. Now stop talking so I can kiss you."

Margaret was happy to oblige. When Robin's lips touched hers, heat raged through her, and when Robin's lips parted, hers did too . . . and the world melted away. When their mouths finally drew apart, Margaret's heart was pounding, her fingers were in Robin's hair, and her face felt as hot as Robin's looked. The story she could tell her friends now! She slipped her hands down to Robin's cheeks and held her face. A lump formed in her throat. She'd never felt such a fierce love for anyone.

Something was tugging at her hair; she realized that Robin was disentangling her fingers. Margaret had possessed only a vague awareness of Robin's hands in her hair when they were kissing. Lost to her bliss and desire, she wouldn't have noticed a train racing toward them!

Robin leaned in again. They shared a sweet kiss, then Robin pulled Margaret into a hug. Margaret lay her head against Robin's shoulder and sighed contentedly. She'd left so much behind and faced an uncertain and frightening future, but there wasn't another time period or place she'd rather be, than in Robin's arms in 2010.

Chapter Eight

PAM WAS EXAMINING HERSELF IN HER bedroom's full-length mirror when a knock at the door startled her. "Coming!"

She opened the door to Bella. "A letter for you," Bella said, presenting it to Pam with a flourish.

"Thank you." Excited, Pam shut the door. Her heart sank when she saw that it wasn't from Jasper, but a letter from Toronto. When the hell would she see Jasper again? Since the dinner at Oliver's the day they'd arrived, she'd seen him only twice, and never alone. She was about ready to poke her eyes out with one of those dreaded embroidery needles! He'd better be looking for a place to live so they could marry, pronto—but shouldn't she be with him when he looked at properties?

With a sigh, she read the return address on the envelope. Hmm, it was from a Miss H. Morgan. The woman must have gotten the address from Jasper's father, or perhaps Margaret's parents. Pam ripped the envelope open and unfolded a piece of flowered stationery.

Margaret,

How could you? When I heard, I was horrified. I thought we were friends! Four months pregnant? How long were you carrying on with Jasper? Did you think about how it would affect me and Teddy? The looks I get! I make sure everyone knows that I value my innocence and that having you as a friend was an unfortunate lapse in judgement. Teddy and I can hold our heads high, which is more than I can say for you and Jasper.

Your poor parents. Did you think of them? No, of course you didn't. You were too busy giving in to your carnal desires.

If you were thinking of returning to Toronto for my wedding, don't! The last thing Teddy and I need is a woman of such low moral character staining our perfect day. You're a liar, and a harlot, and I don't ever want to see or hear from you again.
Helena

Jesus. It was a miracle anyone had children in this time period. Pam was tempted to write back and tell her to fuck off, but she'd probably be arrested. Who would have guessed that pretty, dainty, flowery paper could convey such venom? *Margaret, if you've ever wondered who your true friends were, you can scratch Miss Helena Morgan off your list. One transgression and you were history.*

Pam refolded the paper, stuck it back in the envelope, and reluctantly opened the door and stepped into the hallway. Another exciting day at Pembleton Manor with dour Doris, whose fiancé was a barrel of laughs, too. Pam had started to believe that he was a figment of Doris's imagination, but she'd finally met him the day before yesterday. Elliot was uptight, brusque, and spoke to Doris as if she were a five-year-old. He was also handsome, but that didn't make up for his lousy personality. What did Doris see in him? She was plain and almost twenty-five. Maybe she was desperate, but there had to be better prospective husbands than Elliot.

After a quick detour out the back door to deposit Helena's lovely letter in the trash—after ripping it up, of course, to save it from prying eyes—Pam went to the dining room, where Doris was already tucking into breakfast.

"Good morning," Pam said breezily.

Doris jumped and dropped her fork, then quickly pulled an open book at her elbow over something else. Another book? What was she hiding? Doris glared and picked up her fork. "Good morning," she mumbled.

Resisting the urge to ask what Doris was reading, Pam pulled out a chair and sat, plucked an orange from the fruit bowl, and began to peel it. "Would you like to go for a walk after breakfast? I'd love to see more of the grounds." *And to get out of this freaking house.*

"Yes, all right," Doris said, sounding as if she was about to undergo a root canal.

Ava, a waifish girl who worked in the kitchen, stepped into the room. "A boiled egg and toast for you this morning, Miss Wilton?"

"Yes, please." Pam leaned to her left as Ava poured her a cup of coffee, and took the opportunity to glance at Doris's open book. There was definitely another book hidden underneath it. Pam could hardly contain her curiosity. Was Doris reading something naughty? What passed for porn here? People wearing shorts? Men probably had access to lewd sketches of nude women, even photos. Pam would be surprised if the equivalent existed for women, and a woman of Doris's breeding wouldn't be caught dead with such items, anyway. What *had* she been reading? When Ava straightened, Pam quickly refocused on her orange, not wanting to alert Doris that she'd noticed the other book.

Doris made no pretense of wanting to converse, so Pam munched her way through breakfast in silence. As she was dabbing her mouth with a napkin after finishing her last piece of toast, a voice out in the hallway made her want to push back her chair and leap into the air.

The butler who'd taken Pam's hat the day she'd arrived stepped into the room. "Mr. Bainbridge," he announced, then turned on his heel and left. Jasper appeared in the doorway, clutching his hat in front of him. He inclined his head. "Ladies."

"Good morning," Pam and Doris said in unison.

"Forgive the unannounced and early visit, but I've only just received confirmation that we can view several properties today. I was waiting until I knew for sure before telling you," he said to Pam. "I hope you're available today."

Available? When could they leave?

"Sit down and join us," Doris said, her tone indicating that her suggestion was more polite than heartfelt.

"No, thank you. We'll have to depart soon if we're to have time to see all the properties."

"We can go for our walk tomorrow," Pam said to Doris, trying her damndest to sound disappointed.

Doris nodded. "I hope one of the properties is suitable."

Pam bet she did.

"I hope so, too." Jasper raised his brows at Pam. "Shall we?"

Oh, yeah. Pam murmured a good-bye to Doris and took the time to adjust her hat in the foyer mirror, even though she wanted to run from the house. A car waited outside. Drat. Pam had hoped for an enclosed carriage, where they could relax . . . and neck!

"I borrowed the motor from Oliver," Jasper explained as he opened the passenger door and offered Pam a supporting hand. He rounded the car and climbed into the driver's seat.

"Where've you been?" Pam said. "I'm going crazy."

Jasper chuckled. "I've missed you, too. It's difficult to get away. Oliver's been keen to introduce me to friends and tradesmen who can help me get a start with my cabinetmaking." He pulled away from the house. "I think Hortense is eager for us to marry and move. She's being pleasant and hospitable, but the novelty of my presence has worn off."

The novelty of Pam's presence had worn off for Doris five minutes after Pam had arrived. Hortense, on the other hand, might have an archaic name, but she was kind and sociable, and held her own with Oliver.

"Have you looked at churches?" Jasper asked. "We can't move until we're married."

If the historical record was correct, they'd be in their own home after honeymooning in New Brunswick in December. "Doris and I spent two afternoons slogging from church to church. St. Mark's has dates available in December. It's small, but cozy." And where they'd marry. "Elliot wants a summer wedding. If he and Doris act fast, they might get one of the few remaining summer dates." Doris could have booked their date already, if she didn't need the almighty Elliot's permission to sneeze.

Jasper grunted, then sharply turned the steering wheel.

"Where are we going?" Pam asked as they turned away from the main entrance and onto a path that led deeper into the Pembleton Estate.

"To a secluded guest house that's currently unoccupied," Jasper said with a grin. "Our first viewing appointment is at 1:00." He gave Pam a sidelong glance. "I can't imagine what we'll do until then."

Pam wanted to grab him and kiss him, but her damn hat would get in the way and they'd probably crash into a tree. "I love you, Jasper Bainbridge," she said, her smile splitting her face. Living in 1910 was proving to be more trying than she'd expected, but being with him made it all worth it.

MARGARET GLANCED INTO the empty study and moved on to Pam's bedroom. Robin was sitting on the bed, sorting plastic cards into two piles. "What are you doing?" Margaret asked.

"Deciding which cards to keep. Basically, anything with Pam's picture has to go." She sighed. "I should have done this earlier, but I couldn't face it. I mean, if anyone finds her purse here, we're screwed, and it's time to transition her identity to you."

Margaret sank onto the bed and put her hand on Robin's back. "Perhaps we shouldn't have destroyed the book."

"Just because I miss Pam doesn't mean I think you should go back." Robin turned and handed Margaret one of the cards.

Margaret peered down at it. "What's this?"

"Your health card. Luckily Pam still had the old-style one, so no photo. It means it's okay for you to get sick. Not that I want you to."

Margaret read the name on the card: *Pamela Elizabeth Holden*. She looked up. "Do you have a middle name?"

"Uh, yeah."

"What is it?"

Robin cleared her throat. "Elenora."

Elenora? Then . . . "That's an old name."

"My great-grandmother's name."

"Really?" Margaret breathed. So Robin *was* related to Victor Tillman's family; in fact, she was a direct descendant! Should she tell Robin that she'd met her great-grandparents?

"My great-grandfather's name was Victor." Robin's eyes narrowed. "But I suspect you already know that. You mentioned that he'd gambled all his money away."

Margaret cringed. "I meant no offence."

"None was taken. At the time, I didn't know if there was a connection. I knew my great-grandmother's name because I got it. I had to ask my mother if she knew about a Victor Tillman. Tillman is her name, not my father's." Robin's mouth tightened. "I changed my name. I don't think he cared."

So excessive drinking ran down her mother's side of the family. Robin had avoided the curse, perhaps deliberately; Margaret had never seen her touch a drop of alcohol. "When will you introduce me to your parents?" she asked, dismayed that she hadn't already met Robin's mother, at least. Her father didn't live in Toronto.

Robin tensed. "You might meet my mother on my birthday. As for my father, I don't know. Next time he calls, I'm thinking of saying I don't want to see him. Pam always thought I should do that, and I probably should." She heaved her shoulders and tossed a card onto the smaller pile on the right. "You're around the same height as Pam, but you're a bit thinner. That won't matter."

It did mean that most of Pam's clothes were baggy on her, except for a few items Pam had kept that "she hoped to eventually fit into again," according to Robin. Margaret handed back the card.

"Have you thought any more about cutting your hair?" Robin asked.

"I thought perhaps it would be nice to cut it before our night out." Margaret couldn't help but smile. Robin was taking her out to dinner before the dance. Their first date.

Robin smiled in return. "Good." She dealt with the three remaining cards in her hand, then turned to Margaret again. "After considering the options, I've decided we should try to get you a passport. I used to bitch at Pam for never going anywhere. Now I'm glad she didn't." Margaret's breath quickened as Robin ran her fingers through her hair and rested her hand on the back of Margaret's neck. "You'll need passport photos, but let's get your hair cut first. I should be able to get you an appointment next week."

Margaret swallowed. "All right."

"The only sticky part of the passport application is the references. We can use two of Pam's friends that she doesn't see very often. Chances are, they won't even be called."

"What if they are?" Margaret asked, her heart thumping.

"They'll answer questions about Pam, not you. The worst that can happen is your application is rejected."

Robin sounded reassuring, but she must be worried. Margaret pushed down her own fear, determined to support Robin, not to add to her burdens. "How long will it take to get the passport?"

"If you applied in person, a couple of weeks. But we'll apply through the mail." Margaret quickly nodded. Robin's forehead creased. "It'll take longer, but you have a health card and a birth certificate, so there's no rush. If you didn't need ID with a photo, we wouldn't bother with the passport. Not yet, anyway."

What would she need for them to marry?

"Anyway, enough of this." Robin turned back to the two piles; the sensation of her touch lingered on Margaret's neck. "I'll cut up this pile later. The other one is yours. You'll need a purse." She chuckled. "Though if you were to try wearing pants, you might decide your pockets are enough."

"Perhaps I should try on a pair," Margaret said.

Robin whipped toward her. "Really? Or are you putting me on?"

"I might not like them, but I will try a pair. I don't know if the ones Pam bought will fit me, though."

"Why don't you start with a pair of sweats, just around the house? Throw on a pair in the morning, so you don't have to get up at the crack of dawn to get ready to see me off."

Margaret *would* feel more comfortable—and decent—if Robin saw her in a pair of sweatpants rather than in only her nightie, and an extra hour of sleep would be welcome. "Perhaps I will try that." Her hand went to her head. "Oh, but my hair."

"Margaret, you don't have to look perfect in the mornings. I don't."

Yes, but it was almost impossible for Robin's hair to appear messy.

"You always look beautiful." Robin tapped Margaret's nose.

She flushed with pleasure. "Thank you."

"Should we start preparing for the dance?" Robin asked.

"Yes." Margaret rose when Robin did.

Robin looked down at the two card piles. "We'll go through the cards that are yours later. First, dancing! Let's go down to the exercise room."

She dutifully followed Robin downstairs. The hairs on the back of her neck stood up as she crossed the threshold into the exercise room. She avoided entering it, afraid that she'd double over with nausea and find herself back in 1910 without Robin. For that to happen, Pam would have to read the rhyme, and perhaps be in the drawing room in 1910. But she'd fled to Halifax with Jasper, and apparently they'd started a family. Would she ever want to leave him and their children behind? Margaret and Robin hadn't yet researched what had become of those in the past. Perhaps she'd suggest to Robin that they do so soon, despite the pain it would cause them. If she could reassure herself that Pam had remained in 1910, she could stop worrying that her life here might end at a moment's notice.

Robin slapped her thighs. "We need music," she said sheepishly. "Just a minute." She left the room.

Margaret eyed the door, fighting the overpowering urge to wait for Robin in the hallway. When Mitzy sauntered in, Margaret crouched and held out her hand. "Mitzy," she hissed, and scooped the cat into her arms when Mitzy came over to sniff her fingers. "I'll give you a treat later," Margaret whispered, feeling guilty. For now, she wanted to cling to Mitzy, hoping that doing so would anchor her in 2010.

Robin returned carrying a rectangular metallic object. She set it on the chair and blew away a layer of dust. "I haven't used this in ages. I hope it still works." She unwound the electrical cord, plugged the machine in, and pressed a button. Several lights at the top of the machine came on. "Good."

"What is it?"

"It's a radio and CD player."

"CD?" Margaret bent and released Mitzy.

"CDs contain music."

"Oh, yes. We've already talked about this."

Robin shrugged. "We've covered so much, I'm surprised you remember any of it. Be back in a minute." She left again.

To keep her mind occupied, Margaret peered at the machine without touching it. Robin came back with several CDs. "Will there be a band at the dance?" Margaret asked as Robin inserted a CD into the machine.

"No. There'll be a DJ, someone who selects and plays the music."

How queer, to dance in a room with no musicians.

Robin stepped away from the machine and clapped her hands. "Okay. Let's dance." Margaret reached for her, but Robin shook her head. "No, stay where you are."

"What?"

"When the music is fast, we dance apart." She pressed a button.

Music filled the room, or at least what they regarded as music here. Much of what Margaret had heard sounded like wretched noise, and most pieces included vocals. She was beginning to appreciate the appeal of the more popular songs, though, and even hummed to a few under her breath in the mornings, when Robin had the radio on before leaving for university. "What are the steps?"

"There are no steps. Just move to the music." Robin raised her arms and waved them around; her feet and legs moved in time to the beat.

Margaret stared at her. Surely she should try to mimic her, otherwise what was the point of dancing together?

"Just swing your hips." Robin swung hers to demonstrate, making Margaret's heart flutter. "Move your legs to the beat." She laughed. "Just move! Step to the beat."

Feeling awfully silly, Margaret stepped to one side, then to the other, following the beat.

Robin nodded encouragement. "Do something with your arms. Do this." She swung her arms to her left, then to her right.

Margaret self-consciously did the same, surprised that Robin didn't burst out laughing. But then, how could she, with her own arms flailing around. Though Robin's swaying hips were oddly alluring. Margaret watched her, not paying attention to her own movements until Robin smiled and said, "That's it!"

She couldn't help but smile back, despite her embarrassment and confusion. How could Robin praise her? With no steps to follow, apparently simple movement passed as competence. "Will everyone dance like this?"

Robin nodded.

So they would all just dance however they wanted? She had to admit that she took pleasure in Robin's dancing and enjoyed moving to the music, despite her conviction that she must appear foolish. Observing a full dance floor would probably prove illuminating. At least she wouldn't have to worry about humiliating herself, since she couldn't see how that would be possible.

"Sometimes we might dance in a group, rather than only with each other. People generally form a circle."

Oh. The thought of dancing across from others intimidated her.

The song ended. "A slow one," Robin said when the next song began. "Now come to me."

"Are we going to waltz?" When Robin nodded, Margaret held up one hand.

Robin shook her head. "Hug me."

"I thought we were going to waltz."

"We are."

Margaret didn't mind giving her a hug before they danced. She slipped her arms around Robin's neck and leaned into her.

"Okay, now we move together," Robin murmured. "Sway."

Bewildered, Margaret followed her lead and realized that they were slowly turning in a circle. "Is this waltzing?"

"Yes."

"I like this."

She felt Robin's chuckle. "So do I."

FROM THE CORNER of her eye, Pam eyed Doris sitting on a nearby chair with her nose stuck in yet another book. Doris read at every opportunity; she obviously enjoyed it more than sewing, embroidery, and other feminine pursuits. This time Doris hadn't quickly hidden another book when Pam had walked into the room, which wasn't surprising, since Jasper, Oliver, Hortense, and Elliot were due any minute, and then they'd be off to a swanky restaurant in town for dinner. Since that morning at the breakfast table, Pam had only caught Doris with the other book once; unfortunately she hadn't glimpsed the book's title. She was dying of curiosity!

Hearing heavy footsteps approaching, Pam straightened and clasped her hands in her lap. Oliver and Elliot strode into the room. "Ladies," Oliver said.

Pam inclined her head. "Good evening."

Elliot frowned, then marched up to Doris, yanked the book from her hands, and glared at her. "You knew when we were expected," he growled. "Is this any way to greet us?"

Doris's cheeks flushed a deep crimson. "I'm sorry. I—"

"Don't bother." Elliot tossed the book onto the table next to the chair and turned to Oliver. "Stupid woman," he muttered, shaking his head. Oliver shrugged.

Her blood boiling, Pam looked at Doris, expecting her to speak up, but Doris stared down at her lap.

"You won't have time to read when you have a house to run and children to raise," Elliot said.

"And a husband to tend to," Oliver added.

"Oh, enough." Hortense had stepped into the room and stood at Oliver's side. "Reading in one's own drawing room isn't a sin."

"It is when guests are expected," Elliot said.

Hortense's face tightened at Elliot's refusal to be conciliatory. "Doris will make a wonderful wife and mother. She'll know her priorities when she's married, won't you, Doris?"

Doris raised her head and nodded. Pam inwardly winced at her resigned and bleak eyes. Doris could be difficult to read, but not this time. She didn't want to get married, at least not to Elliot. Why was she engaged to him? It didn't matter how much money the clown had, she could do better. "Where's Jasper?" she quickly asked when Elliot opened his mouth to answer Hortense's question for Doris. God only knew what he intended to say.

Hortense turned to Pam. "He's here. He'll join us in a minute."

Everyone but Doris gazed at her, smiles playing on their lips. What did they know that she didn't? The answer came when Jasper joined them a minute later, striding in with one hand suspiciously behind his back. He nodded to the others, then stopped in front of Pam and extended his other hand. She grasped his fingers, expecting him to kiss her hand and wondering about the reason behind the sudden formality, but he pulled her to her feet and cleared his throat.

"As you know, P—Margaret and I left Toronto in a hurry, and we left something very important behind." He moved his hand from behind his back and extended it, a small, gift-wrapped box on his palm. "The bow unravelled a bit on the way. Bella kindly helped me retie it," he murmured.

Aware of everyone's eyes upon her, Pam accepted the gift and unwrapped it. Her breath caught in her throat when she spotted the box inside; she swallowed as she lifted its lid with a trembling hand.

Jasper dropped to one knee. "Will you marry me?"

As she gazed down at the ring with its bright red ruby, she recalled a conversation she'd had with Jasper and the others about her favourite gemstones. Jasper had initiated the conversation—sly devil. Fortunately "diamond" wasn't at the top of her list; this ring was truly hers, not version two of Margaret's. "Of course I will," she managed to whisper, then fought tears as he stood, took the box from her, and slipped the ring on her finger as everyone clapped.

"We'll order the best champagne tonight," Oliver shouted, evoking another round of applause.

When Doris came to Pam and murmured a few words of congratulations, Pam's throat tightened at the envy in Doris's eyes. Doris had the requisite diamond ring and a fiancé with the desired pedigree, but they both knew who had the better man. Pam's heart went out to her. She impulsively leaned in and gave her a quick hug. "Thank you," she said, determined to win Doris over and be a friend. Doris needed one.

Chapter Nine

"*NO, MOVE YOUR HIPS,*" *ROBIN SAID, then nodded when Margaret swayed. "You're doing great." Margaret started to unbutton her blouse. Robin's mouth dropped open. "Let me," she whispered. Desire made her clumsy; she fumbled with the first button, finally pushed it through, and moved on to the next.*

Margaret ran her finger down Robin's cheek. "Hurry!"

Robin could barely breathe, let alone focus on a button. She—

Suddenly another woman was speaking.

Confused, Robin turned around. What—

Fuck! Her eyes snapped open. She tugged on the cord to ring the bell and grabbed her knapsack. Seconds later, she stood on the sidewalk and blinked into the sun as the streetcar glided away. Why did streetcar stop announcements and alarm clocks always intrude into dreams at the worst possible moments?

With a sigh, she slung her knapsack over her shoulder and shoved her hands into her pockets. Usually she dropped in on Mom on her way home, not in the mornings, but she wanted to talk to her before Mom had her first drink of the day. God, Robin dreaded the upcoming conversation, but she couldn't delay it any longer.

She hesitated outside Mom's apartment door, then inserted her key, turned it in the lock, and rapped on the door before opening it. "It's me," she called, stepping into the hallway and closing the door. When she met only silence, a familiar icy fear gripped her and made her heart pound. "Mom!" She glanced into the living room and kitchen, then raced up the hallway.

Mom lay sprawled facedown on her bed, fully dressed. *"Mom!"* She crossed to the bed and reached out to shake her, then jerked her hand away when Mom suddenly rolled onto her back.

"What the hell is all the shouting?" Mom groaned. "Jesus Christ, Robin, what time is it?"

"It's around 8:30," Robin said, eyeing the half-empty glass of beer on the night table in dismay. "You're not drinking already?" She went over and raised the blinds.

Mom threw her arm across her eyes. "Close those fucking blinds, already! What the hell are you doing here so early?"

"I was hoping to catch you before you started drinking," Robin said, unable to keep the disapproval from her voice. She reluctantly lowered the blinds.

"I haven't had a drink. I haven't even gotten out of bed, for Christ's sake." Mom groaned again.

Robin folded her arms. "I don't have to be in class for an hour. Do you want some breakfast?"

"I want to sleep!"

"Okay. Is Chris here?"

"He's at his girlfriend's." Mom lifted her arm and squinted into the gloom. "What are *you* doing here?"

"I want to talk about my birthday."

"Oh, Christ, is it that time again? How old are you going to be?"

"Twenty-seven."

"Twenty-seven? Christ. Where'd the time go? Jesus, I'm old," Mom wailed. "What do you want to talk about?"

She wanted Mom to somehow be nice to Margaret. "Look, I know I usually drop in here, but I was wondering if you'd like to come visit me, for a change." It would be easier to control the length of the visit if she and Margaret came here, but the living room and kitchen were always a mess. Even if Robin were to clean up and then go fetch Margaret, Mom would probably turn the place into a dump before they arrived.

"And have Pam lording it over me? She's bad enough when she comes here. Freaking goody two-shoes," Mom said petulantly.

Pam and Cathy were—well, now Cathy was the only one who occasionally braved this apartment. "Pam's run off with some boyfriend. She's not living there right now."

Mom barked a laugh and pushed herself into a sitting position. "Good riddance. I got tired of that bitch interfering in our lives, making you think you're better than us."

Robin gripped her arms. "I don't think I'm better than you," she said evenly.

"Look what university did to your fucking father," Mom continued, ignoring her. "It's doing the same thing to you." Her voice rose in pitch. "Don't want to come here for your birthday. Oh, no. God forbid you spend your birthday with us."

"I didn't say I don't want to spend my birthday with you."

"Have you seen your father lately?"

"I had dinner with him last month."

"I already know about that!" Mom snapped. "Since then."

"No."

"You think you hate him, but you'll end up the same way. That's why I told you, you want to go to university, then you can get the fuck out of my home. And you fucking left, didn't you, because you think you're better than us."

Robin shifted her weight and sighed, tired of having the same conversation for the millionth time, but her buried resentment stirred. *I stayed for six fucking years before I left, Mom. Six fucking years cooking your meals and picking up after you and cleaning up your puke and making sure Chris was okay, on top of working two fucking jobs, while my friends went to university.* She pressed her lips together and bit her tongue.

"So no, I don't care if Miss Snobby Bitch is gone. You left us." Mom tapped her chest. "You left us!" she shrieked.

"Okay, then I'm bringing someone here with me, and I want you to be nice to her."

Mom stared at her. "What, you mean a girlfriend?"

Robin swallowed. "Yes."

Mom's eyes grew shrewd. "There must be something special about this one. You've only ever brought a girlfriend here once."

Because Annie had dumped her the moment they'd left the apartment. Robin hadn't blamed her. Not many people appreciated a drunk calling them names. Robin hadn't dated since Annie had told her to fuck off. She'd decided to wait until . . . She refused to think about it. She hadn't expected Margaret to parachute into her life and sneak through her defences like an undercover agent.

Robin wished she could keep Margaret away from Mom forever, but that would mean doing the one thing she couldn't do: cut Mom out of her life. "Her name's Margaret. Since Pam isn't coming this year, I thought I'd bring her along, that's all." She glanced around. "If I come over beforehand to do a little housework, do you think you can keep the place clean for five minutes?"

"Don't get bitchy with me, Robin. You don't know what it's like for me. We used to be a family. We lived in a house, not a fucking dump." Mom's lips trembled. "Do you have any idea what it's like for me? Nobody cares about me. Chris is with his girlfriend. You fucking left both of us. I don't have anyone. Nobody. My fucking kids don't even care about me. I could die and nobody would care."

"That's not true." Robin dropped her arms to her sides. "Shit, Mom, why don't you go to that centre I told you about."

"I'm not going there! Mixing with fucking druggies and god knows what else. Why would I go there?"

"Because your drinking is a problem."

"So I like to have a drink now and then. So what?"

Robin groaned. "You don't just have a drink now and then. Why don't you try AA?"

"I am *not* a fucking alcoholic! And I am sick and tired of you coming over here and telling me what to do and looking down your nose at me. Get the fuck out! Now!"

"Mom—"

"Get out!"

"Fine." Fuming, Robin marched from the room. Jesus, why did she even bother?

"Robin!"

Halfway down the hallway, Robin turned. Mom shuffled up to her. "I want a coffee."

Robin hesitated, then shrugged off her knapsack. "Okay. One coffee coming up."

Mom followed her into the kitchen. "You're coming over on your birthday, right? You wouldn't miss seeing your mom on your

birthday." She threw an arm around Robin's shoulders. "I'll be nice
to your girlfriend, okay?"

Robin resisted the urge to grimace and lean away when she received
a full blast of Mom's rancid breath. Ugh. "Why don't you go shower?
The coffee will be ready when you're done."

"I do need a pee." Mom let go of her and shambled away. "Oh!"
she said, turning around when she reached the archway that opened
on the hallway. "When you come on your birthday, don't forget to
bring a cake."

STILL WALKING ON air after Jasper's public proposal, Pam swept
into the drawing room, looking forward to a trip into town. Oh, it
was empty. She'd expected to find Doris in her usual chair, oblivious
to her surroundings. Doris's book lay open on the cushion. Maybe
she'd gone to the bathroom. Pam was about to sit down when her
eye caught a ribbon of red near Doris's book. Hmm . . . the book
Doris normally hid had a red cover. Pam listened for footsteps, then
hurried over to the chair and pulled out the book stuffed down the
side of the cushion, eager to find out what naughty reading Doris
was concealing.

She frowned down at the title. A medical book? A quick flip
through the pages told Pam that Doris wasn't reading it for the pictures, unless she had a really weird fetish related to body parts. *Oh,
god.* Pam closed it and shoved it back down the side of the cushion.
Why would Doris hide a medical book? Shit, someone was coming!
Pam rushed over to her usual chair and plunked into it.

When Doris entered the room and saw Pam, she stiffened and her
eyes immediately went to her chair. Her shoulders relaxed. "I thought
you were going out for the afternoon with Jasper."

"I am." They'd seen a property they liked and were ready to discuss purchasing it—or rather, Jasper was. "He should be here soon. I
thought I'd come in and have a chat with you. I missed you at lunch."

Doris crossed to her chair and lifted her book. "I took a lunch
down the garden with me."

Pam hoped her disappointment wasn't showing on her face. She
wouldn't have minded a picnic, but Doris resisted every overture of
friendship, limiting their conversations to trivialities and using her

books as a barrier. Before Doris could stick her nose in the book she held, Pam said, "Jasper and I lunched with a charming lawyer yesterday. Jeffrey Marshall. He'll handle the real estate transaction, should Jasper buy. He said he might run in the next federal election. If he does, he'll have my vote."

Doris laughed. "Did you say that? I bet he didn't appreciate it. Mr. Marshall doesn't think women should have the vote. He's spoken against it many times and will probably explode, if it ever comes to pass."

What? Women couldn't vote? Jesus, she should have paid more attention in history class. All she vaguely remembered were boring wars and treaties. "I didn't say it out loud," Pam said, hoping to cover her gaffe. "I only thought it."

Doris moved her book from her lap to the table. "Do you think women should have the vote?" Her eyes bored into Pam.

Was "no" the politically correct answer? Oh, who cared! No matter what she said, Doris would still view her as an inconvenience. "Yes, I do."

Doris's eyes widened. "Really?"

"Do you?" Pam asked, not sure if she'd impressed or offended.

"Of course! Why shouldn't we have the vote? Why should only men be involved in choosing the government? We have to live with its policies and its failures, so why shouldn't we have a say?" Doris's face flushed. "As for not being persons under the law—have you ever heard anything so absurd? What are we, then? Men think they're intelligent, yet they're so stupid! Can they truly be proud of their accomplishments, when they have to deny half the population in order to achieve?"

Pam stared at her in astonishment. She'd never seen Doris so animated, so passionate. Doris's demeanour shocked her almost as much as finding out that she wasn't considered a person. It was a good thing Robin wasn't here; she'd flip out big-time.

"If women had been allowed—were allowed—the freedom to do what they wanted to do, to study, to create, to dream, how many of those achievements would have belonged to them?" Doris said.

Pam nodded. "I agree."

Doris went still. "You do?"

Yes, and she wondered why Doris was engaged to a brash, chauvinistic pig like Elliot. "Secure, confident men don't need to hold women back. Only weak ones do." Pam smiled at Doris's enraptured expression. She never would have pegged Doris as a raging feminist. "I wonder how much further along we'd be if we all worked together."

"Yes! It's foolish to—"

Bella knocked on the open door. "Mr. Bainbridge," she announced.

Pam felt almost disappointed when Jasper strolled into the room. She was finally making headway with Doris. She turned to her. "We can continue our conversation later."

Doris nodded and picked up her book.

In the hallway, Jasper pecked Pam on the cheek. "If all goes well today, the sale should close by the end of the week. We can attend St. Mark's on Sunday and book the date."

Since they'd marry at St. Mark's on December 15th, she assumed the property would soon be Jasper's. Not theirs, Jasper's. No vote. Not a person. While she was thrilled to have discovered a potential key to improving relations with Doris, their conversation had left Pam unsettled. If not for Jasper, would she want to remain in this time period? Was he the only draw? Had she really been born after her time?

MARGARET FOLLOWED ROBIN into the hair salon and instinctively covered her nose and mouth. She recognized the smell of shampoo, but too many other scents assaulted her nostrils. The lights, the machines, the noise . . . Overwhelmed, she gripped Robin's arm with her free hand.

"Robin!" A slender man in a blue t-shirt and tight jeans bounded toward them. "How are you doing, hon?"

"I'm good. This is Margaret. Margaret, Steve."

Steve's mouth dropped open. "Oh my god, hon, the hair! Are you sure there aren't any birds in there? I hope I won't be destroying a protected habitat." He studied her, rubbing his chin. "What are we doing for you today?"

Didn't he know she wanted her hair cut?

"What style do you want?" Robin prompted, picking up on Margaret's bewilderment.

Oh. "I'm tired of my long hair," Margaret said, repeating what she'd rehearsed with Robin. She reluctantly let go of Robin's arm. "I want something lower, er, maintenance."

"What length are we talking about? With all that hair, I could sculpt it."

Robin rolled her eyes. "We're not entering her in a competition."

"I know, hon, but I'd love to play in that hair for a while. Haven't seen this much hair on a single head in ages. You wouldn't understand," he said with a knowing chuckle. Margaret couldn't help but chuckle along with him. Suddenly his fingers were in her hair. "Do you want to look at some magazines, see if there's anything you like?" he asked as he lifted her hair and let it drop, then repeated the action.

"I think you want something simple, don't you?" Robin said. "Nothing that requires a curling iron. Just wash, blow-dry, and brush."

"You want it longer than Robin's, though," Steve said.

Blood pounded in Margaret's ears. "Yes!" She relaxed when she caught him winking at Robin. "Perhaps shoulder length."

To Margaret's relief, he removed his fingers from her hair and stepped back. "Are you sure, hon? It'll take you a while to grow it back. If you don't like your new style, I can't glue your hair back on."

Did he call everyone hon? "I'm sure." Cringing at herself in the mirror wouldn't be the worst thing to bear. If she hated it, she *could* grow it back.

"It'll be a good look for you. It'll let your pretty face shine."

Robin smiled. "I agree."

Embarrassed and not wanting to appear vain, Margaret refrained from nodding.

"Okay, cut and thin." Steve clapped his hands. "Let's get started. Hang your coat, hon, and then I'll wash your hair."

"How long do you think it'll take you to cut her hair?" Robin asked. "A while."

"So I have time to do a bit of shopping?"

Steve nodded as he waved his arm toward the coat hooks. "At least an hour, hon. I'm glad you warned me."

Warned him? And Robin was going to leave her here?

"I'm just going to a couple of stores," Robin murmured as Margaret removed her coat. "You'll be fine. Steve will talk your ear off. Just say uh-huh every once in a while. I'll be back well before you're finished, I promise. On the off chance that something bizarre happens and I'm held up, here's money for the cut, and the tip." Margaret's eyes popped out of her head when Robin handed her seventy dollars. "Pay him and wait here for me. But don't worry. I'll be back."

Margaret slipped the bills into the pocket of the cardigan she'd knitted for herself and often wore over her dress to keep her arms warm. Despite Robin's assurances, her stomach churned as she followed Steve to the back, settled herself into the proffered chair and, after a moment's confusion, tipped her head back over a sink. What would she do if he asked a question she didn't understand? By the time he finished washing her hair, she'd decided that, should she not understand him, she'd pretend not to have heard and change the subject with a question.

"Are you sure about this, hon?" he asked, after transferring her to another chair and covering her with a protective cape.

"I'm sure."

"Okay, then." He picked up a pair of scissors.

Robin was right; Steve was capable of conducting a conversation on his own. Good thing, too, since Margaret only half listened as she sat mesmerized by the transformation taking place in the mirror. What would Mother think, if she could see her now? The state of Margaret's hair would probably be the least of Mother's concerns. *Mother.* A dull ache flared in Margaret's chest. Sometimes she desperately wanted to know what had happened to those she'd left behind in 1910; other times she wondered if it would be better to remember them as they were, and imagine that they'd lived long and contented lives. When Robin tried to find out about Pam's life, Margaret would decide whether to let her family rest in peace.

To her relief, Steve was still cutting her hair when he welcomed Robin back. Oh, but she must look a sight, with her limp, wet hair looped up with clips; she would be terribly embarrassed if Robin came over to say hello. Her cheeks reddened. She expected to see Robin's reflection in the mirror, or to sense her next to the chair, but Robin didn't approach. When Steve was selecting another pair of scissors, Margaret glanced toward the waiting area and smiled to herself. Robin was reading a women's magazine, probably bored or thinking about something else. Margaret couldn't be sure, but she suspected that Robin didn't want to make her feel self-conscious by staring.

Half an hour later, Steve turned off the blow-dryer and surveyed his handiwork. "You look wonderful, hon." He spun Margaret's chair to the right. "Doesn't she look wonderful?"

Robin tossed her magazine onto the pile sitting on a coffee table, rose, and walked beaming toward Margaret. "Wow! You look beautiful. I can't believe the difference. I know you loved your mass of hair, but Steve was right. Your beautiful face really shines now."

And was probably beet red! "Thank you," Margaret mumbled, still amazed that Robin could openly admire her without shame. Steve was smirking; he knew Robin wasn't only a friend. According to Robin, he was also a dev—homosexual. But he wasn't the only one within earshot. Others could be listening, too.

"Just blow-dry it after a shower and you'll be all set to go," Steve said. "Thank you for letting me play in your hair. I feel like I've cut four heads of hair, not one." With a flourish, he whipped off the cape, then went to the cash register at the front of the salon. Margaret looked to Robin, then remembered that she had seventy dollars. She pulled the money from her pocket and held it out to Robin, but Robin shook her head and said, "Why don't you pay him?" When Margaret hesitated, Robin smiled encouragingly. "I'll be right next to you. This is one area where nothing much has changed, except the prices."

That was true; people were still people and money was still money. As she'd already noticed, many changes over the last one hundred years were superficial. She should reserve her feelings of intimidation and fear for those that weren't. She squared her shoulders, went to the counter, and behaved as if she were in 1910, paying for a service. The exchange took place without a hitch.

On the way to her coat, Margaret glimpsed herself in a mirror and paused. For the first time, she felt like a 2010 native. The feeling was fleeting; outside on the sidewalk, with cars whizzing by, she remained close to Robin, afraid of losing her and depending on her guidance. But that momentary sense of belonging would only grow over time.

Robin kept gazing at her. "Absolutely stunning," she said, and tightened her arm around Margaret's shoulders while they waited for a light to change.

Margaret glanced around, unaccustomed to such a public display of affection from anyone. "What did you buy?" she asked, referring to the plastic bag hanging off Robin's right arm.

"Oh, just some vegetables for the sauce I want to make tonight. And while I was out, I went into the camera store here." Robin pointed ahead of them. "They take passport photos, so that's our next stop."

"You want to do that now?"

"There's no time like the present."

No, there wasn't.

Chapter Ten

PAM LEANED FORWARD IN HER CHAIR to clink glasses with Jasper, Oliver, and Hortense, then sipped her wine and watched the couples sweeping around the dance floor. This ball reminded her of the Halloween Ball she'd attended with Jasper in Toronto. It wasn't as lavish, but the crowd was younger and more energetic, and she actually knew people.

Oliver had driven them to the ball. Now that Jasper had closed the deal on the property and knew how much he could spend, he was eager to buy a car. With a home waiting for them, their wedding booked, and private drives on the horizon, they were both in the mood to celebrate. The invitation to attend the annual Sailor's Ball couldn't have come at a better time.

She frowned over the rim of her glass when Elliot and Doris joined them. When it came to Doris, Elliot was all manners and charm tonight, but he always behaved impeccably when they were out in public. In addition to family, he apparently felt comfortable berating her in front of Pam and Jasper, but only showed his true colours behind closed doors. Pam worried for Doris. When she lived with him, would he constantly run her down?

"Shall we dance?" Jasper asked.

She nodded, wanting to recapture the magic of the ball in Toronto and pretend men like Elliot didn't exist. On the dance floor, she reached for Jasper with both arms, then laughed along with him when he caught one of her hands. "Habit," she said gaily, captivated by his rugged handsomeness, the colourful evening gowns dotting the dance floor, the music, and the ambiance. As she followed Jasper's steps, determined to appear as if she'd danced this way for years, her mind wandered back to the Toronto ball—and Robin and Margaret. "Remember Margaret sneaking off to the guest house so we could attend the ball together?" she murmured, knowing full well that wasn't why Margaret had faked a bad stomach. If she hadn't fallen in love with Robin, she probably wouldn't have tolerated Pam and Jasper's growing affection. Would Pam be here, in Jasper's arms, if Margaret hadn't been a closet lesbian? Pam sometimes wondered if her desire to be with Jasper and Margaret's desire to be with Robin had somehow influenced the rhyme's effect. Robin definitely belonged in 2010, which could explain why she and Margaret had gone forward, while Pam had remained behind.

Jasper leaned in and whispered, "I still can't believe Margaret is in the future. She must miss her family and friends."

And him? "I think about them in the present tense, too." She couldn't grasp that they didn't exist; she sometimes wondered what they were doing and thought of them as alive, but elsewhere, as if the world consisted of time periods rather than continents. She had to remind herself that Robin hadn't been born, and where was Margaret? In some type of alternate dimension until October, 2010, when she'd suddenly materialize in the exercise room as if she'd beamed down from the starship *Enterprise*? How was she coping? Did the rhyme book tempt her, or had she quickly adapted to the future?

Pam had to figure out what she'd do with her life. Obviously she'd marry Jasper and have children, but washing faces and darning socks wouldn't fulfill her. She wanted to do more, but what? So far, she'd learned about the best seamstresses and tailors, where to dine when in town, how to sip coffee and chit-chat, and that she didn't have the vote. Her embroidery was improving, too. Give her a few months and she might be at the same level as Abigail's daughter.

It was time to get her head out of the clouds. She wasn't on holiday; she'd live here for the rest of her life. Next time she was in town, she'd keep her eye out for posters and billboards advertising women's organizations or volunteer work. Charlotte had mentioned donating to a thrift shop; maybe Pam could help out there. She'd also broach the subject with Jasper, to see if he had any ideas, but only after they were married and settled. He admired independent women; she was

positive he'd support her desire to contribute to society beyond raising children.

But if she'd misjudged him and he balked and broke off their
engagement? She'd want to go home—to 2010. Her motivation to
throw herself into this time period would vanish the moment their
relationship did. The rhyme book would beckon, Pam would succumb,
and Robin and Margaret's lives could be ruined. So yeah, until she
had a wedding ring on her finger, she'd keep her mouth shut about
needing to be more than Holly Homemaker.

MARGARET DRANK HER soda and tried to follow the conversation
between Robin, Cathy, and the other women at their table. The
loud music wasn't hampering her comprehension, though it didn't
help. The unfamiliar words, the cultural references, and the way they
sometimes grasped what another was saying and responded before
she'd finished speaking, often left Margaret befuddled. Fortunately
nobody had put her on the spot, and she managed to appear sociable
by asking the occasional question. But clearly she had a lot to learn
before she could hope to engage someone in interesting conversation,
and seeing Robin talking to her contemporaries had opened Margaret's
eyes to how different her conversations with Robin were. Robin must
sometimes feel as if she were speaking to a child.

The contrast hadn't been as apparent when they'd met Cathy for
tea, perhaps because it had only been the three of them, and Robin
had introduced topics she'd discussed with Margaret during their
evenings in the study. Margaret hadn't realized it at the time, but in
hindsight . . .

Here, Robin couldn't control the conversation, and perhaps she
didn't want to. She must enjoy discussing music, books, movies, and
TV shows without worrying that she wouldn't be understood. They'd
also discussed their jobs, their studies, interesting places to visit on
the Internet, new gadgets . . . It must be a nice change from explain-
ing a simple concept that everyone in 2010 understood, or filling in
the gaps in Margaret's historical knowledge, or rephrasing an idiom.

Oh, she was overstating the difficulties. When they talked, it
wasn't always as teacher and student. They discussed their days, the
news, their childhoods, and their values, and they did more than sit

and chat. They went for walks, had watched a couple of contemporary movies—and planned to see one in a theatre—and Margaret had read and enjoyed a modern mystery Robin had recommended; she'd already started another one by the same author. Robin was also teaching her how to use the computer and had shown her how to go on the Internet, allowing Margaret to answer some of the questions the newspapers raised without bothering Robin. And despite her initial lukewarm impression of TV, she'd agreed to watch several documentaries, had quite enjoyed them, and now eagerly checked the weekly schedule, usually finding at least one or two shows she wanted to curl up on the sofa with Robin and watch.

But observing Robin with her friends, seeing how naturally she interacted with them, gave Margaret pause. Would Robin tire of her role as instructor? Did she sometimes wish that Margaret was from this time? Though they'd embarked on obtaining Margaret photo identification, and Robin spoke as if they'd remain together in the future, she'd never raised the subject of marriage. It had last come up in 1910, when they'd thought they'd be wrenched apart. Had Robin meant it, or had she gone along with it because she hadn't expected Margaret to be in her life? Perhaps she was waiting until Margaret had the required identification to formally propose, but why hadn't she mentioned it at all?

Would they have to share a bed first? The morality regarding sexual relations was more lax in this time, but Robin hadn't even hinted at the prospect of giving themselves to each other in that way. Had reality tempered Robin's enthusiasm for their relationship?

Margaret tried to focus on the conversation again, but now she was completely lost. She gazed past Cathy, at the dancers flailing to the music. When she'd first entered the gymnasium, clinging to Robin's arm, she'd been struck by two observations: that there were no men in attendance—she'd quickly laughed at herself—and that some women wore skirts and dresses, making her feel more at home. Seeing women being openly affectionate with each other had startled her and she'd tried not to stare. It hadn't taken her long to grow used to the sight, but that hadn't stopped her from blushing when Robin had put her arm around her at the table. Cathy had thought it was cute, but Margaret had been mortified.

She jumped when Robin nudged her arm. "Do you want to dance? It's a slow one." Several of the women were already rising.

Margaret nodded, grateful for the respite from the conversation. "I'm sorry I'm not contributing much to the discussion," she felt compelled to say as she reached for Robin on the dance floor.

"You're doing fine. Most of us haven't seen each other for a while, so we're catching up."

And they spoke the same language.

"It's only natural that you'd listen more than speak. Nobody minds. They all know you just came out." Fortunately Robin had explained to her what "coming out" meant. "They know it's your first dance." Robin's arms tightened around her. "You looked like you were enjoying yourself when we danced with Francine and Debbie."

"I was." She'd always enjoyed dancing, and was still unsure whether the lack of required steps was foolish or liberating. "I'm not the only one in a dress."

Robin chuckled. "No."

"I do like to wear the sweatpants in the morning, but I still feel more comfortable in a dress. I'm sorry—"

Robin squeezed her and pressed her lips against Margaret's ear. "I love you just the way you are."

Did she? Normally such words from Robin would have Margaret flushing with pleasure, but doubts were beginning to mar her rosy picture of their life together.

PAM DESCENDED THE stairs and walked up the hallway to the library, hoping to find an interesting book to take with her to the lovely pond she'd discovered yesterday afternoon. Doris hadn't shown her the picturesque area with its wooden bench and majestic trees, but then, Doris deliberately hurried off in the other direction whenever she spotted Pam. Despite their conversation about women's position in society, Doris still wasn't interested in Pam's friendship. When were her parents due back? Maybe they'd keep Pam company. Better yet, maybe she'd be long gone by then, married to Jasper and decorating their own home.

A shout set her heart racing as she approached the drawing room. It sounded like Elliot. Pam paused outside the doorway.

". . . learn to put your desires aside! You are going to be my wife!"
Silence.

"You have nothing to say in your defence? You are the only woman who didn't agree to accompany Gwen to the lecture today. Are you that selfish, that you'd rather read than learn how you can aid the church in its work in India?"

"Margaret declined to—"

"Margaret is new here, and doesn't share your selfishness—yet. I may have a word with Jasper and suggest that she board with someone else, lest she fall under your influence."

Oh, for god's sake. Without thinking, Pam walked into the room. "I'm not falling under her influence, Elliot."

He spun around. Doris gazed up at her from the chair, where she sat with her hands demurely clasped on top of the open book on her lap.

"I'd rather help the people of Halifax than those in India," Pam said. "When Jasper and I are settled, I'll be looking for opportunities to do so."

"You see!" Elliot spat, flinging his arm toward Pam. "She's not a selfish woman who cares for nobody but herself."

Oops. In trying to absolve Doris of any influence over her behaviour, she'd given Elliot more ammunition. "She declined to attend one lecture. That doesn't mean she's selfish."

Elliot's mouth pressed into a thin line. "Margaret, I appreciate your desire to support your friend. It's admirable, and what I would expect of a lady. But you don't know Doris as well as I do. Books matter to her more than people." He looked down his nose at Doris. "Including her future husband."

"I'm sure that's not true," Pam said, sure that it was.

He smirked and shook his head, then suddenly grabbed the book from Doris's lap, snapped it shut, and held it under her nose. "Will this keep you? Will this give you children?" Pam tensed when his eyes went to the book Doris had shoved down the side of the cushion. He tossed the first book onto the table and slid the other book from its hiding place. "What's this?" He read the title; his face darkened. "What's this?" he shouted.

Doris swallowed and stared at her lap.

"You were told, Doris! How could you disobey me? You are not to read these books!"

Pam couldn't stand by and watch. "Why shouldn't she read the books?"

"Because she is going to be my wife!" he roared. "She doesn't need to know any of this." He growled and flung the arm holding the book across his chest. For a split second, Pam thought he was going to sideswipe Doris with it. She stepped forward, then stopped when he picked up the other book and tucked both books under his arm. "Obviously leaving you on your own, unsupervised, wasn't a good idea. The moment your parents left for Europe, I should have made other arrangements for you. I'll discuss the matter with Mama and Papa. If they're agreeable, you'll move in with them. I'll find temporary lodgings in town."

Doris's eyes widened; she shot to her feet. "No, Elliot, please. I'll—"

"Unfortunately that will leave you here on your own," Elliot said to Pam, as if Doris wasn't in the room. "I apologize, but it must be done."

"I don't want to go, Elliot. Please don't make me go."

Pam winced at Doris's pleading tone, her white face, and the fear in her eyes. She shouldn't have to beg her fiancé to let her live in her own home. "Doris is a grown woman."

"With no sense!" Elliot snapped. "I was warned, but I didn't listen. Well, I'm not making the same mistake Thomas Simmons made. I'll put an end to this right now." He turned to Doris. "You'll have ample time to pack your things by Friday. I can always drive you round, if you forget anything." He raised a finger. "No books. Mama will help you unpack, to make sure." He strode from the room.

"Elliot!" Doris hurried after him.

Pam reached the hallway in time to hear the front door thump shut. She raced toward it. Tears prickled at her eyelashes when a wailing Doris fled up the stairs, her sobs echoing around the spacious entrance hall.

Bella came to see what the fuss was about. Her eyes met Pam's as she shook her head and disappeared through the doorway from which she'd emerged. Pam stared up the stairs, wondering if the rhyme had suddenly dumped her in the middle of the dark ages. Numerous questions jammed her mind, one crying to be answered above the rest: who the hell was Thomas Simmons?

Chapter Eleven

MARGARET PULLED ON HER COAT AND slipped the ten-dollar bill Robin handed her into a pocket.

"Are you sure about this?" Robin said. "I can go with you."

"We've walked to the corner store together at least twenty times. It's only two blocks away."

"But why do you want to go alone?"

"Because I have to start going out by myself." She wanted to show Robin that she could do it, that she could go and buy a loaf of bread without Robin holding her hand.

Robin's face creased with worry. "It gets dark early now."

"Yes, it does. But it's 1:30 in the afternoon."

"Take my phone."

"Robin, I'll be back in less than five minutes." Margaret blew out a frustrated sigh when Robin bounded up the stairs. She had a good mind to leave, but Robin would come after her. "Thank you," she mumbled when Robin returned. The phone joined the money. Margaret turned toward the door.

"Don't talk to anyone." Robin hovered behind her. "Just go to the store, get the bread, and come back."

"What will you do when I go out while you're at university?" When Robin sucked in her breath, Margaret regretted her affectionate teasing. She patted Robin's arm. "Don't worry, I won't unless I've discussed it with you first. Now, I should go. I'll be back before you've even shut the door. Oh, what about a key?" She'd never unlocked the front door, she realized.

"Don't worry about that. It'll be unlocked."

"No, lock it."

Robin hesitated. "Okay." She reached into her pocket, pulled out a keychain, and removed a key. "Here."

Margaret silently accepted it. Excited, nervous, and eager to leave before Robin stopped her, she opened the front door and stepped onto the porch. Unlike that very first day she'd stepped outside with Robin, the sun wasn't shining, and a light dusting of snow covered the path. She should have asked for a pair of gloves, but she wasn't turning back now. Her fingers wouldn't freeze, especially with her hands in her pockets.

Her hand curled around the phone in her pocket when she reached the sidewalk and turned toward the store. She passed only one other person, a man who didn't make eye contact or speak, as usual. She was soon pulling open the store's glass door, reminding herself that people were people, money was money, and she'd bought a loaf of bread with Robin several times.

The shopkeeper smiled at her, much to Margaret's delight. She returned the smile, selected a fresh loaf, and paid for it, thanking the shopkeeper for the change. "Have a nice day," the woman chirped, and Margaret returned the sentiment. Outside, she paused to breathe in the cool air and savour her success. *I did it!* Not quite. She wasn't home yet.

At the corner, she looked both ways and waited for a car to turn, then crossed the road and continued up the sidewalk. Movement up ahead caught her eye. What—was that Robin, darting up the front path? Margaret wanted to strangle her! How could she become the independent woman Robin wanted her to be, when Robin didn't trust her to walk two blocks by herself on their own street?

As she climbed the front steps, she tried to quell her dismay. If it wasn't for Robin's tendency to imagine the worst, Margaret would teach her a lesson by standing out of sight on the porch and waiting for her to rush out in alarm. Instead she unlocked the front door and stepped into her safe haven. She rolled her eyes when she glanced into the living room and spotted Robin on the sofa, supposedly engrossed in a book. Robin preferred those e-reader things. "Bread," she announced, then stifled a giggle at Robin's feigned look of surprise and decided not to reveal that she'd caught Robin watching over her.

"Your first foray out into the world by yourself," Robin declared with a smile as she rose. She gave Margaret a quick hug. "I should give you Pam's keys. Remind me, next time we're upstairs. You were serious when you said you won't go out without telling me, right? At least until I stop hyperventilating about it."

Margaret may have only walked two blocks on her own, but those two blocks were a significant step toward asserting the independence that Robin wanted and narrowing the time gap that separated them. "I promise I'll talk to you first. Now, let me start the casserole for tonight."

"Do you need help?"

Not really, but she'd welcome Robin's company. "Yes, I do." Margaret cradled the bread in her right arm and slipped her left around Robin's waist. She smiled when she felt Robin's arm around her shoulders. It felt so natural to walk up the hallway to the kitchen, arm in arm. She wanted to be with Robin for the rest of her life, not as a close friend or a family obligation, but as Robin's partner, her confidante, and yes, her lover.

SNIFFLING INTO A handkerchief, Pam leaned forward on the wooden bench and gazed into what she'd come to think of as her little pond. Though she'd known it was coming, she hadn't expected today to hit her so hard. Sure, when a scent, conversation, or sight in town evoked a memory of her life in 2010, she often felt nostalgic, even melancholy. But today was different. She felt lonely and depressed; she ached inside, and wondered if she truly belonged here or if she was crazy.

The chill breeze chased ripples across the pond's surface. Pam hunched her shoulders and lifted her coat's collar, then blew her nose. Hairs stood up on the back of her neck. Someone was behind her! Her heart in her mouth, she twisted around. Fear gave way to surprise. Doris mumbled a hello and lowered herself onto the bench.

If Pam hadn't known that Elliot was coming for Doris tomorrow, she could have been forgiven for thinking that Doris had already moved out. Since that scene in the drawing room, she'd glimpsed Doris once, and only because she'd forgotten her gloves when going out for an evening walk with Jasper. Poor Doris must have thought the coast was clear; she'd hurried up the hallway as soon as the front door opened.

Doris clasped her hands on her lap. "I wanted to have a word before I leave tomorrow," she said quietly.

Pam could hardly bear to look at Doris, who was white as a ghost. Her pale skin made the shadows under her puffy eyes more ominous, and the weariness etched into her face . . . Pam reached out and patted Doris's hands.

Doris sat stiffly. "I'm sorry you had to witness that altercation in the drawing room. It must have been awkward for you. Thank you for defending me, though you didn't have to."

Her lifeless voice made Pam forget about her own reasons for feeling down. "Of course I did." God, she couldn't sit by and watch Doris ruin her life. Doris wouldn't appreciate her meddling, but she wasn't Doris's favourite person, anyway. "Doris, what are you doing with Elliot? He treats you like a child. You can do better. I thought you were the sort of woman who'd want a man who respects you." She braced herself to be told to mind her own business. When Doris swallowed and stared down at her lap, Pam wanted Doris to tell her off, to defend herself, anything! But the fight was gone from her. "There are other men—"

"No." Doris shook her head. "No."

"Why not? You're only twenty-four. You can wait for someone better."

"I doubt anyone else will have me." Her chin trembled.

Pam glanced down at the used handkerchief in her left hand. *Um, no.* "I've used it," she said apologetically, lifting her handkerchief a few inches. Then she continued, before Doris tried to derail the conversation by asking about the reason for Pam's moist eyes. "Why wouldn't anyone else have you? You're from an upper class family with a good reputation." Not that such things should matter. "How did you get involved with Elliot? Didn't you realize early on that he's a . . ." *Jerk?* ". . . he doesn't treat you well?"

"My parents arranged our engagement. I was . . . I was engaged to someone else once, but he broke off our engagement." Her eyes closed and her knuckles whitened.

"Did you love him?" Pam asked softly, suspecting the answer.

She nodded, then opened her eyes. "But I misjudged him, or perhaps the depth of his love for me."

"What happened?" When Doris remained silent, Pam hoped she wouldn't clam up, just when things were getting interesting. But she'd sought Pam out to talk, and that must mean that Doris was desperate, or just didn't care anymore. Pam stared into the pond again, not wanting to pressure her.

"You'll laugh at me," Doris finally said.

"No, I won't. I promise I won't. What is it?"

Doris swallowed. "I want to be a doctor."

"A doctor!" Pam breathed. Okay, now the medical book made sense.

Doris tentatively met her eyes. "I have a university degree. So do some of the women you've met. But they got theirs for something to do before they married."

"And you got yours because you hope to go to medical school," Pam drawled.

Doris nodded.

"Well, that's commendable."

"You think so?"

"Yes!" But what did this have to do with Doris and her broken engagement? A sick feeling formed in the pit of Pam's stomach. "But your first fiancé didn't think so?"

"I thought he did. He was supportive when I was in university, even bought me some medical books. I thought he was taking my aspiration seriously, but he wasn't. He thought it was a passing fancy, that I'd give up on the idea once we married, and focus on our family and the housework." Her mouth twisted. "I thought he honestly supported me, that he would have been proud to have a doctor as a wife. That he loved me, so he'd want the best for me, just as I wanted the best for him. I couldn't have been more wrong." She wiped away a tear that rolled down her cheek.

Pam squeezed Doris's arm, then held it. "When did he realize you were serious?"

"When I showed him the application for medical school. It was horrible. He shouted at me and tore it up. I thought he'd be pleased." Her bewildered voice exposed the betrayal she still felt. "I thought once he'd calmed down, we could talk about it, but the next thing I knew, he'd announced to everyone that our engagement was off. My parents were horrified. He was a good catch," she said wryly.

"He doesn't sound like one to me," Pam said, warmed when the hint of a smile touched Doris's lips. "You must have been terribly hurt."

"Yes. And things changed for me. I was often overlooked when invitations went out for parties. Nobody called on me. It became apparent that I'd moved to the bottom of the list of desirable wives. Thomas turned so many against me."

Thomas Simmons, Pam presumed. But . . . "Why haven't you applied to medical school? Why did you hide your medical book?"

"Father refuses to pay the tuition. He forbade me from entertaining the notion again."

How could you forbid someone from having a desire?

"He arranged the engagement with Elliot." Doris sighed. "Elliot returned to Halifax earlier this year, after spending time in the United States. He wants a family. But he doesn't want a relationship. I'll be a maid and breeder, nothing more. I suppose my desperate circumstances made me one of the few who might accept those terms."

Desperate circumstances? They were sitting next to a freaking pond on a god-knows-how-many-acres estate with a flipping mansion and several guest houses, to boot. But none of it was Doris's. She was expected to marry and become the responsibility of her husband. Still . . . "Doris—"

"A couple of months ago, after Mother and Father had left, I was in town and found that medical book among the items donated to the thrift shop. I couldn't resist it. I must have read it a hundred times, even though it hurts."

"Doris!" Pam let out an exasperated sigh. "Why are you giving up on your dream? I know you're dependent on your parents, but if you truly want to be a doctor, there has to be a way. What about what you said about women and achieving?"

Doris snorted softly. "I'm afraid I'm a coward. Words are easy, Margaret. If I were to break my engagement with Elliot, Father would probably disown me. What would I do? Where would I live? It would be too high a price to pay."

Pam gaped at her. "From where I'm sitting, you'll pay a much higher price by marrying Elliot and being trapped in a life you hate." With a man she'd likely loathe. "Yes, if you decided to pursue your dream, you'd have rough times ahead, but at least you'd have a chance

at happiness and fulfillment, and maybe a man who supports you.
Maybe he wouldn't be rich, but so what? You have to think about
what's best for your life, not only for today, but ten, twenty, thirty
years from now." As she had, when she'd announced that she'd remain
in 1910, rather than return to her own time? She wished she could tell
Doris how familiar she was with turning one's back on everything
one knew because of the promise that lay around the corner.

For a moment she felt like a fraud. Who was she, to counsel Doris
to throw everything away, when she'd been sobbing into a hanky
not ten minutes ago? Well, she wasn't saying it would be easy. There
would be doubts, the agony of loss, the wobbly moments when Doris
would be convinced that she was absolutely insane. But it was better
than regret.

"There's no point thinking about it," Doris murmured.

"Yes, there is!"

"No, I can't do it. I'll never be able to afford it. Father won't tolerate
it while I'm under his roof."

"Do you have any money at all?"

Doris's brow furrowed. "I have a little put aside, but not enough
for food, lodgings, and tuition."

"Jasper told me your parents are due back in a few months."

Doris nodded. "February."

"Take that time to find a job and get yourself a room."

"No, I can't—they won't approve. Elliot won't approve."

"Doris." Pam hesitated, then covered Doris's hands with hers. "You'll
slowly die with Elliot. You'll hate him. You'll resent your children."

"I don't even want children. I wouldn't mind if I never marry,
either," Doris blurted. A sea of red washed over her face. "You must
think me a terrible woman."

"No, I don't. Forget what everyone else wants you to do. They
don't have to live your life. Go to medical school. Surround yourself
with people who support you, starting with me and Jasper." He'd
loved the independent Emily and would marry a woman from 2010.
Seeing Doris suffer with Elliot would pain him as much as it would
Pam. "The universe—God wants you to be happy."

Doris pulled her hands from underneath Pam's and turned toward her to search Pam's face with curious eyes. "Who are you?" she
murmured.

"What?"

"You're not Margaret Wilton, and you're . . . different."

Shit! Pam's heart raced. She forced a shrill laugh. "What do you mean? Of course I'm Margaret Wilton."

"No, you're not," Doris said, her voice quietly confident. "When I was seventeen, I went to Toronto with Mother and Father, to see Oliver. That's when I first met Jasper. Of course, he didn't know Margaret then—if he's ever known her at all—and so he had no way of knowing that, while on that trip, I frequently visited with a Miss Violet Dodson, the daughter of one of Mother's friends. On one such visit, several other young ladies were in attendance, including a Miss Margaret Wilton."

"Margaret Wilton isn't an unusual name," Pam said, grasping at straws.

"The Margaret Wilton I met had the same address that you claim. I only remember it because Father later told me that one of his friends lived on the same road."

Shit, what do I do? "How long have you suspected that I'm not Margaret Wilton?" Pam asked, stalling.

Doris pursed her lips. "When Oliver told me you'd be coming to stay with us, I remembered my time in Toronto, but it *was* almost eight years ago. I sort of remembered what Margaret looked like. When we were first introduced, you weren't what I was expecting. But you're about the same height, and have the same colour hair, and I told myself that my memory might be vague, and that Margaret was only fifteen when I met her. Women's faces do mature. And Jasper believed you to be Margaret—or so I thought."

At a loss, Pam could only stare back at Doris. Was she about to be turned over to the local police?

"I saw him help you, at the ball. He positioned your hands. Margaret wouldn't need such instruction." Doris's mouth turned up at the corners. "And she could embroider. We spent an hour in each other's company doing so."

Fuck. "If you don't believe I'm Margaret, why haven't you done anything?" Pam said, doing her best to sound indignant.

"What would I do, tell Oliver? He dismisses everything I say, and you and Jasper would only deny my accusation. Go to the police? You must have identification that supports the name, otherwise you wouldn't be able to marry. I'd be painted as a hysterical woman suffering delusions, and Elliot would have another reason to doubt my suitability as a wife." Her gaze left Pam's face. "Perhaps I am delusional. As my conviction that you aren't Margaret grew, I asked myself, what had happened to the real Margaret? What had you done with her? But you don't strike me as the sort capable of physical violence."

Jesus, did Doris think she and Jasper had murdered Margaret? "If you're not intending to do anything, why accuse me? What if I am some type of crazed murderer?"

Doris's eyes grew bright. "Curiosity, I suppose. It'll be my undoing."

It was more likely that Elliot would crush Doris's curious spirit under his heel, and Doris's willingness to confront Pam was another indication that she no longer cared about what happened to her.

"Who are you? What happened to Margaret?"

Pam gulped. There was no point trying to wriggle out of it; Doris knew she wasn't Margaret. But what to tell her? "Margaret's fine," she began, answering the easier question first.

"So you're not Margaret!" Rather than freaking out, Doris seemed rather pleased with herself. "Who are you, then? And where's Margaret? Why are you pretending to be her?"

"Let me start from the beginning." *Only lie when you have to. Make Jasper look good.* "Jasper and Margaret—the real Margaret—*were* engaged. But they weren't in love. It wasn't an arranged engagement like yours and Elliot's, though. They actually liked each other. It was more an 'It's time to get married, we have genuine affection for each other, and our parents approve' sort of arrangement. But then they met me and a friend of mine. Jasper and I fell in love. So did Margaret and my friend."

Doris blinked. "So why didn't Jasper and Margaret break their engagement? Why are you pretending to be Margaret?"

Details, details. "Margaret knew her parents wouldn't approve of my friend. And I, uh, don't have proper papers."

"You're some type of fugitive?" Doris asked, wide-eyed.

"Not exactly. I'm not from Canada. I didn't legally immigrate here. That's all I can tell you." Pam hurried along. "Anyway, Margaret knew she and my friend would have to elope. She wanted to disappear. She didn't want her parents to worry or to come after her. So we decided that she'd run away with my friend, and that Jasper and I would also run away, to someplace where we could start over. It also worked out for Jasper in terms of his cabinetmaking. Just *that* would have driven us from Toronto. We haven't lied when we've said that his father was incensed by his decision to leave the family business."

"And Jasper told her parents that you were eloping here?" Doris frowned. "They'd still want to come for the wedding, and to visit."

"Not after Jasper told them we'd been naughty and I was four months pregnant."

Doris chuckled. "Oh, dear."

"I've been disowned, which is what Margaret wanted. They're not looking for her now. She and my friend are building a new life together." Pam's eyes welled with tears. *Damn it!* She blinked them away.

"You miss them," Doris said gently.

Pam pressed her lips together and nodded. "It's my friend's birthday today." Or at least it would be, and she'd no longer be there to run interference between Robin and mommy dearest. *God, Robin, I hope you and Margaret are doing okay.*

"What's his name?" Doris asked.

"Robin," Pam said, silently apologizing to Robin and grateful for her unisex name.

"Robin . . . ?"

"Tillman."

Doris chortled. "I've heard of the Toronto Tillmans. Oliver and his old school friends have mentioned them, and that friend of Father's visited last year and told us about the gambling scandal. Is Robin related to them?"

"Yes," Pam said, once again in that twilight zone where she could tell the truth and it made perfect sense, as long as she didn't mention that Robin hadn't been born yet.

"Victor Tillman's a drunk, along with half his family."

Pam quietly sighed. Amazing, how little had changed for the Tillmans over the past—um, how little *would* change over the next hundred years, but Robin was determined to break the cycle. "Robin isn't a drunk. He doesn't drink alcohol."

"Now I understand why Margaret ran away with him," Doris said. "But wouldn't she need her documents to marry him?"

"Not where they went. They left the country."

Doris's brows drew together, but she remained silent.

"So you see, Doris, I know what it's like to leave a life behind for something—or someone—you truly want. I'm not giving you empty advice, and I won't tell you it's easy. It's a leap of faith to believe that, even though your life will be turned upside down for a while, it will eventually be righted, and I mean that in every way possible."

Doris's eyes grew distant.

"Are you going to tell anyone?" Pam asked. "About me?"

"No. I won't ruin four lives."

But she'd ruin her own?

Doris refocused on Pam. "What's *your* name?"

A lump formed in her throat. "Pam. Pam Holden."

"Short for Pamela?"

Pam nodded.

"Well, now we know each other's secrets," Doris said.

"That means we have to be friends."

Doris gave her a shy smile. "I could use a friend right now."

Pam squeezed Doris's hands. "You have one."

"Will you see Jasper later this afternoon?"

She wished. "I'm happy Bill Crawford agreed to take him on as an apprentice, but between that and reinvesting the money he had in his father's company, I'm lucky to see him for an hour in the evenings. But the wedding will be soon." Pam bit her lip when she felt a grin coming on. Poor Doris wouldn't be looking forward to her wedding to Elliot. "Will you think about what we've talked about?"

"I'll give our conversation some thought," Doris said, but Pam could tell that she'd already resigned herself to a life she didn't want.

Chapter Twelve

Margaret stepped into the apartment building's lobby when Robin swung open the glass door and waved her inside. "We can take the stairs, it's on the second floor," Robin mumbled, the first words she'd spoken since they'd boarded the streetcar near home. No, she'd warned Margaret that they were approaching their stop, but otherwise had silently stared out the window.

Yesterday Robin had returned home from university late, because she'd stopped in to see her mother. "I wanted to make sure she remembered we were coming tomorrow," she'd said, and then had told Margaret for the tenth time that her mother could be difficult. As of half an hour ago, Margaret had been cautioned for the thirtieth time. She knew the woman was an alcoholic, but surely she'd remain sober for her daughter's birthday, especially when she was expecting a guest.

When Margaret had woken early that morning to make Robin's breakfast, she'd expected Robin to be in a jolly mood—it was her birthday! But a cloud had hung over her all day. Robin dreaded this visit, and her apprehension was contagious.

Margaret steeled herself when Robin stopped outside an apartment door and smiled weakly. She rapped at the door and opened it. "Mom?"

"She's in the bathroom." A man came into the hallway from a room to the right; Margaret immediately saw his resemblance to Robin. "Happy birthday, sis." He reached for Robin and hugged her.

"Thanks for the card—and the lottery tickets."

"You're welcome. Did you win anything?"

"Ten bucks."

His face lit up. "All right!" He turned to Margaret and swept his arms toward her. "This must be Margaret."

Margaret opened her mouth to say hello, but Chris wrapped her in a hug and squeezed the breath out of her.

"Jeez, Chris, don't break her," Robin said.

Chris let her go. Surprised by the intimate nature of his greeting, Margaret croaked, "Pleased to meet you."

"Robin has told me all about you," Chris said.

She doubted that.

He put his hands on his hips and stared at her. She expected him to say something, but he just nodded, then dropped his hands and brushed past Robin. "Where are you going?" Robin asked.

"To Emma's."

"*What?*"

He pulled on his coat. "It's Saturday night. I tried to get her to come over here, but . . ."

Robin groaned. "I was hoping you'd be here," she gave Margaret a sidelong glance, "to help."

"I know. I'm sorry. She's only had a couple."

"Oh, shit."

Margaret heard a door open behind her.

"Gotta go." Chris patted Robin's shoulder, swung the apartment door open, and hastily disappeared through it.

Robin shook her head and looked past Margaret. "Hi, Mom."

Margaret turned in time to see a woman wave and walk into the same room from which Chris had emerged.

After hanging their coats, Robin led Margaret into the living room and surveyed it with an exasperated sigh. "Oh my god. This room was spotless when I left yesterday."

Her mother looked up from the chair into which she'd plunked. "Don't start, Robin." She squinted at Margaret. "Aren't you going to introduce us?"

Robin heaved another sigh. "Mom, this is Margaret. Margaret, my mother, Janice Tillman."

Margaret inclined her head. "Pleased to meet you, Mrs. Tillman."

Robin's mother barked a laugh. "My, aren't you proper. Call me Janice, sweetheart." She picked up the glass next to her and took a long sip, then held it up. "Do you want one?"

"No, thank you."

"We're going to have pop," Robin said.

"Well, you're no fun. Sit down!"

Robin gathered up the newspapers strewn across the sofa, set the pile on the coffee table, and beckoned for Margaret to sit next to her.

Janice sipped her drink again and eyed Robin over the rim of the glass. "Twenty-seven, eh? Twenty-fucking-seven. Where the hell did the time go? Jesus, I'm old." Another sip. "One minute you're changing diapers, the next your kids are leaving you, just like that." She snapped her fingers. "Did Chris tell you he's thinking of moving in with Emma? He's known her five minutes and he wants to move in with her."

"Sometimes it doesn't take long to know you want to be with someone," Robin said, making Margaret wonder if she was talking about herself, about them.

"Are you two living together?" Janice asked.

Robin hesitated. "Yes."

"Out with Pam, in with Margaret, eh?"

"Pam and I weren't together, Mom, and you know it."

Janice shrugged and drained her glass. "Do you know how long your father and I dated before we got engaged and married? Four months," she said, at the same time Robin mouthed it. "We thought we were in love, and we were! But those wedding vows?" Her eyes narrowed. "Empty words, kids. Remember that." She frowned at her glass. "Christ, I could use a cigarette right now."

"Don't tell me you've started again," Robin said.

"No! I quit six years ago," she informed Margaret proudly. "Haven't smoked since, but I still get the craving. And don't tell me I should give up drinking, too," she said, looking down her finger as she pointed at Robin. "I have to have some indulgences in my life."

Robin's jaw tightened.

"Well, well," Janice said, raising her brows. "Normally I get the lecture now. Don't want to upset Margaret, eh?"

"Mom!" Robin stood. "Do you want a Coke?" she asked Margaret.

"Yes, please."

Janice picked up her glass and held it out to Robin. "I'll have Coke too, but you can add rum to mine."

Robin yanked the glass from her mother's hand and stalked from the room. Margaret wanted to run after her. She swallowed, smoothed her dress, and hoped she didn't look as uncomfortable as she felt.

"So you're living with Robin, now that Pam's out of the picture, eh?" Janice said.

Margaret nodded.

"Do you know Pam?"

"Yes."

"Do you think she's a bitch?"

Margaret stiffened. "Pardon me?"

"I think she's a bitch, looking down her nose at me and filling Robin's head with nonsense. We were happy together, the three of us," Janice said, making a circling motion with one of her fingers. "But Pam lured Robin away, and now she's run off with some guy! I could have told Robin she was no good, but as far as Robin's concerned, Pam can do no wrong. Nope, when Pam farts, lightning bolts shoot out of her ass."

Margaret could only gape, not sure that she'd ever experienced a mixture of mortification and amusement before.

"Good riddance. I'm glad you're here, instead of Pam. You won't tell me to shut up, right?" Janice pitched her voice higher. "'Shut up, Janice.' That's all Pam ever says. 'Shut up, Janice.'"

Fortunately Robin returned carrying two glasses, because Margaret didn't know how to respond. She couldn't imagine telling Robin's mother to shut up, but at the same time, she suspected it would be a bad idea to relinquish her right to do so. She accepted the Coke Robin handed her with a murmured, "Thank you," sipped it, and set it on a coaster on the coffee table.

"Did you hear from your father today?" Janice called when Robin left to fetch her own drink.

Robin didn't answer until she'd returned and sat down. "He sent me a card."

"I hope it contained a fucking cheque."

Robin nodded.

"How much?"

"Mom."

"How much?" Janice roared.

"Why do you want to know? You'll only get upset."

"Do you know how much, Margaret?"

She did, but she wasn't about to divulge the amount. Would Robin's mother be upset because it was too much or too little?

"Don't bring Margaret into this," Robin said.

Janice's mouth pinched. She glared at Robin. "You always protect him."

"No, I don't. You know I don't."

"Yes, you do." Janice lifted her glass and gestured with it at Robin. "You say you're not close, but you're two peas in a pod, aren't you?"

Robin snorted. "No, we're not."

"Be careful, Margaret, because she's a lot like him. I hope you don't piss her off, because you'll be out the door, if you do."

"Mom!"

"What? She has a right to know."

"To know what?" Robin snapped. "Damn it!"

"Who left?" Janice shouted. "You did!" She finished her drink in one go, slammed the empty glass on the end table, and launched into a tirade against Robin.

Margaret looked on in horror, wincing when Janice called Robin a bitch and an ungrateful daughter. It was Robin's birthday. Couldn't Janice put aside any perceived slights for one evening—not that the name-calling would ever be acceptable, or the hurtful accusations. Why wasn't Robin defending herself? Surely she didn't believe her mother's words—or had she heard them so many times that she no longer listened? Margaret suddenly understood why Pam had felt compelled to speak up. Margaret couldn't sit in silence, either. "Janice," she said, then louder, "Janice!"

Janice clamped her mouth shut and shifted her attention to Margaret.

"It's Robin's birthday. Can you—"

"Don't," Robin murmured, placing her hand on Margaret's leg.

"No, let her speak." Janice leaned back and grasped the arms of the chair. "What is it, sweetheart?"

"It's Robin's birthday. It's not the time for arguments."

Janice's eyes narrowed. "Oh, well, pleased to meet you, Pam number two. Who are you, to come in here and tell me what I can say in my own *fucking* apartment? Didn't your mother—"

"Mom, don't!" Robin shouted. "Shit!" She stood. "Let's have cake. Margaret, why don't you come and help me?"

Margaret picked up the drink she'd barely touched and eagerly followed Robin to the kitchen.

"I'm sorry," Robin said as soon as they were out of Janice's earshot. "I'm sorry."

"It's all right," Margaret said, knowing that her assurance wouldn't assuage Robin's embarrassment. "Where's the cake?"

Robin opened the refrigerator and slid out a cardboard box. She set it on the counter and lifted its lid. Margaret read the *Happy Birthday, Robin!* written in icing. "Your mother went to some trouble for this."

"Yeah," Robin mumbled. She set the cake onto a plate she lifted down from a cupboard, then cut several pieces, dropping them onto the smaller plates Margaret held out to her. Margaret rashly kissed her on the cheek and rubbed her arm. "We work well together."

Another mumbled response. Robin added a fork to each plate. "Just a second," Margaret said when Robin picked up two of the pieces. She drained her glass as a way of gathering her courage and, after setting it in the sink, picked up the remaining piece of cake.

When they entered the living room, Janice eagerly reached for her piece. She cut away a mouthful with her fork and popped it into her mouth. "Mmm, chocolate, my favourite. You did good, Robin."

Fortunately Margaret was already seated and had rested her plate on her lap, otherwise she might have dropped it. Robin had bought her own birthday cake? Margaret turned to her. Rage and sympathy surged through her at the sight of Robin's red face and her stiff, hunched shoulders. Margaret wanted to touch her, hug her, do something! But Janice might poke fun, and Margaret had gained enough understanding of Robin to know that it would only make things worse.

Robin was a proud woman, one whom Margaret dearly loved. She would gladly have baked a cake for her, creating it from scratch and decorating it with love. But Robin had said there was no need, that her mother would provide the cake—except she hadn't. Margaret had wondered why Robin had visited her mother yesterday when they'd be seeing her today. Apparently it had been to do the housework and organize her own birthday!

Margaret chewed a bite of cake, but she'd lost her appetite, and her willingness to socialize. She forced the cake down and listened to Janice ramble about her pet peeves and all the slights committed against her, real and perceived, by Robin's father, Robin, Chris, her parents . . . the postman!

Robin didn't protest when Janice demanded another drink. The more intoxicated Janice became, the more wildly her mood swung between belligerent and weepy. Contributing to the conversation was risky; a seemingly innocuous statement could set off a tirade or tears. When Janice asked for yet another drink, Robin finally put Margaret out of her misery by telling Janice they were leaving and, if she wanted a drink, she'd have to get it herself. Janice stumbled into the hallway with them. Margaret thought Janice intended to see them out, but she continued into the kitchen—for another rum and Coke, no doubt.

"Time to make a break for it," Robin murmured, her small smile failing to mask the bleakness in her eyes.

They quickly pulled on their coats and fled the apartment. Robin shoved her hands into her jacket pockets and didn't speak a word the entire way home. She'd raised the drawbridge, shuttered the windows, and hunkered down for a lengthy siege. Margaret would try to find a way in, but not tonight. It would be like poking a wounded animal with a stick.

When they arrived home, Robin hung her jacket and said, "I'm tired. I'm going to bed."

"Can I have a minute of your time?" Margaret asked. "Just a minute."

Robin's lips compressed, but she nodded.

"I have to fetch something from my bedroom." She hurried up the stairs and retrieved Robin's present from its hiding place. She'd looked forward to giving it to her, had imagined them returning home in high spirits and capping off the evening by sharing a tea—the perfect time to watch Robin unwrap her gift. If only Margaret had known . . . On the way home, she'd contemplated holding onto it until Robin's mood brightened, but withholding a birthday present because someone was hurting didn't make sense, and Robin would surely guess Margaret's reason for doing so and not appreciate it.

When Margaret went downstairs, Robin was in the living room, fidgeting on the sofa. Margaret handed her the present. "Happy birthday," she said, inwardly wincing at the hollowness of the words.

"Thank you." Robin unwrapped the gift, unfolded the knitted cardigan, and lifted it up by its shoulders.

"I altered the pattern a bit, so I hope it fits. I removed some of the more feminine features and added a collar."

"It's lovely."

"I know I didn't buy the wool."

"It doesn't matter. You crafted it and put in the time." Robin hugged the cardigan against her chest and blinked rapidly. "It's the thought that counts. You thought of me."

A lump formed in Margaret's throat at the sadness in Robin's voice. Her heart ached for her. Love was joyous, but it had another side—Robin's pain pierced Margaret's soul as if it were her own. Watching Robin struggle with her composure . . . Oh, the helplessness, the certainty that anything she said or did would deepen the hurt, embarrassment, and shame that Robin didn't deserve to feel! She wished they could start the day over. If only she'd known.

Robin folded the cardigan and dropped it onto the wrapping paper on her lap. "I was thinking that we should have invited more people than just Cathy to lunch tomorrow," she said, her eyes on her present. "I should introduce you to more people." She swallowed. "I'm not the only lesbian in Toronto. I'm just the first one you met. It's a big city. There are a lot of us." She nodded, as if reaching a decision. "I'll introduce you to more people."

Margaret loved Robin! She'd fallen in love with Robin before she knew Robin was a lesbian. She hadn't fallen for her because Robin was the first lesbian she'd met.

"If you don't mind, I'll try this on tomorrow. I really need to go to bed. But it's lovely. Thank you."

"You're welcome," Margaret said, but Robin wasn't listening; she'd already scooped the cardigan into her arms and risen.

"Good night," Robin murmured.

Margaret managed to stem her tears until she could no longer hear Robin's footsteps, then she let them flow and quietly wept—for Robin, for herself, and for the battle that lay ahead. How did one overcome years of emotional battering and neglect?

Robin had lost a strong ally—Pam—and it was up to Margaret to take her place. Remaining silent and staring in horror like a frightened rabbit wouldn't do. Janice would *not* run Robin down unopposed in Margaret's presence again! Next time, Margaret would immediately speak up, over Robin's protests, if she had to. Of course, she was assuming this evening hadn't completely scuttled her and Robin's chances of spending their lives together. As much as the thought of seeing Janice again turned Margaret's stomach, she desperately hoped there would be a next time.

Chapter Thirteen

Pam watched in dismay as Elliot helped Doris into his car. When Doris raised her hand in farewell, Pam forced a smile and returned the gesture. Her peripheral vision caught Jasper doing the same. They stood in silence, their eyes on the car as it slowly proceeded up the long driveway. "I could use a drink," Pam murmured to Jasper, aware of Bella dusting a table in the entrance hall that probably didn't have a speck of dust on it. She'd come to see Doris led to the slaughter, no doubt. "Let's go to the drawing room."

Once there, Pam lowered herself into a chair with a sigh.

"She's not going to prison," Jasper said, though he didn't smile.

"It will feel like a prison to her." Pam accepted the glass of white wine he poured. "I don't know, Jasper, she's bright, she has dreams, and she'll waste her life away with that moron."

Jasper chuckled. "It's her choice."

"It's not that simple! To do what she wants, she'd have to give up so much."

"You did it."

"That's different. What I did was like snapping my fingers and making everything and everyone I knew disappear. If I hurt anyone by doing so, I'm not there to see their pain. If I let people down, disappointed them, they can't tell me. I can pretend they're all deliriously happy for me and living wonderful lives." She sipped her wine, then reconsidered and drained her glass. "Doris wouldn't have that luxury. She'd have to face down Elliot, his family, her parents, hold her head high despite the looks and whispers."

After refilling Pam's glass, Jasper poured himself some wine, sat in the chair nearest Pam, and leaned forward. "Are you sure she won't tell everyone about you? Maybe you should have insisted that you were Margaret."

"How? She met Margaret."

Jasper shrugged. "When Margaret was fifteen."

"And knew how to embroider." Remembering the panic in his eyes when she told him about her conversation with Doris, Pam rested her hand on his knee. "She won't say anything. She believed my story, and ever since we talked, she's warmed up to me. In a funny way, my confirming her suspicions has made her trust me more. I didn't lie." And she wasn't concerned that Doris would spill the beans because they'd exchanged secrets. In this time period, Doris admitting that she'd prefer not to marry and have children was akin to admitting that she was contemplating mass murder. A woman who'd rather spend her life working than as a wife, mother, and housewife? Dear me, call the exorcist! Despite Pam's confidence that Jasper would support her aspiration to be more than his wife and the mother of his children, even she, a woman of the future, was sitting on that tidbit until after she had the ring on her finger and he couldn't run the other way, screaming.

She caressed his leg. "I'm glad you were able to come over. I didn't want to sit alone and cry into my wine."

He covered her hand with his, then grasped her fingers. "I know I've been busy trying to establish myself here. But I couldn't turn down the offer from Bill, especially when he was skeptical about a gentleman wanting to roll up his sleeves. It's important that I earn his respect."

"I know."

"And I have to get the money sorted out. I know I'm no longer an investment banker, but I still can't stand to have money sitting around not earning its keep. Everything I'm doing . . ." He lifted her hand to his mouth and kissed it. "It's for us, and our children."

Jesus, she'd never thought she could swoon at the same time her eyes teared up. "I know. Seeing what's happening to poor Doris . . . I know how lucky I am."

A mischievous smile played across his lips. "I guess this would be a good time to tell you that I agreed to help Bill with an order tomorrow, so I won't be able to see you until the supper at Oliver's."

Pam put her wine on the table so she could air-slap him across the face. "You cad!" They both grinned. "Oh, it doesn't matter. I won't mind curling up with a good book for the afternoon." And she could sleep in! Now that Doris was gone, she wouldn't feel the need to drag herself out of bed and present herself at the breakfast table—not that Doris had been there half the time, anyway. Who cared what Bella and the other servants thought? "You'll stay for dinner tonight though, right?"

He nodded. "I thought we could talk about the house. And I want you to start thinking about what you'd like for a wedding present."

Ooh.

"Anything, Pam."

"Let me think about it," she purred, then frowned.

Jasper's face slackened. "What?"

She heaved a sigh. "I just watched Doris marched out the door, and here I am, rubbing my hands together in glee about my wedding present. Life isn't fair."

"No, it isn't."

"Did Oliver say why Doris and Elliot won't be at dinner tomorrow? It seems odd. They always invite them."

"They did invite them. Apparently Elliot turned them down."

God. Elliot's plan to brainwash Doris must include cutting her off from her family and friends. Pam had been told in no uncertain terms that she wasn't to visit until Doris was settled. She knew what that meant. No outside influences until Elliot had successfully turned Doris into a Stepford Wife.

ROBIN SLIPPED INTO her jacket and turned to Margaret. "Are you sure you don't want to come?"

"Leave her be." Cathy zipped up her jacket. "She's already said no twice."

"I'd like to clear the table and load the dishwasher," Margaret said. "You'll have tea and cake waiting for you when you get back."

"We can help you with the dishes and the tea," Robin said.

"Robin!" Cathy grasped Robin's arm and pulled her toward the door. "Come on. Give the woman five minutes to herself."

"We won't be long," Robin said over her shoulder. Why had Cathy so enthusiastically agreed to Margaret's suggestion that they go for a walk, and why was Margaret so eager to shove her out the door? Outside, she pulled up her collar, rammed her hands into her pockets, and skulked next to Cathy.

"God, you're a dumbass sometimes, you know that?" Cathy said.

Robin raised her brows. "What have I done now?"

"You can't tell when someone wants us to have a private chat?"

What? "Why would Margaret want us to talk?"

"Probably for the same reason I do. If she hadn't thrown the perfect opportunity into my lap, I would have figured out some other way to get you alone."

"Well, clue me in, because I have no idea what's going on."

Cathy sighed and shook her head. "Typical. Robin, you look miserable, and you're making Margaret miserable. Or maybe she's miserable for the same reason you are—I don't know. But I do know that you were fine when I talked to you on the phone yesterday afternoon, and that you were off to your mom's last night." She tapped the side of her nose. "Now, I'm not Hercule Poirot, but it doesn't take a crack detective to figure out that the visit probably didn't go well."

Robin snorted. "That's the understatement of the year." The disastrous evening rushed back. "I can't subject Margaret to that."

"What do you mean? You're not thinking of breaking up with her because of your mother?"

"Margaret's special."

"I can see that."

It would be so much easier if she could tell Cathy the entire story. "It doesn't matter."

Cathy grabbed Robin's arm. "Yes, it does! Are you planning to stay single until your mother finally drinks herself to death?" She blew out some air. "Shit. Sorry, I shouldn't have said that, but I can't believe you're going to mess up a good thing because of her."

"Margaret and I . . . it's complicated."

"I'm not blind, deaf, or stupid. Margaret came on the scene real quick and you're already practically married. You don't need to tell me what's going on, okay? I know you love her and she loves you, and that's good enough for me. I'm not out to rock the boat. I've concluded that she came out to her family, who are probably filthy rich and move in hoity-toity circles, and they threw her out."

Robin chuckled.

"What? You have to expect speculation in the absence of information. And it's romantic." Cathy clasped her hands over her heart. "The society chick comes out to her parents because she's fallen in love with a woman from the other side of the tracks. When she's tossed out on her ear, her lover rescues her. It's all rainbows and kittens, but then boom, mommy comes on stage and scares the kittens away."

"You're really weird, you know that?" Robin said with a laugh. Cathy's story had a ring of truth to it, except they'd fallen in love before Margaret had *chosen* to leave her former life behind.

"I'll admit the story has a few holes in it, like how did Pam come to be friends with a society chick? And yes, I'm weird. I'm also worried you'll do something stupid, like choose your mom over Margaret. I think Margaret's worried about it, too."

"She's probably having second thoughts about me."

Cathy slowly shook her head. "No, I don't think so. I think she's hoping I'll talk some sense into you."

"My mother's my problem. It's not fair to expect someone else to—"

"Put up with the crap you do?" Cathy was silent for a moment. "You're not your mother's keeper. And you're not Chris's mom. He's moving on. You need to do the same."

But who would look out for Mom? As for Chris, Robin had to admit that his hasty exit had irked her. She always stood by him—made sure he was taking his medication, gave him a little money here and there, and went over when he needed moral support. He couldn't manage one night for her? His girlfriend, who probably wouldn't be around for long, came before the sister who'd always been there for him. Yeah, he was moving on. He wouldn't be the one to find Mom unconscious, or worse.

"What happened last night that was so bad?"

Despite her still raw humiliation and shame, Robin shrugged. "The usual." And more. She'd wanted to die when Margaret had realized she'd bought her own cake. *Happy Birthday, Robin!* Pathetic. When the baker had asked who it was for, she'd said, *"My niece."*

"The usual, eh?" Cathy said softly. She pulled a rumpled tissue from her pants pocket and offered it to Robin. "It's not used, honest."

Robin took it from her and wiped her eyes.

"What happened? Your mom's nonsense usually rolls off your back."

"It's tougher with an audience."

"You mean an audience you really care about."

Yeah, that did ramp up the embarrassment factor—considerably. "Margaret wanted to make me a cake. I told her not to bother, that my mom would get one." Why was she telling Cathy this? Did she want Cathy to tell her it was okay? "I bought the cake. I usually do." She paused. "It's tough for Mom."

"Jesus, Robin, tough? Why? All the woman has to do is drag her ass down to the bakery and pay for a fucking cake. Jesus! If she can make it to the LCBO, she can make it to the bakery." Cathy groaned in exasperation. "Please don't tell me you buy her booze."

"No, I don't. I told her a long time ago I wouldn't do that."

"Well, tell her you're not buying your own cake anymore," Cathy growled. "Jesus, listen to me. I'm not mad at you, I'm mad at her. I'm frustrated with you. Frustrated!" She muttered under her breath, then let out a loud sigh.

"She started to rip into Margaret when Margaret stood up for me. I told her—Mom—to stop."

"You stopped her? Why don't you do that for yourself?" Cathy asked.

"I'm used to it."

"You shouldn't be used to it."

"Anyway, you can see why Margaret will never want to see my mother again and doesn't have a lot of respect for me."

"She said that?" When Robin remained silent, Cathy said, "You haven't talked to her about it, have you?"

"It's not easy," Robin mumbled.

"I can see how it would be uncomfortable, but she's your partner. You love her. She loves you. If you think you'll be together for a while, she'll have to deal with your mother."

"I can't talk to her about this."

"Why not?"

Because Margaret didn't need to know that the woman she depended on was a pathetic, insecure moron who didn't know what she
was doing, but was very good at pretending she did. She didn't need
to know that she'd left a wonderful life to join a family of screw-ups.
"She depends on me. She hasn't been out for long, and this is the first
time she's lived away from home."

"God, Robin, she's not a child. Neither is your mom. Neither is
Chris. Margaret seems very capable to me, and if you don't mind me
saying so, she'd probably be damn supportive, if you'd only give her
a chance. Why do you always have to go it alone? Why is it okay for
you to support everyone, but nobody can support you?"

*"Oh, so you don't want to go to the store for me. Then what the fuck are
you doing here? What do you mean, you're too tired after work to clean
up the spill in the bedroom? You're useless, you're no good to anybody. I
don't give a shit about your problems. You think you have problems? Your
problems are nothing. Make yourself useful and get me a drink. Nobody
wants to hear about your fucking problems."*

Cathy patted Robin's arm. "Talk to Margaret. Trust her."

No, Margaret had given up so much that she deserved better. She'd
soon realize that when she met more women, women with normal
family members who supported and encouraged each other, looked
forward to spending holidays together, celebrated each other's achievements, and didn't call each other names. Robin loved Margaret and
wanted the best for her. She'd help her become independent, be there
to watch out for her, and quietly fade from her life when Margaret
found love and happiness with a decent woman Robin trusted. She
would not drag Margaret into the abyss known as the Tillman family.
When Margaret had confessed her feelings in the Bainbridge guest
house, Robin should have insisted that they never see each other again.
She wouldn't let Margaret pay for her selfishness.

PAM FORKED A mouthful of apple pie into her mouth and wanted
to moan in ecstasy when the pastry instantly crumbled. Heavenly.
Much better than the frozen crap she'd stuck into the microwave.
She wouldn't mind expanding her limited culinary skills; in fact,
she'd probably have to—knowing how many minutes to microwave
something wouldn't do her much good here. Now she'd have the time

to cook proper meals. In 2010, the last thing she'd wanted to do was slave in the kitchen after dragging herself home from work. Dinner in five minutes with no effort and minimal dishes, or in an hour with a dishwasher load? Tough choice—not. But now she had *no* choice. "Did you make this?" she asked Hortense, knowing Oliver's means were more modest than his parents', though they did employ a cook and a housemaid.

Hortense nodded.

"The pastry is perfect."

Enjoying their own pieces, Jasper and Oliver murmured their agreement.

"Do you want the recipe?" Hortense asked.

In 2010, she would have giggled and wondered about the asker's sanity. "Yes, please."

"I'll copy it for you. If you don't use it, your cook can."

Pam wasn't sure she wanted servants in their faces. A cleaning lady who came in a few times a week would be nice. Their house, while not as large as Oliver's parents', had enough rooms that Pam could see herself doing housework all day to keep up with the dust. But she wanted privacy, at least for the first few years. She'd try this cooking thing and see how it worked out. "Does your cook mind you in the kitchen?"

"She's not live-in, so sometimes I do the whole meal myself. When she's here, she usually doesn't mind if I do the dessert."

Oh, I could handle a part-time cook. "Jasper and I—"

Shouting from the hallway drowned out the rest of her sentence. Startled, she twisted toward the door. A red-faced Elliot marched into the room, the housemaid on his heels. "I'm sorry," the housemaid wailed. "I tried to calm him down."

"It's all right," Hortense said, gesturing for the housemaid to leave the room. Her voice hardened. "What is it, Elliot? Where's Doris?"

His hands went to his hips. "That's a good question. I thought she'd run here, but apparently I was wrong." His eyes settled on Pam. "This is *your* fault."

Her heart pounded. "Pardon me?"

He pointed at her. "You, filling Doris's head with nonsense."

"What's happened, Elliot?" Oliver asked.

"Doris has run off, that's what's happened. I didn't believe it when Mama told me, but it's true. She's gone."

Oh my god, Doris had actually freed herself from her chains! In one day! Maybe she'd known that the longer she waited, the more difficult it would be.

"Why is it Margaret's fault?" Hortense asked.

"She said that Margaret helped her to find the courage to pursue the life she wants, which doesn't involve a husband and children. The fool woman actually believes she can be a doctor." He barked a laugh. "I came to talk some sense into her, but I'm glad she's not here. She'll be more trouble than she's worth. You can have her. And I'd be careful about the company you keep."

"Don't be rude," Hortense snapped.

"I'm trying to warn you, though perhaps it's Jasper I should warn. If I were you, I'd reconsider my choice of bride. I doubt you'll get the loving wife and mother you expect."

"Enough!" Oliver rose from his chair.

"Don't beg me to take Doris back," Elliot said to him. "I don't want her. I doubt anyone will."

Oliver's eyes blazed. "I wasn't going to ask you to take her back. I want you to leave!"

"With pleasure. Tell Doris I wish her well in her life of spinsterhood. As for you, Margaret, I'll be sure to warn everyone not to expose their unmarried daughters to your influence." He whirled and stomped from the room, leaving behind a shocked silence.

Still standing, Oliver shook his head.

"I told you betrothing her to him was a bad idea," Hortense said.

"We were trying to help her, all right?" he snapped. "We don't want her destitute."

"She won't be destitute if she gets her medical degree and practises."

"And how will she do that? Mother and Father won't pay, and we can't either, not when we're—" He gulped down some air, then carried on. "Not when we're hoping to become a family of three soon, and I still need capital to invest." He gazed at Pam. "I don't know what you said to her, but I hope you didn't give her false hope."

"It's not her fault, Oliver," Hortense said. "It's what Doris wants. It's what Doris has always wanted. She needed someone to bolster her courage. It should have been us." She pushed back her chair. "We can discuss Doris's future later. Right now, let's find her and make sure she's all right."

"She must be at the house." Oliver quickly dabbed at his mouth with a napkin and threw it down on the table.

Pam stared miserably at the half-eaten pie that had been so enticing only a minute ago, then blinked back tears as she slid back her chair. Some of them were for Doris; the rest, because Jasper hadn't defended her. While Hortense and Oliver had spoken up, he'd sat silently. Not a word. Not a peep. Even now, as they walked down the hallway, there were no whispered words of support, no reassuring pats. What was she doing here? This wasn't a movie.

Her words to Robin, on Robin's last morning in 1910, came rushing back: *He might be okay with that at first, but when we reach the point where I'm yelling at him for throwing his dirty underwear on the floor, he might wish he was back here and wonder why he gave it all up.*

Why had she given it all up—Robin, her house, her friends, her work? Had she thought shedding her old life for a fairy tale would make her happy? There were no fairy tales. Santa Claus and the tooth fairy didn't exist. Parties always ended. They called it the "honeymoon period" for a reason.

Did Margaret feel the same way? Was she wishing she'd used the book? Had Robin disappointed? Had Margaret realized that other people can't make one happy, that happiness must come from within? Pam's life in 2010 hadn't been so bad. Okay, she'd been in a rut. If she'd wanted to, she could have made changes, held out for the right man, done some soul-searching and figured out what she really wanted from life. But that would have been hard and taken time. Instead she'd left it all behind for a dream world that was becoming a nightmare.

She should have read the rhyme until everyone was returned to their own time. If she'd sucked Robin back, they would have tried again, varied who read the rhyme and where they stood, until she and Robin were back in 2010 and Margaret and Jasper were here.

Well, she still had the book. She could put this right. Robin and Margaret hadn't even realized what had happened yet; they wouldn't know for a hundred years. So reading the rhyme wouldn't affect them.

It wasn't as if they were already happily married and she'd wrench them apart, right?

Though, what if they were? What if all time periods somehow coexisted? Would time travel be possible, otherwise? Did it matter? Being in the wrong time period was unnatural and made happiness impossible. Returning them all to their own time would be doing everyone a favour.

Her resolve hardened as she climbed down the steps to the car in the light of a full moon. Tonight, when the servants were in bed, she'd dig out the book from the trunk and read the rhyme. She wouldn't be in Margaret's drawing room, but instinct told her that it wouldn't matter. There were two time travellers in the wrong time. The rhyme knew who they were.

Her carriage was about to turn into a pumpkin, but she'd rather live with her eyes open than closed. The historical record had been truly accurate all along. Pam Holden wouldn't marry Jasper Bainbridge. The real Margaret Wilton would.

Chapter Fourteen

MARGARET CARRIED TWO MUGS OF STEAMING tea into the study and set Robin's down on the coaster near her elbow. "Thank you," Robin murmured.

Margaret glanced at the comfy armchair, wanting to sit and chat for a few minutes. But Robin's mood hadn't changed since her birthday; she was still withdrawn, perhaps depressed, and rebuffed every attempt at meaningful conversation. Margaret had hoped that Cathy would get through to her, but the drawbridge was still up, the windows still shuttered, and the battering rams weren't making any progress. Well, Mother had called her stubborn for a reason.

She sank into the armchair and blew on her tea. "This afternoon, I continued that course you found . . ." What was that word again? " . . . online. I know it's not a proper course, but I'm improving. I'm typing faster, and I only made a few mistakes." For a moment, she thought Robin would ignore her, but then Robin laid down her pen and looked up.

"That's great! Last week you were still typing with two fingers."

Margaret chuckled. "Yes."

"It *is* a proper course. Just because it's online doesn't mean it can't teach you anything."

"I suppose I still need to touch things to consider them real and valuable," Margaret said, thrilled that Robin was speaking in complete sentences, rather than single words and grunts. "If the same course was on paper, I wouldn't question its value."

Robin touched her mug and apparently decided her tea was too hot to drink. "I was thinking that we should probably find you a," her fingers formed air-quotes, "proper typing course, along with a word-processor course. And maybe we should take a look at community college programs to see if there's a certification program you're interested in. Something that will help you find a job and won't take you years to complete."

"I'm doing the sewing course."

"Yes, but that won't help you find a job. What it will do is get you used to sitting in a classroom and interacting with classmates. After that, you'll feel more comfortable enrolling in a certificate program."

To hide her dismay, Margaret sipped the scalding tea. "I know I'm a burden—financially." She hoped she wasn't a burden in other ways. "I'm trying to contribute however I can, by taking care of the house and meals, so you'll have more time for your schoolwork." When Robin reached out her hand and then slowly pulled it back, Margaret cursed the table that separated them, certain that Robin had wanted to touch her.

"You're not a burden. I appreciate everything you do. Don't feel you have to do it."

Of course she had to do it! She wasn't the sort to twiddle her thumbs, and she wanted to take care of Robin and contribute to the running of their household. Robin didn't make it easy. When she was home, she always wanted to help with the cooking, and she seemed determined to do at least some of her own laundry and part of the housework.

Robin continued on. "But you need to become independent. You don't want to be tied to me."

Margaret gripped her mug. "Why shouldn't I want to be tied to you?"

"I could be run over by a truck tomorrow," Robin said.

She wasn't fooling Margaret. "So could anyone else."

"Right. So it's best that you can take care of yourself. Then you don't have to worry."

She wasn't worried, not about Robin being run over by a truck. Was it possible? Yes, and if it happened, she'd be in dire straits—but her grief would cripple her, not anxiety over how to buy the next loaf of bread. Thrown into the rapids, she'd quickly learn to swim, as she was doing now at a less frantic pace. Robin always wanted to plan for the worst, but that wasn't what she was doing now. "If it will make you feel better, I will find a certificate program that appeals to me." And hope that, by the time she finished her sewing course, Robin would have lowered the barrier she'd erected between them and embraced their relationship again.

But the sinking feeling in Margaret's chest told her that perhaps she was fooling herself. Could Robin overcome years of Janice? Could she cast off the burdens she placed on herself? Even after Janice's death—and despite Margaret's disgust with her, she wished her many more years of life—Robin wouldn't be free. She'd stagger under the weight of guilt and regret.

Perhaps they shouldn't have destroyed the book, not because Margaret wanted to go back, but because she didn't want to add to Robin's worries. Well, it was too late now. The book was gone. She couldn't flee even if she wanted to, and she didn't. She'd be miserable in 1910; she wanted to remain here, with Robin. But she didn't know what to do, how to get through to Robin, and whether her love would survive Robin's self-imposed siege. Margaret was stubborn; she would scale the castle's wall and hang on until her muscles ached and her fingernails bled, but Robin might pry her fingers away and watch her fall.

PAM LISTENED AS Oliver and Hortense reassured an ashen-faced Doris that her entire family wouldn't abandon her. They'd found her sitting at the dining room table, still as a statue, maybe waiting for Elliott to burst in and drag her back to prison. Relief and surprise had flitted across her face at the sight of her brother, sister-in-law, Pam, and Jasper.

"He'll order you off the grounds," Oliver was saying. "Father's dead set against you entering medical school."

"So is your mother," Hortense said from the chair next to Doris. "He's just more vocal about it."

Oliver nodded. "You're right, they'll both be livid. They won't accept it, Doris, and Elliot won't take you back. You'll be homeless and alone."

"I'll find work," Doris said. "I can find a room in a boarding house."

Oliver opened his mouth, then closed it. His support for Doris, both here and in front of Elliot, had taken Pam by surprise. Maybe

Doris's flight had finally gotten through to him how much his sister wanted to be a doctor and not married, or at least not married to some society snot who'd use her as a baby-making machine.

"It could take years to earn the tuition," Hortense said.

Doris shrugged. "I'll be working toward something I really want."

"You don't want to live in a lice-ridden hovel, though. If we had room—"

"Even if we did, it wouldn't matter. Father will order her off the grounds," Oliver said again. "Doris—"

"I'll do what I have to do," Doris said evenly, her white-knuckled hands belying her bravado.

Pam glanced at Jasper, who stood silently at her side. She was keeping her mouth shut because she didn't want to remind everyone that she was responsible for this mess. Better that they remain focused on supporting Doris. As for Jasper, she couldn't blame him for not stepping into the fray, but shit, she could be angry at him for leaving it up to Oliver and Hortense to defend her to Elliot. She'd assumed that Jasper would support Doris's aspirations, but now she wondered. Did she have him all wrong? Maybe he was a man of whatever time period he was in, prepared to accept women as equals in 2010, but not here in 1910. But what of his story about Emily? He admired independent women, or so he'd said.

Hortense sighed. "We'll do whatever we can to help, but I fear it won't be enough."

Doris finally unclasped her hands; her fingers must be stiff. "Not forcing me back to Elliot is enough." She patted Hortense's arm. "Knowing that you and Oliver won't turn your backs on me is a great relief."

"Of course we won't," Oliver said. "I'll admit, I have my doubts that you'll find happiness, but I suppose it's your life. But are you sure? If you pursue this course, you may never find a husband."

Hortense gave him an indulgent look. "If she wasn't sure, she'd still be at Elliot's parents'." She glanced at the clock hanging on the wall. "We should take our leave. I'll come around tomorrow, Doris."

Doris nodded. "All right."

With mixed emotions, Pam joined everyone in the entrance hall. As Oliver and Hortense reassured Doris with their parting words, Pam said good-bye to Jasper. Her throat tightened when his lips brushed hers; she couldn't resist slipping her arms around his neck and holding him, her eyes closing when she felt his stubbled cheek. When they drew back, she briefly held his face in her hands and whispered good-bye in her mind. She loved him, perhaps more than she could ever love anyone. But she didn't belong here. She'd strain against the attitudes of the day, prove a challenge for Jasper, and eventually bite through her tongue. If her futuristic advice hadn't ruined Doris's life, it had certainly made it ten times harder, and Pam couldn't promise herself that she wouldn't advise other women to eschew the expectations of their society and pursue their dreams.

As she watched Jasper, Oliver, and Hortense descend the steps to the car, she told herself that leaving him now would be better than disappearing when they were married. She'd leave a note, tell everyone that she couldn't face life without her family and had returned to Toronto to beg their forgiveness. Only Jasper would know where she'd truly gone; the black rhyme book left behind in her bedroom would be the only clue he'd need, and Margaret's reappearance would clinch it. God, it had better be Margaret. What if Robin came back? What if Jasper went forward? *Don't panic.* They'd keep trying until everyone was where they were supposed to be, remember? They'd do what they should have done in the first place, instead of trying to cheat time.

"I could use a drink," Doris said behind her.

Pam pasted a smile on her face and turned around. "So could I."

They went to the drawing room. Doris poured two glasses of wine and handed one to Pam. They clinked glasses and drank. "Doris, I hope I didn't—when we spoke, I didn't mean to push you."

Doris shook her head. "You gave me the courage to do what I wanted to do."

"I thought you might eventually come around, but I wasn't expecting it to happen so quickly."

"I don't know." Doris's eyes grew distant. She absently sipped her wine. "Elliot and his father were out at their club, so it was just Mrs. Bradley and me for dinner. She started going on about how Elliot expects his shirts and trousers to be pressed, and his favourite meals, and oh, I felt ill, physically ill. I thought, is this it? Suddenly someone was pushing back her chair and saying, 'I'm sorry, Mrs. Bradley, but I can't marry your son.' It was me!" Doris's wide eyes conveyed how surprised she was at her own hubris. "Mrs. Bradley looked like a fish out of water, gasping for oxygen. Finally she wheezed out a *what?* I shouldn't have brought you into it, but I needed one final burst of courage to take that first step and march from the room. I told her that we'd discussed it and you understood. I suppose I didn't want her to think me completely mad. I'm sorry."

"No. We did discuss it, and I did encourage you to pursue medicine. If you needed me with you in spirit, so be it." Pam chuckled. "I doubt I'll ever be invited over to the Bradleys', though." Not that it mattered.

Doris's eyes danced. "No." She drained her glass. "I have to find work. I have to find a place to live. Oliver's right, Mother and Father will be too angry to look at me." She set her glass on the nearest table and clasped her hands in front of her. "Oh, I feel sick, excited, scared, alive! I haven't felt this alive since before Thomas disappointed me."

Pam's vision blurred. "You know what you're meant to do with your life, Doris." And so did Pam. She set her empty glass next to Doris's. "I'm going to bed now." She grasped Doris's shoulders. "It might be difficult, but don't give up. You can do it."

Doris's eyes narrowed. "Are you all right?"

"I'm fine. Just tired." With a nod and one final glance around the drawing room, Pam left, eager to start on her letter to Jasper.

She'd expected to spend at least an hour writing it, but ended up going for short and to the point. She loved him, but she'd made a mistake. This time period wasn't for her. Pam wondered if Margaret was—or would be—experiencing the same sort of time shock. Ideally Margaret would return to the drawing room in Toronto. But then, how did Margaret end up marrying Jasper in Halifax? Oh, her parents thought she was pregnant. They'd probably rip into her for running home, tell her she wasn't welcome, and put her on a train back to Halifax. Or maybe Margaret would return here, to Pam's bedroom at the Pembletons'. Poor Margaret. No matter where she found herself, she'd be so confused at first, but she'd figure it out, and Jasper would be here to rescue her. In her letter, Pam told him to take care of her.

As Pam sealed the envelope, she pondered where to leave the letter. If she held it while she sat on the bed and read the rhyme, it would probably fall to the carpet. The floor wouldn't be a good place for her missive. She wrote *JASPER* across the front of the envelope and propped it up on the desk. Then she went to her trunk, opened it, and lifted out the black book she hadn't set eyes on since the day she'd arrived.

She lowered herself onto the edge of the bed and stared down at the rhyme book resting on her lap, then opened it with shaking hands.

Chapter Fifteen

MARGARET SLOWLY DESCENDED THE STAIRS, CHIDING herself for falling behind in her usual morning schedule. She dragged herself into the kitchen, determined to prepare Robin's breakfast before she came down. A bead of sweat trickled down her brow; she wiped it away. What was the matter with her? She'd gone to bed at her usual hour, yet when the alarm clock had sounded, she'd squinted into the light with tired eyes, surprised that it wasn't the middle of the night. She could have rolled over and slept for hours.

She opened one of the lower cupboards and lifted out the frying pan, then clutched her stomach with her free hand when a wave of nausea washed over her. *No! I don't want to go back! I don't want to go back!* The frying pan slipped from her shaking fingers and crashed to the floor. *No! Please, no!* Her stomach lurched; she squeezed her eyes shut. Banging, sounding far away. Then a weight on her shoulder.

"Margaret! Are you all right?"

She cracked open an eye. Robin peered at her. "Robin!" Margaret clung to her. *Don't let the rhyme take me. Don't let it take me!*

"What's the matter?" Robin shrieked.

"I feel nauseous. The rhyme . . ."

Robin drew back and pressed her hand against Margaret's forehead. "You feel hot. You're running a fever. And you're so pale!" Her forehead puckered. "It's not the rhyme. You're sick."

That realization gave her a small measure of relief. "No wonder I don't feel myself this morning." Robin must think her a hysterical woman.

"Most people with a fever and tricky tummy figure they're ill, not that they're about to be hurtled through time." The amusement in Robin's eyes quickly faded. "Come on, let's get you back into bed."

"No. I'll be—"

"Margaret, don't be stubborn. You're not well." Robin steered her toward the hallway. "If you want, we'll get you settled on the sofa. Then you can watch TV."

"All right. I'd like to change my nightie."

Robin nodded. "While you're doing that, I'll bring down a blanket and your pillow."

When they reached the bottom of the stairs, Margaret gave her a sidelong glance. Robin was wearing only a long t-shirt. She must have rushed from the bathroom when she heard the frying pan hit the floor. Margaret would change into a clean nightie and sweatpants, and would do away with the latter after Robin left.

Robin paused on the upstairs landing. "I only have two classes today. I can skip them."

"No, no. I'll be all right. Go to school."

"But what if you feel worse?"

"I have your phone number."

Robin grimaced. "I don't know."

"I'll be fine. I'm sure it's a stomach ailment that will clear up in a day or two."

"You are, eh?" Robin lifted an eyebrow. "You know, this does bring vaccinations to mind. I bet you're not vaccinated against anything. Because of herd immunity, you probably have nothing to worry about, but when you feel better, you're going to the doctor."

The thought of seeing a doctor frightened her, but she didn't want Robin to worry. "All right." After shutting the bedroom door, she wanted to lie down and close her eyes, but she wouldn't sleep all day and would grow bored up here. She'd rather spend the day on the sofa. When nature called, the small ground-floor powder room would do.

Five minutes later, she climbed into the makeshift bed Robin had prepared on the sofa and laid her head on the pillow with a weary sigh.

"Do you think you can eat or drink anything?" Robin asked.

Another wave of nausea assaulted her. "No."

"You have to at least drink. Let me go to the corner store to get some ginger ale. It'll help."

"Okay." She threw her arm across her forehead and listened to Robin bound up the stairs to get dressed. The episode in the kitchen had erased any doubts she may have had about remaining in this time period and utterly committing to Robin. She dearly missed her family and friends; not saying a proper good-bye to them would always haunt her. But the panicked moment in the kitchen, when she'd thought the rhyme was summoning her back, had made her deepest desire crystal clear. She wanted to remain here—with Robin. Perhaps they wouldn't live a fairy-tale life, but then, she'd never imagined one. She'd simply known that she wanted to be with the woman she loved, and her desire had never wavered.

"Be back in a minute," Robin said from the hallway.

Margaret must have dozed off, because Robin was suddenly there, stirring a glass of ginger ale. "Why are you doing that?" Margaret asked.

"I'm flattening it. It should help calm your stomach. If it doesn't, there are a few other things we can try."

Margaret opened her mouth to ask how Robin knew so much about easing nausea, then clamped it shut and accepted the glass with a nod. She cautiously sipped it. When her stomach didn't revolt, she drank a bit more, then lowered the glass. Best to pace herself. "Don't be late for school." *Oh!* "Eat something."

"I'll grab something there." Robin hovered over her.

"Go, Robin. I'll be all right."

"Call me if you need me, okay? Don't hesitate."

"I won't." She shied away when Robin leaned in to hug her. "You don't want to get sick."

Robin kissed her cheek. "It might be fun, cuddling up under that blanket with you." She quickly looked away, perhaps regretting the lapse in her defences that thrilled Margaret and gave her hope. Oh, how she wanted to get better and be on her feet again! Robin still wanted to be with her, she knew it!

"I'll see you later," Robin mumbled.

From the sofa, Margaret watched her throw on her jacket and grab her knapsack. Then she was gone.

After another sip of ginger ale, Margaret lay back and closed her eyes. As long as she didn't move, the nausea remained at bay. She started to drift. The sound of the cars driving outside blended in with—her eyes snapped open; she sat up, her heart pounding. Someone was in the house!

Robin dropped her knapsack to the floor and pulled off her jacket. "There's no point. I'll just worry about you," she said sheepishly. "I didn't mean to scare you."

Margaret slowly exhaled and lay back again. "I seem to be falling asleep at the drop of a hat."

"Shit, and I woke you up. Sorry. I know you wanted me to go to school, but I can't." She shoved her hands into her pockets. "What can I say? I'm a worrywart."

Margaret loved her worrywart. Her eyes slid shut. "Go eat something," she murmured.

"Okay. Then maybe I'll, uh . . . I don't know. I don't want to wake you up again."

"Since I'm not in the bedroom, maybe you can play that game on your computer."

"Maybe I will—when you're asleep and I'm convinced you'll be okay."

Margaret inwardly smiled. She dozed off, knowing she was in good hands.

PAM FOLDED HER arms to guard against the chill, hoping an even frostier cold wouldn't soon wrap itself around her heart. When she spotted the pond through the trees, she quickened her pace, trusting Jasper to keep up. "This is it," she murmured, sweeping her arm toward the thin layer of ice floating atop her oasis. Maybe bringing him here hadn't been such a good idea; their conversation might ruin her favourite spot. "I almost read the rhyme last night," she blurted, then watched her misty breath float away. The words hung between them.

"Why?" Jasper finally said.

She winced at the tremor in his voice. "Because you didn't defend me," she said, her own voice shaking as her eyes filled with tears. She blinked them back and gazed at the pond. "Oliver spoke up. Hortense spoke up. You sat there while Elliot ripped into me."

"I didn't know what to do. I wanted to come to your defence, but I'm always afraid that I'll give us away, that they'll find out you're not Margaret and take you away from me."

She turned to him.

"It's bad enough with Doris knowing," he said. "I can hardly sleep. I'm not cut out for this."

"Not cut out for what?" Pam asked sharply.

"Lying. Calling you Margaret, when I want to call you Pam."

His distressed face eased her anger and disappointment—a little. "It sounds like neither one of us thought things through."

"You want to go back," Jasper stated.

She shrugged. "I don't know. I honestly don't know. Yes. No. When we're together, I feel as if we can conquer everything. When we're not, I wonder what the hell I'm doing here. When you didn't stand by me . . ." She shook her head. "I'm not one to run away from problems, especially when I've already touched lives here in a way I wasn't expecting. I realized that when I opened the book." And she didn't want to spoil things for Margaret and Robin. How would she explain to Robin that she'd given her and Margaret a chance, only to cruelly snatch it away because she'd awakened from her fairy-tale dream? "I also realized I've been naive, thinking I could just leave my own time and adopt this one, without blinking." She slapped her chest. "Do you know what it feels like, finding out you're a not a person?"

"Of course you're a person."

"Not according to the law! I can't even vote." But since she usually voted for whoever looked the cutest on TV, and there was no TV here, did it matter? She smiled.

"What?" Jasper asked indignantly.

"I was just thinking about Robin's reaction when I told her how I decide who to vote for." She hadn't realized Robin's mouth could open so wide. "I can adapt, Jasper, but I need to know you'll support me one hundred percent. I'm probably going to ruffle feathers. I'm not good at keeping my mouth shut. If you want a demure wife who drinks her tea with her pinkie up and applauds when her rights are trampled, I'm a bad choice for a fiancée."

He grasped her shoulders. "I love you." His Adam's apple bobbed. "I hope you love me."

"I do," she said softly.

"I have to adapt, too. Everything happened so quickly! I don't have to adjust to the time period, but my life was tipped on its head. You gave me the courage to go after the life I want, which includes you as my wife. If I were to say something that cast suspicion on you, I'd never forgive myself. But you're right. Last night, I behaved cowardly. I'm sorry."

See? Now she believed they'd live happily ever after—until the next time 1910 slapped her across the face or Jasper disappointed her. But seriously, they *would* occasionally disappoint each other. "I want to be more than a wife and mother." There, she'd said it. She met his eyes.

"You want to work?"

She wouldn't go *that* far. "Not necessarily. But I want to contribute to society beyond raising children."

"Do charity work. Join the temperance movement. Lots of women do."

"The temperance movement? You mean, no booze? I don't think so. I'm not a lush, but a tipple now and then doesn't hurt."

"Help me with my—our investments."

"Really?"

Jasper nodded. "I can't tell you how much I enjoy working with Bill. I could do without worrying about the money. I can teach you."

"I know a little about investments, so sure. And I'd already thought about getting involved with some type of movement. To help women." Not to prohibit liquor. "I promise I won't be a pain by taking all sorts of unpopular public stands. I figure there are quieter ways to help improve women's lives." She suspected Doris might be able to point her in the right direction.

A smile spread across Jasper's face. "It sounds like we're still getting married."

Of course they were. He'd married someone on December 15th, and it hadn't been the real Margaret. When Pam had lifted the rhyme book's cover, she'd known right away that she couldn't do it. She loved Jasper. Margaret and Robin loved each other. Given time, they'd all muddle through. In her hands, in that book, had sat the power to take that time away, but to what end? They'd always wonder, what if? "I've never doubted that I love you and want to marry you. I've only doubted that I can be happy here."

"I won't fail you again," Jasper said firmly.

She caressed his cheek. "Yes, you will. I'm sure I'll have my moments, too. But we'll get through them." Pam sighed, leaned into him, and rested her head on his shoulder. "Sometimes I wonder if I'll ever forget 2010 and think it was all a dream. But then I think, no, I'll never forget the people, especially Robin and Margaret. I wish I could have said a proper good-bye."

"I'm sure they'll feel the same."

Don't, girls. Don't let the past hold you back. I know you would have said good-bye, if you'd had the chance. I know.

Jasper rubbed her back. "Can we talk about our honeymoon now? Bill was telling me about a picturesque little town in New Brunswick."

"Let's go there," Pam said, not caring where they went as long as they were together. Okay, so they'd discussed another event she'd already known about—their honeymoon in New Brunswick. She felt as if she were cheating, and worried that the universe would be angered and come back to bite her. But how could it, when the universe had obviously wanted Margaret in 2010 and Pam here? Thank god she and Robin hadn't looked at cemetery records. Knowing when she and Jasper would die . . . just no. They had their whole lives ahead of them. When Robin did do a cemetery record and obituary search—and Pam was positive that she would—she'd find that Margaret and Jasper Bainbridge had died married after a happy life together.

MARGARET GRIMACED AND rubbed her arm. Her new doctor, who was female, much to Margaret's delight, hadn't been joking when she'd said that the vaccination might cause some tenderness. And this was only the first one. She'd have a flu shot in a couple of weeks and wouldn't be as nervous about that appointment. Nobody had batted an eye when Margaret had presented herself as "Pam Holden" and handed over her health card. Fortunately Robin's doctor, who'd never met Pam, had accepted her as a new patient. Best of all, after a thorough examination and blood tests, Margaret had been given a clean bill of health. No, she was more worried about the January dental appointment Robin had insisted she make. Despite Robin's assurances, Margaret was sure she'd be tortured.

The kettle clicked off. Margaret took her time making the tea, not looking forward to the conversation with Robin that she'd delayed too long. Now that she was well over her stomach bug and a doctor had declared her healthy, it was time to lay her cards on the table, so to speak. No more, "I'll wait until I'm sure I'm better."

Robin wasn't in the study; she was in the living room, sorting through Christmas decorations for the artificial tree Margaret hadn't believed existed when Robin first told her about it. But there it was, standing in the corner they'd cleared, waiting for its lights and—oh, no tinsel, or anything else Mitzy might swallow. Margaret had joked that soon there'd be artificial people. When Robin had said, "Well, there are blow-up, life-sized dolls, but you don't want to know," Margaret had taken her at her word.

She paused in the archway. Robin was hunched over a string of lights, muttering under her breath. If she was already irritated, maybe now wasn't a good time to—no. No more excuses! Margaret set the teas on the coasters on the coffee table and knelt next to Robin. "Problem?"

"Yeah, one freaking light isn't working, and now I have to figure out which one. This is the type where one light not working means none come on. We need new lights! These are ancient!"

"Let me do it," Margaret said, after watching Robin for a minute and grasping the method she was using to find the bad light. Robin eagerly handed over the string. Margaret set to work, unscrewing a light and screwing in the light Robin handed to her. No, not this one. She moved to the next. "I want to talk about your mother," she said, focusing on the lights and glad her hands were occupied.

"Why?" Robin asked flatly.

She'd anticipated Robin's response. "Because she's coming between us. I want to understand why." When Robin sucked in her breath, Margaret knew she'd surprised her. Perhaps Robin had expected a lecture about her mother's treatment of her, or her mother's alcoholism. But Margaret knew there was no point starting there. She'd tackle those in time. First Robin had to open herself to the possibility of their love again.

"Jesus, Margaret, do I need to spell it out for you? You were there on my birthday."

"Yes, I was," Margaret said evenly.

"Then you should understand why."

Suspecting she'd see anger, Margaret resisted the urge to give her a sidelong glance. "I understand that your mother's a drunk and she treats you terribly. What does that have to do with us?"

Robin jumped up. "What does that have to do with us? Are you serious? Do you think I'll subject you to that? Do you think I'll let her treat you the same way she treats me? I told you, there are other lesbians out there, normal people with normal families that don't have vodka for breakfast."

Margaret looked up. "I love *you.*"

"Shit." Robin grabbed her head. "I said I'll always be here for you, no matter what happens."

"I want more than that."

"Of course you do! You left so much behind. You deserve more."

That wasn't what she'd meant. Dismayed, Margaret dropped the string of lights to her lap. "I want *you,* Robin. If you don't want me, say so. Don't hide behind your mother."

"I'm not!" Robin shouted.

Good, Margaret had broken through. "Aren't you?"

"No!"

"All right," Margaret said, even though she didn't believe her. "Then tell me why you've held me at arm's length since your birthday. Did I do something wrong? Or perhaps now that we've come to know each other better, your feelings for me have changed."

"No!" Robin's hands clenched. "Damn it!"

Margaret picked up the lights and unscrewed a blue bulb, sure it was where she'd left off. She replaced it with the bulb she'd palmed. Had Robin tested this bulb? What if it was the one that didn't work?

"You can do better," Robin said quietly.

"I love *you.*" And she was frustrated beyond measure! "Do you want to be with me?"

"It's not that simple."

"Why not?"

Silence, then, "I have to think about what's best for you."

"That's up to me, isn't it?" She moved on to a red bulb. "I know I'm learning my way around this time period, but I'm a grown woman. I can decide what's best for me."

Robin sighed. "Why do you want to be with me, Margaret?"

Despite the tension in the room, Margaret smiled. "If you're asking me to explain love, I can't. I just know that my heart leaps when you're near, and how much I look forward to seeing you when you come home, how my life would be so much poorer without you in it, and how much I want to be here for you, how I want to share in every aspect of your life."

Robin barked a laugh. "Including my mother?"

"Yes, Robin, including your mother." When Robin didn't reply, Margaret stole a glance at her, and refused to be discouraged by Robin's glare and folded arms. She unscrewed a yellow bulb. "Perhaps you'll give us a chance, instead of assuming defeat. Do you want us to be together? Do you want to try?"

Robin's hands went to her hips. "It's not a matter of—"

"If your mother wasn't . . . your mother, would you give up on us so easily?"

"I'm not giving up!"

Margaret couldn't resist lifting her head and raising a brow.

Robin crouched next to her and met her eyes. "I don't know what to do. I do love you, more than I can express. That's why I don't want to drag you into this mess."

Margaret's throat tightened.

"Back in 1910, I should have told you to go back to the main house. If I hadn't been so selfish, we could have avoided this."

"Avoided what? This terrible life together? I'm sitting here with Christmas lights in my hands, in a warm house, with a nice hot cup of tea, with the woman I love at my side, whom I'm free to be with. Yes, I can see how you regret subjecting me to this terrible existence."

Robin threw up her hands. "You're impossible to argue with, you know that? Not to mention you have quite the sarcastic streak running through you."

"Now you sound like *my* mother," Margaret said. Robin's eyes brightened; the atmosphere palpably lightened.

Robin heaved her shoulders. "Speaking of Christmas, if you think my birthday was bad . . ."

Margaret dropped the lights and reached for her, hoping Robin wouldn't leave her looking foolish with her arms outstretched. She breathed a sigh of relief when Robin tipped forward onto her knees and embraced her. No, she couldn't explain love; she just knew that her heart felt like bursting and that the woman in her arms meant the world to her. Robin hadn't been selfish back in 1910; she'd allowed Margaret to truly live and be herself. It would have been a wondrous gift, had Margaret remained in 1910. To live honestly for the rest of her life . . . yes, she'd given up much, but oh, what she'd gained in return. Janice wouldn't deny her and Robin a life together, not while Margaret had anything to say about it. She drew back. "Do you usually go to your mother's on Christmas?"

Robin nodded. "After her mom died, Pam went with me, which actually made things worse."

"Why don't you invite your mother here this year?"

Robin shook her head. "She won't come."

"Are you sure? If she's here, we could limit her alcohol consumption, or at least slow it down."

"Margaret, she'll be drunk before she even gets here. Christmas brings out the worst in her. All the wrongs committed against her, her broken family, how much better Christmases used to be . . ."

Margaret could imagine Janice rambling on about her awful life and how she had nothing, thereby dismissing her two children as they dutifully sat and listened to her. Would that be how they'd spend their Christmases? In that case . . . "Why don't we have our Christmas on Boxing Day, then?"

"You mean, me and you?"

Margaret nodded. "With the visit to your mother out of the way, we'll be able to relax and enjoy ourselves, have a day just for us that doesn't involve unpleasantness." There was no point trying to pretend that visiting Janice would be anything but unpleasant and uncomfortable. Robin had lowered the drawbridge; Margaret wouldn't reward her trust with platitudes and empty reassurances. She would share Robin's burden—willingly. "Let's start a new tradition. One that's ours."

"I like that idea," Robin said, then she groaned. "My knees are getting sore." She shifted to a cross-legged position.

"Here." Turning, Margaret lifted Robin's tea and handed it to her. "Drink this before it gets cold." She sipped her own tea, then returned her attention to the lights and screwed the spare bulb into the second to last socket. The string lit up. "Oh!" She gazed at the lights, pleased that the conversation had gone well. Robin surveyed the string with troubled eyes, the glow from the multicoloured lights reflecting off her cheeks.

Margaret wasn't naive; Robin would still fret over her mother's behaviour, and she'd be horrified if—when—Margaret exchanged cross words with Janice. But the conversation had renewed Margaret's hope that she and Robin would marry and spend their lives together. Robin would come to accept that Margaret loved her, wanted to be with her, and didn't regret destroying the book. In fact, insisting that they burn the book was one of the best decisions she'd ever made.

Chapter Sixteen

FEELING LIGHT-HEADED, PAM STUMBLED INTO the street with Doris. "God, Doris, I feel so guilty. I never should have encouraged you to—"

"Do what I really want to do?" Doris clucked her tongue. "Don't worry, I'll find somewhere."

Pam wasn't so sure. They'd looked at several rooms she wouldn't rent for Mitzy. Noisy, dirty, a pot for a toilet . . . Jesus. She'd figured Doris's parents would eventually come around—okay, she hadn't figured much at all before she'd shot off her mouth—but Doris and Oliver insisted that their parents would throw Doris out on her ear and tell her to lie in the bed she'd made. Fortunately they'd be in Europe for Christmas, but they'd return in February, which didn't leave Doris much time to find lodgings on her limited budget. Then she'd have to work for at least six months to scrape together the tuition for the first year, or at least her portion, since Oliver was chipping in. Not only that, she'd have to work while studying in order to pay for her subsequent years, and would drag herself home every night to sleep in a dump. How long would it be before she cursed the day she'd listened to her new friend from Toronto and told herself that maybe Elliot wouldn't have been so bad, after all.

"I've been thinking that I might not apply to medical school right away. It might be better if I apply when I've earned enough money to cover all the tuition and to keep myself for a few years."

"That could take forever!" Pam wanted to scream. Doris's parents were loaded. If only they'd see sense. Didn't they want their daughter to be happy? Stupid question.

Doris shrugged. "It will take time, but if I'm accepted to medical school, I don't want to fail. I'll want to fully devote myself to my studies. Working full time now will be better than working part-time later—" she turned to Pam and raised a finger "—and should mean that I'll be able to save what I need more quickly."

Doris would live in a hovel, while mom and dad dined on caviar.

"I'm going to apply to work in one of the factories."

Pam had overheard women talking about the back-breaking, monotonous work, the long hours, the heat . . . The thought of Doris slaving away for pennies made her sick. "There has to be something else." No, really, she felt ill. "Do you mind if we sit down for a minute?" she said feebly.

Doris peered at her, then grabbed Pam's arm and steered her over to a bench outside a butcher shop. Pam gratefully sank onto it and closed her eyes.

"Margaret."

Maybe she'd picked up some bug.

"Margaret. Pam!"

Pam opened her eyes. "Shh."

"Oh, for heaven's sake! It's your childhood nickname, isn't it? One that Jasper's now using, too?" Doris smiled, but her forehead was creased with worry.

Despite the sudden urge to deposit her breakfast on the sidewalk, Pam returned her smile. Jasper would jump at the opportunity to use her real name; he was terrified of slipping up.

Doris was still staring at her. "You're awfully pale."

"I feel nauseous. I always feel this way in the mornings, lately. Maybe it's stress. The wedding's only a couple of weeks away now."

"Sick in the mornings?"

Pam nodded.

"When was your last menses?"

"What?"

"Your last period."

"Um . . ." Oh. My. God. "You don't think . . ."

Doris lifted her eyebrows. "You're pregnant."

AFTER ONE LAST *look in the mirror, Margaret lowered her veil and*

*turned to Mother. "I'm so glad you're here, Mother. When I introduced
you to Robin . . ."*

*Mother smiled. "As long as you're happy. Come. It's time." She ex-
tended her elbow.*

*Margaret slipped her arm through Mother's and slowly walked to her
bedroom door, careful not to trip over her wedding dress. A misty-eyed
Sally swung the door open for them, and Margaret stepped into the church.*

*Father turned to her as he walked her up the aisle. "I wish you all
the best, my darling."*

*"Thank you, Father." Halfway to the front of the church, she searched
for Robin. There she was, up near the altar, in a suit, of all things. Well,
what had Margaret expected, a frilly dress? Hubert stood next to Robin;
he'd better not have forgotten the ring. She wanted to smile and wave at
Robin, but Robin was facing the altar.*

*Another few steps and Margaret was almost at Robin's side. A smile
spread across her face as Father lifted her hand and offered it to Robin.
Robin turned and—Jasper nodded at Father and reached for Margaret's
hand. No!*

Margaret's eyes snapped open. She bolted upright and pressed her
hand against her forehead, her breathing quick and ragged. A dream.
Just a dream. What time was it? She twisted toward the clock on
the night stand. Only 10:45! She'd turned off the light at 10:30, and
had apparently fallen into a deep sleep and had a dream—a nightmare—that had felt so realistic. It had also spooked her. Had she
seen an alternate life, what would have happened if she'd remained
in 1910? Good Lord, she hadn't been transported back, had she? No,
the clock was digital, but she turned on the light for good measure,
never imagining that she'd be so pleased to see Robin's computer. But
it wasn't enough. She needed to see Robin.

Climbing out of bed, she padded down the hallway and peered
into Robin's room, intending to reassure herself that Robin lay sleeping
and then go back to bed, feeling silly. But Robin was awake, reading
a notebook by the light of the small bedside lamp.

Sensing Margaret's presence, Robin looked up. Her brows drew
together. "You all right?"

"I—I had a bad dream." She should go back to her bedroom, especially since she stood there in her nightie, but her heart still pounded
and she wanted to be with Robin.

"What was it about?"

"It doesn't matter." Not knowing what to do with herself, Margaret leaned against the doorframe. "What are you reading?"

"I'm just reviewing my notes for my exam tomorrow."

"I'm sorry. I shouldn't have disturbed you." But she couldn't bring herself to walk away, either.

"It's okay. I'm ready for it." Robin frowned at Margaret. "That must have been some dream. You sure you don't want to tell me about it?"

"I was back in 1910." Margaret shook her head. "It was only a dream."

"But . . ."

"It frightened me. You'll think I'm foolish, but I wanted to make sure you were still here."

"If I wanted to be sucked back, I'd prefer Thursday. I could use an extra month to prepare for the exam I have on Friday."

Margaret chuckled. Her breath quickened when Robin grinned at her. Heat rushed to her nether regions as she imagined what was underneath Robin's baggy t-shirt. Her gaze went to Robin's chest; she dragged her eyes back to Robin's and saw the desire she knew was in her own eyes.

"Do you want a hug before you go back to bed?" Robin asked.

They stared at each other. Robin's words before their fateful first kiss came rushing back. *Can I hug you good-bye? I promise not to mess up your hair.* If she were to hug Robin now, her hair *would* be messed up; she wouldn't return to her own bedroom that night. She knew it, and Robin knew it.

Margaret glanced down the hallway in the direction of her bedroom, then pushed herself away from the doorframe and went to Robin.

MARGARET OPENED HER eyes and blinked into the morning light. Robin's face came into focus. After a confused moment, Margaret realized that Robin wasn't in the bed; she was kneeling next to it. "Hey, sleepyhead," Robin said.

"Good morning," Margaret mumbled. She sat up, and noticed that Robin was dressed, and that she . . . wasn't. She pulled the blanket up against her chest and cleared her throat. "How long have you been up?"

"About forty-five minutes. I have to leave for my exam. It's a good thing I'd already set the alarm before you showed up, otherwise I might have forgotten to do it."

Margaret vaguely remembered a distant beeping, but she'd thought it was the microwave in her dream. "You must be tired." When they'd turned off the light, it was past 1:00.

Robin grinned. "I am, but it's a nice tired."

Blood rushed to Margaret's cheeks, and to other places she didn't want to think about, not with Robin about to leave.

"I made you tea." Robin jutted her chin toward the night table on the other side of the bed.

"Thank you."

"Oh, and uh . . ." Robin stood and rounded the bed. "You'll probably want this." She lifted Margaret's nightie from the floor next to the dresser. "I guess it landed here." She held it out to Margaret, who swiped it from her hand. She almost managed to keep a straight face, but collapsed into a giggle when Robin grinned again. The blanket fell away, but her initial self-consciousness and embarrassment had passed.

When Robin leaned over to embrace her, Margaret eagerly met her halfway and held her close, relishing the sensation of Robin's wool sweater against her skin. When she'd knitted it for her, she hadn't dared to imagine that one morning it would press against her bare breasts, after she and Robin had shared a night of lovemaking. She would have survived life as a nun in an Anglican order only because she wouldn't have known what she was missing.

"Exams can be really inconvenient sometimes," Robin murmured. She drew back, a mischievous glint in her eye. "I'll want an early night tonight. You'll probably be tired, too."

"I'm sure I will be," Margaret said faintly.

"I wouldn't mind sleeping in my own room again. The bed *is* a double. The nights are getting colder. And the room already sort of belongs to both of us."

"Mine in 1910, and yours in 2010."

"Time to make it ours?" Robin asked, gently stroking Margaret's cheek with her finger.

Margaret closed her eyes. "I would like that." If not for Robin's exam, she'd grab Robin's sweater and pull her into bed again. It would be a long day.

"I'd better go, or I'll be late." Robin's kiss was gentle.

After Robin left, Margaret lay back and swallowed the lump in her throat. The talk they'd had over the Christmas lights had made a difference. If Robin didn't believe they had a future together, she never would have invited Margaret into her bed.

PAM SURVEYED HER and Jasper's entrance hall and clapped her hands. "I'm going to have so much fun decorating. I hope to include pieces from my favourite cabinetmaker. At least one in each room."

Jasper guffawed. "That will take some time. I'm busy with Bill's jobs."

She drew back and placed her hand against her chest. "Who said I was talking about you?"

He grinned. "I can dedicate a couple of hours each Sunday to working on a piece for us. I used to hate working on the weekend for a client, but when I'm sanding and sawing and staining, the hours fly by."

"I'm glad." Pam looped her arms around his neck. "I hope you don't regret taking me on."

"Not at all." He pulled her into a hug. "My life is already ten times better than it was in Toronto, and we're not living together yet. I thought Margaret and I could build a decent life together, and perhaps we would have been content. But not like this."

Thank god she hadn't read the rhyme that night. She wanted more than contentment, not only for herself, but for him, and for Robin and Margaret. She'd been naive to expect that she'd effortlessly adjust to this time period. Her love for Jasper was strong, but he couldn't be everything to her. She needed more and she was starting to find it. She valued her growing friendship with Doris and had learned of several charitable endeavours related to improving life for women that she wanted to explore after their honeymoon. And then there was motherhood. Maybe now would be a good time to tell Jasper. She drew breath.

"Our wedding's only a week away," Jasper said; Pam felt his smile. "Have you decided what you want?"

Okay, the baby news could wait a minute. "Yes, I have."

He let her go and stepped back. "Jewelry? Clothes? A motor?"

A car? "I wouldn't mind a car, but that's not what I want. I don't want jewelry or clothes, either."

His brows drew together. "What, then?"

She took a deep breath. "I want us to be Doris's patrons."

"What do you mean?"

"Jasper, it'll take her years to scrape together the money she needs for medical school, and she needs somewhere to live."

"You're not suggesting she live with us!"

"Not in the main house, no. But remember that, um, cottage on the east grounds?"

"It's a shack!"

Pam chuckled. "Trust me, it's already in better shape than most of the rooms we've looked at. We can fix it up. We don't need it for ourselves."

"There's no plumbing, no electricity."

Details, details. "We can have that put in, right?" His silence encouraged her. He wasn't saying no. "Did you have plans for it?"

He scratched his head. "I hadn't thought about it, beyond it being an eyesore. Well, it did cross my mind that I could turn it into a workshop."

Oh. "You don't want to have to drive all the way out there to work. Build one closer to the house." She softened her voice. "Then I can stroll over and visit you, bring you snacks." Poor Doris would have a ways to walk before she even reached the main house, but then she could have their driver—Pam added that thought to her growing list—take her to school. It was better than slaving away in some factory while the desire to go to university was sucked from her. "Oliver said he'll chip in, but he can't do it on his own, and both he and Doris are convinced that their parents won't allow her to live on their grounds."

"Are you sure that's what you want?" Jasper asked, his expression pained. "For your wedding present?"

"Right now, it's the best thing you can give me. It'll make me happy."

"You feel guilty because you encouraged Doris to—"

"Pursue her dream? Live the life she wants? No, I don't. I feel bad about how Elliot reacted, and that there may be a permanent rift between her and her parents, but god, Jasper, she would have wilted and died in that marriage." She paused to draw a breath. "But at first I did feel guilty. I figured that I didn't fit into this time period and that I'd have to keep my mouth shut and follow the norms. But that's not true. I'm not going to rock the boat and start demanding changes—braver women than I will do that, and in 2010 I should have known enough to thank them from the bottom of my heart. But I can help behind the scenes, starting with Doris."

"I suppose we can afford to help Oliver pay for her tuition," he grumbled.

Yes! "And her school materials. We can provide her with an allowance. She won't need much."

"If you think she'll want that shack . . ."

"Oh, I think she'll jump at the chance," Pam said, sensing victory. Maybe now would be a good time. "I hope you don't have to build your workshop before you can start working on pieces for us, because we're going to need one of your creations soon."

"Oh?"

She gulped and reached for his hand. "A crib."

"A crib?"

She nodded. "A crib."

"You mean . . ."

"I don't know how far along I am. I'd guess about six weeks."

"Six weeks." He looked behind him, maybe for a chair. Pam gripped his hand tightly, in case he decided to drop to the floor. "Six weeks," he repeated, awe straining his voice.

"Yeah. Now, about Doris . . ."

"Yes, yes, of course. I'll drive out and have another look at the shack—cottage—today," he said absently, waving his hand. "Six weeks."

"Yes, Jasper, six weeks," Pam said, wondering if she should slap him to snap him out of it. "If we weren't already getting married next week, we'd be putting together a quickie wedding."

"I thought I'd have to tell my parents you'd miscarried—if they asked." His eyes grew sad, but only for a moment. Since they'd fled, he'd written to his parents twice, but hadn't received a reply. Pam planned to suggest that he telephone them on Boxing Day. She didn't want their first Christmas Day together ruined. "Six weeks," he said again.

Pam sighed, then wheezed when Jasper suddenly caught her up in a bear hug. "We'll have to start thinking of names," he said, then leaped back. "Oh, I'm sorry. I shouldn't squeeze you like that."

"You won't hurt the baby," Pam said, pulling him back into a hug. "As far as names go, we have a bit of time yet." Though she already had two in mind, one for a boy and one for a girl. She knew she'd eventually get her way with the girl's name, at least. "Doris knows. Other than that, I guess we'll wait a couple of months after the wedding to announce it. I'm not sure how we'll explain a full-term baby seven months after we married, though."

"The same way everyone else does," Jasper quipped. Their laughter echoed around the empty hallway.

They held each other in silence, basking in the present and the promise of a bright future. Pam was fully committed to both. She would never touch the black rhyme book again. "Before I forget . . ." She reluctantly left Jasper's arms to pick up the paper bag she'd set on the floor near the door. Jasper accepted it with a puzzled look. "Get rid of it," Pam said.

His face darkened when he peered inside the bag.

"Don't destroy it. It might be the copy I ended up with in 2010. If it is, it doesn't matter who you give it to or what you do with it. Somehow it'll get to Jake's." And change all their lives.

He looked up at her. "I don't know what I'll do with it. It's too dangerous to give to anyone."

"Maybe you can find a store that specializes in this sort of thing. They must exist. They did in Toronto."

"I'll try. But what if it's not *the* copy. What if—"

"Whoever ends up with it, whatever happens, we know how 2010 turned out. It'll be okay."

"Maybe I'll just bury it somewhere."

"Go ahead. In fact, you could destroy it, I suppose, because we know I got my hands on a copy in 2010, regardless of what we do with this copy." Wait. "Then again, I may have ended up with it because we knew enough not to destroy it, just in case. Do you know what I mean?" When he stared blankly at her, she sympathized. She wasn't sure she knew what she meant, either. You needed a freaking PhD in time travel to understand this stuff, and even then, you probably wouldn't fully understand it. She didn't, and she'd done it!

"I don't know what I'll do with it yet, but I do know I want it out of our house." Jasper grasped her elbow and walked her to the door.

"Let me take my future wife—and a future mother—to lunch. We have lots to discuss."

They certainly did, and she looked forward to her future roles, roles that were actually in her past. No, her future. She was a woman of 1910 now.

Chapter Seventeen

AFTER PULLING OFF HER COAT AND hanging it, Margaret took a moment to savour the silence. Janice's sharp voice still rang in her ears, and the moaning, the weeping . . . Robin hadn't exaggerated when she'd said that Christmas brought out the worst in her mother. Would Margaret ever see Janice's best? On the bright side, supporting Robin had kept Margaret's mind off her own family. She'd indulged herself with a little cry in the shower that morning, thinking of all the Christmases she'd missed, then reminded herself that she would have been in a nunnery. *New traditions, remember?*

Robin slid the closet door shut. "Glad that's over."

Margaret silently and guiltily agreed. They shouldn't feel that way about spending Christmas Day with Robin's family, but oh, what a family! As far as Margaret was concerned, Robin was a miracle. No, that wasn't fair. Robin's strength and determination to not waste her life staring into a glass had prevented her from following in the footsteps of her mother and ancestors, not luck or divine intervention.

Margaret pecked Robin on the lips. "Why don't I make us tea? We can drink it in front of the Christmas tree." She'd also check to see that the turkey was thawing nicely for their Christmas on Boxing Day dinner.

"That sounds nice." But Robin bit her lip.

"What?"

"Mom drank an awful lot today. I know we said Boxing Day would be for us, but if I don't make sure she's all right tomorrow, I'll worry."

Margaret was about to remind Robin that Chris would be there when she remembered that he'd fled to his girlfriend's soon after dinner, saying he'd be staying there for a few days. She couldn't blame him. "Why don't you phone her?"

Robin shook her head. "She never answers the phone."

Because she wanted her daughter to go over and wait on her hand and foot. Margaret quashed her irritation before it got the better of her. There was no point fighting against a situation that had gone on for years, not when doing so could ruin their Boxing Day. Robin wouldn't relax until she'd assured herself that Janice was okay. As for Janice, Margaret had time to slowly influence the dynamic of her relationship with Robin. Changes wouldn't come overnight, and they certainly wouldn't happen tomorrow. "Let's pop over in the morning." She raised a finger. "But we're not staying."

"You don't have to come with me."

"I'm going with you!" Margaret snapped. Otherwise she'd probably end up spending Boxing Day on her own.

Robin visibly relaxed. "Okay. Good."

Margaret inwardly cursed her harshness. She should have realized that Robin's feeble protest wasn't genuine. "I'll go make the tea," she said softly.

Ten minutes later, she carried two mugs into the living room with a smile. Her face slackened at the empty room. Bewildered, she set the teas on the coasters, then turned around and jumped at the shadowy figure hovering in the archway. Robin stepped into the room; the Christmas tree lights danced on her face and sweater. "I've been keeping something from you." She held out an envelope.

Puzzled, Margaret examined it. It was addressed to Pamela Elizabeth Holden, from the Government of Canada.

"It came a few days ago," Robin said as Margaret carefully ripped open the envelope.

"Why didn't you give it to me then?" Margaret pulled out a passport, opened it, and blinked at her photograph next to Pam's information.

"Welcome to 2010."

Margaret looked up. Robin's anxious face worried her. She slid the passport back into the envelope and turned to drop it onto the sofa.

"I wasn't sure—" Robin swallowed. "I wanted to see how Christmas went."

"I don't understand." If today had gone badly, would Robin have withheld the passport? To what end? "I can't go back to 1910. We destroyed the book."

Robin vigorously shook her head. "No, I wouldn't want you to." Then . . .

Robin shoved her hands into her pockets. "I knew when your passport came that I'd have a decision to make. Well, I already knew what I wanted. I guess I just wanted to make sure before I . . ." Her voice dwindled away. Margaret winced when Robin slipped a hand from her pocket, grabbed one of the teas, and gulped some down. Oh, that must have burned. Robin's eyes watered as she set down the cup and thrust her hand back into her pocket again. She cleared her throat. "Will you marry me, Margaret?"

Margaret's heart instantly cried *Yes!*, but her head prevailed. Lord, how she wanted to scold Robin for basing her decision on how Christmas went! What would have happened if Robin wasn't satisfied with how the day unfolded? Would she have given up on them, decided for Margaret that marrying her would be a bad idea? If not for Margaret's conviction that love was behind Robin's overprotective attitude, that she truly wanted the very best for her, Margaret would tell her she'd think about it.

Robin's lips trembled. "I don't have much money. I know we'll sell the house and we have Pam's money, but I have a student loan to pay, and I'm not finished university yet, and—"

Margaret couldn't bear her distress any longer. "I don't care about that, Robin. Somehow we'll manage. But am I truly who you want? I used to worry that there's too much to learn about this time and the hundred years I've missed, that I'll never be able to discuss a range of topics with the ease that your friends do. I don't worry about that anymore. I know I'll be able to, in time. But there are some things about me that won't change, that will always mark me as a woman of the past."

"Like what?"

"Like wanting to take care of you like a wife would take care of a husband."

"We take care of each other."

"You want me to find a vocation, and I understand that I should. It's unfair to expect you to financially support me. But I don't want a vocation. I want to take care of you."

Robin's brow furrowed. "You mean, be a housewife?"

Margaret nodded miserably at the incredulity in Robin's voice; it shattered her dream. "I would tell you that once you've finished your studies and have more time, I'll perhaps go to school and learn a vocation, but I would be lying. I don't know, perhaps I will, but it's equally possible that I'll still want to be a housewife. I'll understand if that isn't acceptable to you."

"No, I'm—I'm surprised, that's all," Robin sputtered. Her hands left her pockets; she grabbed Margaret's shoulders. "I guess I assumed that since you can do whatever you want in 2010, you'd want to work, or even go to university. But it's all about choice, right? That's what women fought—are fighting for. Telling you that you have to work would be just as bad as telling you that you can't."

Perhaps her dream wasn't dead.

"And you can change your mind later."

Or perhaps it was. "I might not."

"I know. I just don't want you to think that you can't." Robin's mouth turned up at the corners. "If you grow bored of taking care of me, I'll understand."

"It will mean you keeping me."

"I won't see it that way." Robin's voice softened. "We'll both be contributing to our home. And as far as I'm concerned, Pam's money is our money. She wanted both of us to use it. Legally speaking, it's all yours." Robin's fingers dug into Margaret's shoulders. "Will you marry me?"

Her throat tight, Margaret nodded and managed a thready, "Yes." Then she was in Robin's arms, pressing her cheek against Robin's. "Yes, I'll marry you." Was she weeping? She hadn't thought of herself as sentimental. She'd waited apprehensively for Jasper's proposal and had contemplated their future together in a rather detached fashion. But theirs had been a calculated match between two friends who'd assumed they'd become more to each other. Robin's proposal and the promise of a life together filled her with an indescribable joy that took her breath away. *Thank you, Pam. Thank you for reading the*

book, for falling in love with Jasper, for everything. I hope you shared a
wonderful life together. I promise that Robin and I will remember you
both by doing the same.

"I'll take you out to get an engagement ring," Robin said.

"No. I don't need one. I'd rather you spend the money on something else."

"We can put it toward our wedding bands."

"Yes, let's do that." Margaret smiled. "I'll look forward to choosing them with you."

"Christmas hasn't turned out so bad, after all," Robin murmured.

"What would you have done if the visit with your mother hadn't passed your . . . test?" Margaret couldn't help asking. She didn't mind when Robin took her time answering, content to rest her head on Robin's shoulder and relax as Robin stroked her back.

"I would have asked you to marry me," Robin finally said. "It would have taken me a few days to convince myself that I wasn't going to completely ruin your life, but I would have asked you, because it's what I want. I love you. I want to be with you. If I wasn't married to you, I'd miss you every day. I know I said I'd be there no matter what, but I want to be there as your partner. I want us to go through life together."

Margaret's eyes grew misty again; she always felt humbled when Robin trusted her enough to poke her head out of her shell. "I love you, too."

"When do you want to get married?" Robin chuckled; her back vibrated under Margaret's fingers. "Now that it's decided, I want to do it!"

So did she. "I would like nothing more than to marry you as soon as possible, but I would prefer to change my name first, if that's all right with you."

"Uh, yeah, marrying Pam Holden *would* be weird. I'd much rather marry Margaret Wilton."

That wasn't the name Margaret had in mind.

ROBIN STARED AT the rainbow flag on the bedroom wall and hugged herself. She'd leaped from her chair the moment Margaret had said she'd found it. "Is it horrible? Did she die in childbirth? Did she die young of something we can cure now with a pill?"

"Are you sure you want to know?" Margaret asked.

She'd only wonder. "Yes."

Margaret beckoned to her. "Come, sit down."

Robin hesitated, then forced herself to return to her chair. But she wouldn't look at the screen. "You must think I'm a baby, especially after what you just found out." They'd first looked for Margaret's family. Her parents had lived full lives, and so had her older brother Daniel, who'd married and had four children. But her younger brother Hubert had died in the First World War, leaving behind a bride of five months.

They'd taken a break.

Margaret patted Robin's knee. "It's more immediate for you. You lived with Pam here, in this house. You're surrounded by her things. There are few memories of my family here."

Robin covered Margaret's hand with her own. Brave words from a stoic partner. The knowledge of Hubert's death in the war had shaken her. "We can do this tomorrow."

"Why, when Pam's obituary is right here? Do you want me to read it to you?"

"Yeah," she said, trying not to crush Margaret's hand.

"Bainbridge, Margaret." Margaret paused. "Passed away in her sleep in her 85th year."

"Eighty-five," Robin breathed. "That means she was actually 88, right? Because she was three years older than you. And she died in . . ."

"In 1972."

"Jesus, she almost survived to the year she was born! I wonder what would have happened if she had." Eighty-eight. Thank god Pam hadn't died at thirty of a vitamin deficiency or something like that.

"Beloved wife of the late Jasper Bainbridge," Margaret continued. "Cherished mother of Elizabeth, Catherine . . ." Margaret slid her hand from underneath Robin's and slipped her arm around Robin's shoulders.

"What?" Robin barked.

"Elizabeth, Catherine, Robin—"

"Oh, shit." Robin's eyes filled with tears. "She didn't forget me."

"Of course she didn't. All right, Elizabeth, Catherine, Robin, Gerald, and Grace."

"Five kids? Wow. Gerald was her dad's name."

"Dear mother-in-law to Thomas, Patricia, Julia, and Matthew. I wonder who belongs to whom. We can try to find out."

Robin wiped her eyes. "Yeah."

"Grandmother to . . ." Margaret smiled. "It's a long list."

"Bookmark it. I'll read it later. Does it say where she is?"

"She's buried in Halifax. I wonder when Jasper died."

Robin covered her mouth with her hands while Margaret searched for Jasper's obituary. Pam was buried in Halifax. She couldn't quite accept it. Pam, eighty-eight, buried in Halifax. Jesus.

"He died in 1960," Margaret said. "He was eighty."

"She outlived him by over ten years. That must have been hard for her."

"She had a large family, Robin. She wouldn't have been alone." Margaret pursed her lips. "Her children have probably died, but grandchildren might still be alive, and their descendants, of course."

"When she was born, it's possible her children were still alive. They could have been senior citizens when their mother was in the maternity ward!" Was Pam ever tempted to come to Toronto and "bump into" her parents and grandparents? Did she want to warn her father not to get into the car after his business dinner on a snowy night in 2001? How had it felt, watching history unfold and knowing she couldn't warn anyone about upcoming tragedies? Everyone would have thought she was crazy, even if she'd tried. Robin was sure she hadn't. Pam would have known that she couldn't change history. *Shit, I miss you, Pam. I won't be naming any kids after you, but as long as I'm alive, you will be too.*

Margaret tapped away on the keyboard.

"What are you looking for now?" Robin asked.

"I'm trying to find a photograph of her when she's older."

"I don't want to see a photo. I want to remember her the way she was here."

"Then turn around. I want to see one, if I can."

Robin did as she was told. Why did Margaret want to—oh. To reassure herself.

"Here's one, on a Bainbridge family website." Margaret was silent for a moment. "I'm going to bookmark this. It might tell us who married who. If you don't want to see photographs, don't visit this site."

"Okay. The photo you found. Is it her?" Robin held her breath.

"Yes, it's her. And it's safe to look now."

Robin spun her chair around. "She never used the book."

Margaret's eyes were moist. "No. I'm afraid you're stuck with me."

"Good." She reached for Margaret, pulled her close, and held the woman from the past who'd somehow gotten under her skin and stolen her heart. "Good."

Chapter Eighteen

PAM EXAMINED HERSELF IN THE MIRROR while Doris fluttered around her, making last minute adjustments to her wedding dress. The muffled organ music set her heart racing. Jesus, she was about to get married! Who would have thunk it? "So you're sure you've never heard the word 'epidural'?" she said to Doris.

Doris shook her head. "Not in relation to childbirth. Why do you ask?"

"I thought I heard someone reference it in that context," Pam said, her heart sinking. No freaking epidural? Then the child she was carrying must be that daughter of hers, because no epidural meant no more babies after this one. She'd go through it once, and if Jasper desperately wanted more children, maybe—just maybe—twice. That would be it! No more after that.

The door swung open; Charlotte burst in. "Are you ready yet? Poor Jasper's wilting up there." Her mouth formed an "O" at the sight of Pam. "Oh, Margaret," she said, her eyes tearing up. "You'll never forget this day."

No, Pam suspected she wouldn't. "Tell the others to get ready," she said. Charlotte bustled out to tell the embroidery group, today doubling as Pam's bridesmaids, that their walk down the aisle was about to begin.

Doris met Pam's eyes. "I'll miss you two while you're away."

"We're only going for a couple of weeks. We'll be back for the New Year."

"I can't thank you enough for—"

"That's what friends are for." Pam smiled. "And you won't thank us when you're peeing into a chamber pot."

Doris chortled. "I do love your straightforward manner."

"It'll only be temporary." Pam lifted a brow. "The chamber pot, that is."

Doris's eyes danced. "Are you ready, then?"

Pam took a deep breath and nodded. Doris leaned in to give her a quick hug. "Thank you for asking me to be your maid of honour."

"I couldn't imagine it being anyone else. Come on. It's time for me to get married."

When they reached the top of the aisle, Pam accepted Oliver's extended arm, took her bouquet from Doris, and waited while Doris positioned herself between the bridesmaids and the bride. "Unfortunate that your family couldn't put aside their anger to attend," Oliver murmured.

"I prefer it this way. They would have snubbed Jasper." The loud introduction to the Wedding March drowned out Oliver's reply.

Pam's walk down the aisle was a blur, both mentally and visually. Oh god, it was really happening. She remembered how surreal she'd felt when it had been time to send Jasper and Margaret back to 1910. Little had she known! Today felt surreal in a good way.

When she reached Jasper's side, he dazzled her with his smile. Man, her husband-to-be-in-five-minutes cut a dashing figure in that suit. Could her heart beat any faster? Somehow she said her rehearsed words, held out a trembling hand so Jasper could slide the wedding ring onto her finger, and kissed him at the appropriate time, all while in a daze.

When the minister introduced Mr. and Mrs. Jasper Bainbridge to those gathered and applause rang in her ears, she smiled through her tears and thought back to that night when she'd found the wedding announcement on the Internet. When she'd read the words on the phone's display—the cold words of history—she'd viewed a kaleidoscope through a black and white lens. She loved Jasper, she was coming to love Doris, and she'd eventually love these people who'd gathered here on her very special day. If only Robin and Margaret were—no, don't go there. Robin would want this for her. Robin was here, smiling down on her. *And I'll be at your wedding, Robin. There'd better damn-well be one, or I'll be freaking pissed!*

To reinforce that wish, she imagined Robin standing with the other women when it came time to throw the bouquet and, in her mind, she threw it to her. Nope, scratch that. Robin would be hopeless; she'd rather it bounce off her head than catch it. Pam formed an image of Margaret instead, then tossed the bouquet over her shoulder. She turned around in time to see Doris dodge it. A beaming young lady she didn't recognize triumphantly held it up. As Pam clapped along with everyone else, she closed her eyes for a moment and smiled at Margaret clutching the bouquet to her chest. *You have a wonderful life, girls. I will, starting with a honeymoon with my dashing husband, and then a child.* Just the one. Okay, maybe two, but that would be it. No more!

July, 2011

MARGARET STARED DOWN at the gold band on her finger and touched it to make sure it was real. They were married. She and Robin. Married. When she felt a chin on her shoulder, she looked up and turned, expecting to see Robin. Cathy smiled at her. "Congratulations, Mrs. Tillman. And you really *are* Mrs. Tillman. How did you manage that, Robin?"

Robin shrugged and lifted her hands, palms up. "I didn't manage anything. She wanted to change her name to that."

"I'm old-fashioned," Margaret said, then grinned when Robin did, pleased that Robin was no longer upset about her decision to take the Tillman name. When Margaret had first told Robin of her intent, Robin had vehemently tried to dissuade her. But Margaret hadn't budged. Why take the name Wilton again? That name belonged to Pam and a life that Margaret had left behind. It had made perfect sense to take Robin's name, though if Mother could see her now . . . !

"Tillman is a proud name," Janice growled. "You should be proud to have it." Behind her, Chris rolled his eyes.

"I am, Janice," Margaret said, grateful that Janice had shown up—and come sober, though how long that would last was anyone's guess. She suspected they'd help a tipsy Janice home.

An elevator door dinged open. "Let's get to the restaurant," Robin said, ushering everyone inside.

As they rode to the ground floor of City Hall, Margaret gave Robin's hand a quick squeeze. Oh, how she'd looked forward to this day! If not for the rhyme book, she would have travelled to her wedding in a horse and carriage and walked down the aisle of a grand church in a wedding dress designed by one of Toronto's most prestigious designers. Hundreds of guests would have watched her wed the firstborn son of a respectable and wealthy family; every unwed woman in the church would have envied her. Afterward, the wedding party and guests would have enjoyed a lavish, multi-course dinner and danced to live music in a palatial ballroom, dressed in clothes bought specifically for one of the society events of the year. The society pages would have dedicated a full page to the wedding. Margaret would have tried, oh-so hard, to be a good wife to Jasper, while wondering why her experience of love fell so short of that described by her friends.

Today, she'd ridden the streetcar to City Hall with Robin and greeted the small group of family and friends that waited outside the civil marriage chamber. Her voice had shaken with emotion when she'd vowed to love and cherish a woman who wore a blouse and trousers. Now they would all ride the subway to a restaurant, where'd they laugh and chat while they dined on a fifteen dollar per head buffet. Margaret didn't believe it was possible for her to feel happier, more optimistic about the future, or more in love—though somehow, her love for Robin would continue to grow, a mystery that humbled and delighted her.

Did she wish that her family had been here to see her marry? No. They wouldn't have understood. To be herself, she'd had to leave them, and she was grateful to live in a time in which fewer lesbians had to choose between their families and themselves.

The elevator doors opened; everyone spilled out into the large lobby. "Too bad Pam couldn't be here," Francine, who was becoming Margaret's friend in addition to Robin's, said. "Couldn't she and her husband have flown over? First she leaves it to you to sell the house, then she misses your wedding."

Robin shrugged. "Her husband couldn't get the time off."

"Man, she must have it bad, not wanting to leave his side for five minutes," Cathy said.

"Don't knock Pam. She felt so guilty she couldn't make it that she's paying for our honeymoon," Robin said with a twinkle in her eye that only Margaret fully understood. "And I can honestly say that if it wasn't for Pam, we wouldn't be together."

Margaret's throat tightened. Normally embarrassed by overt public displays of affection, she didn't protest when Robin squeezed her and planted a wet kiss on her cheek.

"She gave us first and last month's rent too, as a thank-you for handling the house sale," Robin added.

"You should have taken an apartment in my building," Janice muttered.

That was the last thing they'd wanted to do! They'd leased a nice two-bedroom apartment not far from the university. They'd had the keys since the beginning of the month, but they hadn't wanted to upset Mitzy by moving her to a new home and then abandoning her to go on their honeymoon. She'd be more comfortable in the only home she knew, with Cathy coming in every day to feed and cuddle her. Margaret and Robin—and Mitzy—would move into their new home in August.

They'd spent the last week painting their apartment, and Margaret had loved every minute of it. They were even making friends in their apartment building! A young woman who'd noticed their comings and goings had invited them in for tea and cookies and had shocked Margaret by brazenly asking if they were a couple, or roommates. Melissa hadn't batted an eye when Robin had honestly answered her; in fact, they were going to Melissa's for dinner the Saturday after they moved in.

"Where are you going for your honeymoon, again?" Francine quickly asked when Janice looked as if she was about to launch into a tirade about their apartment choice.

Robin grabbed Margaret's hand. "Halifax. It'll be Margaret's first time flying."

Cathy's eyes widened. "You've never been on a plane?"

Margaret tightened her grip on Robin's hand. "No."

MARGARET COULD FEEL Robin's tension as they approached the spot marked on the map they'd obtained from the cemetery's office. If not for the flowers she cradled in her arms, she'd slip her arm through Robin's in the hope of calming her, though the gesture probably wouldn't do much good. Shock had jolted Margaret when she'd come upon the family plot in Toronto and read the names of those she'd lived with a mere eight months ago. Worn lettering on dull tombstones had marked the graves as old, but her memories were fresh. Mother's voice murmured in her ears, Father's pipe smoke crept up her nose, and Hubert's pranks brought a smile to her lips. She even missed Daniel, who, in recent years, had been too busy working and dating to bother with his younger sister. *In recent years.* Not according to the dates on those tombstones. "There it is," she said, spotting the Bainbridge plot.

Robin stopped walking.

Margaret turned around. "I'll understand if you don't want to . . ."

"No, we came here to do this." Robin took a deep breath, then marched up to the large stone with *BAINBRIDGE* chiselled across its top. Her shoulders stiffened; she put her hands on her hips.

Margaret waited a moment, then stepped to her side and read the stone:

BAINBRIDGE
In loving memory of

JASPER BAINBRIDGE
Born February 23, 1880
Died March 18, 1960

His wife MARGARET "PAM" WILTON
Born May 12, 1887
Died August 22, 1972

Their daughter CATHERINE JUNE BAINBRIDGE
Born November 2, 1913
Died January 27, 1982

Margaret swallowed the lump in her throat, then glanced at Robin to make sure she was all right, and winced at her pale face. "Do you want to lay the flowers?"

Robin nodded, lifted them from Margaret's arms, and crouched down to place them at the foot of the tombstone. When she didn't straighten, Margaret crouched next to her and slipped her arm around Robin's shoulders.

"They called her Pam," Robin murmured; Margaret could hear the tears in her voice. "I wonder how that happened. And why is only one daughter with them?"

"She didn't marry, remember?" Margaret looked beyond the main stone. "Some of the others are here, too."

"It doesn't seem right. She—" Robin's voice choked off.

"She led a full life, Robin," Margaret said softly. "In that photograph I found, Pam was surrounded by family. She was smiling, she looked happy. She was all right." Her words weren't making any difference; Robin's shoulders still shook and tears still flowed. "She wanted to be with Jasper. She named a son after you. She gave one of her daughters my name as a middle name. She didn't begrudge us this, our life together. She wanted us to have it."

Robin nodded and wiped her eyes.

"She lived the life she wanted, and she expected us to do the same."

"I know. I just wish we could have all lived our lives together. I never got to say thank you, or good-bye."

Margaret had no words of comfort to offer, since she felt the same way. At the cemetery in Toronto, Robin had asked if she wanted to find her family's descendants. She didn't. She'd never contact them, because they'd never feel like family. Her family was in the past. She didn't regret leaving them; after Robin, she would have been miserable in 1910. But oh, how she wished she had known that the rhyme would send her back into the future that night. She would have told her family and friends that she loved them, made her peace over any perceived slights and forgiven those who'd committed them, thanked her parents for loving and raising her, and left behind some explanation for her sudden disappearance, perhaps given a letter to Jasper to pass along. But there wasn't any point wishing for something she could never have and allowing it to overshadow the rest of her life. That wouldn't be honouring Pam's incredible gift.

Margaret's eyes settled on Jasper's name on the tomb. He deserved some credit too, for marrying Pam as Margaret Wilton, and for not using the book. "We'll never need a reason to think of them, because we always will, but perhaps we should choose one day each year on which we do something in memory of them."

"Another new tradition?" Robin was silent for a moment. "I'd like that." She straightened; Margaret followed her lead. "Who else is here?" Robin murmured. Hand-in-hand, they read the nearby tombstones, all Bainbridges except for one.

"Doris June Pembleton," Margaret read, puzzled. "I wonder why she's buried in the Bainbridge plot?"

"Maybe another child?" Robin suggested.

"No, look at the birth date." The name Pembleton rang a bell, but Margaret couldn't remember where she'd heard it.

Robin pointed. "Hers has an epitaph: *Cherished friend, Bainbridge aunt, trusted physician.*"

According to the death date, she'd died four years before Pam. "We'll have to research her," Margaret said. "We could do more research on Pam's descendants, too."

Robin shook her head. "I don't want to know. If I were to run into them, I wouldn't know what to say." She swallowed. "Let her rest in peace."

Robin returned to the main tombstone and crouched in front of it again. Margaret kept a respectful distance as Robin rested her hand on the top of the stone and closed her eyes. Robin wasn't religious, but whatever was behind the gesture, she seemed to draw comfort from it. She opened her eyes, stood, and held out her hand. "Come on, Mrs. Tillman. It's time to get on with the life Pam's given us."

"Just a moment," Margaret said as she slipped her hand into Robin's. She lowered her head, closed her eyes, and thanked Pam for giving her the opportunity to live in honesty and to love the one she wanted. Pam and Jasper would live on in her, in Robin, in their love for each other. They would cherish Pam's gift until they, too, breathed their last. *Thank you.*

They walked from the Bainbridge plot, neither having to speak to know that they'd never visit it again. They carried Pam and Jasper in their hearts.

Outside the cemetery's gates, Robin pulled a pamphlet from her back pocket and showed it to Margaret. "I picked this up at the hotel. It's a place that offers horse and carriage rides. You want to go on one?

Margaret chuckled. "You want to go on a horse and carriage ride?"

"Well, I figured you went on a plane, so . . ." Robin hailed a passing taxi. She waited until they were settled in the backseat before raising the subject again. "What do you think? You want to go on a ride?"

"All right," Margaret said, warming to the idea.

Robin gave the stable's address to the taxi driver. It didn't take long to reach their destination and arrange for a ride. The carriage driver supported Margaret's elbow as she climbed into the carriage. "You ever been on one of these, love?" he asked.

She smiled. "Once or twice."

CARRYING TWO GLASSES of lemonade, Pam stepped out into the sunny spring afternoon and strolled across the back garden to where Jasper worked. A smile spread across her face when she spotted him bent over the crib he was making for their first child. "It's beautiful," she breathed when she reached him.

Jasper turned to her and wiped his brow, then accepted the glass of lemonade she handed to him. He took a long drink. "I'm not quite finished, but it'll be ready in time."

That time couldn't arrive fast enough. She already felt like a tank, and she wasn't due for another two months. She sipped her own lemonade and moved to sit on a wooden chair near the crib.

"Don't!" Jasper barked.

She froze.

"Two of the legs are wobbly, that's why it's out here. It might collapse."

Was he implying something about her weight? Could she blame him? She was surprised nobody had broken a bottle of champagne against her side and christened her the good ship Margaret.

Concern crossed Jasper's face. "You shouldn't be on your feet. Maybe you should go inside, where you can sit down."

"I'm fine, Jasper. I'm pregnant, not ill, and I was just sitting down. I'll—" Movement behind him caught her eye. Doris strode toward them, her spring coat flapping around her ankles.

She triumphantly held up an envelope. "It came," she shouted.

Pam gasped. "And?"

"I was accepted." Before Pam and Jasper could stop her, Doris plunked into the wooden chair. Pam winced, but the chair held. "Oh my." Doris fanned herself with the envelope. "I'm going to medical school."

Pam gave her glass to Jasper and held out her hand. "Let me see it."

Doris leaped to her feet and thrust the envelope into Pam's hand. "I have to send a letter of intent," she said, pacing as Pam read the acceptance letter. "I'll say yes, of course. Why wouldn't I? Of course I'll say yes."

Pam lowered the letter in time to see Doris return to the chair. Jasper lunged forward, but with two lemonades in his hands, all he could do was cringe when Doris plopped herself into it again. It held.

"Do you want a glass of lemonade, Doris?" Pam asked.

Doris shook her head. "I have to tell Oliver." Her mouth tightened. "I'd tell Mother and Father, if they were speaking to me."

Doris's parents had reacted more vehemently than Pam had expected. They'd banned her from their estate—a rather futile gesture. By the time her parents returned from Europe, Doris was already happily decorating the "shack" that Jasper, Oliver, and Bill had turned into a decent cottage. Her parents had also turned their backs on her, rebuffing her every attempt to see them. When Pam and Doris had run into Doris's mother downtown and Mother had crossed to the other side of the road without a word, Doris had stopped trying. Her parents' rejection hurt, but Doris hadn't given up on her dream. Pam admired her for it.

When Pam handed the letter back, Doris fell silent and read it, maybe trying to convince herself that it was true—she would become a doctor. Nothing would stand in her way now. She slid the letter back into the envelope and stood. "Off to Oliver's, then."

"Come for dinner tonight."

"I will." She hurried away, then turned, strode back to them, and threw her arms around Pam's neck. "Thank you. Thank you." She

hesitated, then gave Jasper a hug. "I couldn't have done it without—
I'm going to medical school! Good Lord, I'm going to medical school."

"Go tell Oliver," Pam said, grinning along with Jasper.

"All right, all right." Doris whirled and marched away. Without
looking over her shoulder, she thrust her arm into the air and waved.

Amused, Pam smiled at Jasper. "Did I tell you that she asked if
she could be there when the baby is born, and I said yes? She wants
to witness a birth."

"Will they allow her in?"

"It's Doris. Somehow she'll elbow her way in. You'll be there too,
right?"

The blood drained from his face. "Why would I be there?"

"In 2010, the fathers are usually there."

"Then I'll be there when you have a baby in 2010," he said.

Pam tried to muster outrage, but couldn't. Considering that he was
pale and swaying on his feet at the mere thought of being with her as
she gave birth, it was probably better that he pace outside, especially
since there would be a lot of screaming. No epidural? Jesus.

Jasper handed Pam her lemonade. After they'd finished their drinks,
he set their glasses on the grass. She ran her hand along the top of the
crib. "It'll look beautiful in the nursery." Suddenly she did feel a little
heavy on her feet. Apparently the chair wasn't as hazardous as Jasper
had suspected, so she sat on it. Something gave. Uh-oh.

"Pam!"

Jasper's strong arms were suddenly around her, preventing her
from landing on her ass. She and Jasper surveyed the flattened chair.
"It didn't collapse when Doris sat on it!" Pam said indignantly.

"Yes, well—"

Pam leaned into him and pressed a finger to his lips. "One crack
about my weight and this baby I'm carrying will be an only child!"

He kissed her finger. "I was going to say that Doris weakened it."

Her eyes narrowed.

"I wonder if it will be an Elizabeth or a Robin who first uses this
crib," he said, apparently eager to change the subject.

"So you're okay with the names? It's too bad we can't call a daughter
Margaret. She'll have to settle for having Margaret as her middle name."

"If we have a girl, are you sure you don't want us to call her Pamela?"

"God, no. That's still my name, and thanks to Doris, everyone's calling me Pam now. Nope, Elizabeth or Robin." She smiled. "You'll think I'm batty, but I talk to Robin—the 2010 Robin—all the time."

He met her eyes. "Any regrets?"

"No."

"I wonder if Margaret will regret her choice."

"She won't."

He lifted his brows. "You sound confident of that."

"Because she's where the universe wants her to be, just as I am." Otherwise the rhyme wouldn't have worked its magic. She missed Robin dearly. If she could have one wish, it would be for Robin to somehow be here, but still live out her life in 2010. Pam was forging new friendships, but nobody would ever replace Robin. They were, and forever would be, connected through time. But Pam was at peace with the choice she'd made, and hoped with all her heart that Margaret would be at peace with hers and live a long and joyous life with Robin. *Do me proud, girls. Do me proud.* "I miss Robin, but I'm happy, Jasper. I truly am."

"If we have a girl, we'll have to keep trying until we have a boy you can name Robin," Jasper said, a glint in his eye.

"Um, listen, buddy, two's my limit. It would be nice to have one of each, but if it doesn't happen, it doesn't happen. I'll settle for two girls. Or boys," she hastily added. Jasper didn't know they'd have at least one daughter.

His brows drew together. "Oh. Whenever I think of children, I always imagine myself with more than two."

"How many do you want?" Pam shrieked.

He shrugged. "I don't know. Five?"

"Five?" She snorted and pinched his cheeks. "In your dreams, Jasper Bainbridge. In your dreams."

Other titles by Sarah Ettritch

The Salbine Sisters
Rymellan 1: Disobedience Means Death
Rymellan 2: Shattered Lives

Visit Sarah online at www.sarahettritch.com and
www.facebook.com/settritch

Thanks for reading!

Lightning Source UK Ltd.
Milton Keynes UK
UKOW051426090112

185015UK00001B/155/P

9 781927 369029